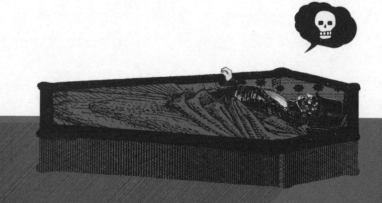

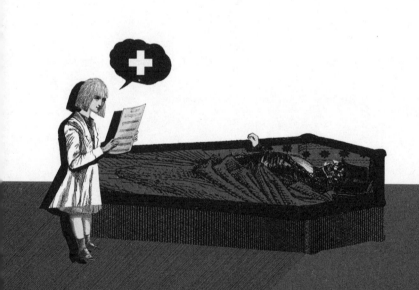

STRANGE PRACTICE

A
DR. GRETA HELSING
NOVEL

VIVIAN SHAW

www.orbitbooks.net

Copyright © 2017 by Vivian Shaw
Excerpt from *Bad Company* copyright © 2017 by Vivian Shaw
Excerpt from *Prudence* copyright © 2015 by Tofa Borregaard

Author photograph by Emilia Blaser
Cover art and design by Will Staehle
Cover copyright © 2017 by Hachette Book Group, Inc.

Orbit
Hachette Book Group
1290 Avenue of the Americas
New York, NY 10104
orbitbooks.net

Simultaneously published in Great Britain and in the U.S. by Orbit in 2017.
First Edition: July 2017

Orbit is an imprint of Hachette Book Group.
The Orbit name and logo are trademarks of Little, Brown Book Group Limited.

The publisher is not responsible for websites (or their content) that are not owned by the publisher.

The Hachette Speakers Bureau provides a wide range of authors for speaking events. To find out more, go to www.hachettespeakersbureau.com or call (866) 376-6591.

Interior illustrations by Will Staehle

Library of Congress Cataloging-in-Publication Data

Names: Shaw, Vivian, author.
Title: Strange practice / Vivian Shaw.
Description: New York : Orbit, 2017. | Series: A Dr. Greta Helsing novel ; 1
Identifiers: LCCN 2016058218| ISBN 9780316434607 (paperback) | ISBN 9781478943655 (audio book downloadable) | ISBN 9780316434614 (ebook (open))
Subjects: LCSH: Women physicians—Fiction. | Medicine—Practice—Fiction. | Patients—Fiction. | Cults—Fiction. | Murder—Fiction. | BISAC: FICTION / Fantasy / Contemporary. | FICTION / Fantasy / Paranormal. | FICTION / Action & Adventure. | FICTION / Fantasy / General. | FICTION / Fantasy / Urban Life. | GSAFD: Paranormal fiction | Fantasy fiction.
Classification: LCC PS3619.H39467 O73 2017 | DDC 813/.6—dc23
LC record available at https://lccn.loc.gov/2016058218

ISBNs: 978-0-316-43460-7 (trade paperback), 978-0-316-43461-4 (ebook)

Printed in the United States of America

LSC-C

10 9 8 7 6 5 4 3 2 1

For Laura Amy Schlitz, who told me not to stop.

Under the darkened city of London, old machinery roared on. Fans the size of small rooms spun into the darkness, pushing air through dead tunnels where no trains moved; rats, used to the dull echo of the machines, preened their whiskers atop switchboxes in dim chambers all but forgotten by the bustling world above.

In a city built on layers of itself, era after era pressed down into the dark like sedimentary rock by the march of progress, the space underground was scarcely less crowded than the daylit streets. Tunnels and conduits, pipes and cables, a man-made warren of networks, stretched from one side of the city to the other; some were in active use, some abandoned, left to the rats and the slow, inexorable seeping of water through the earth; some forgotten about entirely, used to store old paperwork. Years of secrets lay stacked on one another in moldering cardboard boxes, their identifying tags long fallen and scattered on the concrete floors in an unrelieved and endless night.

No one knew now exactly what remained in the tunnels, and no sensible person would go down there alone—but certain esoteric subsectors of society had always gravitated to such places. As long as there was secrecy, there would be a need for holes to hide in.

CHAPTER I

The sky was fading to ultramarine in the east over the Victoria Embankment when a battered Mini pulled in to the curb, not far from Blackfriars Bridge. Here and there in the maples lining the riverside walk, the morning's first sparrows had begun to sing.

A woman got out of the car and shut the door, swore, put down her bags, and shut the door again with more applied force; some fellow motorist had bashed into the panel at some time in the past and bent it sufficiently to make this a production every damn time. The Mini really needed to be replaced, but even with her inherited Harley Street consulting rooms Greta Helsing was not exactly drowning in cash.

She glowered at the car and then at the world in general, glancing around to make sure no one was watching her from the shadows. Satisfied, she picked up her black working bag and the shapeless oversize monster that was her current handbag and went to ring the doorbell. It was time to replace the handbag, too. The leather on this one was holding up but the lining was beginning to go, and Greta had limited patience regarding the retrieval of items from the mysterious dimension behind the lining itself.

The house to which she had been summoned was one of a row of magnificent old buildings separating Temple Gardens from the Embankment, mostly taken over by lawyers and publishing firms these days. It was a testament to this particular homeowner's rather special powers of persuasion that nobody had succeeded in buying the house out from under him and turning it into offices for overpriced attorneys, she thought, and then had to smile at the idea of anybody dislodging Edmund Ruthven from the lair he'd inhabited these two hundred years or more. He was as much a fixture of London as Lord Nelson on his pillar, albeit less encrusted with birdlime.

"Greta," said the fixture, opening the door. "Thanks for coming out on a Sunday. I know it's late."

She was just about as tall as he was, five foot five and a bit, which made it easy to look right into his eyes and be struck every single time by the fact that they were very large, so pale a grey they looked silver-white except for the dark ring at the edge of the iris, and fringed with heavy soot-black lashes of the sort you saw in advertisements for mascara. He looked tired, she thought. Tired, and older than the fortyish he usually appeared. The extreme pallor was normal, vivid against the pure slicked-back black of his hair, but the worried line between his eyebrows was not.

"It's not Sunday night, it's Monday morning," she said. "No worries, Ruthven. Tell me everything; I know you didn't go into lots of detail on the phone."

"Of course." He offered to take her coat. "I'll make you some coffee."

The entryway of the Embankment house was floored in black-and-white-checkered marble, and a large bronze ibis stood on a little side table where the mail and car keys and shopping lists were to be found. The mirror behind this reflected Greta dimly and greenly, like a woman underwater; she peered into it, making a face at herself, and tucked back her hair. It was pale Scandinavian blonde and cut like Liszt's in an off-the-shoulder bob, fine enough to slither free of whatever she used to pull it back; today it was in the process of escaping from a thoroughly childish headband. She kept meaning to have it all chopped off and be done with it but never seemed to find the time.

Greta Helsing was thirty-four, unmarried, and had taken over her late father's specialized medical practice after a brief stint as an internist at King's College Hospital. For the past five years she had run a bare-bones clinic out of Wilfert Helsing's old rooms in Harley Street, treating a patient base that to the majority of the population did not, technically, when you got right down to it, exist. It was a family thing.

There had never been much doubt which subspecialty of medicine she would pursue, once she began her training: treating the differently alive was not only more interesting than catering to the ordinary human population, it was in

3

many ways a great deal more rewarding. She took a lot of satisfaction in being able to provide help to particularly underserved clients.

Greta's patients could largely be classified under the heading of *monstrous*—in its descriptive, rather than pejorative, sense: vampires, were-creatures, mummies, banshees, ghouls, bogeymen, the occasional arthritic barrow-wight. She herself was solidly and entirely human, with no noticeable eldritch qualities or powers whatsoever, not even a flicker of metaphysical sensitivity. Some of her patients found it difficult to trust a human physician at first, but Greta had built up an extremely good reputation over the five years she had been practicing supernatural medicine, largely by word of mouth: *Go to Helsing, she's reliable.*

And *discreet.* That was the first and fundamental tenet, after all. Keeping her patients safe meant keeping them secret, and Greta was good with secrets. She made sure the magical wards around her doorway in Harley Street were kept up properly, protecting anyone who approached from prying eyes.

Ruthven appeared in the kitchen doorway, outlined by light spilling warm over the black-and-white marble. "Greta?" he said, and she straightened up, realizing she'd been staring into the mirror without really seeing it for several minutes now. It really *was* late. Fatigue lapped heavily at the pilings of her mind.

"Sorry," she said, coming to join him, and a little of that heaviness lifted as they passed through into the familiar warmth and brightness of the kitchen. It was all blue tile and blond wood, the cheerful rose-gold of polished copper pots and pans balancing the sleek chill of stainless steel, and right now it was also full of the scent of really *good* coffee. Ruthven's espresso machine was a La Cimbali, and it was serious business.

He handed her a large pottery mug. She recognized it as one of the set he generally used for blood, and had to smile a little, looking down at the contents—and then abruptly had to clamp down on a wave of thoroughly inconvenient emotion. There was no reason that Ruthven doing goddamn *latte art* for her at half-past four in the morning should make her want to cry.

He was *good* at it, too, which was a little infuriating; then again she supposed that with as much free time on her hands as he had on his, and as much disposable income, she might find herself learning and polishing new skills simply to stave off the encroaching spectre of boredom. Ruthven didn't go in for your standard-variety vampire angst, which was refreshing, but Greta knew very well he had bouts of something not unlike depression—especially in the winter—and he needed things to *do*.

She, however, *had* things to do, Greta reminded herself, taking a sip of the latte and closing her eyes for a moment. This was coffee that actually tasted as good as, if not better than, it smelled. *Focus,* she thought. This was not a social call. The lack of urgency in Ruthven's manner led her to believe that the situation was not immediately dire, but she was nonetheless here to do her job.

Greta licked coffee foam from her upper lip. "So," she said. "Tell me what happened."

"I was—" Ruthven sighed, leaning against the counter with his arms folded. "To be honest I was sitting around twiddling my thumbs and writing nasty letters to the *Times* about how much I loathe these execrable skyscrapers somebody keeps allowing vandals to build all over the city. I'd got to a particularly cutting phrase about the one that sets people's cars on fire, when somebody knocked on the door."

The passive-aggressive-letter stage tended to indicate that his levels of ennui were reaching critical intensity. Greta just nodded, watching him.

"I don't know if you've ever read an ancient penny-dreadful called *Varney the Vampyre, or The Feast of Blood*," he went on.

"Ages ago," she said. She'd read practically all the horror classics, well-known and otherwise, for research purposes rather than to enjoy their literary merit. Most of them were to some extent entertainingly wrong about the individuals they claimed to depict. "It was quite a lot funnier than your unofficial biography, but I'm not sure it was *meant* to be."

Ruthven made a face. John Polidori's *The Vampyre* was, he insisted, mostly libel—the very mention of the book was sufficient to bring on indignant protestations that he and the Lord Ruthven featured in the narrative shared little more than a name. "At least the authors got the spelling right, unlike bloody Polidori," he said. "I think probably *Feast of Blood* is about as historically accurate as *The Vampyre*, which is to say *not very*, but it does have the taxonomy right. Varney, unlike me, *is* a vampyre with a *y*."

"A lunar sensitive? I haven't actually met one before," she said, clinical interest surfacing through the fatigue. The vampires she knew were all classic draculines, like Ruthven himself and the handful of others in London. Lunar sensitives were rarer than the draculine vampires for a couple of reasons, chief among which was the fact that they were violently—and inconveniently—allergic to the blood of anyone but virgins. They did have the handy characteristic of being resurrected by moonlight every time they got themselves killed, which presumably came as some small comfort in the process of succumbing to violent throes of gastric distress brought on by dietary indiscretion.

"Well," Ruthven said, "now's your chance. He showed up on my doorstep, completely unannounced, looking like thirty kinds of warmed-over hell, and collapsed in the hallway. He is at the moment sleeping on the drawing room sofa, and I want you to look at him for me. I don't *think* there's any real danger, but he's been hurt—some maniacs apparently attacked him with a knife—and I'd feel better if you had a look."

Ruthven had lit a fire, despite the relative mildness of the evening, and the creature lying on the sofa was covered with two blankets. Greta glanced from him to Ruthven, who shrugged a little, that line of worry between his eyebrows very visible.

According to him, Sir Francis Varney, title and all, had come out of his faint quite quickly and perked up after some first aid and the administration of a nice hot mug of suitable and brandy-laced blood. Ruthven kept a selection of the stuff in his expensive fridge and freezer, stocked by Greta via fairly illegal supply chain management—she knew someone who knew someone who worked in a blood bank and was not above rescuing rejected units from the biohazard incinerator.

Sir Francis had drunk the whole of the mug's contents with every evidence of satisfaction and promptly gone to sleep as soon as Ruthven let him, whereupon Ruthven had called Greta and requested a house call. "I don't really like the look of him," he said now, standing in the doorway with uncharacteristic awkwardness. "He was bleeding a little—the wound's in his left shoulder. I cleaned it up and put a dressing on, but it was still sort of oozing. Which isn't like us."

"No," Greta agreed, "it's not. It's possible that lunar sensitives and draculines respond differently to tissue trauma, but even so, I would have expected him to have mostly finished healing already. You were right to call me."

"Do you need anything?" he asked, still standing in the doorway as Greta pulled over a chair and sat down beside the sofa.

"Possibly more coffee. Go on, Ruthven. I've got this; go and finish your unkind letter to the editor."

When he had gone she tucked back her hair and leaned over to examine her patient. He took up the entire length of the sofa, head pillowed on one armrest and one narrow foot resting on the other, half-exposed where the blankets had fallen away. She did a bit of rough calculation and guessed he must be at least six inches taller than Ruthven, possibly more.

His hair was tangled, streaky-grey, worn dramatically long—that was aging-rock-frontman hair if Greta had ever seen it, but nothing *else* about him seemed to fit with the Jagger aesthetic. An old-fashioned face, almost Puritan: long, narrow nose, deeply hooded eyes under intense eyebrows, thin mouth bracketed with habitual lines of disapproval.

Or pain, she thought. *That could be pain.*

The shifting of a log in the fireplace behind Greta made her jump a little, and she regathered the wandering edges of her concentration. With a nasty little flicker of surprise she noticed that there was a faint sheen of sweat on Varney's visible skin. That *really* wasn't right.

"Sir Francis?" she said, gently, and leaned over to touch his shoulder through the blankets—and a moment later had retreated halfway across the room, heart racing: Varney had gone from uneasy sleep to *sitting up and snarling viciously* in less than a second.

It was not unheard-of for Greta's patients to threaten her, especially when they were in considerable pain, and on the whole she probably should have thought this out a little better. She'd only got a glimpse before her own instincts had kicked in and got her the hell out of range of those teeth, but it would be a while before she could forget that pattern of dentition, or those mad tin-colored eyes.

He covered his face with his hands, shoulders slumping,

and instead of menace was now giving off an air of intense embarrassment.

Greta came back over to the sofa. "I'm sorry," she said, tentatively, "I didn't mean to startle you—"

"I most devoutly apologize," he said, without taking his hands away. "I do *try* not to do that, but I am not quite at my best just now—forgive me, I don't believe we have been introduced."

He was looking at her from behind his fingers, and the eyes really *were* metallic. Even partly hidden she could see the room's reflection in his irises. She wondered if that was a peculiarity of his species, or an individual phenomenon.

"It's all right," she said, and sat down on the edge of the sofa, judging that he wasn't actually about to tear her throat out just at the moment. "My name's Greta. I'm a doctor; Ruthven called me to come and take a look at you."

When Varney finally took his hands away from his face, pushing the damp silvering hair back, his color was frankly terrible. He *was* sweating. That was not something she'd ever seen in sanguivores under any circumstance.

"A doctor?" he asked, blinking at her. "Are you sure?"

She was spared having to answer that. A moment later he squeezed his eyes shut, very faint color coming and going high on each cheek. "I really am sorry," he said. "What a remarkably stupid question. It's just—I tend to think of doctors as looking rather different than you."

"I left my pinstripe trousers and pocket-watch at home," she said drily. "But I've got my black bag, if that helps. Ruthven

10

said you'd been hurt—attacked by somebody with a knife. May I take a look?"

He glanced up at her and then away again, and nodded once, leaning back against the sofa cushions, and Greta reached into her bag for the exam gloves.

The wound was in his left shoulder, as Ruthven had said, about two and a half inches south of the collarbone. It wasn't large—she had seen much nastier injuries from street fights, although in rather different species—but it was undoubtedly the *strangest* wound she'd ever come across.

"What made this?" she asked, looking closer, her gloved fingers careful on his skin. Varney hissed and turned his face away, and she could feel a thrumming tension under her touch. "I've never seen anything like it. The wound is... *cross*-shaped."

It was. Instead of just the narrow entry mark of a knife, or the bruised puncture of something clumsier, Varney's wound appeared to have been made by something flanged. Not just two but four sharp edges, leaving a hole shaped like an X—or a cross.

"It was a spike," he said, between his teeth. "I didn't get a very good look at it. They had—broken into my flat, with garlic. Garlic was everywhere. Smeared on the walls, scattered all over the floor. I was—taken by surprise, and the fumes—I could hardly see or breathe."

"I'm not surprised," said Greta, sitting up. "It's extremely nasty stuff. Are you having any chest pain or trouble breathing now?"

A lot of the organic compounds in *Allium sativum* triggered a severe allergic response in vampires, varying in intensity based on amount and type of exposure. This wasn't garlic shock, or not *just* garlic shock, though. He was definitely running a fever, and the hole in his shoulder should have healed to a shiny pink memory within an hour or so after it happened. Right now it was purple-black and...oozing.

"No," Varney said, "just—the wound is, ah, really rather painful." He sounded apologetic. "As I said, I didn't get a close look at the spike, but it was short and pointed like a rondel dagger, with a round pommel. There were three people there, I don't know if they all had knives, but...well, as it turned out, all they needed was one."

This was so very much not her division. "Did—do you have any idea why they attacked you?" Or why they'd broken into his flat and poisoned it with garlic. That was a pretty specialized tactic, after all. Greta shivered in sudden unease.

"They were chanting, or...reciting something," he said, his odd eyes drifting shut. "I couldn't make out much of it, just that it sounded sort of ecclesiastical."

He had a remarkably beautiful voice, she noticed. The rest of him wasn't tremendously prepossessing, particularly those eyes, but his voice was *lovely*: sweet and warm and clear. It contrasted oddly with the actual content of what he was saying. "Something about...*unclean*," he continued, "*unclean* and wicked, *wickedness*, foulness, and...*demons*. Creatures of darkness."

He still had his eyes half-closed, and Greta frowned and bent over him again. "Sir Francis?"

"Hurts," he murmured, sounding very far away. "They were dressed . . . strangely."

She rested two fingers against the pulse in his throat: much too fast, and he couldn't have spiked *that* much in the minutes she had been with him, but he felt noticeably warmer to her touch. She reached into the bag for her thermometer and the BP cuff. "Strangely how?"

"Like . . . monks," he said, and blinked up at her, hazy and confused. "In . . . brown robes. With crosses round their necks. Like *monks*."

His eyes rolled back slightly, slipping closed, and he gave a little terrible sigh; when Greta took him by the shoulders and gave him a shake he did not rouse at all, head rolling limp against the cushions. *What the hell,* she thought, *what the actual hell is going on here, there's no way a wound like this should be affecting him so badly, this is—it looks like systemic inflammatory response but the garlic should have worn off by now, there's nothing to* cause *it, unless—*

Unless there had been something on the blade. Something *left behind.*

That flicker of visceral unease was much stronger now. She leaned closer, gently drawing apart the edges of the wound— the tissue was swollen, red, warmer than the surrounding skin—and was surprised to notice a faint but present smell. Not the characteristic smell of infection, but something sharper, almost metallic, with a sulfurous edge on it like silver tarnish. It was strangely familiar, but she couldn't seem to place it.

Greta was rather glad he was unconscious just at the

moment, because what she was about to do would be quite remarkably painful. She stretched the wound open a little wider, wishing she had her penlight to get a better view, and he shifted a little, his breath catching; as he moved she caught a glimpse of something reflective half-obscured by dark blood. There *was* something still in there. Something that needed to come out right now.

"Ruthven," she called, sitting up. "Ruthven, I need you."

He emerged from the kitchen, looking anxious. "What is it?

"Get the green leather instrument case out of my bag," she said, "and put a pan of water on to boil. There's a foreign body in here I need to extract."

Without a word Ruthven took the instrument case and disappeared again. Greta turned her attention back to her patient, noticing for the first time that the pale skin of his chest was crisscrossed by old scarring—*very* old, she thought, looking at the silvery laddered marks of long-healed injuries. She had seen Ruthven without his shirt on, and he had a pretty good collection of scars from four centuries' worth of misadventure, but Varney put him to shame. *A lot of duels,* she thought. *A lot of…* lost *duels.*

Greta wondered how much of *Feast of Blood* was actually based on historical events. He had died at least once in the part of it that she remembered, and had spent a lot of time running away from various pitchfork-wielding mobs. None of *them* had been dressed up in monastic drag, as far as she knew, but they had certainly demonstrated the same intent as whoever had hurt Varney tonight.

A cold flicker of something close to fear slipped down her spine, and she turned abruptly to look over her shoulder at the empty room, pushing away a sudden and irrational sensation of being watched.

Don't be ridiculous, she told herself, *and do your damn job.* She was a little grateful for the business of wrapping the BP cuff around his arm, and less pleased by what it told her. Not critical, but certainly a long way from what she considered normal for sanguivores. She didn't know what was going on in there, but she didn't like it one bit.

When Ruthven returned carrying a tea tray, she felt irrationally relieved to see him—and then had to raise an eyebrow at the contents of the tray. Her probes and forceps and retractors lay on a metal dish Greta recognized after a moment as the one that normally went under the toast rack, dish and instruments steaming gently from the boiling water—and beside them was an empty basin with a clean tea towel draped over it. Everything was very, very neat, as if he had done it many times before. As if he'd had practice.

"Since when are *you* a scrub nurse?" she asked, nodding for him to set the tray down. "I mean—thank you, this is exactly what I need, I appreciate it, and if you could hold the light for me I'd appreciate that even more."

"*De rien,*" said Ruthven, and went to fetch her penlight.

A few minutes later, Greta held her breath as she carefully, carefully withdrew her forceps from Varney's shoulder. Held between the steel tips was a piece of something hard and angular, about the size of a pea. That metallic, sharp smell was much stronger now, much more noticeable.

She turned to the tray on the table beside her, dropped the thing into the china basin with a little *rat-tat* sound, and straightened up. The wound was bleeding again; she pressed a gauze pad over it. The blood looked *brighter* now, somehow, which made no sense at all.

Ruthven clicked off the penlight, swallowing hard, and Greta looked up at him. "What *is* that thing?" he asked, nodding to the basin.

"I've no idea," she told him. "I'll have a look at it after I'm happier with him. He's pushing eighty-five degrees and his pulse rate is approaching low human baseline—"

Greta cut herself off and felt the vein in Varney's throat again. "That's strange," she said. "That's *very* strange. It's already coming down."

The beat was noticeably slower. She had another look at his blood pressure; this time the reading was much more reasonable. "I'll be damned. In a human I'd be seriously alarmed at that rapid a transient, but all bets are off with regard to hemodynamic stability in sanguivores. It's as if that thing, whatever it is, was directly responsible for the acute inflammatory reaction."

"And now that it's gone, he's starting to recover?"

"Something like that. *Don't* touch it," Greta said sharply, as Ruthven reached for the basin. "Don't even go near it. I have no idea what it would do to you, and I don't want to have two patients on my hands."

Ruthven backed away a few steps. "You're quite right," he said. "Greta, something about this smells peculiar."

"In more than one sense," she said, checking the gauze. The bleeding had almost stopped. "Did he tell you how it happened?"

"Not really. Just that he'd been jumped by several people armed with a strange kind of knife."

"Mm. A very strange kind of knife. I've never seen anything like this wound. He didn't mention that these people were dressed up like monks, or that they were reciting something about unclean creatures of darkness?"

"No," said Ruthven, flopping into a chair. "He neglected to share that tidbit with me. Monks?"

"So he said," Greta told him. "Robes and hoods, big crosses round their necks, the whole bit. Monks. And some kind of stabby weapon. Remind you of anything?"

"The Ripper," said Ruthven, slowly. "You think this has something to do with the murders?"

"I think it's one hell of a coincidence if it *doesn't*," Greta said. That feeling of unease hadn't gone away with Varney's physical improvement. It really was impossible to ignore. She'd been too busy with the immediate work at hand to consider the similarities before, but now she couldn't help thinking about it.

There had been a series of unsolved murders in London over the past month and a half. Eight people dead, all apparently the work of the same individual, all stabbed to death, all *found with a cheap plastic rosary stuffed into their mouths.* Six of the victims had been prostitutes. The killer had, inevitably, been nicknamed the Rosary Ripper.

The MO didn't exactly match how Varney had described his attack—multiple assailants, a strange-shaped knife—but it was way the hell too close for Greta's taste. "Unless whoever got Varney was a copycat," she said. "Or maybe there isn't just one Ripper. Maybe it's a group of people running around stabbing unsuspecting citizens."

"There was nothing on the news about the murders that mentioned weird-shaped wounds," Ruthven said. "Although I suppose the police might be keeping that to themselves."

The police had not apparently been able to do much of *anything* about the murders, and as one victim followed another with no end in sight the general confidence in Scotland Yard—never tremendously high—was plummeting. The entire city was both angry and frightened. Conspiracy theories abounded on the Internet, some less believable than others. This, however, was the first time Greta had heard anything about the Ripper branching out into *supernatural* victims. The garlic on the walls of Varney's flat bothered her a great deal.

Varney shifted a little, with a faint moan, and Greta returned her attention to her patient. There was visible improvement; his vitals were stabilizing, much more satisfactory than they had been before the extraction.

"He's beginning to come around," she said. "We should get him into a proper bed, but I think he's over the worst of this."

Ruthven didn't reply at once, and she looked over to see him tapping his fingers on the arm of his chair with a thoughtful expression. "What?" she asked.

"Nothing. Well, *maybe* nothing. I think I'll call Cranswell at the Museum, see if he can look a few things up for me. I will, however, wait until the morning is a little further advanced, because I am a kind man."

"What time *is* it?" Greta asked, stripping off her gloves.

"Getting on for six, I'm afraid."

"Jesus. I need to call in—there's no way I'm going to be able to do clinic hours today. Hopefully Anna or Nadezhda can take an extra shift if I do a bit of groveling."

"I have faith in your ability to grovel convincingly," Ruthven said. "Shall I go and make some more coffee?"

"Yes," she said. Both of them knew this wasn't over. "Yes, do precisely that thing, and you will earn my everlasting fealty."

"I earned your everlasting fealty last time I drove you to the airport," Ruthven said. "Or was it when I made you tiramisu a few weeks ago? I can't keep track."

He smiled, despite the line of worry still between his eyebrows, and Greta found herself smiling wearily in return.

CHAPTER 2

Neither Ruthven nor Greta noticed when something that had been watching them through the drawing room window for some time retreated, slipping away before the full light of dawn could discover it; nor were there any passersby there to watch as it crossed the road to the river and disappeared down the water stairs by the Submariners' Memorial.

In the early hours of that same Monday morning, the owner of a little corner grocery shop in Whitechapel came down to unlock the steel security grates over his display window and start preparing for the day. He had just rolled the grates up when he saw something in the street that at first he thought to be a stolen department store mannequin; on closer examination it turned out to be the body of a naked woman, her eyes nothing but raw red holes, with something pale spilling from her gaping mouth. He didn't look closely enough to make out that this was a cheap plastic rosary: as soon as he'd finished being sick, he stumbled back inside and rang the police. By the time most people were awake, it was plastered all over the newsfeeds: RIPPER STRIKES AGAIN! DEATH TOLL RISES TO NINE.

A few streets away from the grocer's shop and his unpleasant early morning discovery was the tiny office sign of Loders & Lethbridge (Chartered Accountants), one floor up from Akbar Kebab and an establishment offering money transfer and check-cashing services. The Whitechapel Road accounting firm predated its neighbors by approximately forty years, but times were tight all over, and it had been deemed wise to move the offices upstairs and let the ground-floor space to other businesses. This meant that the entire atmosphere of the firm was permanently permeated with the smell of kebabs.

Fastitocalon, who had worked as a clerk for the firm for almost as long as it had been around, didn't really mind the grease and spice in the air, but he did object to taking it home with him in his clothes. He'd made the best of it by demanding of old Lethbridge that he be allowed to smoke in his office. This Lethbridge had grudgingly permitted, mostly because he enjoyed the occasional cigar himself—and perhaps on an unconscious level because he'd found that keeping "Mr. Frederick Vasse" more or less content seemed to be correlated with fewer boils on the back of his, Lethbridge's, neck.

Lethbridge was actually one of the more accommodating employers Fastitocalon had known in his time. It wasn't all that easy to find someone willing to hire a middle-aged and unprepossessing person with an oddly greyish complexion and a chronic cough, even if reassured that he wasn't actually contagious. Lethbridge had overlooked the physical short-comings and hired him because of his uncanny gift for numbers, which had worked out in everyone's favor.

As a general rule Fastitocalon did his best not to read people's minds, partly out of basic good manners and partly for his own sake—most people's thoughts were not only banal but *loud*—but he knew perfectly well what Lethbridge thought of him. When he thought of Frederick Vasse at all.

Right now, for example, Lethbridge was thinking very clearly *if he can't stop that goddamn racket I'm sending him home for the day*. Fastitocalon's cough never really went away, but there were times when it was better and times when it was worse. He had run out of his prescription antitussives and kept meaning to call his doctor to get more of them, but hadn't gotten around to it; the cough had been bad for several days now, a miserable hack that hurt deep in his chest no matter how many awful blue menthol lozenges he went through.

The thought of going home was really rather appealing, even if his flat was currently on the chilly side, and when Lethbridge came into his office a few minutes later scowling intently he argued against it—but didn't argue very long.

Ruthven moved through the empty drawing room, picking up the debris of first aid supplies scattered on the floor around the sofa, the discarded gauze-pad and alcohol-wipe packaging looking oddly tawdry in the light of day. He was very much aware of the fact that he had not actually been *bored* for coming up on ten or eleven straight hours now, and that this was a profound relief.

It had become increasingly apparent to him over the past weeks that he had, yet again, run out of things to *do*, which was a perilous state of affairs. He had staved off ennui for a while this time by first renovating his house again and then by restoring an old Jaguar E-type, but the kitchen was as improved as it was going to get and the Jag was running better than new, and he had felt the soft, inexorable tides of boredom rolling in. It was November, the grey end of the year, and November always made him feel his age.

He had considered going up to Scotland, moping about a bit in more appropriate scenery. Going back to his roots. There were several extremely good reasons *not* to do this, but faced with the spectre of serious boredom Ruthven had begun to let himself imagine the muted melancholy colors of heather and gorse, the coolness of mist on his face, the somewhat excruciatingly romantic ruins of his ancestral pile. And sheep. There would be sheep, which went some way toward mitigating the Gothic atmosphere.

Technically Edmund St. James Ruthven was an earl, not a count, and he only sort of owned a ruined castle. There had been a great deal of unpleasantness at the beginning of the seventeenth century that had done funny things to the clan succession, and in any case he was also technically dead, which complicated matters. So: ruined castle, to which his claim was debatable, almost certainly featuring bats, but no wolves. Two out of three wasn't bad, even if the castle didn't overlook the Argeş.

Ruthven wasn't much of a traditionalist. He didn't even *own* a coffin, let alone sleep in one; there simply wasn't room to roll over, even in the newer, wider models, and anyway the mattresses were a complete joke and played merry hell with one's back.

He took the crumpled wrappers into the kitchen and disposed of them. Having seen Varney properly installed in one of the guest bedrooms, and been reassured that his condition—while serious—was stable, Ruthven had spent a couple of hours looking through his own not inconsiderable library. The peculiar nature of the weapon Varney had described didn't fit with anything that immediately came to mind, but something about the *idea* of it was familiar.

Now, having killed a few hours, he judged it late enough in the morning to call August Cranswell at the British Museum, hoping to catch him in the office rather than somewhere in the complicated warren of the conservation department. He was rather more relieved than he would have liked to admit when Cranswell picked up on the third ring, sounding distracted. "Hello?"

"August," Ruthven said. "Am I interrupting something?"

"No, no, no—well, yes, but it's okay. What's up?"

"I need your help with a bit of research. As usual."

"At your service, lordship," said Cranswell, a smile in his voice. "Also as usual. What's the topic this time?"

"Ceremonial daggers. To be more exact, ceremonial daggers dipped in something poisonous." Ruthven leaned against the kitchen counter, looking at the draining board by the sink: Greta's surgical instruments lay side by side on the stainless steel, once more boiled clean. It had been a long time since he'd been called upon to sterilize operating tools, not since the Second World War, in fact—but the memory was still vivid in his mind seventy-odd years later.

Cranswell's voice sharpened. "What kind of poison?"

"We don't know yet. But the dagger itself is extremely peculiar."

"You are not being even slightly reassuring," Cranswell said. "What happened?"

Ruthven sighed, removing his gaze from the probes and tweezers and directing it at the decorative tile work on the walls instead. He sketched out the events of the past night and morning as briefly as he could, feeling obscurely as if the details ought to be communicated in person, as if the phone line itself was vulnerable. "Varney is stable, at least," he concluded, "and all the...foreign material...has been removed and taken for proper analysis. Greta says he should recover, but nobody knows quite how long it'll take, and she pointed out the rather obvious similarities between this business and the Ripper cases. But the dagger is why I'm calling you."

"Wow," said Cranswell, sounding somewhat overwhelmed, and then rallied: "Tell me everything you can. I don't have our catalog of arms and armor memorized, but I can go and look."

"Varney didn't get a good look at it—he described it as a spike, or a short weapon like a rondel dagger. But the blade itself was cross-shaped. Like two individual blades intersecting at right angles. I have no idea how one would go about making such a thing."

"I've seen something like that, but it wasn't a knife," Cranswell told him. "Lawn sprinklers have spikes like that to anchor them in the ground. I'm guessing your friend didn't encounter a ritual lawn sprinkler stake, however."

"The likelihood is slim. But if you could look through the daggers you've got hidden away and see if anything even close to this exists in your catalog, I'd appreciate it—but mostly I want you to check the manuscript collection."

"Manuscripts," Cranswell repeated. "You think this thing might show up in one of them?"

"It's the monk costumes. I can't get the medieval warrior-monk orders out of my mind, you know, taking up arms in the service of some flavor or other of god. Varney said they went on a bit about unclean creatures of darkness and purification and so on, which is difficult to credit in the modern age, but then again this whole wretched business is somewhat unbelievable."

"I'll have a look," said Cranswell. "If we have anything it'll be in storage; none of the manuscripts on display are likely to have anything useful to offer, but I'll check."

"Thank you. I...do know you're busy," Ruthven said, wryly. "I appreciate it."

"I could kind of use a break right now, actually. I'll call you this afternoon if I find anything, okay?"

"Splendid," he said. "If you aren't doing anything tonight

and feel like being social, come over. I'll make you dinner in partial recompense for your time."

Cranswell chuckled. "Done," he said. "Any opportunity to avoid eating my own cooking, you know. Okay, I'll go see what we've got."

"Thank you," Ruthven said again, meaning it. He set the phone back in its cradle, feeling somewhat guilty at having dragged another person into this business but mostly relieved to have Cranswell's assistance and his access to a staggering number of primary sources.

Greta rubbed at the hollows of her temples, leaning against the lab bench and watching her ex-boyfriend twiddle knobs on his microscope. "Well?" she said.

"Well what?" Twiddle, twiddle. "How do you expect me to do any sort of analysis if you keep interrupting me to say 'well'? In fact I can't make out anything useful in this. Just looks like a sharp piece of silvery metal to me. I'll have to run it through the GC-MS." Harry sounded interested.

She came forward; after a moment he moved to let her have a look down the scope. As he'd said, it wasn't much use: a triangular fragment of white metal, presumably the tip of some kind of blade, with a weird greyish coating on bits of it. The coating was what worried Greta. Other than metal and blood, it had smelled sulfur-sharp and *familiar*, as if she'd been around that scent some time before, but she couldn't place it. And Varney's reaction to whatever it was had indicated a fairly complicated inflammatory response.

"*Can* you?" she asked. "Last time I had to get some spectrometry done I had to wait ages for my samples to be processed, there was a queue of several labs ahead of me, and anyway it must cost something awful."

"Maybe at King's College you'd have to wait, but this is the Royal London," Harry told her with a smirk. "As it happens we don't have a queue for the mass spec just at the moment and this is weird enough to be interesting, so I'm willing to take it on."

"You're magnificent," said Greta, straightening up. "Completely *magnifique*."

Harry laughed. "You didn't get any sleep at all, did you? I can tell. Go away and let me get on with my work. I'll ring you as soon as I get any results out of this mess."

She nodded, stifling another yawn, and collected her vast and untidy handbag. "Right. I'll be in touch, Harry, and thanks. I really do appreciate it."

He was already packing up the sample to prepare it for the gas chromatograph–mass spectrometer, and just nodded—the same annoyingly distracted little nod she remembered without love from the time they'd spent together. Greta shoved her hands into her pockets and headed out of the laboratory, making a conscious effort to think about something—anything—else.

Greta's personal life was practically nonexistent, given the demands of her career, and in any case it had been a losing proposition trying to date someone completely outside the world she worked in. She had had a handful of relationships in her adult life, none of them lasting more than a few months and all of them largely unsatisfactory. It was difficult to keep coming up with new and inventive cover stories for her day job, for one thing, and while she defaulted to *I run a private clinic for special-needs patients* and relied on doctor-patient confidentiality to avoid having to discuss what it was she actually did, Greta found the effort of it exhausting. She had allowed Harry to think that the nature of her clinic tended toward the discreet treatment of diseases one simply did not talk about, but dinner-table *how was your day* conversations had been a daily minefield to negotiate, and the benefits of being involved with someone had simply not measured up.

He was a useful acquaintance, however, and Greta had from time to time presumed on that acquaintance to get some lab work done—and been very, very glad that Harry didn't ask questions, particularly those starting with "why."

She made her way out of the lab building without paying much attention to her surroundings until she was outside again, looking up at the façade.

The original structure of the Royal London Hospital wasn't a particularly prepossessing building, made out of yellow-brown brick with some cursory pilasters stuck on the front in a stab at classical gravitas. Over the years new bits had been built on here and there, including a vast series of rectangular additions clad in blue glass that contrasted very oddly with the Georgian design of the original building. It was ugly but it was also clearly thriving, busy, and not relying on optimism and duct tape to keep going.

Her own clinic in Harley Street was about as spartan as you could get, and the only reason she was located in that particular hallowed realm at all was that her father had owned the property outright and left it entirely to her on his death, along with just about enough to pay the taxes. These days her neighbors were mostly other specialist clinics rather than the personal offices of famous and/or knighted medical men, but she was still very conscious of her own comparative unimportance. Premises in London's historic medical VIP area were a bit exhausting to live up to, especially when she couldn't afford to keep the place looking quite as glossy as the rest of the street, despite the protective illusion wards on the door. What money she could spare after expenses and upkeep went toward helping her more disadvantaged patients with necessities.

Greta let herself entertain a thoroughly idiotic fancy of building some modern blue glass boxes on the roof of the property to create a solarium for her mummy patients, and shook her head. Harry was right. She needed sleep.

She had called her friend Nadezhda Serenskaya early that morning to see if she could possibly take Greta's office hours for the day; Nadezhda, who was a witch and thus well acquainted with London's supernatural community, and Anna Volkov, a part-rusalka nurse practitioner, regularly stepped in to help Greta out, but generally with more notice. Now she took out her phone again and dialed the clinic.

It rang three times before Nadezhda came on the line, and Greta knew it would have gone to voice mail if she was with a patient, but there was still a stab of guilt at having to make her friends do the receptionist part of her job as well as the actual doctoring.

"Greta," Nadezhda said, sounding unruffled. "What's up?"

"Hey, Dez. At the moment, not a lot." She couldn't suppress a yawn. "Thanks again for stepping in on zero notice. How's it been so far?"

"Hush, you know I *like* the work, I'm glad to help. Pretty quiet, some walk-ins but mostly I'm amusing myself tidying up your sample cabinets and dusting your office, which is hilariously disorganized. Are you okay? What's going on?"

"I'm fine," she said. She could picture Dez bustling and had to smile. "I just didn't get any sleep last night—house call, and a bad one; it's something I've never seen before. I think we're out of the woods, but I'm waiting on test results."

"Which are going to take forever," said Nadezhda. "So you ought to go home and get some damn sleep while you can manage it. Don't worry about the clinic, everything's under control, and Anna says she can take tomorrow and the day after if you need them, I've called her already."

There was absolutely nothing in that statement that should make Greta want to cry, but much like Ruthven's latte art it tightened her throat nonetheless. She didn't *deserve* friends like these. "Thank you," she said, and was relieved to hear that her voice sounded entirely ordinary. "I'll...find something to eat, and then yeah, okay, I will go home for a little while. Thanks, Dez." What she really wanted to do was hurry back to Ruthven's to see how Varney was doing, but she knew perfectly well that Ruthven would call her if there was any change.

"No worries. You call me if you need anything, all right?"

"I will," she told the phone, and "Good-bye," and swallowed hard. This was fatigue and low blood sugar. Nadezhda was right: food first, and *then* rest.

With a sigh Greta turned and started off along Whitechapel Road. There was a fairly decent pub just a block away, the Blind Beggar, which ought to be able to provide her with some lunch; then perhaps she might actually have a chance to drive home and get some sleep.

It surprised her not in the slightest when this prospect became, once more, totally unattainable.

A familiar rattling cough from behind her made Greta stop and look back to see the grey figure of her most frequent patient: coatless, suit-jacket collar turned up and hat jammed over ears, trudging along glumly against the November wind. She said a few unladylike words and trotted back to Fastitocalon, nudging her way through midday shoppers.

"Fass, what the devil are you doing out in this weather without a coat? You sound dreadful."

"Thank you, I'm sure," he said, giving her a look. "What a nice surprise it is to see you, Dr. Helsing, as always you brighten up the day like a little ray of sunshine." Then he started to cough again, and whatever else he might have had to say was lost. It was an unpleasant sound, bronchial and sharp, almost like fabric being ripped.

Greta put her arm around him. "Right, enough of this,

come with me." She propelled him briskly in the other direction, toward the nearest pharmacy, wishing to God she'd had another cup of coffee. He went biddably enough, although he did point out that people were staring at them. "I don't give a damn about staring," she said. "Look, sit down. I won't be long."

Fastitocalon subsided into one of the chairs in the pharmacy's little waiting area. He was glad to sit down; he was, in fact, considerably older than the fifty-something he appeared to be. Greta was saying something to the pharmacist, scribbling on a blue pad and fishing in her enormous handbag for her credentials. He watched her, the pale hair almost colorless under the fluorescent lights, the rapid gestures with which she emphasized her points, and thought how very much she was like her father. Wilfert Helsing had been Fastitocalon's dear friend as well as his physician, and he'd known Greta all her life—and in the years since Wilfert's death, had done his best to keep an eye on her.

In a manner of speaking. He really *did* try not to slip into people's heads by accident, but Greta was different. He had offered, and she had accepted, the tacit protection of his mental presence: a distant and mostly imperceptible flicker of awareness in the very back of her mind, the sensation that she was not alone.

He thought—not for the first time—about the novelty of being ordered about by the same girl who had, at six months of age, been sick all over the shoulder of his totally irreplaceable

1958 Italian topcoat, the girl he'd once delighted by turning all her plastic play blocks into brightly colored lumbering beetles, the girl he'd tutored with indifferent results in the arcane discipline of sixth-form calculus. The woman who had turned to him on a cold and awful day for what support he could provide, who had said, *Fass, help, I don't know what to do.*

Humans lived so *fast.*

Another fit of coughing shook him and he retreated behind his handkerchief, cursing a number of factors, including London's weather, his own stubbornness, and the events of the Spanish Inquisition. Suddenly Greta was there, beside him, and she pushed the familiar bright plastic of an inhaler into his hand.

"Here. And there's a longer-acting nebulizer as well. Why didn't you tell me you'd run out of meds? And you've been smoking. I intend to shout at you at considerable length about that."

The magic chemicals were doing their job, though. Soon he could stop coughing and wipe at his streaming eyes. "I thought you were already shouting. We're making a scene."

"No," said Greta, helping him up and nodding to the pharmacist. "I have not yet begun to shout, and a scene would involve somebody throwing things and/or being tossed out of a window; this is just a mild disturbance. Come on, I'm making you eat lunch, and after *that* I can shout at you. And you can tell me all about why you're walking around in November sans sensible outdoor clothing, and I can tell you about the wretched day...er...night and morning I've had."

The Blind Beggar was crowded, but mostly the patrons were around the bar, watching a football match. Greta was able to find them a table in the back without much difficulty, and ordered coffee for herself and tea with a good slug of brandy in it for Fastitocalon.

"Right," she said, when the drinks had arrived. "You go first."

He eyed her. "Can I demur on the basis of a terribly sore throat?"

"Nope. Drink your nice fortified tea and give me the facts. Just the facts."

"You're a hard woman, Greta Helsing." Fastitocalon did as he was bidden, wincing as he swallowed, but the brandy spread a wonderfully heartening warmth through him. "That's . . . really rather nice. There isn't much to tell, anyway. I was temporarily out of ready cash due to an unexpected rent increase last week, and my winter coat was relatively new and still worth a bit." He shrugged. It wasn't as if this situation was exactly novel. "I expect I'll manage."

Greta pinched the bridge of her nose. "Fass. Really, listen to yourself. You are not living in a Russian novel, okay? You don't have consumption and your flat's on the second floor; it's not remotely mistakable for a garret. Ruthven is going to go absolutely spare if he hears about this, you know."

"Yes, which is why you aren't going to tell him," said Fastitocalon. "Please, Greta, be a good girl and just forget the whole thing; it's hardly important. Nor the first time it's happened. You should've seen me in the 1820s, stuffing bits of rag round the windowpanes to keep out the drafts. That was proper Russian-novel stuff. This is just a capricious landlady."

"Maybe if you weren't old enough to know better *and* didn't have COPD *and* didn't have any way to cloud men's minds and fog their understanding of rent increases, I'd say pawning your only winter coat in London in November might be an acceptable course of action." Greta looked up as the waitress came back. "Same again, and the beef and barley soup and granary roll. Fass?"

"Hmm? Oh..." He shrugged. "What she's having? I wish you wouldn't call it that."

"Call what what?" Greta asked as the waitress finally quit staring at Fastitocalon and retreated, order pad in hand.

"COPD. It sounds like a law enforcement team. In my day we referred to my trouble as chronic bronchitis."

"Well, it is. Bronchitis is an obstructive pulmonary disorder. Which reminds me, when did you run out of your meds and why didn't you tell me you'd run out?"

He looked down. "A week ago? Some sort of mix-up. They said there weren't any refills left on that prescription and they'd call you to get you to authorize it. Didn't they?"

"Not that I'm aware of," Greta said, taking out her prescription pad again and writing busily, eyebrows drawn together in a scowl that reminded Fastitocalon once more suddenly and vividly of her father.

"Anyway, it's fine," he said. "I'm quite all right. Er. Lethbridge sent me home, though."

Greta finished scribbling and pushed several blue prescription slips across the table, still scowling. "There. That's three months' worth. And good for Lethbridge. I might revise my opinion of him if he goes on showing that level of common sense. You're going to eat something nourishing and then you are going straight home and..."

She paused and ran a hand through her hair. "You don't have much heat there, do you?"

"Oh, of course I do. It's just that most of it escapes up the holes in the ceiling where they didn't seal it round the drainpipes and goes to heat my upstairs neighbor's flat instead."

"Oh, Jesus Christ," said Greta, despairingly. "What else? Have you got to crawl up the steps over broken glass both ways while carrying weights in your teeth?"

Fastitocalon laughed—and it was a testament to the powers of modern medicine that the laughter didn't turn into another hacking fit. "Broken glass? Oh, we would've *killed* for broken glass when I was young," he said in a terrible Yorkshire accent.

"*Luxury,*" said Greta, and this time both of them burst out laughing.

Not so far away at all, in a small room lit with brilliant blue, a naked man-shaped thing knelt, head bowed. Its skin was an angry red that looked dark purple in this light, blotched and shiny with blisters. It was moving very slightly, swaying back and forth with the rhythm of the beating of its heart. Dancing, jumping shadow-shapes played over a concrete floor and metal walls that curved in a low arch overhead. The air stank of ozone: the smell of bright energy, of lightning storms.

The object before which it knelt was squatting in a cabinet like a malevolent deep-sea creature, alien, tentacular, glowing: filled with moving, flickering blue light. Within a thick glass vessel a glaring blue-white spark danced, far too bright to see clearly, accompanied by a strange atonal humming that was both awful and hypnotic.

Distantly, over that humming, footsteps approached; distantly the thing registered that it had heard them. They did not matter at the moment, nothing mattered, not when there was the light to look at, the *light*, the *blue light*.

"Every thing that may abide the fire," said a voice, replacing the footsteps in its awareness, "shall go through the fire, and be made clean; the flame shall burn up their wickedness."

Slowly it woke into a higher level of consciousness, swimming upward from dark stillness lit only by that blue. It stood with effort, and where it had knelt there was a mark, a stain of fluids soaked into the concrete floor.

It turned toward the voice, still dazzled with blue light, unable to see what it was facing: another man-shaped thing, this one clothed in the coarse brown habit of a Benedictine brother, its own shiny pink and white scars concealed from sight. Beneath the hood there was another gleam of blue: twin blue pinpoints of light.

"In the fire thou shalt be purified, as silver tried in a furnace of earth," the newcomer said.

There was a pause before the thing remembered speech and how it worked. "I am...purified," it said, slowly. Its voice was cracked, uneven, as it gave the ritual reply. "My sins are burned with fire."

The hooded monk inclined his head, once: a nod, or a bow. "Behold, thine iniquity is passed from thee, and I will clothe thee with raiment; let the high praises of God be in thy mouth, and the holy sword of the Lord God in thy hand."

"Praised be God," said the thing, completing the ritual, and its knees began to buckle with the unaccustomed strain of standing upright after so long on the ground. The monk caught it easily, lifted it in his arms like a child. There was a soft series of wet little percussions as fresh blisters broke, dragged across the monk's rough-woven habit, and the thing moaned. Everything was dark, with moving stars.

"Take comfort," said the monk, and turned, and bore it away into the darkness. "Blessed are the pure in heart: for they shall see light in the darkness, walk the paths of night without fear. You shall see with new eyes. You have a purpose."

Only now did the thing realize that the little bursts and sparks of light all around it were not from the tunnel they were passing through. It blinked, and each blink was agony, and it *could not see.* The blue light had burned away its sight, ablated tissue and nerve and vein, sunk the sun behind the horizon for ever.

Then the monk's words began to make sense. New eyes.

A new sight with which to see a cleaner world.

CHAPTER 3

Ruthven set the kettle on a burner and lit it with a blue pop of gas. "Really, it's no trouble at all," he said. "I've got so many rooms in this place that never get used. Sir Francis could probably do with some company, anyway; he seems to be a thoroughly melancholy sort."

Fastitocalon was leaning in the doorway of the kitchen, resolve crumbling by the minute. Of course he didn't *need* the wretched vampire's charity, he could get on perfectly well by himself, he'd *been* getting on perfectly well by himself for the past several hundred years, but... it was awfully comfortable in here. Really very comfortable indeed. And he thought that Greta just might have had a point with her insistence that he must not get chilled. He'd argued with her most of the way here on the tube and he was now feeling rather short on arguments.

"You're wavering, aren't you," Ruthven said, and smiled: wry and sympathetic. His teeth were very white and very

40

even, the upper canines ever so slightly longer than a human's. "Sit down, for heaven's sake, and stop arguing with yourself."

"I'm not wavering," Fastitocalon murmured, but he did sit down at the big scrubbed-pine kitchen table, rubbing at his aching chest. *"I'm* a melancholy sort as well, come to think of it. I might make him worse. What happened, anyway? Greta didn't actually talk much about the whole episode, except to say that she'd been up all night; she was mostly too busy telling me off."

The vampire leaned back against the counter, arms folded. "He was stabbed. By persons unknown, with a weapon unlike any I've seen before—which reminds me, where the hell is Cranswell? He said he'd be here this evening with some useful reference books, but it's getting on for six o'clock and there's no sign of him." A strand of glossy black hair escaped its mooring and drooped over his forehead, and he pushed it away with an irritable little flick. The gesture was theatrical, Fastitocalon reflected, if unconsciously so. Come to think of it, Ruthven *did* have the exaggerated black-and-white looks of a silent-film actor.

His attention was wandering: the whine of the boiling kettle recaptured it just as Ruthven was saying something about a temperature of eighty-seven degrees Fahrenheit, which as far as he, Fastitocalon, knew was pretty much febrile-seizure territory for vampires. "Good heavens," he said, taken aback. "But he's...recovering?"

"Yes. Now that the poisonous bit of metal is out of him, he's improving, but almost as slowly as a human. He ought to have healed within a few hours, at most, from the time it happened; that was in the middle of last night, and he's still flat on his back."

"Did...do...you have any idea why?" Fastitocalon looked up at Ruthven, thinking again how good he'd have been in the earliest of the early films, those big shiny silver eyes rimmed with dramatic makeup. Murnau would have adored him. "I mean, why *Varney* in particular? I didn't know he was even still in England. Or alive, for that matter."

"I don't know. They apparently knew where he lived, broke in to his flat to poison everything with garlic, and then attacked him while he was still incapacitated from the fumes. But the particularly odd thing is that they were dressed up, he said, sort of like monks. Long brown robes, hoods. It's a bit topically relevant, given the whole Ripper business. Greta is sure there's a connection."

Ruthven poured out tea into a mug, a sharp lemony smell filling the kitchen, and then added generous amounts of both honey and brandy. Fastitocalon hadn't really been listening; he reflected dreamily that he'd never met a sanguivore quite so ineffably *domestic*, silver-screen looks and all. Ruthven ought to be wearing pearls and a frilly apron. Possibly with little bats on it.

Slowly Fastitocalon was beginning to suspect himself of being ever so slightly feverish, if the quality of his thought process was anything to go by. Nevertheless, the hot mug was extremely welcome, and he wrapped his hands around it and breathed in the steam gratefully. "Thank you. I, ah, I've decided to give up protesting. It would in fact be awfully nice to stay here tonight and not have to deal with balky electric fires and obstreperous upstairs neighbors."

"I'm glad to hear it." Ruthven eyed him thoughtfully. "You ought to have some aspirin or something. Where's Greta gone?"

"Back to her flat to collect some things. She said she might as well move in for the duration if you're having houseguests, which struck me as somewhat presumptuous." He coughed. "I wonder what her poor clinic patients are doing while she's fussing over me. And Sir Francis, of course, who is *actually* in need of expert care."

"I gather she has friends who can step in to run the place when she can't be there," Ruthven said. "I shouldn't worry about that; she has things well in hand. Come and sit in front of the fire."

Fastitocalon had run out of energy to protest, and just nodded and shuffled on after the vampire into the drawing room and let himself be installed in a chair beside a cheerful applewood fire. His chest ached, muscles sore from the exercise of coughing, and the warmth of the fire and the brandy were extraordinarily welcome.

In fact he was almost asleep when the doorbell rang three times in rapid succession, followed by someone banging on the door with a fist. Ruthven said a forceful word or two and hurried round to see what on earth the matter was, peering through the peephole. Fastitocalon heaved himself out of the chair and followed him, blinking sleepily. Another curse, and Ruthven yanked open the door.

For the second time in as many nights a desperate figure fell forward into the entrance hall. It had begun to rain, a nasty, icy, slimy sort of rain that got down collars and under hoods and up sleeves, and the newcomer was soaked and shivering.

Once Ruthven had scanned the street for any sign of danger and then shut and bolted the door, he helped the new arrival to his feet: a tall, young black man with curly hair. "You do know how to make an entrance, Cranswell," he said. "Are you all right? What happened?"

The young man looked down at Ruthven, and then at the plastic-wrapped bundle he was still clutching to his chest. "Followed," he managed through chattering teeth. "Think I lost them but—pull the b-blinds."

Ruthven's brows drew together. He turned back to the drawing room doorway, hurrying across to the windows. "Followed by what?" he said over his shoulder as he drew the curtains one by one. "Did you get a good look at them?"

"No," Cranswell admitted, shivering. "Or not clearly. At all. I don't...even really know what I saw, Ruthven." His accent was tinged with American, not strong enough to indicate he'd been there recently or that he had originally hailed from that side of the Atlantic, but noticeable. The current uncertainty in his voice didn't suit him in the least, Fastitocalon thought.

Ruthven finished with the curtains and came back over to them. "What did you bring? Did you find anything about the weapon?" He glanced at Fastitocalon and sighed, passing a hand over his face. "I'm sorry," he said. "August Cranswell, may I introduce Frederick Vasse, an old friend of mine. Vasse, this is Cranswell. He's a junior curator at the British Museum, and my manners have apparently deserted me."

"Hi," Cranswell said, glancing at Fastitocalon for a distracted moment before looking back down at the bundle in his arms, as if to reassure himself it was still there. "I looked through the collection and found a couple of books I really, really, really am not supposed to even have access to, and I kind of…got them out anyway—I can't believe I did that—and I think maybe I have what you're looking for, but it's pretty gruesome."

"So was the attack on Varney, I gather." Ruthven nodded toward the fire. "Sit down and get yourself warm; you're shaking. Tell me what happened."

"I don't know," Cranswell said, still hugging the books to his chest. "Like I said, I don't really know what I *saw*. I was… in the basement, which is creepy to begin with, especially if you're alone, and obviously I shouldn't have been there. I didn't want anybody to know what I was up to. It took me a while to track down the books I wanted, and the whole time I kept thinking I heard someone coming. Or like…a tapping sound. Like water dripping in a cave. Every time I stopped to listen there was nothing there."

Fastitocalon watched him, no longer feeling even slightly dreamy. Cranswell sat down in one of the chairs by the fire and set the books aside, holding out his hands to the flames: long, well-shaped hands, ringless, smooth with the tight skin of youth. "It would have been okay if I just kept *hearing* stuff," he went on. "But—I didn't have more of the lights on than

I absolutely needed, and it's dark down there even with the lights *all* on, and I saw—just these two pinpoints of light down one of the aisles. Like eyes. Just for a moment, and then they were gone, but I saw them again a moment later from another direction. I... kind of freaked out, and, well. Got out of there in a hurry."

Ruthven had been listening to this in silence, and now went over to the sideboard and splashed whiskey into a glass. "Go on," he said, coming over to press the drink into Cranswell's hand. "I think we'd better hear the rest of it."

Cranswell looked up at him, blinking, and then wrapped his fingers around the glass. The cut-crystal facets glittered as his hand shook. He swallowed half its contents, coughed explosively, and then settled back in the chair looking slightly steadier.

"I was okay when I left the Museum," he continued, looking down. "But as I was walking down Drury Lane, I started... seeing little points of light again. Blue light. More than one of them. In pairs, just for a moment. Nobody else seemed to see anything out of the ordinary, I mean, it was dark and raining and everyone was in a hurry to get wherever they were going, but nobody else seemed to notice the... eyes." He shivered, once, hard, like a dog coming out of deep water. "Then I happened to look down a side street where all the lamps were out, and there were *lots* of them. A whole swarm of little points of light. They were watching me—I don't just think, I *know*—and then they *moved*, they were coming toward me, and—that's when I ran."

He drank off the rest of the whiskey and shut his eyes for a long moment. "But I got you the books you wanted. Sorry I'm late."

Fastitocalon watched Ruthven's face go through a rapid series of expressions, ending up with a kind of fond exasperation. "Never mind that," he said. "Thank you for bringing them, and I want you to stay here tonight, Cranswell; I don't know what's going on, and I *don't like it*."

Greta's flat in Crouch End was quite a long way away from both her clinic and Ruthven's house, and at times like this she often found herself thinking that she'd really rather suck it up and deal with the vagaries of public transportation for the commute instead of driving; she'd spent the past half an hour stuck in traffic on Farringdon Road, and her fingers on the wheel were crossed that her phone wouldn't ring with urgent summonses to anywhere.

She had turned the radio off ten minutes earlier after flipping through the stations to see if she could find any useful traffic information, and now turned it on again in search of something other than car horns to listen to.

"...a *second* killing today," someone on the news was saying, her smooth announcer's voice not quite smooth enough to hide a kind of horrified fascination. "That's ten murders now in six weeks. Neil, what do we know so far about the latest cases?"

"Well, Sheri, both seem to point unquestionably to the serial killer popularly known as the Rosary Ripper, from what the Met have released so far. The first victim of the day was found in Whitechapel, as we reported previously, early this morning. The second body was found in Soho just hours ago, and the MO and the signature rosary left at the scene of each crime are consistent with the other cases. Investigations are still under way to locate the source of the rosaries."

I should hope so, too, thought Greta, staring at the radio, her eyes wide. *Two more murders, one done in broad daylight? How the hell is he—or they—getting away with this?*

Before last night, before she had had any reason to suspect that there was more than one individual involved in the killings, she had thought about it only at a distance. She'd felt strongly if obscurely that whoever was doing the killing was male. Most serial killers *were* men; those few women who committed multiple murders tended to do it with poison, as far as Greta knew, and for monetary gain. This—whoever it was, or *they* were—seemed to be doing it for the sheer hell of the thing, and so far it looked like they weren't slowing down at all.

The unpleasant thought occurred to her that perhaps the unsatisfactory result of the attack on Varney had spurred them on to more active efforts, to make up for that particular failure. They hadn't killed *him*, but hey, perhaps two humans were worth as much as one vampyre to whoever was behind this business.

Neil the announcer was continuing: "Police have issued safety recommendations for the public, which are available on their website as well as all main news agencies. It is strongly advised that people travel in groups and stay in well-lit areas as much as possible. Remain alert and aware of your surroundings at all times."

"This may be the most prolific serial killer who has been active in greater London since Dennis Nilsen, often referred to as the British Jeffrey Dahmer," his colleague put in, still with the tinge of fascinated horror in her voice. "Nilsen murdered at least twelve young men in the years between 1978 and 1983. So far it seems that the so-called Rosary Ripper's motivation in these murders does not appear to be sexual, unlike Nilsen's crimes, but police have declined to speculate on the real motives behind the recent spree of killings. We can be sure of one thing, Neil, I think."

"What's that?" he asked.

"London is a *frightened* city."

Greta turned the radio off. "London," she told the darkened dial, "contains multitudes." The apparent presence of a lunatic or lunatics plural running around the city stabbing people to death was certainly *unpleasant*, but the world in which she moved was rather more complicated than that inhabited by Neil and Sheri and the majority of their listening public.

Until now, the vicissitudes of the surface world had not impinged noticeably on the version her patients inhabited, and she liked it that way. The idea that the Ripper was responsible for the attack on Varney did not so much frighten Greta as *offend* her.

And it had to be stopped. It had to be stopped for a number of very obvious reasons, but among them was the fact that such a crossover from the ordinary human world to that of the supernatural represented a clear and present danger to the rest of the supernatural community. Secrecy was safety, and a breach in one was a breach in both.

Her first priority was Varney's recovery. Once he was well again she could turn her attention to the problem of somehow tracking down whoever was responsible.

Greta had no illusions about her own capacity to go up against something like this herself. That was going to have to be Ruthven's job; Ruthven, or one of the other people she knew who were capable of casually unscrewing somebody's head.

Up ahead the traffic was finally beginning to thin out. Greta relaxed a little. It shouldn't take her long to collect what she needed, and the drive back would be a lot less wearisome.

Night had fallen completely by the time she parked across the road from her block of flats, a row of white-painted town houses labeled improbably as Grove Mansions. The driver's-side door was being its usual recalcitrant self. Greta banged it shut without bothering with the lock and let herself into the building. She was only going to be here for a few minutes to collect some spare clothes and some more tools and books, and anyway no one in their right mind would want to steal the Mini. The one time it had been lifted, years ago, the thief had promptly left it just a few streets away, in apparent disgust.

Her ground-floor flat was a mess, as usual, clothes hanging over chairs, books and papers stacked on every horizontal surface. It was the kind of impersonal, abstract clutter left by somebody who lived alone and didn't use the place for much of anything other than eating or sleeping, who spent the majority of her life somewhere else. Greta's limited house-keeping instincts were applied almost entirely to her clinic; by the time she got home at night, she didn't have the energy to face tidying up or doing anything more complicated in the kitchen than microwaving frozen dinners. There was a certain weary sense of guilt that accompanied these solo meals, gener-ally consumed at the kitchen table or cross-legged on the bed, hunched over whatever book she was reading at the time. Lec-turing her patients on healthy eating habits always felt more than a little hypocritical.

The prospect of staying at Ruthven's house and eating Ruthven's reliably excellent cooking was therefore a particu-larly attractive one, even if the reason for her stay was both worrisome and unpleasant. It didn't take her long to throw a couple of changes of clothes into an overnight bag and grab her toothbrush and comb. The mental picture of the luxu-rious spare bedrooms at the Embankment house rose again, and Greta made a face at her thoroughly inelegant pajamas. Whenever she stayed with Ruthven, she always felt vaguely as if she ought to be draped in lace and ruffles, or possibly diaphanous peignoirs, whatever *they* were, in order to live up to the surroundings; and then inevitably felt rather frivolous for minding the fact that she couldn't.

Her phone was still blessedly silent as she headed back down the stairs. She took it out and looked at the screen, in case she'd turned off the ringer by mistake, but nobody had called or texted her. She knew that Ruthven would have gotten in touch if Sir Francis took a turn for the worse, but she couldn't help worrying while he was still above eighty-four degrees. To be entirely honest, she couldn't help worrying about him in general. This was not a situation she had ever seen precedent for, and she simply didn't know what sort of clinical course to expect. And there was Fass to consider, too, although she was pretty sure this latest exacerbation wouldn't turn into anything seriously worrisome now that he was back on his meds, if only he would be *sensible* about it.

Not that he ever had been, of course. She could remember her father shouting at him twenty years ago for doing precisely the same passively self-destructive things for which she currently found herself shouting at him, with roughly similar levels of success. Fastitocalon's attitude had appealed powerfully to Greta during her early-teen sulky rebellious stage. Now it just exasperated her, in an affectionate sort of way. It was a little strange, being the one to do the shouting, which she avoided thinking about more than she could help.

She was still considering Fastitocalon as a role model for moody fourteen-year-olds when she got back to the car and let herself in. There was an unpleasant sharp and acrid sort of smell, sort of like something burning, and she wondered for a moment if the engine could have somehow overheated on the way up here without her noti—

At this point her thought process cut off absolutely, because something in the backseat rustled, and something very, very cold and sharp was suddenly pressed against the side of her neck.

Greta went completely still. The world seemed to have slowed down to half its normal speed and developed an eerie, glassy clarity. Her blood roared distantly in her ears.

"What do you want?" she said, and was surprised to hear her voice sounding steady and calm. Whoever was holding the sharp thing against her neck was also breathing heavily, as if with effort. The sharp smell had an undertone of rancid saltiness, like something pickled that had gone fulsomely rotten in a dark cellar corner.

"Thou hast done evil above all that were before thee, above all thy sins, and dealt with a familiar spirit, and with wizards; thou hast visited the dwellings of the wicked and given succour, thou hast wrought much evil in the sight of the Lord," he said, and the knife pressed a little closer.

Beyond the sound of her own heartbeat Greta was aware of the faint ticking of the clock in the dashboard, the sounds of traffic on the main road, a hundred yards away; it might as well have been on the moon. She was entirely alone, more alone than she had ever been in her life. *There is no one who can help me,* she thought, feeling herself skidding closer to the edge of some mental precipice. *No one at all.*

Dimly, in another part of her mind, the thought surfaced for a moment and flicked its tail: *What evil? I'm not the one holding a knife to someone's throat.*

"This is the punishment of the sword, that ye may know there is a judgment," the man went on. The voice sounded to her as if its owner couldn't be older than his early twenties, reciting something learned by heart, and Greta wondered who had done the teaching, and why.

Her hand, in the darkness, still held the bundle of keys. Now, very slowly, very slowly indeed, her fingers began to move, even as her mind raced. "Why are you doing this?" she asked, still surprised at just how calm she sounded. "Who sent you?"

He hissed, a gust of rancid breath against her cheek, and the blade he was holding against her throat twitched. "In the name of the Lord God, the Sword of Holiness casts you from the surface of this world," he said in her ear. "Into unending torment and the eternal fire."

The Sword of Holiness, she thought. *The Sword of Holiness, not the Rosary Ripper, and it* is *a group of them, Varney's three attackers and God knows how many more.* She wondered if the ten people who had been featured on the newscast had heard those words, too, before they died—*the Sword of Holiness casts you from the surface of this world*—and in that moment Greta's determination froze solid and immovable. She would *not* be the eleventh, if she had any say in the matter.

Her fingers closed in the darkness around a small squat cylinder, hooked to the same ring as the keys to her house and the Harley Street premises. Her heart thudded rapidly in her chest as she turned the little cylinder between fingers and thumb, hoping desperately that it was still good after spending a year being bounced around in her purse. Everything was still so clear and so slow. Like being inside cold, thick, heavy glass.

She had to make him lean as close as possible, if this was going to work, get his face right down next to her shoulder. "I don't understand," she said, and her voice was as small as she could make it. "What do you mean? What have I done?"

Whoever it was drew in a deep breath—to explain, or condemn, or recite—and in the same instant her right hand came up holding the little can of pepper spray, pointing over her left shoulder, and pushed the button.

After that everything happened very fast. The hiss of the spray was almost completely lost in the bellow of surprise and agony from her assailant; the blade he was holding against her neck scored a thin line of bright acid pain before it fell to the floor, forgotten in his desperate attempts to stop his face from burning. In that instant she, too, cried out, her own eyes and throat on fire from the spray mist—and scrabbled for the door handle, yanked it open, and mostly fell out of the Mini. Oh, it hurt, Jesus *Christ* it hurt. What had he cut her with?

He was still thrashing around in the tiny backseat of the car and howling. Her first instinct was to run, in any direction, get as far away from here as she possibly could, but the part of Greta's mind that had coolly objected to the accusation of *evil* took over. She was not in immediate danger, unless he had friends nearby; the incapacitant spray had done what it said on the tin, and she needed very much to know who and what it was that had attacked her.

Despite the flailing she could make out that he was wearing some sort of dark garment with wide sleeves and a hood, which fell back to expose a head utterly devoid of hair and plated with ugly red and white ridges of scar tissue. Between his clawing fingers tears flowed and glistened in the car's dome light—and then her stomach seized up again in a knot of ice, because between his fingers she could *also* see a bright blue glow, where no light had any business being.

That's not human, she thought. *That's wrong.*

That meant it wasn't a question of crossover, as she had thought on the journey here. Not humans attacking supernaturals and throwing the whole careful structure of secrecy into precarious imbalance. That meant supernaturals attacking *both worlds at once.*

She had to know more. Reluctantly—extremely reluctantly—Greta took a step back toward the car, and then another, the canister of pepper spray still clutched in her right fist. She made herself reach out to open the back door, stared at the writhing form of the man, at the rough-spun fabric of his brown woolen robe, the rope cincture round his waist, the livid scars on face and hands. Those were burn scars, and they were recent, too.

He had dropped whatever he'd been holding to her throat when she got him with the spray, and Greta badly needed to get her hands on it—she had to know as much as possible about the weapon that had injured Varney. A glint of metal on the floor almost under the driver's seat caught her eye. Some kind of dagger. The man was still clutching at his face—if she could just reach past him and *grab* it—

Searing pain shot through her scalp as he seized a handful of her hair and wrenched her head round to look him in the face. It was not a nice face to look into. It would not have been a nice face to look into even had it not been twisted and piebald white and red, or if his eyes had not been giving off *visible blue light.*

"Witch," he choked out. "Filthy...sinful...witch. All of you will die. All of you. The world will be, will be cleansed..."

I'm not a witch, I'm not *a witch,* Greta thought on a jagged hysterical wave of adrenaline. *Nadezhda is the witch, and she's quite clean already—*

She shut her eyes tight, and held her breath, and emptied the rest of the pepper spray right into his face.

He screamed again, a high, thin animal noise, letting go of his handful of her hair, and now Greta was sobbing as she scrabbled under the seat for the weapon he'd been carrying, as she backed away from the car, heedless of the rain that had begun to fall. The lights of the main road, the blessedly ordinary sounds of traffic, beckoned to her, no longer as coldly inaccessible as the surface of the moon.

She dropped the knife, whatever it was—she hadn't even looked at it too closely—into her bag, and ran.

CHAPTER 4

August Cranswell was now on his third large scotch of the evening, and at the comfortable remove of that much twelve-year-old Macallan he was able to observe matters with rather more equanimity.

They were in Ruthven's kitchen, the two books he had brought with him carefully laid open on the table. Ruthven's peculiar friend—who was *grey*, actually faintly grey in complexion, and who apparently was into cosplaying Edward R. Murrow, 1950s pinstripe suit and all—had turned out to be much better at Latin than Cranswell himself was, and he'd gladly yielded up the duty of translation.

"This is all rather formulaic," Vasse was saying. "It's talking about the equivalent of mystery cults, secret societies, that sort of thing, and then it goes into discussing warrior monks, much more to the point."

"When you said that on the phone earlier, Ruthven, I kind of remembered seeing this a year or two back," Cranswell said.

"Took me a while to find it. The other book has the pictures of daggers I was talking about, but this one talks about orders of various Swords."

" 'The Livonian Brothers of the Sword,' " Vasse said, his fingertip not quite touching the ancient paper of the page. "Yes. Early thirteenth century, during the Northern Crusades. It says they got sort of subsumed into the Teutonic Knights, but they weren't the only set of monks at the time who were going around armed to the teeth. The description gets quite lurid in places," he added.

"Right," said Cranswell, who had managed to read most of the page in the uncertain light of the basement but was fully aware he hadn't grasped the nuances. "Several other orders came into being around that time. One of them called itself the Order of the Holy Sword, which looks way cooler in Latin, like a lot of things."

"Gladius Sancti," said Ruthven, peering over Vasse's shoulder. "The sword is to be taken literally, I presume, although what got Varney wasn't a sword so much as a dagger. Or a spike. It left an X-shaped hole in him, which is not something I've seen before."

" 'Holy sword' sounds a bit more impressive than 'holy spike,' " said Vasse, "*vallus sanctus,* but in point of fact *gladius sancti* means 'sword of holiness.' Which is a bit different."

"The general idea gets itself across, details of grammar notwithstanding," said Ruthven, drily. "Presumably they were running around with holy edged weapons *of some description* back in the thirteenth century. I still can't really picture this

Vivian Shaw

thing. I've never seen a wound like that before, and I have seen a great many wounds in my time."

"It's—look, it's easier to just show you," Cranswell said, and turned a few pages in the other book he had brought. Part of him, behind the pleasant insulation of whiskey, was still more than a little astonished that he'd done this deed at all, brought irreplaceable artifacts out of climate-controlled storage without any kind of authorization—*taken them off museum premises,* what had he been *thinking*—but he had been having the kind of day where really, really stupid decisions looked remarkably inviting. His first exhibit, the first one he had ever been assigned to research and put together on his own, the first opportunity he had had as a junior curator to demonstrate that he actually knew what he was doing, wouldn't go up until the new year, but today had been an unremitting hell of logistical pitfalls regarding tiny details of the exhibit, and all in all Cranswell had *needed* the break. And the distraction. And now he wasn't *entirely* sure he could get the damn things back safely and keep his job. The sour adrenaline from the chase through the dark was still sloshing around in his bloodstream, which didn't help matters.

He was using a clean butter knife to turn the pages, rather than touching them with his fingertips, and it took a few moments for him to find the section he wanted: a double woodcut. On the left-hand page was depicted what appeared to be a somewhat standard flaming sword, of the sort wielded by angels at the gates of Eden, and on the right...

"It *is* a spike," Ruthven said. "No. It's a *stake.*"

Cranswell looked sharply at him. Ruthven's eyes were wide and dark, the pupils swallowing up all but a fine ring of silver. After a moment he blinked hard, and they shrank smoothly back to normal. "Tell me," he said conversationally, turning to Vasse, "what else does the book have to say about these individuals?"

Rain spattered against the second-floor windows, blurring the streetlamps into splashes of light, turning the expanse of the Thames into a featureless black field. Through the brocade curtains of a massive four-poster bed, the blotchy light fell across Sir Francis Varney's features, and did them no favors whatsoever.

Varney lay with his silvering hair spread messily over the pillows, white hands twisted in the bedclothes, alternately tossing and lying deathly still as whatever he was dreaming came and went in waves. The gauze taped over his wound had been replaced not long ago, but now a dark stain was once again beginning to spread over the cloth. His fingers twitched, plucking at the covers, and slowly crept back to the dressing as if the wound beneath had begun to burn.

Down in the street a car's wheels spun and skidded in the wet, and the yelp of rubber was followed by the hollow bang of metal on metal as it plowed into the back of a taxi. The report was sharp and loud enough to jerk Varney out of his dreams, and he sat up with a gasp, staring into the darkness, not at all sure where he was. A bright spike of pain from his shoulder made him swear and clap a hand to the place. Then he remembered everything.

First there had been the sudden shock of the garlic, like tear gas, blinding and choking with its acrid stink; then, reeling from that, he had only just been able to make out the forms of the attackers through streaming eyes, far too late to be able to escape them even if he hadn't been incapacitated. Indistinct dark figures, robed and hooded, and voices chanting. *Unclean, accursed, creature of the Devil, spawn of the pit.* And then pain had burst and flowered in his shoulder, bright hot drilling pain, and the shock had cleared his vision enough to glimpse the ugly spike buried in his flesh before everything had gone sick-dark and cold.

Varney could only just remember coming to, and stumbling away from the poison smeared on the walls and door, and finding his way through the night to the only place he could think of that might offer him succour in this dreadful city. Then there had been a pale man with a high forehead and strange eyes—Ruthven, Lord Ruthven, as he'd so desperately hoped, still at this address after so many years—and hot blood, *proper* blood, wonderfully rich and heartening, and then a strange woman with pale hair, a thin, worried face. A doctor. She had looked hardly old enough to bear the title, and he had—oh, God, he'd *snarled* at her, hadn't he, it had been a couple of years now, he'd been doing so *well*—and then there had been a confusing kind of dizziness that made everything go away for a little while.

He shivered, cold and hot at once, and ran a hand through his tangled hair. He was apparently wearing someone else's pajamas, which wasn't a reassuring realization in the slightest, and the silk felt unpleasantly damp where it clung to his shoulders and back. Too warm. He must have been sweating. That in itself was worrisome.

It had been a very long time since Varney had been actively hunted, but one did not forget the heavy fear in one's belly, nor the acute awareness of tiny sounds and movements. He heard soft footsteps approaching the bedroom door now and froze, knowing his legs would not support him if he did try to run, if there had been anywhere to run to.

The knob turned almost soundlessly, and the door opened a fraction, enough to throw a bar of cheerful yellow electric light across the carpet. Varney's pupils contracted painfully at the sudden light and he shrank back against the pillows.

"Ah," said a voice, and the door opened the rest of the way, silhouetting a familiar form. "You *are* awake. How are you feeling?"

Varney shut his eyes, relief flooding through him, as Ruthven came over to the bed and frowned at the stain of blood on the bandages. "Somewhat improved," he said after a moment, glad his voice sounded more or less steady. "Again, I cannot possibly thank you enough for your hospitality."

"Nonsense." Ruthven sat down beside the bed. "One of the junior curators at the British Museum's something of a friend of mine and he's been good enough to borrow some very useful books for us. We've found something in one of them that looks to me as if it might be the kind of dagger used in your attack. Do you feel up to looking at a few woodcuts?"

"Of course," Varney said, and made an effort to sit properly upright, which shot another bolt of pain through his wound and sent glittering sparks drifting across his vision. Sound faded out for a moment or two. How long had it been since he'd died, the last time? He was *decaying*, that's what it was. Decay of the system.

"I want Greta to dress that properly again," Ruthven was saying, his big silver eyes narrowed. He reached over to rest the back of his hand against Varney's forehead. The touch was unexpected, and Varney blinked up at him, astonished by the chill of the hand, gentle as it was. "And you still feel awfully warm to me," Ruthven went on. "I'll bring the books up for you, but you mustn't get worked up about it, all right?"

Varney let his eyes half-close and listened to the slow beating of his own blood in his ears. It *was* warm in here. "Of course. I promise to behave."

Ruthven quirked a long eyebrow at him, but said nothing further, and after another moment the door shut behind him. Varney was left in the dimness.

Ever since the attack he'd been fighting off a dull awareness that the words used by his assailants were accurate. He *was* a monster, accursed of God, unclean, a dead thing walking the earth to feed on the living; each time he had been hunted before, his hunters had a reason. In all his long existence

Varney had never done anyone more good than harm, nor even wanted to.

A vast wave of melancholy, bland and grey as tears, broke over him; it was a very familiar feeling.

Downstairs Ruthven found Fastitocalon carefully copying out the description of the Order of the Holy Sword, or possibly Sword of Holiness, into a pocket notebook.

According to the text, the Gladius Sancti had been considered a bit weird even by the standards of the day, and had gone around setting fire to bits of the countryside and generally making a nuisance of themselves. It had been somewhat of a relief when they apparently gave up and disbanded; they had, however, merely gone underground into full-on secret-society mode. The book mentioned in particular that they had resurfaced in the seventeenth century, at the height of witch hunting, and they had not been simply after *witches*: Their quarry was *demons*, by which they apparently meant all sorts of supernatural creatures, or in practice anybody they didn't much like.

Which seemed to be almost everybody. The really interesting part, to Ruthven's mind, had been the details about their rumored possession of an *actual* blessed sword of some kind, like the Spear of Destiny, brought out of the Holy Land— and with it a recipe for a sacred chrism to anoint ordinary blades and render them capable of slaying demons. Ruthven didn't know about *demons*, but whatever had been on the blade used to stab Varney had done him absolutely no good whatsoever.

He was, nonetheless, finally on the mend, Ruthven reminded himself, and said as much to Fastitocalon. "Wants to see what we've got, apparently lucid and *compos mentis*, if feverish. I do hope Greta gets back soon, though. I'd be happier with a medical expert on hand."

Fastitocalon smiled a little. "I shouldn't worry. She's got every intention of attaching herself limpetlike to the household as long as you've got Varney tucked up in your spare room. She was fretting all afternoon about not being here to keep an eye on him, in between delivering lectures for my benefit." He coughed. "You could ring her up and tell her he's awake; she'd probably be glad to hear it."

"I think I ought, yes. Look, can you take that book with the woodcuts up to Sir Francis and see whether it's anything like the weapon he remembers?"

"Certainly, if you're sure he won't be put off by having total strangers visit while he's indisposed." Fastitocalon looked up at Ruthven with a wry smile. "I wouldn't blame him."

"I shouldn't think he'll mind in the least. You'll probably do him a power of good."

Ruthven supposed Greta was stuck in traffic; it was not a nice night to be driving. He went through to the kitchen for his mobile, hearing Fastitocalon coughing as he climbed the stairs, and felt a twinge of worry. Probably he should have bullied Fass into bed, rather than getting him to help out with the research project du jour.

He put on a kettle, listening to the phone ring on the other end. Most likely she *was* stuck in traffic and too busy driving to pick up; he'd just text her instead. He was about to end the call when her voice came on the line, uneven and thickened with tears, and he could feel his pupils contracting with surprise.

"R-Ruthven," she was saying, unsteadily. "I've seen one of them. I've seen one of them up close, he was *in my car*, he was *in my goddamned car*, and I don't know how many others there might be—"

"What happened?" he demanded. "Are you all right? Where are you?"

"On the bus, all the way in the back. I wanted to be around *people*. With lights."

"I'm coming to get you," he said, turning off the stove.

"*No*," she said, and there was real urgency in her voice. "No, don't, stay right there. Don't leave the house, Ruthven. They're probably watching you right now; they know where you live."

"Who, for God's sake? What happened, Greta? What the hell's going on?"

"He said they were the Holy something." She sounded a little more focused now. "Dressed like a monk. Talked in— what sounded like Bible quotes, all about evil and wickedness, just like Varney's attackers—"

Ruthven went cold all over, the little hairs on the backs of his arms prickling as they stood erect. "The Sword of Holiness?" he interrupted her.

"Yes," said Greta, sounding terribly young. "Yes, that was

it. He was—burned. And his eyes were—it's not *possible*, but they were *glowing blue*, I don't know *what* he was, and there's more of them, I don't know how many, Ruthven. It's *them.* The ones who are killing people."

"In the name of purification," he said, not really asking a question.

"Yes," she said again. "That's right. I'm—I'm two stops away from Blackfriars. I'll be there soon."

The line went dead, and Ruthven took the phone away from his ear, staring down at it, his pupils slowly expanding again. It was rare for Greta Helsing to let anyone see, or even hear, her cry. That in itself was enough to send a creeping finger of dread down his backbone, a cold, sick feeling that vast things were spinning out of control.

He shook himself and hurried through to the hall for his coat and keys and an umbrella. Never mind her instructions not to leave the house. If he started behaving like that at his age it was only a short step to hiding in the cellar and hissing at people, and he'd spent enough time complaining about that sort of thing already.

It was, in fact, a dark and stormy night, with a little thunder muttering in the east over the Isle of Dogs, and the people he passed on the street were hurrying to get out of it, heads burrowed down into hunched shoulders. Nobody paid him any attention as he made his way toward the Blackfriars bus stop: just another man in a dark coat, perhaps paler than most, his black hair combed straight back from a high forehead. The overall effect was slightly spoiled by the fact that dampness made his hair frizz.

Ruthven leaned against a handy wall and made himself unnoticeable, fading into the background, just an unremarkable figure in an unremarkable location. He had a few minutes to wait before Greta's bus arrived, and he wanted to keep a good lookout for any more people interested in damaging him and his friends. Nothing seemed to pose an obvious threat, though. While he listened to the rain beat on his umbrella and scanned the road and pavement, he considered again what they'd found out so far.

It was not immediately evident to him why something out of the more obscure and less desirable annals of history had suddenly popped up here, in London, in the present day, but the similarities were beyond question. The people who were responsible for the attack on Varney—and now on Greta, too, which Ruthven couldn't think about too hard just yet—had clearly been reading the same books he'd just seen, and he didn't know if it was worse to imagine that they were *following the example of* the past, or that they were trying to *re-create* it.

And if they were determined to cause this much of a nuisance for Ruthven and his friends, what else might they be up to? There were a large number of people in London who might fall under the broad category of *undead* for the purposes of persecution. He hadn't heard of anyone else being attacked by robed assassins, but that didn't mean it wasn't happening, or hadn't happened already.

He looked up as the blunt snout of the bus hove into view, its windows bright and cheerful in the darkness, and detached himself from the wall. First things first, he'd get Greta home and make sure she was all right, and *then* he would consider the reappearance of murderous monastic orders and try to make sense of it.

The rain intensified, pouring down the gutters and washing rubbish in clots and tangles down into the tunnels below. Greta had to wait for everyone else to shuffle down the aisle and down the bus steps before she could get out—and then half-fell into Ruthven's waiting arms with a distinct lack of grace, burying her face against his shoulder.

He held her close, his arms around her hard and strong as iron bars, his skin very smooth and cool and white, and the familiar smell of whatever he put on his hair was absurdly comforting: something a little like roses, sharp and faintly sweet. She could feel his heartbeat, slow and even and deep, and that steady rhythm seemed to settle her own racing pulse a little.

She clung to Ruthven, her face pressed into his shoulder and her arms wrapped tight around his ribs, and he simply held her for a few minutes, stroking her hair, and then sighed.

"It's a miserable night," he said, reasonably, "and the way our luck's been going, one or both of us are going to come down with something if we stand around here any longer. Come on, we are going back to the house and you are going to have a very large drink. Perhaps two large drinks. I haven't decided."

Greta gave a little unsteady snicker and after another moment unwound herself from him, rubbing at her face, glad it was dark. She was not one of the rare but infuriating people who could cry becomingly, which was one of the reasons she tried very hard not to do it. "All right," she said, "but if anyone comes at us with sharp things I'm going to let you handle it. I've had enough of that for tonight."

Ruthven's mouth thinned, but he didn't say anything, just put his arm around her waist and let her lean on him for the brief walk back.

In the darkness and the pouring rain, not a soul noticed the two pinpoints of blue light slowly withdrawing from a storm drain in the pavement opposite the house, or the emergence, a moment later, of several terrified rats.

In the warmth and light of the entrance hall, he took her coat—and then stared, tipped up her chin with a finger, and swore.

"What?" She twitched away from him. Ruthven looked uncharacteristically *worried*, focused intently on her. "What is it?" she repeated.

"Why didn't you *say* they'd done their best to cut your throat? Oh, Christ and all his little angels. Come and sit down before you fall over, and let me clean that out for you."

Greta stared at him, then took a step toward the side table with its green mirror and pulled her scarf away from her neck. Where the man's blade had bitten, over the great vein just below the angle of her jaw, an angry red furrow marked her flesh. The tissue was puffed and shiny around it, and as the relief of being back in the safety of Ruthven's home began to sink in, she was increasingly aware that it hurt. Well, not so much hurt as *burned*. It felt like lye on unprotected skin.

"Oh," she said, blinking at herself in the mirror, and found the floor suddenly tilting under her feet like the deck of a ship in rough seas. The familiar checkered marble of the entry hall went sparkly grey. Distantly she could hear Ruthven saying some words unfit for polite company, and then the floor gave another dizzying heave and everything went away for a little while.

CHAPTER 5

Greta opened her eyes and blinked, and couldn't work out exactly what it was she was looking at. A flat surface, mostly white, and the edge of some kind of raised pattern, curly leaves and flowers twining into each other.

After a moment or two her eyes decided to focus, and she recognized the plaster-work pattern of Ruthven's drawing room ceiling. This revelation prompted some more blinking.

She sat up, or rather tried to, surprised to find that the room swung dizzily around her, and had to shut her eyes very tight for a moment or two until it decided to settle back down again. Her neck hurt like hell. A brief exploration revealed that somebody had taped a gauze dressing over the cut.

A second, slower attempt at regaining verticality met with more success. Still touching the pad of gauze, Greta looked around. She was lying on the nicer of the drawing room sofas, with Fastitocalon ensconced in an armchair nearby. He looked up as she stirred, and marked his place in the book he was reading.

"Back with us?" he said mildly.

The immediate past was filtering back into her memory little by little. Greta could recall getting off the bus and wrapping around Ruthven like a panicky octopus, and then it was raining on her, and then he'd said something and... everything had gone grey and sparkly, and Greta had no idea how much time she'd lost. She made herself stop fiddling with the bandage, with an effort; she wanted to get a look at the cut itself and make sure it was properly clean.

"I didn't go anywhere," she told Fastitocalon.

"You fainted dead away," he said, reaching over to the coffee table for a cup of something. "Don't worry; you haven't been out more than, oh, I'd say fifteen or twenty minutes. Quite a creditable swoon, if I'm any judge; Ruthven caught you in his arms very prettily indeed, just like in the films. I expect he felt quite pleased with himself. Drink your nice tea; it's good for you."

"I don't faint," Greta said crossly. "Or at least I've never done it before, and I don't plan on doing it again." She took the cup in both hands. "How's Varney?" Thank God *he* hadn't seen that; it was bad enough for Ruthven to have witnessed it, but Varney was a comparative stranger, and she particularly hated doing embarrassing things in front of people she didn't know.

The tea was strong and extremely sweet, with brandy in it, and she realized with a slightly sheepish smile that it was exactly what she'd push on someone else under the circumstances. *Oh, Fass.*

"Varney," he said, "is awake and talking. Ruthven's with him now. He's led an interesting life, apparently. We had quite a nice little conversation about being ancient and decrepit, he and I." Fastitocalon coughed. "And he was good enough to confirm that the account we found in one of that young chap Cranswell's books sounded a great deal like the people who'd attacked him. Some sort of medieval warrior monks wielding magic swords, if you can imagine."

Greta stared at him, and then put down the teacup and looked wildly around the room. "Where's my bag? What happened to my bag?"

"Right here," August Cranswell said, coming through from the kitchen with Greta's battered handbag. She recognized him after a blank moment; they'd met at a party Ruthven had thrown several months back.

"You're awake," Cranswell added, unnecessarily. "Are you okay? What's going on?"

She pushed herself to her feet, grimly fighting off another wave of dizziness, and grabbed the bag out of his hands. Ignoring the others for the moment, she rummaged frantically through the litter of phone and notebook and Chapstick and keys and receipts and bits of string. Her fingers closed around something cold and heavy at the very bottom of the bag, and her hand shook a little as she drew it out into the light.

It was a knife about eight and a half inches long, including the hilt. The blade, or blades, tapered to a sharp point, and resembled two daggers intersecting at right angles, forming an X. Or a cross. Where the blades met the leather-strapped hilt, the metal was a sort of tarnished-looking silver color, but from a little farther down the length of the cross-shaped blade was covered by a dull dark grey coating. It looked powdery, friable. Here and there a little of it had flaked off, revealing the paler metal beneath.

One of the four blade edges had a dark smudge along it, and Greta's other hand rose slowly to the wound on her throat.

London's lost rivers had taken on a romantic sort of mystery in popular awareness. The idea of waters flowing on and on in the endless darkness under the city streets was deliciously eerie, and of course lost and abandoned tunnels and caverns had always appealed to a certain sort of adventurous spirit. Even the names were evocative: the Tyburn, the Fleet, the Effra, the Westbourne, once broad streams in their own right—now bound and channeled in the bowels of the ancient city, but not entirely forgotten. The old rivers flowed now in a muffled roar and chime of water through cathedrals of tile and brick, unseen arches and coigns of gorgeous complexity guiding and shaping their eventual journey to the sea.

Now the unrelieved darkness of one of these tunnels resolved itself around two pinpoints of light, moving with a steady loping rhythm against the flow of dirty water. There was a heavy, almost snoring sound of breathing accompanying the two glowing points as they proceeded through the darkness; that breathing and the slosh and splatter of footsteps echoed and re-echoed in the close confines of the tunnel, so narrow a bore that the creature moving through it had to stoop over; but after a few minutes the pipe abruptly opened into a much larger chamber. It paused, just inside the opening, the little steady pinpoints of light blinking on and off twice, and then moved out into the wider space beyond.

The illumination of those pinpoints was limited to perhaps two or three feet of distance, but the creature did not actually require visible light to perceive its surroundings; it could see quite well. It stood in a high-ceilinged space. Above it stretched an arching, intersecting set of vaults at sharp angles to one another, the old brick glistening with slime. Other tunnels opened into the chamber, black maws in the greater blackness.

It stood there for several minutes—apparently waiting for something. Eventually a second pair of blue pinpoints appeared in the mouth of an intersecting tunnel, higher up on the chamber's wall.

The second creature came to a halt looking down at the first; there was silence again in the chamber, underneath the rush and murmur of moving water. "Well?" the newcomer demanded, after a moment.

"The monster-doctor lives," said the first. "Wounded, but not severely. She is with the demons again. Under their protection."

There was a hiss, and the points of light above it blinked on and off, once, and steadied as their owner regained control of itself. It looked down once more. "She is unclean and shares the habitation of devils; she is anathema; she nurses the wicked." It paused, and when it spoke again the voice was cold and blade-sharp around the edges. "Our brother has failed to destroy her; the task will be given to one more worthy. He will find no welcome for him among our order, but the retribution of sins. Henceforward he, too, is excommunicate and anathema. Find him, and cast him out."

In the darkness of the chamber the first pair of lights moved, and the short, ugly blade of a knife gleamed bright for a moment, drawn from its sheath and then replaced again. "It will be done," it said.

"Go. Instruct the others and then continue your vigil."

"*Lux aeterna*," said the thing, and it bowed, low, before turning and loping away into the dark. Behind it, the twin blue pinpoints of its interlocutor remained still for a moment longer, watching until it was beyond the range of even these rather remarkable senses; shortly afterward complete and utter darkness returned to the chamber where three tunnels met.

In Crouch End, the rain had tapered off to the sort of miserable drizzle common to Novembers all over the world, and the dome light of Greta's abandoned Mini was fading to a dull, tea-colored glow as the car's elderly battery gave up what was left of the ghost.

The driver's-side door was closed; the back door on that side gaped open, and rain had soaked the worn upholstery from blue to black. The car stank of the incapacitant spray residue that coated most of its interior, and also of old sweat and something unpleasantly sharp and acrid, metallic. Here and there on the backseat little shreds of something that looked like damp tissue paper lay mashed into the upholstery. Some of them still showed the raised loops and whorls of fingerprints.

The Mini was parked along the curb of Middle Lane, not far from the gate leading into the adjoining Priory Park. In the mud by the gate itself, a couple of footprints and a twist of some sort of brown fiber caught in the ironwork bore witness to the fact that someone had passed that way since it began to rain.

Nobody was there when a dark, indistinct figure stumbled out of the trees; nobody but a couple of sparrows were disturbed when it slipped on the wet grass and fell into some bushes, or staggered to its feet again, leaving tufts of coarse-spun wool snagged on the branches. No one was there to register its labored, painful breathing, or the words it was muttering in little runs as it made its way across the park. It was, or up until fairly recently had been, a man.

The shiny, lumpy pink scars of recent burns stood out against hairless white skin, piebald and blotchy; his eyebrows and eyelashes had vanished, his teeth showed an odd dark stain at the gum line, and his mouth was twisted up on one side with scar tissue. What had happened to his eyes was perhaps the worst. They were the white of poached eggs, a blank mass of pale, formless, membranous tissue. They were eyes that had, quite literally, been cooked.

And they were also *glowing faintly blue*. At the moment it

was almost impossible to tell, as the remains of his face were scarlet and puffy with the effects of capsaicin spray, the eyes almost swollen shut, a trickle of blood here and there where he had clawed at his skin in a helpless attempt to stop the burning—but little slits of light still showed between the lids. It had been several hours since the attack, and his frantic coughing had subsided, but the pain of the spray on the burn-scar tissue was slower to fade.

He knew very little at the moment other than that the monster-doctor woman had escaped him, and that this had displeased God, with the consequent punishment of physical agony. Words of prayers he had only just committed to memory came back to him, and he was muttering them as he crossed the park, following a distant yet undeniable call in his head. He knew which direction he needed to go in to reach the holy light. As soon as he found the right kind of way down into the tunnels, he would leave the surface and make his way there.

By the time the abandoned Mini's dome light guttered out completely, he had, in fact, gone underground.

CHAPTER 6

Tuesday morning came grey and bleak, the sourceless light of a winter dawn throwing no shadows over the vast arching teeth of the Thames Barrier, rendering Cleopatra's Needle a dull white spike, flattening the baroque shadow-play on St. Paul's dome. Even without venturing into the streets, people could feel the bone-coldness of the city, feel the year's end creeping upward from the soles of their feet.

It was August Cranswell who got up and made the day's first pot of tea, wearing a borrowed dressing gown over his boxers and a T-shirt advertising the fact that Guinness was Good for You. Both Ruthven and Varney were still sleeping the sleep of the undead, and Greta had made Fastitocalon swallow a fairly powerful antihistamine before the lot of them trooped severally off to bed. Cranswell had the house to himself.

He went to fetch the newspaper, pausing for a moment on Ruthven's front steps to watch the early traffic crawl along the Embankment and the poor bastards who had no choice but to be not only up and about but working at this hour toil along the pavement, breathing out great clouds of white in the frigid air. Winter had definitely shoved autumn out of the way and settled in for a good long stretch of bitter chill to wind up the year. Cranswell wondered how the mad monks planned to celebrate Christmas, and decided he didn't want to know.

In the kitchen he put the kettle on and unfolded the newspaper. The headline screamed RIPPER DEATH TOLL RISES TO 11: NEW VICTIM DISCOVERED AFTER YESTERDAY'S TWO KILLINGS.

Cranswell hadn't caught the news of the latest murder on the radio the evening before—he'd been too busy perpetrating theft of antiquities—and now he read with a dull kind of horror about the tenth *and* eleventh victims. It was somehow worse to realize he had almost become *used* to reading about murders, that there was very little shock in his reaction, just intensifying fear.

The article made particular mention of the plastic rosaries found at all the scenes so far:

The Roman Catholic Diocese of Westminster has released a statement condemning the activity of this serial murderer and in no uncertain terms vilifying his or her blasphemous tactic of using rosaries as an accessory to his or her crimes. Some commentators have questioned the actual sanctity of the rosaries involved, given that they are apparently massproduced in Taiwan and retail for 50p apiece, but so far this point has not been directly addressed by the diocese.

The kettle boiled, and Cranswell made the tea, glad for the brief distraction.

He'd been frightened—badly frightened—by the previous night's experience; in fact he thought he had never been quite so scared in his entire *life*, which sparked exactly no desire to go home at the moment. The fact that he didn't *know* what he'd seen, or thought he had seen, was no comfort whatsoever; he didn't want to go out there right now. The Embankment house was much nicer than Cranswell's flat; also he rather strongly wanted to remain under the immediate protection of someone physically capable of tying lampposts in knots.

Ruthven wouldn't mind putting him up for a few more days. He was always encouraging people to come and stay with him; it was not out of any noticeable desire to bite their necks—unless they were into that, maybe—but Cranswell thought partly just because he was lonely. It must *be* inescapably lonely, being *that* old, having watched so many people come and go, quite separate from the ordinary lives all around him. Having to pretend he was one of them, for the most part.

Ruthven was good at pretending. He *didn't*, in fact, tie lampposts in knots; that was precisely the sort of objectionable and dangerous showing off that he condemned roundly in the supernatural community. Cranswell could remember a story Ruthven had told him two or three years ago, in which a group of very young and very stylish vampires had been given the choice of leaving the city in a hurry or having their pretty necks wrung, after a series of unacceptably high-profile incidents. "But you're one of the *Kindred*," their leader had said, according to Ruthven. "You're *above* the humans."

"I expect," Ruthven had told him, "that if you ever actually take the time to think clearly about what you've just said, you will be absolutely paralyzed with embarrassment. You are barely a decade changed and you have been reading entirely too many tiresome novels. We are not above or below the living, we are *beside* them, and if we want to go on existing at all we have to understand that the secrecy must be maintained for *everybody's* sake. I thought the way you're thinking, four hundred years ago and change, and it was only through sheer dumb luck that I survived that thought process. Get out of my city and grow up, if you can manage it."

And then he *had* hit the leader hard enough to break quite a lot of bones, mostly because by then he had realized that rational conversation wasn't doing the trick, and put the lot of them on a lorry heading for the Midlands. Nobody had heard from that particular soi-disant coven again, and Cranswell wondered from time to time whether any of them were still around, and what they'd ended up doing with themselves.

Cranswell's own familial connection with the world of the supernatural dated back to the early nineteenth century, when two Cranswell brothers, Michael and Edward, and their sister Amelia, had leased an unprepossessing property in Cumberland known as Croglin Low Hall, and were unfortunate enough to catch the attention of a local and extremely uncivilized vampire. Amelia was attacked and survived the encounter, although much weakened, and after a trip to Switzerland to get her strength back had with considerable pluck returned to Croglin with her brothers to lure the creature from its lair and put it properly to rest.

After that success they had stayed at the house only a year or two before Michael received an inheritance from a distant aunt; then the family could afford to move to London, where they had remained ever since. Edward—August's great-great-grandfather—had become an authority on mythology and superstition, and the next generations carried on the work of gathering as much knowledge as possible about creatures like the one from Croglin.

Like the Helsing family—who had dropped the *van* from their name in the 1930s, fleeing the Netherlands ahead of the gathering storm of World War II—the Cranswells had found themselves making a transition from *hunters* to simply *scholars*, after having made actual neutral contact with the supernatural. In their case, August's great-grandfather had found himself face-to-face with Lord Ruthven, the latter having been uncharacteristically careless about *being seen* while changing forms, and had managed to convince Ruthven not to immediately thrall away his memory. The subsequent conversation had surprised both parties with its pleasant interest; and after that first meeting a tentative friendship had developed. It didn't take long to solidify, based on mutual respect, and—after a little while longer—mutual trust; Ruthven and the Cranswell family had been good friends ever since.

It had in fact been Ruthven, without the title, who introduced Cranswell's father to the woman he would end up marrying, a Nigerian scholar doing a postdoc at University College London. August himself had first met Ruthven seven years ago; his father had been dying, and August had come home from his master's program at Harvard to be there. Francis Cranswell had introduced Ruthven to his son as an old family friend who would *look after* August and his mother.

This Ruthven had done. Adeola Cranswell's mortgage had been paid off, the death duties taken care of, and her aging car repaired—he had offered several times to replace it, but she told him not to be silly—and August's student debt mysteriously vanished without trace. That in itself would have been enough to endear the vampire to him forever, world without end, but he simply *liked* Ruthven as a person, money or no money. Even after the revelation of his actual nature.

In fact, he owed his job at the British Museum partly to Ruthven's influence, and had been more than happy to oblige whenever asked to do a bit of specialist research. He'd always found his scholarship and time well rewarded—with prettily penned notes accompanying generous and prettily penned checks, or tickets to some particularly desirable show, or reservations for dinner for two at the Petrus.

"Really," Ruthven had said when the question of his nature had first (awkwardly) arisen, early in their acquaintance, "the easiest thing is to think of me as a large well-dressed mosquito, only with more developed social graces and without the disease-vector aspect. Actually the leech is probably a more accurate simile, but the mosquito tends to offer less objectionable aesthetic connotations. It doesn't hurt; the bite wounds heal almost immediately, with only a little itching; people have no memory of the experience. I don't take more from any single individual than they'd give in a Red Cross blood drive, and half the time I just get by on blood packets Greta collects for me."

"But," Cranswell had said, "what about the killing people thing? In all the books and movies?"

"Well, really," Ruthven had told him, looking rather tired, "don't you think it'd sort of attract public attention, all these random individuals dropping dead of sudden blood loss? Any vampire who kills when he or she feeds is a vampire with some rather significant impulse-control problems, plus I'm not even sure it would be comfortably *possible* to down that many pints of the stuff in one go. Even if you don't have access to blood from a bank, it's much easier and wiser to take a small amount from several individuals than drain one person to the point of death, and far less likely to get you noticed by people with the pitchfork-and-torch mentality."

Cranswell had blinked at him. "That...actually kind of makes sense."

"Exactly, which is why nobody suspects it. Do try to keep up, Mr. Cranswell."

He smiled, remembering Ruthven's long-suffering expression, and went to call the office and tell them he wouldn't be coming in.

*   *   *

The Embankment house was three stories high. Ruthven's bedroom faced the river, as did the two spare rooms flanking it; on the other side of the hall the smaller and less ostentatious apartments where Cranswell and Greta had been installed looked over the back garden. Cranswell balanced the tray against his hip and knocked gently on the doctor's door. After a moment she called out "Yes?"

"Cup of tea?"

"Oh," she said, sounding surprised. "Thank you. Come in?"

Cranswell let himself in. The curtains were still drawn, but the lamp on the bedside table was lit, the crystal and silver on the dressing table glittering softly in its low light. Greta was sitting up in bed, a book on her lap.

"Did I wake you?" he asked, looking suitably apologetic.

"No, course not. Here." She cleared off a litter of several other books from the table beside the lamp for him to set the tray down. "Thanks. It's awfully nice of you. I take it the rest of them are still abed?"

"Yup, no sign of anyone else stirring." Cranswell handed her a cup. "I didn't know if you took sugar— How's the neck?"

She made a face and managed to stop herself before she rubbed at it. "Hurts a bit. Mostly just itching. I don't think the stuff on that blade did me any serious harm, and I cleaned it out properly last night." The knife itself, as Cranswell knew, was sealed inside three layers of plastic and safely out of the way in the garage: Greta had insisted on keeping it as far as possible from Varney, Ruthven, and Fastitocalon.

"D'you have any idea what it is?" he said. "The, ah, the coating?"

"Not really. My friend's looking at the bit I took out of Sir Francis's wound. If it's the same stuff we ought to know some-time today what it's made of. But it's not affected me anything like the way it did him."

"Because you're human," Cranswell said, settling on the side of the bed with his own teacup. "Right? I mean, from what the Museum books say, it's pretty certain they designed that stabby spike thing to hurt demons, which I guess includes vampires in the definition."

"Mmh." Greta didn't look particularly happy about it. "It's a pretty vague definition, then."

"Well, vampires, monsters, undead creatures, demons, all that kind of falls together, right?"

"Not from the medical standpoint," Greta said. "It makes rather a lot of difference. Anyway, we know it doesn't do vampyres any good at all, but Varney seems to be on the mend. I really do have to get over to the clinic at least for part of the day. It's flu season for the ghouls, and I need to see Mr. Renenutet about his feet, and...there's so much to *do* and I can't just let Nadezhda and Anna handle everything on their own. Or refer everybody to Dr. Richthorn, the other special-ist. Hounslow's a *long* way for them to go." She tucked hair behind her ear.

"What are you going to do about your car?" Cranswell asked.

Greta looked up at him in shocked realization. "Christ, it's still up there. In Crouch End. Full of pepper spray. I'll have to take the tube."

"You know, I wouldn't," Cranswell said, slowly, realizing this even as he spoke. There was a sort of *formless* fear that had been lapping at his thoughts ever since he'd woken, and the idea of being underground was repellent for no very good reason. "Wouldn't go down into the dark if you don't specifically have to. Take the bus. Or have Ruthven drive you over."

She rubbed at her face, the pale hair slipping forward again to cover her hands. "Maybe you're right. Oh, hell, what time is it?"

"About half past eight."

"Mmh. Okay, I suppose that's not too bad. I'll have a shower and try to wake up and then see Varney, and then go over to the clinic one way or another. You're staying here for . . . for the duration?"

"Yeah. I called in to work, told them I had the flu and I'd be out for a few days. I'm kind of surprised that you're looking to leave the house, to be honest."

"If I didn't have things I really couldn't put off, I'd stay right here, and maybe hide under the blankets," Greta said. "I suppose I've got to call the police about the attack last night as well, and be shouted at for not reporting it at once."

He made a face. "You probably should. And I really do have to get those books back to the museum, but Lord knows how without making it obvious that I pinched them in the first place."

"How'd you get them out?"

"Oh, one of those little cards in each storage locker, you know, Removed for Conservation by Squiggle Signed on Line, that sort of thing. Thank God they weren't actually on display. I'd have had to mess with the security cameras, and I'm not even remotely secret-agency enough." Cranswell dropped his head into his hands and groaned. "I can't actually believe I did that. I'd had a pretty awful day and—sort of acted on impulse, instead of talking myself out of it. I'm kind of amazed I didn't get caught, to be honest. Maybe I could smuggle them back into the conservation department under the cover of a really big coat."

"Maybe you could borrow one of the gents who can alter perceptions of reality," Greta said, not unsympathetically. "If Fass feels up to it, I know he can do things to, say, security guards' awareness of your presence. I'm sure he'd be willing to help."

"Who *is* he?" Cranswell asked her.

"Fass is.... an old friend of the family? To be honest it's really rather difficult to tell exactly *what* he is. I mean, he's known me since I was born, he was one of Dad's good friends, and he's looked like that ever since I can remember. It's... well, you know, it'd be really awkward to sit him down and say to him, 'Hey, I've been meaning to ask you, what sort of creature are you anyhow?' after all these years." He *wasn't* human, that much she knew for a fact—the longevity and lack of aging were a dead giveaway, plus the grey complexion and the supernatural powers—but physiologically it was difficult to distinguish Fastitocalon from any other fiftyish man with a bad chest.

"What does he do again?" Cranswell asked.

"He's an accountant. Absolutely loves numbers, you know? He tried to teach me calculus back in school and I wasn't having any, but I could still see how much he loved the subject. He does math for fun on the back of envelopes. It's his thing."

Cranswell shuddered. "But you said he can...manipulate perceptions of reality?"

"Ye-es," Greta said, finishing her tea. "I've certainly seen him do things like convince people he isn't there, or unlock locks without a key, that kind of stuff. I'm pretty sure if you asked nicely he'd go with you to the museum and help you get those books back to their proper homes."

He wasn't wholly convinced, but nodded after a moment. "Maybe you're right. Not like I have a hell of a lot of choices right now. If I want to keep my job."

"Pretty much what I was thinking." Greta gave him a wry look. "Oh, what a huge, gigantic bloody mess this all is. Thanks awfully for the tea, Mr. Cranswell—"

"August. And it's no problem—I was gonna go see what there is for breakfast, if you have any requests."

She smiled, an actual honest-to-God smile that made Cranswell feel as if the world might not be spinning *entirely* off its proper track after all, and said, "Bacon. Lots of bacon, and at least one egg."

*   *   *

Sometime later, a little more presentable and fortified with breakfast, Greta Helsing knocked gently on the door of Varney's room. There was a faint stirring within, and then a mellifluous, if rather weak, voice called out, "Enter."

Greta entered. He was lying as she'd last seen him, propped up on pillows, his grey-streaked hair spread out in tangled waves, but there was a little more color in his face, which was nice to see. "Good morning, Sir Francis. How are you feeling?"

Varney looked up at her as she approached the bedside. His eyes really *were* metallic, she thought, famously described in the terrible novel as *polished tin*. She hadn't been quite sure of her initial observation, but there it was, unmistakable in daylight. The irises were a dark shining grey like tarnished mirrors, catching and reflecting the light in little gleams as they moved. She wondered what was behind the effect, and if that was part of the specific vampyre physiology. Like the beautiful voice. Was that some peculiarity of the larynx common to the species, or was it just Varney himself?

"I have certainly felt worse, Doctor," he said, and she could hear the capital *D*. "But what of yourself? I understand from Ruthven that you experienced a terrifying attack last night. I do hope you have taken no serious hurt."

Greta shrugged, exercising some effort not to reach up to the bandage on her neck. *Taken no serious hurt*; he sounded so courtly, and she was again vividly aware that she was wearing jeans and a somewhat threadbare sweater, not the ruffles and lace that this house and its decor called for. Vampires and fancy clothing just *went together*; it was one of those things.

"I'm all right," she said. "The spike just scratched me, and whatever's on it doesn't seem to be doing me anything like so much harm as it's done you. Under the tongue, please." She handed him a thermometer, sitting on the edge of the bed.

Varney's eyes narrowed as he looked from her face to her throat, taking in the light gauze dressing taped over the cut, but he accepted the thermometer with decent grace. His teeth were just as white as Ruthven's, but the pattern of the dentition was different. His upper pre-canines as well as the canines were a little elongated. She wasn't likely to forget the sight of those teeth bared in a snarl at her, when she had first woken him out of a feverish doze. That one was going to stick around for a while.

The thermometer beeped, and she reclaimed it for a look, relieved both at the distraction and at the reading. "Not bad at all," she said. "You're down to eighty-three; that's much, much better than you've been. Did you sleep all right?"

Varney lifted a hand and let it fall, limply. She wondered if he was aware of the tableau he presented, and she had to admit the effectiveness of the pathetic gesture, whether or not it was intentional. "I suppose I must have," he said, wearily. "I cannot remember any dreams."

The clinical picture was a solid improvement, at least so far. There seemed to be more black and less grey in his hair, which she'd seen before as a general indication of increased well-being in several supernatural species. "Well, it seems to have done you no end of good," she told him. "I want another look at that wound, and then I've got to go over to the clinic, but I should be able to bring you back some suitable blood."

She was leaning over him, extremely glad that her hair was for once behaving and staying in its messy ponytail, and her gloved fingers carefully, carefully removed the tape holding the gauze down over his wound. Again she noticed the lattice-work of old scars, scars upon scars, a record of what must have been a fairly tumultuous existence, and again she wondered: *a lot of lost duels?*

The last of the tape came away, and she lifted the gauze pad to reveal his wound; she smiled involuntarily at the improvement. The inflammation was significantly reduced, and there was scab formation in the tips of the cross-shape that had not been there even several hours ago. "That's lovely," she said, sitting back and folding the used dressing into a neat square. "Much, much better. I'm very pleased."

Varney peered down at the wound, looking perplexed, and then back up at her. Greta had seen that reaction before, and knew that to anyone else's eyes it would probably still appear fairly unpleasant, but she was profoundly relieved at the extent of the healing process. "Your body's getting on with healing itself quite satisfactorily, if much more slowly than you're used to," she told him, stripping open a fresh sterile dressing. "That should be completely closed over probably by tomorrow, and after that you can get up and resume activity—*light* activity, I hasten to specify."

She taped the fresh dressing over the wound, not bothering with any further application of ointment, and stood up, still smiling. "In the meantime, is there anything you'd particularly like other than the blood? Special teas? Amusing if unimproving literature?"

He stared up at her, and then, rather astonishingly, began to smile back.

CHAPTER 7

S o, uh, Dr. Helsing said you were an accountant."

"That's right. Why, do you need one?"

"No, I . . . was just, uh . . ." Cranswell trailed off.

Fastitocalon smiled a little, to himself, hunching deeper into his borrowed coat as they walked. He was having to exert a little extra energy, although not much, to project a faint don't-notice-me field around the pair of them; he was saving most of his strength for the effort it would take to conceal Cranswell and the precious burden inside his jacket from the security in the museum. "You were just kindly making conversation, and also you are wondering why I'm capable of doing magic, I expect."

"You don't read minds, too?"

"I try not to, in general, as a matter of etiquette. It's not common among accountants, magic, except inasmuch as sufficiently sophisticated mathematical theory does overlap with some areas of magical scholarship. But most people who do taxes and balance books aren't into the purely theoretical end of things."

Cranswell was still staring at him. "I'm okay with the idea that there's magic," he said, "because hell, I *know* there's vampires and were-creatures and all the other things that ordinary people don't actually believe in, but... this isn't wands-and-pointy-hats stuff you're doing, is it?"

"No," said Fastitocalon, "no, it's not. Let's just say I used to be a demon and leave it at that? Long, long, *utterly* uninteresting story." He deliberately avoided looking at Cranswell, hoping to forestall any interruption. "And I'm jolly glad Greta convinced me to come back to Castle Ruthven with her when she did. Given the damage that blade caused to Sir Francis, I expect it would do something just as comprehensively nasty to me. If we see any monk types I shall hide behind you and whimper."

He coughed. It wasn't raining, thankfully, but it was a raw cold morning, and he was very glad it wasn't far to the Museum.

"You sure you're okay to do this?" Cranswell asked, frowning. He had been about to say something else, something about *what do you mean you used to be a demon,* Fastitocalon knew, and was a little glad of the excuse to distract him. "You sound pretty rough."

"Oh, this is nothing," said Fastitocalon. "Back in the day I used to get kicked out of lodging houses in Rotherhithe for making too much noise and disturbing the neighbors. These days life is generally easier, but I do miss opium dens."

Cranswell was definitely looking as if he had a lot more questions on his mind as they reached the bottom of the museum steps. Fastitocalon held up his hand, halting. "All right. It'd be easiest if I could just flip you in and out of the conservation department, but unfortunately I don't think I'm up to it at the moment and anyway I've not been there myself so I don't have a very clear mental picture of the place to aim for. We'll have to do this the longer way."

"What's flipping?" Cranswell wanted to know.

"Translocation," he said. "But this'll have to be good old-fashioned invisibility. Stay close to me and don't make any sudden movements. I need to keep physical contact for this to work, and remember that people won't be able to see you, but they can still *feel* you, so don't bump into anybody."

He took a precautionary dose from his inhaler—it would not do to start coughing noisily in the middle of this operation—put his hand on Cranswell's shoulder, and shut his eyes.

When he opened them again they were ever so slightly orange on top of the grey, like a coat of luster on stoneware. Around the two of them, color and light and sound faded out slightly, as if someone had turned down the volume.

Cranswell was staring at him. He made what he hoped was a reassuring face, and nodded toward the museum.

It had occurred to Greta Helsing with increasing frequency over the past twenty-four hours or so that, having lost her father before she hit thirty, she had developed a tendency to gravitate toward *other* older male figures, presumably to make up for a perceived or unconscious lack of parental guidance in her life. *Older in some cases meaning by at least several hundred years, and probably more.* She didn't know whether this was really something she ought to encourage in herself.

It had been particularly noticeable earlier in the day when she'd found herself arguing with three of these older male figures at the same time that she could, in fact, be trusted to get herself to Harley Street and back without being murdered or walking into anything or falling down a hole.

"Look, I appreciate the concern," she had said for the fourth time. "I do. Believe me. But they're vulnerable to very basic self-defense equipment, and I have a job to do that needs doing. I don't intend to stay out very late and I'm not going to be wandering alone down any alleyways."

Ruthven and Fastitocalon had shared a look with Varney, whose advice they had sought after Greta refused to be cowed by either of them, singly or in concert. It was a look she had seen God knew how many times on the faces of parents dealing with irrational and exasperating teenagers, and it gave her a lovely warm sense of righteous resentment that kept her going all the way to the bus stop. At which point, of course, trepidation had set back in, and she had found herself alternately looking in all directions for people in brown woolen robes and saying lots of bad words under her breath.

The bus had arrived, had not been full of murderers, had gone where it said it was going to, and had stopped where it was promising to stop. Greta decided against calling up Ruthven to inform him she'd arrived in one piece after all.

Her clinic occupied one of the less grand of the houses that lined Harley Street: the ground floor was white-painted stonework with brick above it like most of her neighbors', but the second- and third-floor windows lacked pediments, and Greta tried not to notice just how badly the door needed repainting. Or how dusty the panes of the fanlight above it were. Her brass plate by the door was kept polished, however, and she gave it a rub with her sleeve before letting herself in: She could see her face reflected behind the letters: GRETA HELSING, MD, FRCP.

The friends Greta had prevailed upon to keep the clinic running had been managing between them in her absence. Greta's patients were used to seeing them in the clinic; Nadezhda did a lot of helping out with the magical aspect of some of the mummy cases, as well as maintaining the wards on the front door that prevented ordinary people from getting a close look at her patients as they came and went, and Anna was often there to assist Greta with minor surgical procedures. Today Anna was in charge.

So far Greta had not mentioned anything about the *nature* of her sudden and enforced absence from work, and if they could only work out a way to deal with the situation sooner rather than later, hopefully her colleagues would never need to know.

She was going to buy both of them a very, very large drink

when this was over. Knowing that her practice was in good hands was—well. It was *important* to Greta.

There were only two walk-in patients in the waiting room when she arrived, and Anna was escorting a glum-looking banshee in a scarf back from the examination room.

"Hello, Anna," she said, "and hello, Mr. O'Connor. I hope the strain's getting better? Excellent. Have a happy Christmas. Sorry—I'd meant to get back before now. Has it been crazy?"

Anna was a comfortably large lady who wore purple scrubs in the office and only very infrequently had to suppress urges to stand around in ponds and lure travelers to a watery grave. She gave Greta a hug. "Good to see you, love. No, it's not been too bad, couple of cases of the flu, one or two of that GI bug, poor Mr. O'Connor's vocal strain. Mr. Renenutet did call and I told him you weren't in the office at the moment but you'd give him a ring about his feet when you got in."

Greta nodded, hanging up her jacket and getting into a white coat. "Right, I'll do that once I've seen these two. I'm afraid I can't stay the whole day—you haven't scheduled any appointments?"

"Lord no. No, and people who need to be seen right away I've sent over to Richthorn. I rang him up and he's happy to help out. I'll get you a cup of tea, love."

"You are a gem," Greta told her, and went out to the waiting room to check the sign-in sheet.

Time always went faster while she was working. Once she'd seen her patients—a young were-cat in search of birth control and a thin creature of indeterminate species with strep throat—she rang up the mummy Renenutet to discuss replacing three of the bones in his left foot. She did a lot of restorative and maintenance work on mummies, and kept meaning to find time and money to actually go visit the exclusive—and necessarily secret—Oasis Natrun spa and resort, just outside Marseilles.

Her mummy cases had been among the most rewarding of her medical career. There was nothing in the world like the feeling of knowing you had personally undone the damage of a couple millennia of entropy. Whenever she got particularly depressed Greta would remind herself how lucky she was to be able to *do* things like drastically improving a patient's quality of life with a few hours of work and some extremely basic supplies, and the clouds would lift a bit. She loved what she did in general, of course, she always had, ever since she took over her father's practice, or she wouldn't be here—but sometimes she *really* loved doing it.

"We've been putting this off," she was saying, drawing little metatarsal bones on her desk blotter, planning how she would shape and refine the lightweight nylon replacements. If she ever won the lottery she would set up a 3-D printer to make exact replicas of her patients' bones, but at the moment hand-carved prosthetics were about the best she could do. For some very fiddly procedures she had consulted the one underworld dentist she knew who did veneer and implant work on vampires; Renenutet's feet were less delicate a job. "The longer you put weight and strain on those, the more difficult it's going to be to replace them. I know the prospect of being off your feet entirely for a couple of days while the resins have time to properly cure is not all that appealing, but you really will be much better afterward. Able to lurch around without a cane."

"Do you really think so? It's been ages since I could do any real lurching," he said wistfully. "Mentuhotep did say you did wonders on his back, and of course Ibi's actually able to *move* again, poor man—"

"I'm sure of it. Look, come in next week and we'll have another X-ray and plan out the surgery properly." She was already picturing the technical challenge of the repair work, the subject of burned monks entirely driven out of her head. "You'll be up and about again by Christmas; I ought to have done this in the first place instead of trying to reinforce them in situ, but it won't take me long to extract the damaged bones and replace them with the plastic prosthetics."

The difficult part would be attaching the prosthetic tendons and ligaments—woven elastic strapping—to the existing bone, but Greta had pioneered a couple of techniques for exactly this type of procedure, including dual-cure resin compounds and very tiny titanium screws. "I think you'll find your pain levels will drop significantly once you have the replacements in place, and you'll have a lot more stability. Then we can start thinking about your back."

"It *would* be awfully nice," Renenutet said, "not to sort of feel them *grinding* when I walk, if you know what I mean."

Greta winced. "I can just about imagine. All right, things are...a bit hairy just at the moment but if you make an appointment next week we ought to be able to get started. Do you have any questions?"

"I don't think so," he said. "Oh—when you do the surgery, can you have someone say the proper spells over the new bones before you put them in? It really does help."

"Of course I will. I'm still not good enough at pronunciation to try doing it myself but I'll have Nadezhda do it if no actual mummies are available." She kept meaning to get *better* at Egyptian but never seemed to have the time. Nadezhda wasn't completely fluent, either—but then again she was a witch, and her magic and that of the Egyptian spells seemed to be compatible.

"Thank you so much," he said at the same time as a tap came on her office door and Anna stuck her head in.

"You're very welcome," she told Renenutet. "I've got to go, I'm afraid, but call up to make the appointment next week, all right?" She hung up, and hoped very much that she would be *able* to see him next week. That there would *be* a next week for everyone.

The thought that there might not be made her shiver, and she pushed it away as hard as she could.

Anna was looking apologetic. "Sorry," she said, "but it's a bit urgent. There's a ghoul who says he needs to speak to you in private right away."

"Which ghoul?"

"I didn't catch his name, but he's wearing a sort of cloak thing made out of what looks like rat pelts," Anna said. "He doesn't look very well, but then they never do, do they?"

"That's Kree-akh," Greta said, getting up. "He's the chieftain of the northern city clans. Tell him to come in."

Fastitocalon kept his hand on Cranswell's shoulder, trying not to draw more energy from the contact than he could help—it was difficult not to, but thoroughly impolite, like taking a sip of someone else's drink.

He could see the way quite clearly in Cranswell's thoughts. They threaded their way through the people sitting on the museum steps, not bothering very much about avoiding brushing into anyone just yet. Up the steps to the Great Russell Street entrance, and inside, into the pale-green-painted lobby with the *suggested donation* box; Fastitocalon told himself he'd come back when visible and actually part with a fiver, but right now he had more important things to do. And then they were in a vast white echoing space with a glass ceiling, surrounding a central chamber: what had been the British Museum Reading Room the last time *he'd* been in here and was now apparently used for various other exhibits.

Cranswell led them to the left, into the Egyptian exhibit hall, and Fastitocalon remembered why he didn't spend much time in places like this: the intense, knotted, crisscrossing trails of time and metaphysical significance that hung around collections of antiquities were exhausting to experience, and the older the object the heavier its weight on reality. The things in here were *old*.

They skirted around the group of people looking at the Rosetta Stone and moved on, past Old Kingdom sarcophagi, past statues of Bast, through the Assyrian section, into the Greek statuary. The way was still very clear in Cranswell's head, which made it a bit easier to withstand all the intense and complicated input, and—

Fastitocalon really *did* try not to read people's minds, because it was rude, but this was barely *reading* so much as being unable not to overhear: Cranswell was both fiercely proud of this place and his privilege to be part of it, and profoundly afraid that he had fucked the latter up beyond repair by doing this stupid, impulsive, uncharacteristic thing that he and Fastitocalon were now here to remedy. Taking the books had been a spur-of-the-moment decision, prompted by frustration and stress, not a deliberate, premeditated choice.

Fastitocalon could not say anything aloud, even if he had wanted to let on that he knew what Cranswell was thinking, but he squeezed Cranswell's shoulder again, lightly, as if to say, *Don't worry. I've got you. This will be all right.*

In each of the galleries there had been several discreet security cameras, none of which were registering anything at all out of the ordinary. They passed through more rooms, down a flight of stairs into a rather dated section with worn 1970s-era linoleum on the floor, and Cranswell led him to a door marked STAFF ACCESS ONLY between signs describing Early Greek Inscriptions and Athenian Public Documents. Fastitocalon stood patiently beside him, keeping the contact as he shifted the books he was carrying to balance on one hip and fished out a set of keys from his pocket. The keys jingled, but dully, as if even that little sound could not make it out of the bubble Fastitocalon was maintaining around them.

The door opened onto a dim hallway, and as it closed behind them, leaving the public space behind, Fastitocalon could feel the difference in the atmosphere. There had been something here other than people, and it had been here *recently*.

"This way," Cranswell whispered, unnecessarily, and led Fastitocalon down another narrow flight of stairs. The lights here were fluorescent, yellowish, buzzing, and the temperature had gone up. More doors to unlock, and then they were in a long, low room with cabinets arranged in rows, like stacks in a library. The traces of something not entirely human were much, much stronger here. He could almost *smell* them.

Cranswell hurried along the rows of cabinets, glancing around with the furtive air of someone trying not to be noticed. In here, though, there were no security cameras to worry about, and Fastitocalon let go of him and leaned against the wall for a moment or two, breathing hard.

As Cranswell unwrapped the books from their protective plastic and very, very carefully returned each of them to its proper place, Fastitocalon looked around—not quite seeing what an ordinary person might see. To his eyes, which were now noticeably if faintly lit with orange, there were crisscrossing trails left by everyone who had been down here in the past several days—he could easily make out Cranswell's earlier track, when he had come down to take the books in the first place—and most of them were human, but some of them were *not*. Three of them, in fact.

They had come quite close to Cranswell, last night. Stood there, watching him.

Fastitocalon shivered suddenly, in the warmth of the underground chamber.

The creature Anna escorted into Greta's office would not have won any beauty contests on a *good* day, which this rather obviously wasn't. She turned the lights down a little, coming around the desk, and offered him a hand. The way Kree-akh was moving, as if the air itself was too heavy and the floor beneath his feet uncertain, spoke volumes; the fact that he *took* her hand and let her steady him, help him to a chair, was worse.

Ghouls never *did* look well. Anna had been quite right about that. Almost skeletally thin, wiry ropes of muscle and tendon holding bone to bone under their greenish-grey skin, they gave off a distinct air of the grave. Most of them didn't have much hair, and what they did have was stringy and knotted, clinging like seaweed to their skulls. They were built for moving quite fast through low tunnels, their backs bent and long arms dangling, and even when standing upright the tallest adults were only just about Greta's own height. Their skin was slick and damp, dappled like a frog's, and mostly they wore nothing but necklaces and a kind of loincloth stitched together out of hides whose origin did not bear close contemplation; this one, however, had a long grey-brown fur cloak draped around his shoulders. Whoever made it had not removed the individual rats' tails before sewing the pelts together, and the rows of shriveled dangling tails offered an interesting textural counterpoint to the velvety fur.

In the dimness of her office she could easily see his eyeshine, two points of red light that winked off as he squeezed his eyes shut. He was leaning a little sideways in the chair, hanging on to it with clawed fingers, visibly fighting off dizziness. Greta sat on the edge of her desk, looking closely at him. "What's the matter?" she asked. "What happened?"

"I need more medicine," he said. Or rather *hissed*. Ghoul dentition brought to mind the more alarming types of deepsea anglerfish; their own language was ideally suited to a mouthful of needle-teeth, but pronouncing standard English presented a bit of a challenge. Kree-akh was something close to fluent in it, which was an impressive achievement. "I—ran out," he said. "Two days ago."

"More Effexor?" Greta said, nonplussed. "You should have had at least another two weeks worth on that refill. How did you manage to run out so quickly?"

There wasn't a lot in the literature about the use of antidepressants in ghouls. Greta and Kree-akh had gone through three different medications before they found one that treated his symptoms, which was more or less the same process as she would expect to go through with a human patient, and she had been toying with the idea of writing a case study simply to establish precedent. He had been on venlafaxine for three months now, and they had settled into a regular routine of visits for her to monitor his progress and provide him with the prescription refills, since he could hardly be expected to go to the pharmacy himself. Which was all well and good, except for the part where suddenly stopping venlafaxine brought on really *nasty* side effects.

"I...lost the bottle," Kree-akh said, and she could hear the lie very clearly.

This entire business had been extremely difficult for him, and Greta was still impressed by the bravery it had taken to visit her in the first place asking for help. Ghoul chieftains were not *supposed* to suffer from anything so pathetic—and human—as depression, but he was what she might term a progressive example of the species. Being responsible for three separate ghoul clans in a kind of extended tribe was a hell of a difficult job, made more so by the fact that Kree-akh's rule did not rely on vicious brute force so much as reasoned authority. He had come to her—and Greta was very much aware of the level of trust this had implied—initially complaining of headaches, and then admitted that he had heard there were medicines that might do something for exhausting, anxious misery.

He was still leaning sideways in the chair, eyes shut, greener than usual with nausea and dizziness. "Stay there," Greta said, unnecessarily. "I'll be right back."

She went to look through her store of drug samples, wondering how exactly he had come to lose the pill bottle; ghouls were scavengers, notorious for hanging on to things, even when those things *weren't* of paramount pharmacological importance.

That made Greta think of the stuff on the crossblade, and its pharmacological importance; and *that* made her wonder if the people who had attacked her and Varney could be going after the ghouls as well. It wasn't a nice thought, even though Greta was more confident in ghouls' ability to defend themselves than her own.

After a few minutes she found what she was looking for, and brought him a couple of pills and a glass of water. "Here. Effexor, and meclizine for the nausea."

"Thank you," Kree-akh said, and gave her a very horrible attempt at a smile. Greta smiled back and reached for the phone to call in a new prescription to the nearby pharmacy on Beaumont Street. By the time she'd finished dealing with the pharmacist, he was sitting a little more upright and looked somewhat less miserable.

"I'll go and pick that up as soon as it's ready," she said, "or send Anna, if she's not in the middle of something. In the meantime, can you tell me what happened? I don't...want to pry, but there have been some strange and rather awful things going on, people on the surface being attacked by a group of madmen dressed up as monks—"

Kree-akh hissed, sitting up straight, his eyes glowing brighter in the dimness of her office. "Monks," he said. "It was *monks* did it. Humans, but not—ordinary humans, they *smelled* wrong."

"Did *what?*"

"We were...taken by surprise," he said, looking both furious and somehow embarrassed. "My sentries were overcome, it was—most of us were asleep, and there were many of them, fast and strong, and they could see in the dark as well as we can. I lost two young ones. The rest of us escaped."

"Leaving behind everything," Greta said, slowly, realizing it. "Including your meds. I am...so sorry, Kree-akh. I don't *know* what's happening, or what to do about it—"

"We could not even retrieve the bodies," he said, guttural and harsh. "They are not at rest. Their flesh is. Is *wasted.*"

Greta closed her eyes. That was a particularly terrible insult, to the ghouls—a vicious insult, and a bone-deep sorrow. In a society that ate its own dead as a means of honoring their memories, being unable to claim the bodies of the slain meant their spirits could not be properly freed, that the grieving process could find no natural conclusion. "I'm so sorry," she said again, knowing it was completely inadequate.

When she looked back at him Kree-akh was watching her steadily, and it was not at all easy to hold that gaze—red light, in dark hollows—but she did it anyway. For a long moment he simply looked at her, and then spoke a sentence or two in ghoulish. Greta only caught a little of it: something about *respect*, or *earned trust*, she wasn't sure. One day she really would get around to properly *studying* the languages her patients spoke.

He sighed, and passed a hand over his face, and looked—briefly—very human indeed. "Yes," he said in English. "You

113

are sorry, Doctor, for dead who are not your own, or even your own *kind*. That is … rare, I think."

"There isn't much I can really do to help, I know," she said, "but if there *is* anything, please will you tell me? And—are the rest of you safe?"

"For now, yes. We have moved away from the tunnels they invaded. There are other places in the undercity to make a home; and when my people have settled there will be time to observe these monk-men and find their weakness."

Kree-akh didn't need to add *and avenge our dead*. The combination of needle-teeth and red eyes was suddenly very frightening indeed. "They attacked a friend of mine," she told him, looking away from the teeth. "Or a friend of a friend, at any rate. And one of them had a go at me. If they're the same people, and I cannot think there are *two* groups of homicidal monks with glowing blue eyes roaming London at the same time."

"Blue eyes," he repeated. "Yes. They saw in the dark, with blue eyes. Blue flames. Like—" He waved a clawed hand irritably, searching for the word. "Gas. Like gas burns blue."

"They *look* burned," Greta said. "At least the one who attacked me was covered in what I think were fresh burn scars. I wish I knew *who* they were." Too many bits of information were swirling in her head—too many questions and answers that she couldn't clearly piece together. "Or *what* they were. Because they aren't human, or at least not entirely human, anymore."

Kree-akh hissed to himself, and clittered his claws together:

an unconscious gesture, like lashing a tail. "They tried to harm you?" he said.

"Tried," she told him, and pulled down the collar of her sweater to show him the pad of gauze. He hissed again, looking rather terrible, and she hastened to add, "It's okay, I'm all right, I wasn't badly hurt. And I'm staying with Ruthven. Where it's safe."

He nodded, and the terrible look passed off into an aching kind of tiredness. Greta tucked back her hair and said, rather tentatively, "I'm pretty sure you could, too. Stay there, I mean. You and your people. In the cellar of the Embankment house, if you truly ever are in need of a safe place to hide beyond the tunnels." It wasn't *her* cellar she was volunteering, but she knew Ruthven would almost certainly agree. Almost.

"I will remember," Kree-akh said, and got up, steadying himself on the edge of the desk. "That is better. I feel almost well."

"Good." Greta got up, too, reaching for her phone and tucking it into her pocket. "I'll go round the corner and collect your medicine, shouldn't be very long. You can wait in here or go out to the waiting room, whichever you prefer."

"Here," he said. "Here is...safe. Everywhere else is too bright."

It was obscurely gratifying to have her office labeled *safe*. Greta smiled at him and went out to tell Anna she would be right back.

Her phone buzzed as she was about to leave, and she paused at the door to read the text. Harry had come through for her after all: *Hey, Helsing. Got your mass spec results. Whatever you're into is some fascinatingly weird shit. Emailed you the numbers.*

Greta thought *fascinatingly weird shit* was the understatement of the century.

On an ordinary map of London it would be difficult to make out the precise route taken by the creature that had visited Crouch End the night before. Some of the roads he had taken did not follow anything written down for the general public to see.

He was aware that he had failed in his mission and that God was displeased with him; but God surely knew he had tried, and at least he had wounded the woman—even if he *had* lost the sacred blade in the attempt. When he got back to his brothers he would tell them about it, and do his penance for failing to complete his mission. There would be more vigil in front of the blue light; he longed for it, in a cloudy, indistinct way, even as he feared the pain it would bring.

Not terribly far away, in a different tunnel, another pair of pinpoints of light paused, blinked on and off, tilted, as their owner listened to blue-lit words that echoed inside its head. It had been heading north to evict a couple of ghouls from their refuge in an overflow chamber. Now it turned, retraced its steps through bobbing debris. It had something more important to do than chase off the unclean eaters-of-flesh from the underground passageways that now belonged to its Order; it was charged with intercepting anathema.

In its glass prison, the jumping spark of the light-of-God hissed and crackled and flung deadly light across the walls of its little room. Under the steady atonal humming, another sound rose and fell in electrical singsong, almost like words; a faint sibilant voice, muttering to itself in the blue heart of the glow.

CHAPTER 8

Above, in the city, it was raining again: that slow but insistent icy rain that characterizes London for much of the winter. Not quite cold enough to be actually frozen; certainly cold enough to be utterly miserable for anyone unlucky enough to be out in it.

Varney was, despite Greta's instructions, out of bed. He'd been anxious and irritable all day, ever since the doctor had left against sanguivorous advice to go and...do whatever it was she did, presumably dose other monsters for the grippe and sew up holes in their hides. Wrapped in a borrowed and very beautiful dressing gown that was considerably too short in the sleeves and hem, the vampyre stood at his bedroom window and glowered out at the afternoon.

It had been a very long time since Francis Varney had come across any humans so matter-of-factly involved with the world of the supernatural—perhaps because he took pains to avoid getting to know humans at all. That she was so unafraid of him *troubled* Varney. He was not sure what to make of it. Or of her.

Varney's hand crept to the dressing taped over the wound. His memory of recent events had come back to him with rather more clarity than he would have liked, as the fever receded, and he couldn't help replaying certain aspects of that evening in his mind.

What he had told Greta was true. He *did* try to minimize the number of occasions on which he lunged at somebody, fangs bared, upon being woken unexpectedly, but it was... still an instinct he could not completely quell. The mortification upon realizing what he had just done—to a total stranger—had been rather worse than the physical effects of his wound, for a moment or two.

Then he'd said something stupid, he couldn't quite recall what, and after that things went first blurry and then blank behind a haze of sickening, vertiginous misery. He could just about remember cool hands on his face, a delicate touch on his skin, in the middle of all that pain.

When he'd next become aware of the world he had felt *different* somehow. The wound still hurt dreadfully, but it was a kind of hurt he *knew*, could recognize, from countless other injuries. Between them Ruthven and Greta had helped him up the stairs, and Varney neither remembered nor wished to know which of them had been responsible for undressing him—

He winced away from the thought, and went back to staring out of the window, but couldn't quite distract himself from the question of how to *react* to someone like Dr. Helsing. Did he try to push her away, urge her out of his sphere of influence, insist that she avoid his gaze for her own safety? Did he attempt to eat her? He simply had no basis for comparison.

Perhaps it was just decay of the system affecting his mind, or the fact that he'd been practically in hibernation on and off for several decades now and had not had a great many recent encounters with women, but Varney was finding it increasingly and extremely difficult to avoid thinking about her. He could feel the beginnings of the same inappropriate fixation that he'd had on Flora Bannerworth, all those centuries ago.

She wasn't anything *like* Flora, or any of the other maidens he had pursued with such single-minded devotion—none of them would have countenanced the prospect of becoming a physician, to be sure, and he didn't know if he actually approved of it as a career for a lady—but she was not unattractive, in a pale, pointed fashion.

Ugh, he thought. *Shall I never be free of unseemly desire?*

It wasn't simply desire, either. There was a kind of miserable fascination in this, Varney's mind trying to fit Greta Helsing into any of the available preshaped settings in his view of the world and failing completely. She was *odd,* and he could not work out quite why she did what she was doing, or why anyone would want to. He could more or less understand the desire to repair things that were broken, but the effort, and time, and energy, a human would have to put into first studying and then qualifying and then *maintaining a medical practice* for the undead seemed to him utterly incomprehensible.

Not only the job she did but the lengths to which she must have to go in order to keep that job, and her livelihood, secret from the waking world. It was so *strange*. Everything was strange, and nothing he knew seemed to make any kind of sense, and this house was the only place just at the moment where Varney felt even slightly *safe* or secure. The idea of venturing out into the city beyond these windows made all the little hairs rise on the back of his neck. It was not easy to be a monster. It had never been, but sometimes he simply noticed it more clearly.

Oh, but the world is a cold *place,* he thought.

A suitably cold one, of course. Varney couldn't possibly object on moral grounds to being disliked and disenfranchised—he was dead, he fed on the life of the innocent, the blue-eyed creatures who had wounded him were actually quite right in claiming to do the work of God, but...it was cold, for all that. He shivered, leaning against the window frame and watching the distant scurrying of pedestrians, the beetle-black cabs making their way along the Embankment. Were they, too, aware of the icy and uncaring nature of the universe? They were his prey—or, well, certain among them were—and he himself was now prey of a subtly different kind.

Absently Varney rubbed again at the dressing over his cross-shaped wound. It ached now, rather than that awful dizzying burn, and the ache was accompanied by an increasingly maddening itch.

"You oughtn't to be up," said a voice from behind him, and Varney was sufficiently far gone in his familiar unhappy reverie that he jerked in surprise and turned to find Ruthven watching him from the doorway. His host's sleeves were rolled up and his tie loosened, but the hair remained neatly combed back. "Not that I can blame you," Ruthven went on. "Lying around all day is intensely boring. Do you feel any better?"

Varney almost guiltily dropped his hand from the dressing. "Er," he said. "Yes, thank you. Quite improved."

"I'm glad to hear it. Since you *are* out of bed, would you like to come downstairs and keep me company for a while?"

His immediate instinct was to demur—no, really, he was always better off alone, Ruthven didn't need his melancholy presence—but something about the way Ruthven was looking at him seemed to change his mind. "If you're quite sure...?"

"I am." Ruthven gave him a rueful smile. "And I'm sure I've got some dressing gowns somewhere that are proportioned for ordinary people. You needn't put up with mine."

Varney felt his face go ever so slightly warm in embarrassment.

Downstairs in the drawing room Ruthven had lit a fire and pulled most of the curtains shut to block out the greyness of the afternoon. "Look, I don't suppose you particularly want to think about this all that much," he said, "but I've been messing about plotting all the recent attacks on a map of the city, and I wondered if you'd have a look at it and tell me if anything strikes you as corresponding to a pattern."

Varney settled in an armchair by the fire. "Please? I'm...it's so wearying to feel completely useless."

"Don't I know it. All right, back in a minute."

Rain spattered against the tall windows, and the applewood

of the fire crackled. Varney was conscious of the sheer comfort of the juxtaposition and sat up a little straighter, for once not tempted to rub at the hole in his chest. It really was a nice room, he reflected. He'd not been in any condition to appreciate its harmonious proportions before. Old Turkish rugs, a huge mahogany sideboard clustered with big crystal decanters and stacks of *National Geographic* back issues; books stacked on the floor, books on desks and tables, books packed on built-in bookshelves up to the high ceiling, with an antique set of library steps resting against the highest shelf. There was a comfortably beat-up globe in one corner. The furniture was a disorganized mixture of baroque Victorian pieces, including what appeared to be a genuine horsehair chaise longue, and more comfortable and contemporary sofas and armchairs. A large flat-screen TV lurked in one corner, atop an unobtrusive cabinet containing an entertainment system. It fit Ruthven quite well, Varney thought. A mixture of ages.

Ruthven came back with a laptop, setting it down on an exquisite little inlaid eighteenth-century table, and turned it so Varney could see the screen: it showed a shot of central London on Google Maps. Ruthven had put in little pushpins at the location of each of the "Rosary Ripper" murders, and a further set of markers for the attacks on his friends. Kensington, Crouch End. The path Cranswell had taken from the British Museum was marked in small blue dots.

Varney peered at the computer, and his eyes widened. "My God, there's been ... *eleven* murders now?"

"It seems to be speeding up," Ruthven said. "Multiple killings in one day. And they've found the same sort of cheap plastic rosary at each scene."

Varney squinted at the screen and adjusted the angle. "They must have some way of getting around the city, quickly and easily, without being seen. I doubt they have invisibility cloaks, or a group of very sympathetic cabbie friends, and dressed up like Benedictines they would not escape notice."

"The Underground," said Ruthven. "Right? They're using the tube tunnels. Have to be."

"It does seem likely." Varney turned the laptop back to him. "Although I don't know how easy it would truly be to creep around in the tunnels without being caught."

"Transport for London does get awfully intense about people wandering around restricted areas," Ruthven said, thoughtfully. "Especially since the bombings back in 2005, and the attacks in Europe. I'd imagine they're being extremely vigilant with their security cameras and patrols and so on. Maybe the disused stations...or there's some other tunnels, must be, for power cables and steam..."

Varney sat back in his armchair, thinking. "What I find unsettling is the...the uncertainty of the *nature* of these creatures. These people. They are human, or they are so close as to be able to *pass* for human, and yet the blue eyes are very much *not*."

"I know," said Ruthven. "In the book Cranswell found, the Gladius Sancti were just people, humans like any other order of rather obsessive zealots who took things too far in the name of God. It didn't mention blue-glowing eyes. I have a feeling that would have been included."

"And why is this happening now?" Varney said. "I have been in and out of London for centuries, as have you and, I gather, several other creatures of our kind; why are madmen, human or otherwise, suddenly objecting to our presence now?"

"Why would a secret society like the Gladius Sancti surface in the modern world at all, for that matter, and where the hell did they get those spikes and the magic stuff to put on them, is what *I* want to know." Ruthven sighed. "They were supposed to have brought the recipe for their demon-slaying poison out of the Holy Land back in the thirteenth or fourteenth century, but the book didn't mention what they did with it after that. Or what it actually contained."

"Do you suppose," said Varney, slowly, the idea coming to him like something large and unpleasant rising to the surface of still water, "do you suppose that someone has actually found it?"

Ruthven sat back, looking at him. "The recipe?"

"And the knives. And their...particular scripture. The verses that tell them what to do." Varney could recall only snatches of it, but it had sounded very biblical indeed—but no part of the King James *he* could remember specifically covered *the hunting of demons.*

Ruthven was still looking at him, the silver eyes narrowed in consideration. "I don't think it's *impossible* that something could have survived undiscovered for this long, just...vanishingly improbable."

Varney laughed, a hollow sound that echoed in his chest. "One thing I have learned beyond the shadow of a doubt throughout my existence is that anything that can possibly go wrong *will go wrong*. If there *were* some hidden cache of thirteenth-century manuscripts containing the instructions for this...this holy poison...and the original blades to carry it, and if this cache *could* be found by someone of a mind-set to put them to use instead of into a museum, then..." He spread his hands, shrugging. It was one of the first things he had really come to understand about his half-existence, in the early years; it explained why everything he ever attempted to achieve had ended up the same way, at the point of a sword, the tines of a pitchfork, the flames of a torch.

Ruthven was looking at him with a surprised, and faintly pitying, expression. "Well," he began, and Varney could hear the diplomacy being applied. Ruthven didn't believe him; well, why should he? He had a beautiful house and an espresso machine and two automobiles, and a number of imperial dressing gowns, and actual human friends who enjoyed spending time with him, and he apparently found it *entirely untroubling* that he belonged to a tribe of undead monsters used to frighten children into obedience. Varney was abruptly, suddenly exhausted, tired almost to the point of nausea. The wound in his shoulder itched like fire.

"I don't suppose it matters, much," he said, cutting Ruthven off in mid-platitude. "The fact is that they're here, they have these weapons, and they are...using them. Whether or not they are entirely human. And we need to know how they are getting around."

Ruthven looked as if he had been about to pursue the diplomatic line further, but—thankfully—decided against it, taking the computer back and resuming his search. He had been looking up Underground maps, and unsurprisingly finding only the standard line maps rather than the more useful blueprints indicating where the off-limits tunnels ran. As Varney watched, one of his searches popped up a picture of a complicated intersecting series of brick arches and openings.

Ruthven stared at it, his pupils expanding and contracting rapidly. "I'm an idiot," he said.

"Pardon me?"

"An idiot. Really, I ought to have thought of it at once. You've read your Hugo just the same as I have; what did he famously spend half a damn chapter describing in detail as the easiest way of moving around a city while escaping pursuit?"

Varney straightened. "They can't be using the sewers, surely?"

"Look." Ruthven searched for, and found, a map of the main drainage network of London (circa 1930, but close enough). He centered it on the map of modern-day London and turned down the opacity just enough to let the two superimpose, and turned the screen to show Varney. Every single one of the markers he'd placed at attack or murder scenes was located along a sewer line. Not entirely surprising, given the way the sewers often tended to lie beneath the roads, but the correlation was exact.

"I think the question now is not how they're getting around," he said, "but where it is they're coming and going *from*."

*   *   *

Greta had brought back blood and danishes for the household when she'd come back from the clinic, which meant Ruthven didn't have to go out to eat. *Just as well,* he thought, looking out at the uninviting prospect of a cold rainy night. Even if there weren't mysterious zealots with poisoned spikes out there looking to perforate him, he wouldn't have looked forward to braving the elements; it took some little time to first select and then thrall somebody, and then find somewhere they wouldn't be disturbed for the few minutes it took to drink, and all this was much more tiresome to contemplate in the rain. Besides, it really *did* make his hair frizz.

Everyone was home: Cranswell and Fastitocalon had returned from the museum sans priceless literary artifacts shortly after Greta's arrival, and were in the middle of a conversation about metaphysics. Ruthven listened with half an ear, and then with his full attention, coming to lean in the doorway of the kitchen and watch Cranswell consuming pastries while Fastitocalon explained how demons worked.

After a little while Greta came to join Ruthven, and they exchanged a look. Neither of them had ever actually come right out and asked Fastitocalon to tell them the details of his nature, but Ruthven at least had been curious about it for *decades.* One did not flat-out ask an old friend what they *were.* Perhaps it was different for Cranswell, who had only just met him, or perhaps Cranswell simply didn't mind the impropriety. Either way, this was fascinating.

It seemed that Heaven and Hell both existed, although

much of theology had got hold of the wrong end of the stick. The two sides were not in active competition. "You *don't* go after souls," Cranswell repeated.

"No. Well.... see, this is the biggest misconception people have and I'm fairly sure Sam has left it this way for a reason, but we don't actively try to tempt people into Hell. Hell just provides the torments, or the boredom, either way, which people believe at the most basic unconscious level that they deserve."

Cranswell stared at him, hand frozen halfway through reaching for the last pastry. "You're kidding, right? Hell is what you make it?"

"Well, not exactly. Your fate is sort of whatever you subconsciously know it ought to be." He looked wretched. "This is not my field. I'm...I was an accountant, not an afterlife counselor."

"What if you're an atheist?" Greta said. "What if you don't believe there even *is* an afterlife, that you just die and decompose and are recycled?"

Fastitocalon looked over at her. "Then that's more or less what happens, I think. The idea is not that one side gets more souls than the other in order to win, like celestial checkers or something, but that the influence and power of the two sides remains in balance at all times. The balance is incredibly important. Otherwise very bad things happen. Rivers of blood, rains of fire, horses eat each other. Generally to be avoided."

He looked dreadfully tired, Ruthven thought. Tired, and

ill; this was taking a lot out of Fass, first the business with the artifacts and now having to tell everyone things that were probably supposed to be kept secret. Even as the thought crossed his mind, Fastitocalon began to cough, and Greta nudged Ruthven aside and went into the kitchen to steady him with a hand on his back.

"You need to be in bed," she said, when the fit was over. "I should have sent you there directly when you got back from the Museum, but I'm sending you now. Varney's already taken himself off."

"Mmh," Fastitocalon said, leaning into her hand. "I'm... not going to argue."

Ruthven glanced at Greta, saw the flicker of concern behind the calm doctor-face. It wasn't a good sign when Fastitocalon *didn't* immediately protest that he was quite all right and people shouldn't fuss. "Well, good," she said. "Go on. I'll bring you a cup of something heartening in a little while. Do you—"

"I'm all right," he said, cutting her off, and got up with a brief effort. "I can manage the stairs without expiring, I believe."

Cranswell looked up at him as he rose. "Thank you," he said. "For the—the museum thing. Thank you, Fastitocalon. That was kind of incredible, actually, and I really appreciate you doing it."

Fastitocalon blinked at him, looking surprised. "Oh, well," he said, "you're quite welcome. I'm glad I was able to help. It is so pleasant being *useful*."

* * *

After Fastitocalon had gone to bed, Ruthven made dinner for the human contingent, and when he was finished with the washing up he went to check the locks again, unable to excise a certain formless nagging anxiety. He could not make himself settle to anything. For the first time since this whole business began he was thinking about getting out of London—maybe not Scotland, maybe somewhere *warm and dry*, with scenery. Italy might do. Or Greece. He'd *liked* Greece, even if the last time he'd been there it had been during a less-than-admirable phase of his existence and he had made some extremely poor decisions—but the seas really had been wine-dark, and the olive groves fragrant, and all in all it was a much more pleasant prospect than London in November.

Ruthven filed that thought under *profoundly unhelpful*, and sighed. Running away was out of the question.

Cranswell and Greta were looking through the lab results on the fragment of metal she'd dug out of Sir Francis, and he joined them in the dining room. The table was covered in books—half of which he barely even remembered buying, back in one of his more Gothic phases: witchcraft lore, herbals, and...apparently a paperback of Montague Summers's drivel that he absolutely had no memory of purchasing *at all*. The contrast between their bowed heads, dark and fair, under the warm lamplight made him think of Renaissance paintings.

"Anything interesting?" he inquired.

Greta looked up. "Yeah. This stuff...Ruthven, Harry's

results are kind of incredible. It's like a broad-spectrum anti-supernatural cocktail. There's the iron, for the ones who can't bear cold iron; there's silver, for the weres; there's a bit of lead; and the rest is all a potpourri of classic white-magic herbs. Look at this."

She pushed a couple of books out of the way and slid her notebook across the table to him. "Furanoacridones and the acridone alkaloids arborinine and evoxanthine, plus coumarins—all of that you can get out of plain old *Ruta graveolens*, otherwise known as rue. Rosmarinic acid and carnosic acid, from rosemary—and a whole bunch of stuff you can extract from sage and wormwood, including thujone. There's lavender, valerian, yarrow, all kinds of stuff. And not to leave you out, we've got a *ton* of thio-2-propene-1-sulfinic acid S-allyl ester."

Ruthven looked at her, one eyebrow slightly raised. "Which is what exactly, when it's at home with its feet up?"

"Allicin," she said. "Derived from garlic. What you might call the active principle."

He was suddenly very, very glad the blade was sealed up in plastic and safely locked away in the garage; even just touching it for any length of time would almost certainly make him break out in hives and wheeze for breath.

"These guys really did their homework," Cranswell said, still scribbling notes. "There's a bunch of other stuff in here that I can't identify as specifically toxic to a specific kind of monster—no offense—but none of it looks like something you'd want to have inserted into you on a pointy instrument."

"No kidding," said Greta, touching the side of her neck. "It looks like they're not only loaded for vampire, as it were, but they're also equipped to take down pretty much any other kind of undead and/or generally supernatural being that's known to have a particular physical or chemical weakness. Did you lock the doors?"

"I did," said Ruthven, "but I am suddenly moved by the inspiration to go and do it yet again. And possibly chalk some sort of protective rune on them, if I knew any. Do *you* know any?" he added.

"Not my field." Cranswell shrugged apologetically, but he looked uneasy nonetheless.

Greta rose and went to join Ruthven, and together they checked the locks once more, not only on Ruthven's front door, but his back door and cellar doors as well, and all the windows one by one.

Elsewhere, another door was opened on blue light.

Something—some*one*—hit the floor of the low arched little room with a squelchy thud, and moaned. In the blue light his torn habit looked black, sodden with rainwater and less mentionable things from the journey through the tunnels in the dark.

They had found the nameless man in the overflow chamber, and at first he had been glad to see the dim pinpoints of light approaching; at least until the first blow doubled him over and sent him face-first into the shoals of filth on the floor. After that they had dragged him by the arms, silent, their grip implacable as iron, through the undercity to the inner sanctum.

Two blue-eyed monks looked down at his crumpled form. Without saying a word, they drew dull grey crossblades from their sleeves and knelt to cut the remains of his habit away. First the rope cincture around the waist, then the cowl and hood, and finally the garment itself was stripped off in pieces, revealing half-healed burns still weeping fluid. Still without speaking, they folded and set aside the remains of the clothing.

The humming of the spark in its globe seemed to intensify, as if focusing its attention. Both monks crossed themselves, murmuring something under their breath, and then bent to take his arms and drag him toward the metal cabinet. Hanging from the corners of the cabinet were two stained leather straps, just the right length for fastening round somebody's wrists.

He roused from stupor enough to cringe away from the light, now just inches away, and made a thick choking sound. The straps held firm. The curve of the glass bulb was so close he could feel the heat from it on his skin, in his bones, like desert sunshine. The noise of it filled the world. It resonated in the hollow spaces of his skull, mindless and insistent, and somewhere deep in the remains of the nameless man the thought occurred that it would drive him mad, that this was what the insane must hear inside their heads.

He was not worthy of the light of God, if he could think such things. He deserved the pain.

When the priest with the long braided whip came in, he

was silent, hanging half-conscious from the restraints, but it was not long before the dim ozone-smelling tunnel rang and echoed with screams.

"We separate him, together with his accomplices and abettors, from the precious light of the Lord God and from the society of all Christians; we exclude him from our Holy Order."

Twelve men in rough robes and hoods stood in darkness lit by a single shaking candle flame, their shadows moving on the tiled walls of the sewer tunnel. Twelve men, surrounding a heap of something on the noisome floor. They were together in fellowship, at this time and in this place. The work they did now was entirely the work of God.

"We declare him excommunicate and anathema," their leader continued. "We judge him damned, with the Devil and his angels and all the reprobate, to eternal fire and torment."

The words had the ring of practice, of familiarity. In point of fact this small group of men, or men-shaped creatures, had read words like them many times before, under vastly different circumstances. Not these precisely—in that earlier life, one spent under the sky rather than beneath the city streets, there had never been a need to speak these particular phrases, only praise and adulation—but words *like* these. They knew the text and the cadence and response. It was right. It was true. It was just.

The one who had spoken wore a blue stole around his neck, vivid against his brown monk's habit, bright and strange in the dimness of the tunnel. Now he reached out shiny-scarred fingers into the candle flame, holding them steady and unwavering in the middle of the light for a moment before pinching it out. Darkness flooded in, so absolute as to be almost tangible; then, slowly, pinpoints of blue light appeared in pairs. A small and shifting group of constellations.

"He is unclean," said the figure who had snuffed the candle. In the faint light of their combined eyeshine the stole around his neck was just visible. "Expel him. And then purify yourselves."

Two of the monks broke from the circle and bent to pick up the thing lying on the tunnel floor: a thing that grunted as it was lifted, and left a bloody trail behind it in the dark. A third led them down the tunnel to the circular alcove of a manhole, and without a single word they carried it up the iron ladder and into the larger darkness of the night.

Sir Francis Varney was also damned, with the Devil and his angels and all the reprobate, and it was keeping him up at nights.

As the city slept toward morning, he leaned once more on the windowsill of his room and—his mind running in familiar, well-worn ruts—considered himself. He was a very old monster, and quite a cunning one, except for the part where he always somehow got in the way of his own plans and ended up either dead or on the run from a crowd of irate humans—still, the planning was all right, as far as that went. It was the tiresomely persistent self-loathing factor that really doomed him to continued failure.

Ruthven had been undead for what, four hundred years? More than that. Almost as long as Varney himself. And yet he dwelled here, in this comfortable, gracious house with its warmly living atmosphere, surrounded with the innocent and clean. With the living.

Varney went over it again in his mind, deliberately making himself iterate Ruthven's advantages, like a man probing at a rotten tooth with his tongue. He had his cars, and wireless Internet, and subscriptions to magazines, and a kitchen with food in it, food *that he himself cooked and fed to living people.* How could he manage to be so ... so *ordinary,* when he was an undead fiend from hell? And that didn't even take into account Frederick Vasse, or, properly, Fastitocalon, who by his own admission was *actually* a fiend from Hell, or at least used to be one before a management shakeup in the seventeenth century. Fastitocalon worked as an accountant, for crying out loud. He'd even mentioned that there was an official representative of the nether realms stationed in London to keep an eye on things, and Varney simply couldn't wrap his head around the idea of demons cheerfully walking the streets with the rank and file of humanity, as if they didn't *mind* being what they were.

As if they didn't mind their own selves.

He could not imagine it, could not comprehend considering himself anything other than a stain on the skin of reality, a regrettable blot on the world's copybook. His sins were beyond forgiveness.

Not only the fact of his unholy nature, but the terrible deeds he had done, cried out for retribution. Any one of them would damn him to the fiery pits, but one in particular cried out for vengeance: the episode in his existence—he could hardly call it life—he most regretted; the turning of Clara Crofton. Of all the foul, indefensible, destructive, unforgivable acts he had perpetrated on the world during his various sojourns in it, none could be worse than the sin of changing a human being into a damned, parasitic horror such as himself. To doom her to an eternity of pain and loathing, to take away the last sweet gift any human could receive, the gift of absolution—no, Varney could not forgive himself for that, and would not try. Redemption was beyond him.

He leaned his chin on his hand, watching raindrops creep down the glass. Again and again in the course of introspection he would come up against the same question: Why, if he loathed his existence so profoundly, did he struggle so hard to hold on to it? Why not rid the world of a monster and himself of a tiresome burden? Why, when the blue-eyed monks attacked him, when he was half-mad with pain, so ill he could hardly stand, had he come here for assistance? It would have been simpler to let the poison do its work. Simpler, and perhaps better for everyone.

But then Ruthven would not have been warned of the danger, a little quiet voice said in his mind. *You did that much good, at least.*

It wasn't enough. Nothing would ever be enough.

Varney heaved a sigh so melancholy it actually fogged the windowpane for a moment. He had to leave, and the sooner the better. First thing in the morning, he would make his apologies and tender his profound gratitude, and then he would leave them and find another of his lairs to hide in while he regained his strength.

Before morning, the rain had grown colder—cold enough to rime the edges of street signs and lampposts with ice, glaze the pavements with a thin layer of it, reduce the remaining plants in window boxes to limp sogginess. London never looked at its best in winter, except for those brief mornings when overnight snows had iced each cornice and roof peak, lending the metropolis a spurious and fleeting purity. Today it was particularly unprepossessing. Waking to find himself warmly tucked in the vast and comfortable bed, Varney contemplated the world outside and considered that perhaps he might put off relocation just a *little* bit longer.

When he made it down to the kitchen, Greta and Ruthven were already up, and Varney stood for a moment just outside the doorway. Looking in.

"Very stylish," Greta was telling Ruthven, who hadn't bothered dressing; he was plying the toaster in a heavily quilted and embroidered silk robe that made him look like a short, exceptionally pallid Mughal emperor. "You ought to have a matching nightcap," she added.

"Nightcaps are for people with drafty bedrooms." Ruthven looked over his shoulder and smiled at Varney. "Good morning. Well, not a particularly good morning, the furnace is misbehaving, but we're all still functioning and nobody else appears to have made the papers for being murdered overnight. Could be worse." Varney realized belatedly that it was, in fact, a good deal colder in here than usual.

He came into the kitchen and stopped, awkwardly, not knowing what to do with himself.

"Did you sleep all right?" Greta wanted to know, looking up at him, arms wrapped around herself against the chill. She was in jeans and a faded Cambridge sweatshirt, and looked about eighteen with her hair escaping from its band. Her eyes were blue-grey, sympathetic; innocent of makeup, her lashes were dark gold, and caught the light. "Ruthven says he had bad dreams."

"Quite well, thank you. I really ought to take my leave," Varney said, trying not to notice that she had the faint marks of pillowcase wrinkles printed on one cheek. "I have trespassed on your kindness long enough, Ruthven, and—"

Another voice cut in. "We're all trespassing on his kindness, but thankfully he appears to have a lot of it."

Varney turned to see August Cranswell leaning in the doorway with his arms folded. "And frankly," Cranswell continued, "I'm not about to go out into the nasty wider world until we have some clearer idea of what the hell those idiots in the robes are actually up to. I'd say that goes double for you guys."

Ruthven quirked an eyebrow at him, then turned to retrieve the toast and set it into its rack. "You make a valid point," he said. "Greta's young man sent over the results of his tests last night, Varney, and it looks as if the poison these people are using is even nastier than we had reason to believe."

"He's not my young man," she pointed out, and Varney was aware of having had to squash another sudden surge of murderous animosity. He was generally pretty good at controlling it while he was fully conscious—being woken up was evidently still sometimes enough to set it off—but just now it had flared up like a brief and intense physical pain, a stab of completely idiotic jealousy, and just as quickly faded back to nothing.

This is ridiculous, he told himself, *you scarcely know her,* but all the good sense in all the world could not stop Varney's wretchedly traitorous instincts. If he were not so focused on the problem at hand he might have passed a few not unenjoyable days daydreaming about Greta Helsing and reminding himself of all the very many reasons he should not be doing so, but they had *things* to do, damn it, and Varney was so tired of his own predictable and infuriating predilections.

"He's a handy acquaintance who happens to have access to a mass spectrometer," Greta was saying. "And while I don't really want to venture out at all today, I do need to go up to Crouch End and deal with the car."

Cranswell frowned at her. "What if there's more of them?"

"I hardly think they're going to make another attempt the same exact way as before," she said. "Although you can feel free to come with me if you think I need protecting."

"I don't think it'd help," Ruthven told her. "No offense intended, Cranswell, but of the ambulatory members of the current household, you're not exactly the best equipped to deal with murderous attackers, supernatural or otherwise." He gave Cranswell a rueful, apologetic look.

"Yeah, yeah, I know, I can't throw people across rooms with one hand or anything like you guys, but we know that poison compound isn't designed to drop *humans* with the slightest contact, right? What if you get stabbed, Ruthven?"

"I don't intend to. *I* can't take Greta to sort out her car, anyway; I've got to be here to let the central-heating person into the cellar."

He turned back to the toaster, and it was Varney who watched Greta first blink and then turn colors rapidly, and then look *awkward*. It was not an expression he had seen on that face before. Tiredness, yes, intent focus and concern, but not *embarrassment*.

"Um," she said. "About that. I...may have told Kree-akh he and his people could shelter in your basement. It's possible they're already there. I'm sorry, Ruthven."

Ruthven turned to look at her. "May have? Why would they need shelter?"

"It's— Kree-akh came to see me yesterday," Greta said, still looking cross with herself, "and said he and his immediate tribe had been driven out of their encampment. By human-looking things that had *blue eyes*, and that could see in the dark, and did not smell like humans. Two of Kree-akh's people were killed."

"*Killed?*" Ruthven repeated. "Good God. Is— Are the rest of them all right? Was he hurt?"

"He said they were—well, not all right, no, but safe. For now. He wasn't harmed in the attack himself. But the—the blue-eyed men were dressed like *monks*, he said. It has to be related to all of this, to Varney's attack, to the man in my car." She sighed. "I'm so sorry, Ruthven, I should have told everyone last night, but it got driven right out of my head by the mass-spec results."

"Mm," said Ruthven, eyes narrowed. "No harm done. Of course the ghouls can stay in the basement. I just hope they don't encounter the furnace people. It is so *draining* having to thrall panicky repairpersons into forgetting the things they have just witnessed."

"I really am sorry," Greta said. "I don't normally volunteer other people's houses as sanctuary."

"No, well. You were quite right. I'm glad you made the offer," he said, straightening up. "But this is getting more complicated by the minute. Look, come with me and see if they *are* down there yet, and if so we can all have a nice talk about what they saw and what the hell to do next. Then you go up and sort out your car, and get that business over with, and come back afterward. If Fass is feeling up to it I'd suggest he accompany you; I have to stay here and deal with the furnace."

Greta nodded, finishing her toast and licking butter off her fingers, and Varney had to look away in something of a hurry. "All right. And I do need to go over to the clinic again this afternoon, if nothing else dramatic transpires: I have a job to do."

"Me, too," said Cranswell, "but they're not expecting me in the office this week. I want to do more research in Ruthven's library." He was also lounging at the kitchen table with a cup of coffee, wearing a bathrobe over boxers and a T-shirt, and to Varney showed absolutely no sign of wanting to move. The contrast between him and Dr. Helsing was difficult to ignore.

Humans, thought Varney, watching Cranswell stir another spoonful of sugar into his mug, *are remarkably variable.*

Which made them, of course, *remarkably difficult to deal with.*

The cellars of the Embankment house were extensive, containing quite a lot of cobwebby racks of wine bottles as well as the recalcitrant furnace. Greta had been down here once or twice to fetch a particular bottle, but she had always felt somewhat uneasy in the damp cellar chill. As if something was looking over her shoulder, and plotting how best to wall her up inside a niche.

This was foolish and she knew it, but she was still glad Ruthven went first. He stopped just inside the doorway, sniffing, and sighed. Greta could just about pick up the smell of carrion herself, and there were shufflings and mutterings from the darkness at the bottom of the steps. *It's bad,* she thought to herself, *it's really bad, if Kree-akh actually took me up on that offer so quickly. He must have had little choice.*

"Well," said Ruthven, hands on hips, staring down into the dark. Greta could make out multiple sets of red pinpoints of light now, looking back at them. "I wish I'd had more notice. I could have tidied the place up a bit, but—welcome, now that you're here. How many of you are there?"

More shuffling and hissing conversations in ghoulish, and

then the cobwebbed lightbulb in the center of the ceiling clicked on. Twelve ghouls stood—or huddled—in a rough circle around Kree-akh, who let go of the light's dangling cord.

Greta knew that both they and Ruthven could see perfectly well in almost complete darkness. The light was a concession to her own human handicaps, and she felt slightly touched, in an embarrassing sort of way. "Thank you," Kree-akh said. "Your...protection is appreciated."

Most of the ghouls were young adults; a few were middle-aged, and there was one very elderly individual. One of the younger ones was carrying a bundle on her back that set up a thin little wailing. Greta watched as she unwrapped the bundle to reveal a very small ghoullet: Tiny greenish arms waved uncoordinatedly. Beside her Ruthven caught his breath.

"It's quite all right," he said, sounding rather astonished. "I'm...happy to help. What do you need by way of accommodations?"

The ghoul with the baby was bouncing it on a skeletal hip, trying to quiet the wailing, and shot Kree-akh an apologetic look. The chieftain sighed, turning his attention back to Ruthven. "Water," he said, "clean water, and any meat scraps you don't need."

"I can do better than that," Ruthven said, and turned to her. "Greta, help me fetch blankets and look in the freezer for anything that might suit our guests. I'm going to put on a kettle. Do any of you need medical attention?" he added, to the ghouls.

"Not urgently," said Kree-akh. He had his arm around the

young ghoul, said something to her in their language. Greta wondered if the ghoullet was his child or grandchild, and how old it was, and remembered him in her office saying *I lost two young ones*. "But the thought is kind," he added.

"Kind, nothing," said Ruthven. "I want you to tell me all about what happened, if you are willing, but for the moment let's get you settled and safe—and if you could please *not* show yourselves to the furnace repairperson if and when they arrive I would profoundly appreciate it."

"We are good at hiding," Kree-akh said, as drily as a ghoul could manage. The baby was winding down to whimpers and hiccups, not in full cry, and Greta thought he looked more than a little relieved. "Perhaps less good at not being heard; but we are good at hiding."

Greta pushed away her curiosity—she would have loved a chance to examine an infant ghoul, she'd never seen one before—and went back up the stairs to fetch blankets and supplies. The house had taken on a subtly different air with the advent of each new group of occupants. It was no longer simply the impersonal, gorgeous mansion of an aristocrat. Now it was something slightly more like a *castle*, a fortification to retreat within. A small and complicated little world.

She still didn't know what to *do* about any of this, or where it was going. Greta was a scientist both by training and inclination, and *not knowing* was not an acceptable state; the difference between this situation and any she had experienced before was that she also did not know where to even begin looking for answers.

First things first, she told herself. *Crouch End. The car. Cross that off the list of things to worry about, and perhaps someone else will have thought of something by the time you get back. At least Varney's recovery proves that the poison isn't necessarily fatal, and these monk people* are *vulnerable to an extent. They can be hurt.*

She thought, seeing again Kree-akh in the slanting shadows of the cellar light, with his arm around the young mother and her child, that she would be *eminently* okay with hurting the Gladius Sancti, Hippocratic oath or no Hippocratic oath.

CHAPTER 9

Fastitocalon had borrowed one of Ruthven's coats, too short in the sleeves but at least warmer than anything he currently owned. Greta sat squashed next to him on the bus, which was hot and bright and crowded, full of life. It was unquestionably comforting, even if she did feel mildly carsick. Being somewhere this *normal* and ordinary, full of normal ordinary people who didn't have magic powers and couldn't turn into other things, and whose eyes *didn't* glow in the dark, was a luxury Greta had not honestly considered before now.

It was also really, really hard to make herself *think* constructively about what was actually happening, from the viewpoint of this bus seat. The whole miserable, terrifying business seemed as remote and impossible as a dream, and she knew it *wasn't*, and she didn't know what to *do*...

"I hate this," she said, almost to herself.

Beside her Fastitocalon blinked out of a doze. "Mm?" he asked.

"Nothing. Sorry. Go back to sleep. There's four stops left."

He looked at her closely, peculiarly intent. "It's not nothing," he said. "What's the matter? I am very deliberately not reading your mind, by the way, so you have to actually tell me."

That got a small, not very mirthful chuckle out of her. She welcomed the faint constant sensation of never being *entirely* alone, the awareness of his presence nearby; since her father's death Fastitocalon had been watching over her in Wilfert's place. It was a consideration she appreciated. "It's just— I'm not good with not being able to sort things out, Fass. It's what I *do*, it's what I'm for. I don't necessarily know how to fix everything to start with, but I can *find out*. There are processes by which I can actually gain understanding, but with this... there's no way in. I don't know what to *do* and I want to so very much."

Greta hadn't actually meant to say all of that, but it had come tumbling out in a flood, too fast to snatch back the words. "They've murdered eleven humans that we know of, nearly murdered Varney, driven Kree-akh and his people from their homes and murdered two of *them* as well, and—the surviving ghouls are holed up in Ruthven's basement and one of them has a baby, and I *want to do something*, Fass, I want to *stop this happening*."

He nodded, simply. "Yes," he said. "I know. I do too. It's— there's so much we don't know. Simpler to consider what we know it's *not*, and go from there."

"Well, it's not ordinary wildtype humans," Greta said. "Whatever has happened to them has changed them, I don't know to what extent but it's very obviously an alteration."

"Quite. And the change, or the author of the change, is neither angelic nor demonic in nature," he said, and she blinked at him.

"What? How do you know?"

"I can sense these things," Fastitocalon told her solemnly, tapping his temple with a finger. "Truly my powers are vast. No, it's just that—well, angelic, or heavenly, objects or entities are immediately recognizable to the right type of vision. They're covered in a sort of sparkly golden dust and make me break out in hives. Demonic and infernal stuff is just as recognizable, only I'm not violently allergic to the sparkles, and they're red rather than gold."

She thought again of how many times she'd wanted to ask *what are you*. Fastitocalon smiled a little and continued: "In any case I *know* it didn't come here from either Heaven or Hell, because it would have tripped the monitoring stations and someone would be doing something about it, which they do not seem to be."

As he had described it to Cranswell the night before, the balance thing was key. Which was why every major city and locus of metaphysical importance was monitored by both sides, all the time. A dedicated operative was stationed at each point to keep an eye on the equipment that measured disturbances in reality. "If anything had come through recently, it would have registered," Fastitocalon said. "And been summarily dealt with. No, I think that this is definitely supernatural, but nonbinary."

She was still trying to picture these monitoring stations, and getting a sort of vague mental image of geology postdocs watching seismographs, which didn't at all gibe with her mental image of Hell. The idea that there *could* be anything supernatural that wasn't associated with either of the major players was just as difficult to fit her head around. Flickers of barely remembered Lovecraft came to mind: things that dwelled in the darkness beyond reality, blind idiot gods dancing endlessly to maddening thin flute music, shuffling and stamping on and on as the wheels of eternity ground toward the heat death of the universe.

Some of these thoughts must have been too loud to ignore, because Fastitocalon tipped up her chin with a thin, warm finger and looked earnestly at her. "Don't worry," he said, and then made a face of his own. "I mean, don't worry *unduly*. I don't think you need be concerned that the universe is going to implode, or be overrun with nameless horrors of polysyllabic description. This situation is...awkward and objectionable, but I don't believe either Sam or Above is incapable of handling it, should matters get that far."

She looked at him steadily, thinking, *This is my friend, my father's friend, whom I have known all my life, and he is on first-name terms with the Devil.* "I'm having real trouble thinking of the Adversary and Great Beast that is called Dragon and so on being known as 'Sam.'"

Fastitocalon smiled, that odd little unexpected smile that lit his whole face. "Samael. Translates as something like 'severity of God,' which has a nice ring to it. He likes being an enormous white snake when he isn't being the terribly beautiful androgynous wingèd et cetera. I mean, *large*. Probably thirty feet long, about so big around. Black eyes with red pupils. Not what you'd call subtle."

His voice was warm, fond. Greta thought he must have enjoyed working for this Samael, and she wondered again exactly what had happened to drive him up here to live full-time in freezing garrets doing other people's accounts for them. "Especially when envoys from Above are visiting," he continued. "Being eyeballed by a thirty-foot-long snow-white snake tends to knock a lot of the insufferable out of angels."

She just bet it did. "How does he talk when he's a snake? Their mouths aren't built for it."

"How does he turn into a snake in the first place? How does Ruthven change from sixty or seventy kilos of bipedal humanoid into a few grams of regrettably adorable bat?" Fastitocalon shrugged. "It's not a meaningful question. I could go into the metaphysics, but you complain at me when I talk about sums."

"I do not," Greta retorted, and then had to look sheepish. "Okay, maybe I do. Never mind the how, then. Tell me more about Samael."

"Other manifestations include a pretty convincing human male of astonishing physical beauty, a cloud of floating eyeballs, and a point of light about as bright as a welding arc. The androgynous wingèd creature is his default setting."

"No red socks?"

"No red socks. Nor has he got a tail or cloven hooves. Or horns. A lot of demons do, you know. Really big curly ones are considered ostentatious, but a neat, well-kept set of horns is quite within the realm of respectability."

She was feeling more and more as if this had to be a dream, that her old friend and the bus around them were going to fade out and turn into something else any minute now, but Fastitocalon just nudged her with his elbow and she jerked out of the daze. "This is our stop."

Thoughts of Heaven and Hell were driven right out of her mind by the tiresome logistics of arranging for the Mini to be towed to a garage and have them see if the interior was salvageable. It was drizzling again, that thin, icy drizzle that went right down your collar and drained away all enthusiasm or motivation, and her damp hair stuck to her face and neck.

Fastitocalon was doing that thing where he was really, really difficult to notice at all—not invisible, not missing, just… remarkably easy to ignore. He had his eyes closed and was apparently paying no attention whatsoever to her struggles with the insurance company.

"Yes," she told the phone. "Fine. *Finally*. That works for me. Have them call this number with the report, and leave a message if I can't pick up. Right. No. Thank you."

She hung up and gave the Mini's front tire a kick on general principles before squinting up at the sky. "If you want to get anything done in this country you've got to complain till you're blue in the mouth, as I believe John Cleese once pointed out. C'mon, my flat's not palatial but it's at least warm, I'll make us a cup of tea..."

She realized she was having to do all the work in the conversation, and looked sharply at Fastitocalon, or where she knew Fastitocalon to *be*, even if he wasn't strictly all the way visible just at the moment. "Fass? What is it?"

He held up a hand, slipping back to his ordinary greyish self, eyes half-closed; he looked like a man trying very hard to remember something, or to follow the faintest thread of a musical phrase. Despite her immediate instinct to ask him what the hell he was doing, Greta kept quiet, just watching as he turned slowly, searching for something she couldn't sense. He turned a little farther, and then went still, closing his eyes. When he opened them again, the pupils were little round dots of brilliant orange light, as if the insides of his eyes were on fire, and she took an involuntary step back. The effect was very horrible indeed.

He blinked, and the orange glow cut off. "Sorry," he said. "You've gone a funny color. Sit down for a minute, will you?"

It was one thing to *know* that her old friend wasn't human— she was fine with that, most of her friends weren't actually human at all—but every now and then the essential *strangeness* of him came through and flicked the distant switch in her hindbrain that said *run*. Greta shivered, once, violently, and then control came back. "I'm all right," she said. "Just...how about you warn me next time you're about to do that. What is it? What have you seen?"

"I know which way he went, after you were gone," Fastitocalon told her, looking anxious. "It's faint but distinctive. Look, you get a bus back to Ruthven's, where it's safe. I want to follow the trail a little way, see what I can find out."

"Balls," said Greta. "I'm coming, too. He ruined my car, tried to cut my throat, and said a lot of things a well-bred gent ought not to say to a lady. I want to be there when you find him."

He sighed, and pinched the bridge of his nose. "I don't suppose it's worth trying to convince you it's too dangerous?"

"Not in the least," she said, and took his arm. "Come on, the sooner we find him the sooner you can get in out of this cold weather. The damp's not good for you."

He looked down at her. "You're impossible," he said.

"It's a human thing," she told him, and tugged at his arm. "Let's get a move on."

While Greta paced and argued on the phone, Fastitocalon had let his eyes half-close and his other senses calm and then flow outward, smooth as oil over stone, perceiving not simply on this plane of existence but several above it, where he could sense things other than physical objects in space. The trail of the thing that had attacked Greta was old now, cold and overlaid with the trails of hundreds of other living creatures, but it had a peculiar sort of rancid sharpness to it that drew his attention. He had kept very still, listening to Greta's voice only on a distant, shallow level of awareness, most of his concentration focused on that trail.

Fastitocalon had, in fact, *felt* a little of the attack on her itself, through his connection with her mind. It hadn't been at all clear exactly what was happening, but the sudden spike of vivid terror had been unmistakable. Before he had been able to figure out what, if anything, he could *do* about it, the terror had passed off into what he had come to think of as Greta's *maintaining* mode, and he had known she was, if not safe, then at least not in immediate danger. It had taken him a while to calm down again, nonetheless.

Now he led her along the attacker's trail, trying not to think about how visibly shocked she had been to see him looking actually demonic for once. The jab of fear had passed almost immediately, to be replaced with first the truculent expression he remembered from her childhood rebellions and then, somehow terribly, with an almost exact replica of her father's determined look, as she went back to *maintaining*. It had been bad enough when he hadn't known the cause of it; witnessing that shock and knowing it was his own bloody fault was *worse*. Fastitocalon missed Wilfert Helsing very sharply sometimes. It should be Wilfert watching over her, and not his own self.

The trail led across Priory Park southwest, toward Barrington Road, and as they came out onto the street he lost it briefly. Too much had happened since the thing leaving the trail had passed by. He leaned against a lamppost, ignoring Greta's questions, and slid a little way up the planes again, losing some of his visible presence as he did so, but keeping up a general anti-attention field to limit the effect. Up here there were fewer distractions, and he didn't have to pay attention to things like buildings and cars; all that was locked on the prime material plane. Here he could see/sense the *essence* of individual humans, their pneumic signature, what might in a somewhat earlier era have been called their souls. At once the trail of the thing that had attacked Greta sprang back into his awareness, a bright and somehow toxic blue.

It had come out of the park here, paused, and then continued southward—but not by road. Fastitocalon could see the dim outlines of the buildings and streets, but the blue trail paid no attention to them; it passed *below* these obstacles.

He slid back down to the prime material plane, becoming all the way visible again, and this time remembered to keep his eyes shut until the immediate feedback effects had passed. Greta was shaking his arm, saying something; he turned his other senses back on one by one. "...scaring me," she was saying. "Snap out of it, Fass. Come on, don't do this to me right now."

Fastitocalon drew a deep breath, cold and painful in his chest, and opened his eyes, once he was pretty sure the orange light had passed. He found Greta staring up into his face with a mixture of worry and irritation.

"This way," he said. "We can't follow it precisely, but I have it now, it's clear again. Sorry." Beneath their feet an iron manhole cover hid the low rush and chime of water: a storm sewer. "It's gone underground," Fastitocalon said, toeing the metal cover. "Into the tunnels. That's where they hide. That's where they've *been* hiding, all along."

Distracted from all the things she'd been going to say to him with regard to scaring sixteen kinds of hell out of her with his intermittent vanishing act, Greta stared first at the metal circle and then at Fastitocalon, eyes widening. "In the *sewers?*"

"In the dark places under the city," he agreed, pulling Ruthven's coat tighter around his shoulders. "Sewers, tube tunnels, utility tunnels. Come on, the weather's not getting any less nasty, and I've got its trail again. Let's see where it's been."

Two hours later, wet and chilled and in an extremely unfriendly frame of mind, Greta stood on the corner of St. Pancras Way and the Camden Road, shifting from one foot to the other and wiggling her toes to try to get the feeling back in them. They had been walking steadily ever since leaving Crouch End, and while it wasn't so very far a walk, having to stop every so often for Fastitocalon to reorient himself on the trail and do unsettling things he refused to explain to her—"it has to do with planes" was all he'd said—and the general cold, unpleasant louring weather had made it a thoroughly unenjoyable experience.

Fastitocalon was currently walking in a small circle with his eyes tight shut, an activity that should have drawn more attention than it was, in fact, doing. Even Greta was having trouble seeing him clearly, and she had the advantage of actually knowing he was present; she thought probably he was broadcasting a Don't Notice Me signal, or a Somebody Else's Problem field, or something of the kind. Not that she had any idea *how* he was doing that, not that "how" was an answerable question, or what other magical abilities he had that she'd never been informed of, but—

"Oh," he said, and she turned to see him looking for an instant very ill indeed. The orange light in his eyes was back, but this time it seemed less noticeable, or perhaps she was just getting used to it. "There's more than one."

"It met up with friends?"

"I don't think so," said Fastitocalon. The orange was the only color in his face. "No, I rather think they caught up with it. There's…" He waved his hands in the irritable gesture of someone trying to convey a complex point in a language they don't speak well. "There's nuances to the signature. I can feel at least three of them as well as our chap, and they're all that nasty sort of cyan blue and smell terrible, but… ours fades out and then comes back different. Guttering. It's… I think they found it, and took it somewhere, and then brought it back changed. It's very close."

Greta shivered, a long involuntary wave that raised the hair on her arms. "It's close to us? Now? Underneath the street?"

"No," he said. "It *was* underneath… but it's on the surface now, I'd swear to it, and very nearby. This way."

He began to walk west again along the Camden Road, and she could see he was shivering, too. She'd had enough. They should be on their way back to Ruthven's like sensible people, she told herself. They should stop following the invisible track Fastitocalon said he couldn't quite *see* but *sensed*, especially if the monk was close by. What if he had another of those pig-sticker things and decided to poke holes in *Fass* with it this time? She had seen enough of Varney's reaction to be pretty sure it would do real harm to him and...

Greta sighed and hurried after Fastitocalon. *All right, fine,* she thought. *So I'm curious.* Curiosity had never done anybody any good—M. R. James had written a couple of pithy illustrations of that particular point—but dammit, she wanted to know what was going on.

Fastitocalon was moving deceptively quickly. She caught up with him as they passed under the railway bridge, and she noticed with a sinking feeling that he was beginning to wheeze. This really *wasn't* good for him. She needed to get him somewhere warm and dry as soon as possible, but one look at his face told her it was a waste of time trying to argue the point for the moment.

The rain was intensifying as they crossed the canal. Greta had her hood up; she couldn't hear much over the drumming of raindrops, and she would have put money on it that Fastitocalon couldn't, either. Nevertheless, as they passed the late Victorian St. Michael's Church incongruously squashed between the supermarket and an interior design shop, he stopped dead in the middle of the pavement with his head tilted, clearly listening for some faint sound to come again.

She looked around. Just wet, cold, miserable London, nothing glowing blue.

"There," he said softly, and pointed to St. Michael's. "Inside. It's very faint, but it's there. I think it's badly hurt."

She didn't have to ask if he was sure. He looked bleak and exhausted, shoulders hunched against the rain, and Greta couldn't help a miserable cowardly wish that he would say *don't go in there, it's much too dangerous* or maybe *let's go home and leave it to die on its own.*

No. She shook away the thought and the wash of hot shame that went with it. That wasn't something Fastitocalon would ever say. "Let's go, then."

"I'll stay out here, if you don't mind. Churches tend to give me a nasty headache."

Greta looked at him despairingly. "Fass, please—"

"You'll be fine on your own," he said. "You can do this."

She wasn't even remotely sure of that. "Fass, what if it's got the knife?"

If it had the knife, she realized, cross with herself, *he* was probably in more danger than she would be. He sighed, and for a moment looked not only ill but old—ancient, heavy with the weight of years, the way some of her barrow-wight patients were weighed down.

"All right," he said, pinching the bridge of his nose. "I'll come with you." But Greta knew even as he said the words that she couldn't take the offer.

She made her hands relax from the tight fists they'd curled

into, took a deep breath. "God damn it. No. Never mind. You stay here. I won't be long, I hope."

Greta opened the gate, passing through into the church-yard—a narrow strip of space with a few trees offering some shelter from the rain. She could very vividly remember the cold clarity of her terror when the monk had held the knife to her throat; some of that chill rose again in her despite the day-light and the nearby presence of her friend.

The door handle itself was cold, shockingly cold under her hand, and slick with rain. She gripped it hard enough to hurt, and pulled the door open on empty silence.

When nothing glowing blue and screaming flung itself at her, she let out her breath, took another one, and stepped forward into the gloom. It smelled of brass polish and lilies and age, like all churches she'd encountered: that indefinable tang of wood and stone that had been where it was for many centu-ries, and was not going anywhere for many more. There was nobody in there with her. Fastitocalon had been wrong.

He wasn't frequently wrong. Greta's eyes had adjusted to the gloom, and her ears to the curious echoing deadness of church halls everywhere, and she stood perfectly still, straining both senses to catch what he had caught. At first she thought it was her own breathing, still too fast from fright; then it came again, and the sound curdled disgust in her stomach even as it called out to instincts she had been trained to obey. It was a faint mewling, the sound of something exhausted and in ter-rible pain.

She paced slowly up the aisle, wishing she had the little can of pepper spray to hold on to: Even empty, it had felt comforting. That sound came again, closer now. Closer. She was aware of a smell now, overpowering the lilies-and-polish atmosphere of the church: the smell she'd noticed for the first time bending over Varney's wound, a low, sour reek of herbs and metal, somehow rancid, as if exposure to the air was turning something bad. Underneath that was the unmistakable smell of shit. Of sewers.

She reached the end of the rows of empty folding seats, and looked around: nothing. Nothing in the nave, anyway. The shadowy aisles were separated from the nave by a series of vast arches reaching up to the clerestory windows, supported by huge stone pillars, each easily wide enough for a man to hide behind.

She took a step and then another step around the heavy curve of the last pillar. At first she didn't realize what she was looking at. She thought for one absurd moment that someone had left a heap of mottled-pink rags lying on the floor, and then the heap moved. It moved, and opened its horrible eyes at her, and made that low, mewling sound again, and Greta Helsing only just made it to the rubbish bin by the door in time to lose what was left of her breakfast.

The sounds she made echoed unpleasantly in the dim air of the church, and seemed to go on echoing after she had finished being sick. She wanted Ruthven. She wanted Fastitocalon. She wanted her father, oh *God*, how she wanted her father, because Wilfert Helsing would have known what to do; he *always* had known what to do, her whole life, and now she was left alone with the thing slumped behind the stone pillar and it was going to be up to *her* to make all the decisions.

Greta remembered being a medical student, years and years ago, and for the first time truly understanding the difference between working in a hospital, in a department run by a senior physician, under a set of rules and guidelines and frameworks, and working as a solitary GP. There were no tiresome staff meetings, no interpersonal conflicts, no bureaucratic bullshit to wade through in order to do the job—and there were also no instructions or support from superiors. No one to ask for help, advice, consultation.

She had asked her father how he could bear the entire responsibility alone, *how do you stand it, how do you know you're not going to make mistakes with no one else there to help you,* and he had laughed a little.

I don't, he had said. *I don't know for a fact. But I know that I know how to do this job. I trust in my own skill and experience to help me make good decisions. When it comes right down to it, you must be able to trust yourself, before asking your* patients *to place their trust in you. If you cannot do that, do not pursue medicine as a career.*

She had shivered. *But I don't trust myself, yet. Not entirely.*

*You will get there, Gretalina. Confidence comes with practice and reinforcement of learning. You have the right kind of brain for this, and you also—*he had tapped her solemnly on the chest—*have the right kind of heart.*

In the church, she wiped at her face, finally straightening

up. *I don't have the right kind of stomach for it, though,* she thought. *Still, I'm all there is, and I will have to be enough.*

She set her shoulders, took a deep breath, and began to retrace her steps.

The thing behind the pillar wasn't much more of a delight for the eyes—or the nose—the second time around, but now that Greta knew what to expect, she found that she *was* able to look at it through doctor's eyes, and the horror was clinically acknowledged and registered in the back of her mind.

It...he...was naked, covered in weeping burns and scars from older injuries, and what looked like the raised welts of a whip crisscrossed his back. The last time she had seen this individual he'd been dressed up like a Benedictine brother in rough brown wool, and she wondered where his habit had gone; on a day this cold and wet, she thought it unlikely that he had voluntarily taken off all his clothes.

So someone had...stripped him naked, flogged him bloody, and...what, dumped him here? In the church? Had he crawled in here himself, seeking sanctuary? Fass had said the trail went from the tunnels to the surface and then led here.

The clinician in her pointed out that while she was imagining possible scenarios he was continuing to lose fluids—Christ, those burns had to be getting on for eighteen percent total body surface area, plus who knows how much blood loss from the back wounds—and she needed to do something about that in a hurry. Despite the stink and the fact that his ruined, weeping eyes were *glowing bright blue*, Greta

Vivian Shaw

approached him, with her hands open and spread: *I'm not a threat.* She wasn't sure if he could see her, but when he cringed away farther, she figured he at least could detect movement. That awful mewling cry came again.

"I'm not going to hurt you," she said, lying. She would have to hurt him a great deal just getting him out of here. "I'm a doctor. I want to help. Can you understand me?"

"Unclean," rasped the burned man.

No argument there, she thought, swallowing hard against renewed nausea. "What's your name?"

"Anathema," he said. "Excommunicate." He had trouble pronouncing it, his voice thick and slurring, but struggled determinedly through the syllables.

Greta realized that under all the wounds and scarring he couldn't be older than his mid-twenties, and she thought again of what sort of mind it would take to hurt a person this badly and abandon them naked and bleeding and alone. She didn't know much about excommunication, but she was pretty sure that his soul was considerably better off for dissolving ties with such a group, and changed her tack.

"What *was* your name, before you met them?" He was at least not huddling back into the shadows anymore, and after another moment or two he uncurled himself from his knot with a hiss of pain.

"Don't...know," he said. "Cold. Light's gone. Light of God. Dancing....and that sound, that *sound.*" He stopped, shaking his head in dumb negation of something only he could hear. Fluids spattered the floor. "In my head, all the time, humming. Voice of...of..."

Voice of what? Greta thought, shaking her own head. "It's all right. Never mind about that right now," she said. "We've got to get you out of here. Hang on a minute."

They had to get him warm, first of all. She looked around. There were dusty velvet hangings in the shadows beyond him. Greta gave one a determined tug and it parted company with its rail, collapsing in heavy folds and sending up a cloud of choking dust. *Not ideal, but better than nothing,* she thought. *Sorry, St. Michael. I hope you understand.* With the velvet in her hands she knelt down beside him.

He flinched away, covering his face with his hands, but Greta stayed put, ignoring the smell as best she could. After a moment he peered at her between his fingers.

There were what looked like ligature marks around each wrist. They had tied him up before they whipped him.

"I don't mean you harm," she said quietly, very much aware that this man had tried to kill her, had hidden in the dark and held a knife against her throat. "Will you let me help?"

He stared at her with those terrible eyes for what felt to Greta like an awfully long time before nodding, once. She draped the velvet around his shoulders as gently as she could, knowing any contact with the wounds was painful; he hissed, but didn't try to get away, and after a moment his fingers crept up to pull the curtain more tightly around himself. Even through the cloth she could feel the sick, unnatural heat of his skin, the sharpness of his bones. She wondered what the blue monks ate, and when they had last fed this one.

Greta had been pushing away the question of what in blazes to *do* with him, but now it shouldered its way back to the forefront of her mind. She *could* call an ambulance, she *should* call an ambulance, he needed an emergency room, a burn unit, but there was the issue of the blue-glowing eyes to consider. That wasn't a human thing. That was a definitely and incontrovertibly *non*human thing, and *that* was a problem because any doctor worth their white coat would start asking questions the moment they saw it—and the answers they'd get would lead to other, more prying questions. And experiments. And, very probably, quite literal witch hunts. It would only be a matter of time before investigation into this one particular inexplicable phenomenon developed into searching for *other* inexplicable phenomena.

Her entire practice—in fact most of her day-to-day life—was predicated on the fact that the majority of the ordinary world *did not, and must not, know her patients existed.* Their safety, their well-being, their livelihoods, their whole existence depended on their remaining firmly in the realm of fiction. Taking this...whatever he was...to the nearest hospital would be an unacceptable breach of the cardinal rule of secrecy. She didn't need to think very hard about what it would mean for Fass, for Ruthven, for Varney, for the rest of the vampires in London—and the weres—and the mummies—and the banshees—and the ghouls...

And even if she had personally been *able* to get up and walk away from this man, walk away and abandon him to whatever fate remained, she couldn't do that, either. Eventually he *would* be found, and whoever found him would start asking the inevitable questions—and they'd end up with the same problem. All roads led to the pitchfork-and-torch brigade, except one.

Greta cursed everything to the deepest pits of Erebus and got out her phone.

"Fass," she said when he answered, cutting off his *hello*. "I'm going to need a ride to the clinic, and I don't think this guy can walk. Can you flip someone from inside of a church?"

"I don't know," he said. "I've never tried to find out. No time like the present, I suppose."

The weariness—and the resigned willingness—in Fastitocalon's voice hurt her heart, and Greta promised silently that when all this was over she'd do something, anything, to make it up to him. She didn't look up as the church door opened, or as his footsteps approached; she kept her eyes on the shivering velvet-wrapped form of her patient until Fastitocalon reached them and held out his hand.

She gripped it, thin and chilled and strong, and squashed her revulsion sufficiently to take the burned man's hand as well. The moment all three of them were linked, Greta's vision flared orange-white and she felt herself both pulled and *twisted* as the church around them flickered and was gone.

Translocation under the best of circumstances was a little dizzying; translocation like this, with Fastitocalon ill and at the end of his strength, fighting the metaphysical environment, carrying two people with him, was violently disorienting. Greta had to blink through sparkly grey static for several miserably nauseated moments before she could see properly again.

They were in her office, in the Harley Street clinic, lying on the floor. Sitting up brought on another wave of dizziness, but it passed more quickly this time, and she looked around. It was blessedly ordinary in here, warm and bright and familiar and *safe*, and the rain still pounding against the windows merely made the space more cozy.

Beside her Fastitocalon was stirring, his face a peculiar shade of pale grey, and Greta only just managed to reach over to grab the rubbish bin in time for him to be sick, glad she herself had gotten that part over and done with already this afternoon.

While he was occupied she turned to the burned monk, still wrapped in his purloined ecclesiastical curtain and deeply unconscious. The enormity of the task that lay ahead hit her in the face. He needed *so* much work, and she wasn't at all sure she could manage to provide it on her own. Anna's knock at the door a few minutes later, and her muffled inquiry if Greta was a) in there and b) all right, had never been more welcome.

Anna put the CLOSED sign up and locked the clinic while Greta got Fastitocalon dried off and provided with hot sweet tea and something for his church-induced headache. Together she and Anna turned their attention to the job of first cleaning and then dressing the burned monk's overlapping and extensive injuries. They got fluids into him as fast as Greta deemed advisable, both a little surprised at how stable he actually seemed to *be* despite the multiple burns and lacerations. It was becoming evident that whatever was making his eyes glow was also speeding along the process of healing. Even as they worked, some of the cuts were beginning to scab over, and one minor scratch completely vanished into a shiny pink line as Greta and Anna watched, mouths open.

"That's not right," Anna said, pointing with a gauze pad clamped in her forceps. "That's...vampire-level healing, but this one's a living human. Or at least he used to be."

"I want Fass to have a look at him, when he can see straight. Earlier he was going on about this guy's pneumatic signature, or something, I can't remember—a trail only he could see. Maybe he can tell us what we're looking at."

"I've never seen human eyes do *that*, either," Anna said, going back to work. Neither had Greta; the blue light was somehow still faintly visible through his closed eyelids. She described how the eyes had looked the last time she'd seen them up close, in the backseat of the Mini: the corneas boiled-egg-opaque, a mass of tattered and ridged tissue through which he couldn't possibly have perceived anything beyond blurry light and dark, if that, and yet he had somehow been able to see her nonetheless—see *through* his ruined eyes. Greta wondered if he could see through other things as well, fascination and curiosity warring with alarm in the back of her mind.

"The whole of the eye glows, but the light's not given off by the corneal surface," she said. "More like...I don't know, like the light is generated farther in, passing *through* the eye itself and visible only in the outside air?"

"It must have been what the ghouls saw," Anna said. "Blue eyes glowing in the dark." She shivered, and Greta thought again of the way Kree-akh had held the mother and her child, in the harsh light of the cellar's single bulb, thought of death in the darkness, sudden and swift—

Enough, she told herself. *You have a job to do.* "Pass the saline, please."

CHAPTER 10

Afternoon had turned into evening by the time all the monk's burns and slashes had been cleaned and attended to, and Greta's phone had rung and gone to voice mail several times. She had sent Anna home with fulsome thanks and a promise of overtime pay when Greta could scrape up the extra, and she was alone now with the burned monk and Fastitocalon.

She stripped off her gloves and dropped into the exam room's chair, closing her eyes for a long moment before taking her phone out of her pocket. It felt as if she'd been up for approximately a week; her back and neck hurt, the tension headache that had started in her temples had taken over her entire skull, and fatigue dragged at her as if gravity had been jacked up a couple of notches just in her immediate vicinity.

There were texts waiting as well as voice mail. Oh. Right. It would probably have been a good idea if she'd called Ruthven at some point to let them know where she and Fass were, or weren't, such as dead in a ditch somewhere.

Guiltily she scrolled through the increasingly irate texts, considering asking Fastitocalon to be the one to call Ruthven, but she could hear him coughing monotonously from her office and thought, probably, all things considered, it would be more efficient if she did the talking.

Ruthven picked up on the first ring. "Where the hell are you?"

"The clinic," she said. "Look, I'm—"

"I was just about to go out looking. I rang Sheelagh O'Dwyer and got her and the other banshees to do a sweep and had the damn ghouls pass the word to try to catch your scent. For God's sake, Greta, what have you been *doing* all day that you couldn't bother to answer your bloody phone?"

She winced, rubbing her temple. When he was cross he just stuck to icy sarcasm, but when he was really angry he went up half an octave and the Scots crept into his cut-glass accent.

"I'm sorry, Ruthven, I really am. It's my fault, I completely lost track of time, but could you maybe not shout?" She sounded exhausted even to herself. "We took care of the car thing, then Fass caught the...scent? Trail, track, whatever, of the man who attacked me. We followed it to Camden Town and, uh, long story short, I've got one exhausted demon and one seriously damaged mad ex-monk on my hands and I forgot to call you and I'm sorry."

"You've *got* one?" She could hear excited voices on the other end.

"Yes. An exile from the ranks. He said he'd been excommunicated, presumably because he didn't manage to kill me properly the last time we met."

"Can he talk?" That was Cranswell. "We can probably make him talk."

"Do shut up, Cranswell," said Ruthven, and much of the anger had leached out of his voice. "What condition is he in?"

"Terribly burned, and he's been flogged on top of that, and God knows what pathogens he's been exposed to—but he's healing, amazingly well as a matter of fact. Much faster than he ought to be. He's stable for now."

"Can you move him?"

"If I have to." The voices in the background on Ruthven's end were raised in argument now. "Why?"

"Interrogation," Ruthven said. He sounded tired, too, tired and worn out with worry, and she felt another stab of guilt. "I'd say all three of us here are very definitely *interested* in whatever your catch can tell us about the Gladius Sancti and their plans. Varney in particular would like a personal word with him on the subject of stab wounds."

"And if he doesn't know anything? He seemed really out of it. I'm not sure he can remember much detail."

"Well, we'll work out what to do with him, at least. How's Fass?"

"Exhausted. I want him in bed. He spent much too much time out in the cold and rain today, and then he had to flip all three of us back here. From a church, no less." She rubbed at her temples again, wondering when she'd last been this tired.

"And you?" Ruthven's voice had warmed back up. "No, don't answer that. I can imagine. I'll come and fetch you. If we fold down the Volvo's backseat you can slide your new friend in on a stretcher and I can get all nostalgic about driving ambulances in the Blitz. Won't that be nice?"

She laughed despite herself, as he had meant her to, and had to swallow as her throat ached with a sudden wave of fondness. "You didn't *really*, did you?"

"There's a lot you don't know about me, my darling. Go and pack up what you need. I'll be there in a little while."

It had been easier than Greta had anticipated, getting her patients stowed in Ruthven's elderly 240 wagon (which was that particular shade of pale yellow reserved for eggnog and Volvos). The drive over had been quiet except for Fastitocalon's cough; she had spent it sitting perfectly still with her eyes shut and savoring the experience of not being in charge of the situation. Being managed by other people was often maddening, but sometimes—like right now—Greta luxuriated in the somehow *anesthetic* insulation it brought. She did not have to *think*, and that felt like...oh, like sitting down had felt, after the hours and hours of work: a vast and crawling weight removed.

As they drew up in front of the Embankment house, reality came back, stacking up the weights again in her mind, in her heart. She was going to have to protect the man who'd fairly recently tried to kill her from the attentions of a very angry vampyre as well as August Cranswell's enthusiastic questioning, and it was going to...

She mentally rephrased her analysis from *suck* to *be bloody awful*, and then again to *present a considerable challenge*, and the progression was enough to make her laugh a little at the sheer absurdity of the situation. Ruthven raised an eyebrow at her.

"Nothing," she said, swallowing against a sudden unexpected threat of tears following in the wake of the laughter. The image of balancing on a very narrow ledge between deep valleys rose in the back of her mind, and she pushed it away, willing her voice to sound normal. "It's been a long day, that's all."

"It certainly has." Ruthven patted her hand. "Come on, I want to get some food into you. You've gone the color of good bond paper and these two need their beds."

Fastitocalon protested being lumped in with the quondam Gladius Sancti infantry on the invalid list, but he was handily overridden.

Later that evening, after Ruthven had made dinner for her and Cranswell (no garlic was the only real house rule when it came to food; small amounts of scallions and chives were on the okay list, and it turned out you didn't need *Allium sativum* to make quite a passable Bolognese), she told them her interpretation of what she had seen.

"They're radiation burns, not chemical, and I can't think of a thermal burn situation that would result in the pattern I saw. Full-body burn cases from stuff like falling into boiling hot springs exist in the literature, but the pattern doesn't fit; his *aren't* all over, they're worst on his front, and some parts of his back and legs seem to have been spared." She looked around the table at their expressions. "Judging by the repeated references he made to blue light I'm going to venture the theory that they're UV burns, and that they're due to something like an unshielded welding arc, or extended exposure to a mercury vapor lamp without the outer protective bulb. The pattern is consistent with his having spent a significant amount of time in a kneeling position facing the source, possibly with his hands held together in front of his chest. The burns are worst on his face and neck, his hands and forearms, the front of his lower torso, and the front of his thighs. He said something about a noise, too, as well as the light. A humming or buzzing sound." She paused, and tucked her hair back. "The real question is what the hell a UV source like that is doing underground, and what has it got to do with their kill-all-demons bit? And not incidentally *who they are*, and why they are doing whatever it is they're doing, but mostly I want to know what's responsible for this."

Cranswell was winding up the last strands of spaghetti on his fork, his appetite apparently unaffected by her narrative. "Blue light of God," he said with his mouth full. "Whatever it is, they're being exposed to the source on purpose. Maybe for penance. Like hair-shirts or flagellation, you know, mortification of the flesh."

"'O holy UV-B light source, purify me of sin'?" Greta said, looking skeptical. "I don't think they had those back when this sect got started."

"'S like that Ursula Andress movie." He finished twirling the spaghetti, conveyed it to his mouth, and used the now-denuded fork to gesture. "With Stacy Keach. *Something Something of the Cannibal God*. Ursula and supporting cast were exploring a primitive volcanic island staffed by cannibals, like you do, and found the locals worshipping a dead guy with a Geiger counter stuck in his chest cause they thought the clicking was the sound of his dead heart still beating. You know. Object taking on talismanic significance. Cargo-cult stuff."

"But a *lightbulb*?" Varney said, interest in the subject apparently overtaking mild revulsion at Cranswell's table manners. "And these aren't superstitious cannibal tribes. They're... well... as Dr. Helsing says, we don't know *who* they are. Just that they can spell quite long words in garlic juice on people's walls."

"Religious mania is capable of prompting some pretty messed-up behavior," Cranswell pointed out. "People do all kinds of stuff because God tells them to. Why shouldn't God be a lightbulb? He's already been a whirlwind and a burning bush, just to select two examples completely at random."

"Wait," said Ruthven, holding up a hand, looking into the middle distance with the preoccupied expression of someone tracking down an elusive thread of memory. "Wait. Underground, right. *The* Underground. There's all sorts of electrical switchgear and so on to run the systems down there."

"I think the transport authority would notice a bunch of crazy monk guys genuflecting to their light fixtures," Cranswell said. "Like, even in London that's weird."

"Shut up, I'm thinking." Ruthven's hand, still lifted, tapped gently at the air as if to jar loose whatever he was trying to remember. "Trains and electrical switchgear...electrical switchgear...I've nearly got it."

"I had an electric train when I was a kid. The transformer that came with it was this little dinky piece of shit that was always overheati—"

"That's it!" Ruthven thumped the table, making them all jump. "Sorry. That's what reminded me, when you said *transformer*. I know what the blue light is. I mean, I think it has to be." He beamed at them in satisfaction. "Nothing else fits all the requirements, the blue light and the humming-hissing sound and the mercury vapor and the ultraviolet radiation and the, well, the talismanic significance, as you so precisely put it."

"*What* fits the requirements?" Greta demanded.

"Oh, sorry. It's not a lamp at all, it's a mercury arc rectifier. Electric railways had them, that's what made me think of it. They were pretty much the standard up until, oh, the sixties or seventies, when thyristors took over. Pity, though of course solid state was less dangerous and took up less space. Very few of them are still actually working these days; they're museum pieces, quite apart from the toxicity thing."

"I *don't understand* what you're *talking* about," said Varney, enunciating with irritated clarity, and Greta and Cranswell shot him identical grateful looks.

"Used to have them in carbon arc film projector setups, too; you had to have DC to run the arcs," Ruthven went on, and

180

then apparently finally realized he'd lost his audience. "Look, I'll show you." He took out his phone and did a quick You-Tube search. "Here's the one from the Manx Electric Railway that was still in place up until a few years ago."

All three of them crowded in to stare at the little screen; it was playing a video clip of something that was at once wonderful and terrible and profoundly hypnotic.

Cranswell was looking over Ruthven's shoulder. "It *is* a lightbulb. With legs."

It did, in fact, resemble one: a giant blue-glowing glass bulb, six angled legs jutting out from its walls just above the base, looking vaguely tentacular. The flickering unsteady glow was brightest in the hollow glass tubes of the legs, each of which bent ninety degrees before giving itself up to a graphite fitting and a coiled, curled wire. In the base of the bulb lay a miniature lake of mercury, on the surface of which danced a glaring brilliant blue-white spark. Far too bright to look at for long, the moving spark seemed to describe strange patterns on the liquid metal: sigils that might make sense if you could only watch long enough to follow them, that—despite the danger— made you want to *try*.

When it was over, nobody protested when Ruthven played the video again, turning up the volume so the humming of the thing was clearly audible over the tour guide's chatter.

"Good heavens," said Varney quietly. "I don't think I can blame them for thinking *that* thing could have supernatural powers. What are the legs for?"

"Anodes," Ruthven said. "It turns AC into DC. For reasons

I won't go into, the mercury vapor only conducts current in one direction. It's a valve that only lets current pass one way."

"I'll take your word for it," said Greta. "If that's basically what amounts to a great big unshielded UV lamp, it could probably do the kind of damage I saw. If he'd been exposed to it for... well, quite a while."

Ruthven glanced at her, eyebrows raised. She shrugged, not really wanting to examine the thought too closely. "It would have to be hours. Several hours."

"Like I said," Cranswell put in, "doing vigil or penance or what-have-you."

Purifying them, Greta thought, and winced. "UV sterilizes," she said. "It is literally germicidal; it's actually one of the ways you sterilize things in a lab. Ugh, it does fit, doesn't it? Burning away the dross."

"*How* does this thing confer on them the... the supernatural powers we have witnessed?" Varney asked impatiently. "Their eyes, how does it make them able to see through objects when their eyes are obviously blinded?"

Cranswell nodded. "And how does it make 'em glow blue while it's at it?"

"That is, I think, where the supernatural aspect comes in."

With almost comically coordinated timing, they looked up from Ruthven's phone to see Fastitocalon leaning in the doorway, looking haggard but focused. "Because, make no mistake, they *are* supernatural," he continued. "It takes one to know one."

"What are you doing up?" Greta demanded.

"Providing the demonic viewpoint. No," he added, lifting a hand, "please don't start with the lecturing, I've had rather more than enough of that for one day, and I'm quite capable of rational discourse."

Greta looked mutinous, but just sighed and got up, gathering the plates. "I'll put on a kettle," she said. "If we're going to have a council of war we might as well have a nice cup of tea while we're doing it."

In the tunnels, blackness. No sound save for the dripping of water, the distant roar of the fans that never stop turning, the intermittent rumble of trains passing through in tunnels nearer the surface. Down here there is only blackness, and the slow drip as unseen water patiently works its way through cracks in the concrete, stretching milky fingers of newborn stone down from ceilings, rotting away the man-made rock, fraction by fraction over the years. The creatures that use these tunnels have no need of light to see by. It is dark everywhere but in one chamber, and in that one chamber the light never goes out.

In its glass prison, the dancing point of blue-white brilliance is surrounded by a cold blue glow that turns red into black, burning on and on in the relentless dark. The steady atonal humming that accompanies the light does not change with its flickering intensity.

Inside the blue glow, inside the hum, past the silver trickle of condensing mercury on the glass walls of the bulb, an entity watches, and considers.

It is not an entity that had been present when this installation was built. In fact, it has only been here, in this physical metal-and-glass stronghold, for a matter of months, finding it peculiarly comfortable as a dwelling place. Before that it had ridden through the centuries in many kinds of vessels: weapons, jewels, living creatures, the minds of men. Twined with their thoughts, their ideas, their dreams, unnoticed and unremarked, it watched in the darkness behind their eyes. From time to time it has spoken to them from the mouths of oracles, or been the voice of gods and idols in their heads; sometimes it has merely whispered words to them in the long watches of the night, and planted seeds that bore strange fruit.

It has been around for a very long time, this formless, bodiless entity. It is as old as creation itself—an overlooked fragment of existence, like the scraps on a cutting-room floor—and it has slept from time to time, from age to age, but it is awake once more.

Awake and *hungry*.

Its purpose is and always has been to *consume*, to devour; and all the mischief it has made in all the ages of civilization, and before civilization itself, is merely to generate *hate* and *fear* to feed its unending hunger. It has turned the course of history to its own desires, fomenting unrest, provoking conflict, steering what might have been peaceful agreements toward aggression, over and over again.

It was in the adder that stung King Arthur's knight at Camlann, starting the last battle. It rode in the hearts and minds of those who set fire to the Library of Alexandria. When the

Mongols took Baghdad in 1258 and the waters of the Tigris ran black with ink from ruined books and red with blood from ruined men, ninety thousand dead, it *feasted*. But it can focus its attention far more tightly, and some of its favorite feedings have been spiced by the intense fear that springs up surrounding the work of a single human's hands; the spell cast over a town, a city, by a series of high-profile and mysterious deaths. There is a certain satisfaction it finds in such careful and delicate work.

And the web of threads it has woven through this city, through hearts and minds and the dark holes under the earth, through faith and fervor, is almost complete. Perhaps it is time for the end of this game, for it to take its meal.

The *belief* of these zealous little god-botherers whose ready-made cult it has settled into, as a king might assume a captured throne, has been surprisingly rich and nourishing. It had found them ideally suited to its purposes: a group of men only just formed into a tiny sect intent on following the example of a long-lost secret society. They had been quite ordinary, if *intense* in their devotions to a particular view of God.

The entity has enjoyed them immensely from the beginning, their fervent belief tasting rare and delicious. At first it had merely watched; then it began *influencing* these believers, settling into their hearts and minds, lending them the slightest edge of its (vast, unmeasured) strength—and rendering them no longer entirely human in the process. Now their belief has metastasized from devotion into blank-eyed madness, which it enjoys for its own piquancy; but it is the formless terror, the gathering *fear* that its creatures have induced in the city above that the entity truly desires. The generalized fear brought about by the killings, and the bright, delicious spikes of it each time someone has found themselves being watched—being *followed*—by two pinpoints of blue light. The deaths are delightful; the *fear* is much, much better. It had intended to draw this out a little longer, but perhaps the time has ripened long enough.

It is not only the killings of ordinary people that have stirred up the city to its current rich and wonderful concentration of dread. On its own that would have been reward enough for all the thing's efforts; but here and now it has been able to taste a rarer and more potent vintage. The terror of the living is delicious. The terror of the *dead*, however, is *exquisite*.

When it had first settled into place and was beginning to choose its tools, it had not thought to bother with the effort and concentration required to engage the city's small group of monsters. There were always monsters; there always had been. Mostly it was simply too much work to manipulate them, to play upon their minds the way it played upon the briefer, brighter minds surrounding them; but this time it had hit upon a little band of tools that were in a peculiarly appropriate position to make that leap. It is quite proud. Armed with their pretty poisoned ritual toys, they have done a remarkable job so far both in directly engaging the monsters and in persecuting the humans they apparently valued, and the heady savor of *supernatural* fear is profoundly satisfying to experience— goes, in fact, much further toward sating the entity's unending hunger than anything has done in a very, very long time.

When the entity's chief servant had discovered that the excommunicate still lived, that the monster-doctor woman he had failed to kill had somehow brought what was left of their outcast brother to a place of safety, he had been *furious*, incandescent with hatred, blazing with the most delicious determination to rectify this wrong.

(That the woman must die had been clear from the beginning; she was peculiarly necessary to the monsters, and killing her would send a lovely ripple effect of not only fear but *despair* through the city's undead, which the entity has been looking forward to a great deal. The young man who had stolen the books was much less important, and merely frightening him had seemed sufficient expenditure of effort at the time.)

The rich and heady anger of its chief servant at the initial failure to dispose of the woman had gone some way toward distracting the entity from its hunger—but not for long. Thinking, now, it reaches out for the servant's mind—a red welter of intense and fervent belief that, to the entity, is beautiful—and gives a little tug. It does not have to wait long before the man appears in its chamber, in the chamber of the peculiar talisman it has chosen to inhabit, and falls on his knees in the glare of its light. In his rough-spun habit and cowl he could have been kneeling before any number of altars in the centuries gone by. This chamber is as much a sanctuary as any cathedral of stone and gold and jewel-colored glass.

Come closer, it says inside his head. The servant's scarred face and blank, unblinded eyes are turned up to it, worshipful. *I have a new task for you.*

"Yes, Lord," he says, a whisper, barely audible under the endless hum. "I will not fail You again."

I know. Its voice is gentle. *I have made you the minister of God, a revenger to execute My wrath. Your heart is true, and in your mouth are the names of God, and in your hand the great and strong sword.*

Speaking in the forms and cadences its tools expect has always been easy. It has an ear for language; taking on the role of these people's very specific image of God had posed no challenge whatsoever. It has been many gods, over the millennia. Many.

The servant bows lower before it. Tears gleam on his blue-lit face. "Yes, Lord, thank You, Lord, what would You command me?" In his voice is such joy.

Let them be burned with fire, says the voice inside the light. *Kindle a fire in their company, and the flame shall burn up the wicked, the blood-leeches and their servants, the thief and the Devil's whore and the demon-creature and the excommunicant. Let them be burned with fire. There is no darkness, nor shadow of death, where the workers of iniquity may hide themselves.*

He is nodding, eagerly. "Will the fire not spread, Lord?"

Let it. Now the thing allows some of its pleasure and amusement into its voice. Oh, it has been so *long* since the last time it razed a city, such a long while since the last time it fed anywhere near so well; this will be even more delicious than it had foreseen. Its tools' devotion to their code of purifying this world of evil is both lovely and peculiarly useful for its own purposes. *I have set my face against this city for evil, and not for good, and give it into your hand,* it tells him, in the words of the book he has spent his life studying. *You shall destroy it utterly, and burn the towers of this place with fire, and all that are therein. Let it spread. Let death seize upon them, and let them go down quick into Hell, for wickedness is in their dwellings, and among them.*

"When shall it be done?"

It considers. *First call your brothers back from their work, and let them make ready with prayer and meditation. When the time is right I will set your new tasks upon you.* Now the voice is warmer than ever, genuinely pleased, anticipatory. *By the end of the seventh day, which is the Lord's day, My will shall be done, and you shall—all—know peace.*

CHAPTER 11

When Greta woke up, fully clothed but shoeless, there was a note leaning against the glass of water on the bedside table. *Forgive the presumption. R.*

She sat up, the movement accompanied by a fusillade of cracks from her spine, and winced. Being carried off to bed like a kid who'd stayed up past her bedtime was admittedly to be preferred over spending the night sleeping where she'd dozed off at the dinner table, but that didn't mean it wasn't embarrassing. At least she'd managed to outlast Cranswell, who had drifted off in the middle of an increasingly incoherent conversation with Fass about what did and did not rate as part of the binary Heaven–Hell balance.

Six hours of sleep was not even near enough to make up for the past several days, but it at least made her able to think a little straighter, pushing away some of the fatigue poisons and the dull, formless dread.

She swung her legs off the bed and got up stiffly, padding

over to the window to notice that it wasn't raining and that a weak, watery sun was even trying to poke its way through the clouds, for the first time all week. Slightly cheered up, Greta went to check on her latest patient and found Ruthven sitting by the burned monk's bed reading, yesterday's tie loosened, his shirtsleeves rolled up. Some of his hair had even escaped its usual aerodynamic styling process and drooped over his forehead. Absurdly and suddenly she wished she could draw, wanting to catch the scene on paper: Casual Dracula.

"I've been watching since about three in the morning," he said, not looking up at her until he'd marked his page in the book he was reading. "No change for the worse. He woke up twice and asked for water, mumbled a lot of stuff about damnation and the reprobate and eternal suffering, and went right back to sleep. If that's what this is. Unconsciousness, sleep, I don't know."

Greta came over to put a hand on his shoulder. "Thank you," she said. After a moment he covered her hand with his own, and smiled up at her. The smile was only a little worn round the edges. He had color in his face; his lips were faintly pink. "You're being wonderful about all of this, Ruthven. Thanks for looking after him, despite—"

"Despite everything," Ruthven finished for her. "Yes, well. One tries, you know. One does one's best. I went out to eat after you'd conked out, so Fass took the first watch, but I took over and sent him to bed when I got home. Varney, I think, didn't quite trust himself not to come over all murderous in the middle of the night, and sensibly stayed far away."

Something was kicking her brain. "Where did we even get to last night? I remember them talking about entities that don't belong to either God or the Devil, and you were trying to explain electronics to me and Sir Francis and it wasn't working."

"More or less. Fass was telling me a bit about his version of magic after you'd dozed off. He says it works very much the same way as electromagnetism. Similarly enough that there are—oh, laws, and equations and things describing its behavior, which under other circumstances I'd want to learn a great deal more about." He shrugged. "The point is that there's a lot of overlap between physics and magic, and that suggests to me that perhaps whatever's turned this poor bastard into what he is now is *using* the rectifier and the radiation it puts out to transmit its power. The same way a radio transmitter works."

Greta raised an eyebrow at him. "It's using the UV light to...what, control them?"

"Something like that. Radio transmitters encode information by modulating a carrier wave's amplitude or frequency. My theory is that this...thing, whatever it is, the intelligence behind all the attacks...is altering the output of the rectifier via magic, so that it can directly influence people who are exposed to it."

"Is that even possible?" she asked, wishing she knew more about physics.

"I don't know. It *sounds* vaguely plausible to me, but Fass will be able to confirm it when he wakes up."

"I bet he'll be happy to go on at great length about it. But the end result is, what, that these Gladius Sancti guys actually get something tangible *out* of their idol worship other than a lovely warm sense of self-righteousness?"

"Yes," said Ruthven. "They get turned into tools."

He closed his eyes, opened them slowly. They were very pale in this light, the black-rimmed irises cold and clear like little silver bowls of ice. "Imagine you've prayed all your life," he continued, "that you've been taught to pray, taught to believe that you *must* give praise in prayer and that you are not to expect the blessing of hearing anything ever answer back—that expecting anything to reply to you is hubris and wickedness—but one day there's this little voice, this still small voice, that *does* reply. And you believe it and you love it and you worship it, just as you have been taught to all your life... and it shows you wonderful things inside your head, and takes away your fear and pain. And it tells you how to make things... and where to go... and what to do to people *with* those things, once you get there."

Ruthven's voice was slick with acid, and she blinked down at him. "You... really hate this, don't you?"

"Yes," he said, and got up, book in hand. "I really hate this. I'll put the kettle on and go to check on the ghouls, if you'll excuse me."

Wordless, she stood aside to let him go by.

Ruthven had never talked very much about his distant past, but she knew he had lived and died at the end of the sixteenth century—a time when belief in some form of Christianity would have been pretty much universal in this part of the world. Greta thought it was entirely possible that he could see more clearly from the perspective of the Gladius Sancti than she would ever be able to.

She held a roughly agnostic position with regard to the existence of deities. That a great many supernatural beings existed was self-evident to Greta; that an omniscient and omnipotent and *benevolent* creator was in charge was somewhat less so, based on the chaotic and disorganized nature of the universe. Nor did she feel any desire to pray or attend services, although she had never considered people who did to be particularly foolish or misguided; it was simply a part of other people's lives that she did not share. Trying to imagine what it would be like to have truly believed in something, truly and honestly experienced faith, was difficult for her. Trying to imagine what it would be like, as a believer, to *hear the voice of God* was something close to impossible.

Witnessing the intensity of Ruthven's loathing for the thing that had taken such advantage of these people's belief made Greta just a little glad she *didn't* know what it was like.

She pushed away the thought, with effort, and turned her attention to the man in the bed. The fact that Greta herself had been allowed to sleep through the night was encouraging; either Ruthven or Fastitocalon would have woken her if his condition had deteriorated overnight. In fact, he was rather better than she had expected, and she thought again of the cut healing to a pink, shiny line of scar as she and Anna watched. *Whatever is doing this to these people takes care of its belongings,* she thought. *To some extent.*

I wonder if it knows he's here.

Greta wished she hadn't just thought that. She started another bag of IV fluids dripping slowly, gave him another dose of antibiotics, and checked the dressings on his wounds—which were noticeably further along in the healing process than they had been twelve hours before. She was changing one of the dressings when his eyes opened: just a slit of blue light.

"Back with us?" she said quietly. "Ruthven said you had a pretty quiet night."

The slits widened, and she saw his ruined eyes move, tracking her. Clinically she knew perfectly well that there was no way he should have been able to see a damn thing other than vague areas of dark and less-dark, and even that much was highly unlikely, but he was looking right at her nonetheless.

God, but this was so fucking *creepy.*

Greta kept her face straight, the careful, noncommittal bedside expression reassuring in its familiarity. After a moment he tried to say something, the tip of a dry tongue creeping over cracked lips, and managed it on the second attempt. "Where?"

"You're safe. You're safe and nobody is going to hurt you," she said, and reached over for the glass of water on the bedside table. Somebody—Ruthven, presumably—had located an actual bendy straw to put in it, and Greta's chest ached with a sudden clutch of fondness for the small kind thought. She held the glass for the monk to drink; the awful eyes slipped half-closed again in relief, or possibly even pleasure. Then he sighed a little, a faint wheezing sigh that she thought was the weariest damn sound she had ever heard.

She set the glass aside. This time when his eyes opened, they opened all the way, trained on her face, and she imagined she could *feel* the blue light itself touching her skin as they widened in visible recognition. He made a nasty hitching noise in his throat, shrinking away from her.

"You," he said. It was barely audible. "I know you. The wicked, whose day is come."

"Yes, I know," Greta said, feeling approximately a thousand years old. "It's all right. I know. You were sent to get rid of me."

"Give them...according to their deeds...and according to the wickedness of their en-endeavors," he rasped. "For by fire and by his sword...will the Lord plead with all flesh...and the slain of the Lord shall be many."

She said nothing, looking down at him, and he winced and closed his eyes as if rebuked, and carried on. "But when the righteous...turneth away from his righteousness...and committeth iniquity, and doeth according to...all the abominations that the wicked man doeth, shall he live?"

"I don't know," Greta told him, gently. The words were familiar, as if she'd heard them before, and more than once. He turned his head on the pillow in a slow and deliberate negation.

"All his righteousness...that he hath done...shall not be mentioned: In his trespass that he hath trespassed...and in his sin that he hath sinned...in them shall he die."

There was a game Greta and her father had played a long time ago in which you had to hold a complete conversation using *only* quotations from books or plays, and the first person who couldn't come up with a line—any line—to carry on the discussion conceded defeat. Greta, who had been a voracious reader from an early age, had enjoyed it much more than Scrabble. Neither she nor Wilfert had used Bible quotes to any great extent, lacking the necessary stock of memorized phrases, but as Greta looked down at her patient she thought she could recognize a highly experienced player of the game.

"You didn't commit iniquity," she told him, not ungently. "You might have meant to kill me, but you didn't do it. That's a mortal sin you did not commit. Trespass, well, you did break into my car, but I suppose that's a bit beside the point. We found you in the church, my friend and I, and brought you here to treat your wounds."

That seemed to puzzle him, and he looked up at her uncertainly.

"I suppose I'm wicked to some extent," Greta said. "Most people are. But on the whole I rather think it's your brethren who are workers of iniquity, if they're the ones who have been murdering people. 'Other sins only speak; murder shrieks out. The element of water moistens the earth,'" she added, completely unable to stop herself, "'but blood flies upward and bedews the heavens.'"

He blinked.

"Book of Webster, *Duchess of Malfi*."

He did a bit more blinking, and Greta had to smile. "I

mean it," she said. "If they threw you out, you're the better for it. They were not...doing God's work."

He looked terribly confused. "The land is full of...adulterers," he said after a moment, as if searching for imperfectly memorized words. "Because of swearing the...the land mourneth...the pleasant places of the wilderness are dried up...and their course is evil, and their force is...not right?" His voice rose a little at the end, a question.

"Well, there *are* lots of adulterers around," Greta said. "And lots of wicked people in general. People lie and cheat and steal and commit murder and have wars and refuse to give help to the people who need it. But that doesn't mean you ought to go around killing them and reciting the King James for justification."

"But..." His expression changed, as Greta watched. "But the enemies of the Lord shall perish, and the workers of iniquity be scattered."

"I daresay the Lord will sort that out on his own time," she said. "Here's another one: 'Hypocrisy is woven of a fine small thread, subtler than Vulcan's engine.' Don't you think it seems a little...backward, perhaps...to run around committing mortal sins in order to cleanse the world of sin and evil?"

"We are *commanded*," he said. "The Voice of God."

She nodded. "What if it isn't, though? What if it *isn't* God at all, but something else?"

He screwed up his face—which had to hurt his burns, Greta knew—and shook his head firmly. "That's blasphemy."

At least they weren't playing the Quotation Game anymore.

"What if it's something that's *pretending* to be the Voice, and making you do its dirty work?"

"No!" he said, miserably, and again, softer: "No."

Greta sat back, not willing to push him any further right now. "Never mind," she said, more gently. "You're safe here, like I said, and we'll take care of you, even if they did cast you out of their ranks. Don't worry about it now."

"Excommunicated," he mumbled, but with less distress.

"Okay, excommunicated. I know it matters to you, but it doesn't change anything for us. We'll help you no matter what."

He looked up at her and despite the horrible blue-blank eyes, Greta thought she could see something like hope in his face, just for a moment, before his expression returned to one of pain and grief. He really couldn't have been more than twenty-five, she thought.

When he spoke again his voice had changed. It was no longer the voice of someone playing a memorized part, but someone tired and hurt and frightened. "Eyes hurt," he mumbled. "Everything hurts. Where are we?"

"Victoria Embankment," she said. "In a house belonging to one of my good friends. I'm going to give you something for the pain."

"Embankment. *Chelsea*," he said. Greta blinked.

"Same riverbank, yes."

"Chelsea," he said again. "Something about…Chelsea. Can't remember…"

"It's okay," she said. "Relax. It'll come back to you." She

hoped, anyway. She hoped some things that were a bit more useful came back to him. There was another of those faint sighs, and the hand that was least damaged rose and drifted across the bed in her direction. She stayed where she was, letting his fever-hot fingers find and touch hers, letting him grip her hand.

"Cold hands," he said. "I'm on fire. Don't... don't make me go back, I can't, I can't bear that *hum*..."

"They won't find you. You're safe here," she said, wondering again if it was true. If any of them were actually safe here, if this man's colleagues—or the thing that was running them—were aware of his location.

"Who was..." His breathing was getting faster. "Man. White face, black hair. Gave me water."

"Easy," Greta said, trying to put as much calm in her voice as she could. "It's all right. That's just Ruthven. It's his house."

"Demon?"

"No, just a vampire."

This seemed to confuse him. "Unclean. Spirit of the dead, a devil."

"Well, it depends on your point of view," she was saying, but he squeezed her hand weakly and she shut up.

"In...danger."

"What, from him? I assure you, you've got the wrong end of the stake there—"

"No," and now he sounded slightly irritated and much more with it. "*He's* in danger. You. All...all of you. They want you dead."

Greta stared down at him, a mangled collection of scars in the shape of a man. Again the unwelcome thought surfaced: What else might be looking back at her from behind that face? *They want you dead.*

"We need your help," she said, aware of how small her voice was. "Please. Tell me what you know."

"Can't *remember*," he said, closing his eyes tight. "Can't... Blue light and that humming and it, the—the Lord, the Voice of the Lord spoke unto him..."

"Unto who?"

"Brother. Brother... Johann?" The effort of trying to remember was telling on him. Greta bit down on her questions.

"All right. Don't worry about it now," she said. "It *will* come back. Just rest, okay? You're safe here. We'll protect you."

He seemed about to protest, but just subsided, breathing hard. Greta got up and went around the bed to inject the dose of pain medication into his IV. Soon enough his face relaxed as the stuff took hold.

She had the beginnings of an idea for how to help him remember the things they needed to know, but it would require Sir Francis Varney's help, and she was not at all sure they could count on that. More than once she'd caught Varney eyeing her with an odd kind of awkward intensity, and she hoped he wasn't feeling hostile toward people who provided ex–Gladius Sancti personnel with medical care as well as toward the Gladius Sancti themselves. If the terrible penny-dreadful's account was to be believed, Varney had historically shown very little hesitation in killing people who annoyed him, or at least injuring them badly. At one point he was said to have accidentally murdered his own *son* in a fit of anger, and she hoped the intense stare was not an indicator of imminent violence.

It was *definitely* a different sort of eyeing than she got from Ruthven or Fastitocalon. She wasn't entirely sure how she felt about that, either.

Greta pushed it out of her mind and just sat where she was, watching over her nameless patient, and trying to squash the feeling that unseen things were slipping faster and faster out of control.

She wasn't sure how much time had passed when Cranswell tapped her on the shoulder, making her jump. "Sorry," he said. "I'm supposed to take a turn watching him. If he wakes up, can I ask him all the questions?"

There was something reassuring about Cranswell's lack of mental filter. "No, you may not," she said, and hauled herself out of the chair. "You may ask him a *few* of the questions, but he's really having difficulty remembering anything other than the blue light and the fact that he hurts. At least he's come out of the Bible-quoting stage, but he's not very clear. He said something about Chelsea, too. I want to ask Varney to hypnotize him."

"Varney's a hypnotist? I thought he was a melancholiac."

"Ten points for vocab, but all vampires have some degree of ability in that direction. Actually I don't know how exactly it works—it's called thralling—but it's enough like hypnotism to be useful in the same situations. You've probably seen Ruthven do it—his pupils pulse in and out in a sort of rhythm, and whoever's looking into his eyes goes all vague and smiley. Makes you feel like your head's full of warm pink clouds." She had once asked him to do it to her in the spirit of scientific inquiry, and then once after that when she'd had a particularly horrific migraine, which it took care of with commendable speed. Thralling was a hunting technique, of course, but Greta didn't feel the need to point that out to Cranswell.

"Anyway," she continued, "he's good at it but not anything like as good as I think Varney must be, because have you *seen* Varney's eyes? They're literally reflective. Famously described as 'polished tin.' I just hope he's willing to have a go."

"Pretty sure he won't say no, if it's you doing the asking."

Greta frowned at him. "What's that supposed to mean?"

"Just an observation," Cranswell said, raising his hands in a placatory gesture. "I think tall-dark-and-angsty has developed a thing for you, Doctor."

She stared at him, feeling her ears go pink. "Nonsense," she said. "Of course he hasn't. I'm not his type, anyway; there's a noticeable lack of lacy nightgowns and swooning. He's known to go for the sort of lady who clutches the bedclothes to her snowy bosom and quavers 'the vampyre, the vampyre' through bloodless lips, and I lack even the slightest hint of glamour. Is there anything for breakfast?"

Cranswell eyed her. "We're down to toast and Weetabix.

Somebody is going to have to go grocery shopping, and it's not going to be me."

"No, you're going to sit right here and keep an eye on our friend, and *not* go all Gestapo on him if he wakes up and is capable of sentences."

"Okay, okay," Cranswell said, sitting down by the bed. "You take all the fun out of... being in a pretty ludicrous situation, if you think about it."

"I'm trying not to. I'll bring you up a cup of tea in a bit."

Varney was sitting at the kitchen table when she came in, looking incongruous because, well, Varney just looked incongruous anywhere that wasn't a windswept hilltop or a ruined castle. It was difficult to imagine him *not* appearing profoundly dramatic.

His hair was noticeably darker, though. She'd have to check the literature on that manifestation again, but it was almost always correlated with an increase in general health.

Also, August Cranswell was a twit.

At the moment Varney had his long hands wrapped around one of Ruthven's earthenware mugs, and the rich, coppery smell of blood was heavy in the air. Ruthven must have brought dinner back with him in the night, which was one more thing Greta could cross off her list of things to worry about. You got used to the smell of blood pretty quickly, but she did have to admit it was always a little off-putting at first.

"Morning," she said, sitting down and reaching for the toast rack. Varney watched her butter a slice of somewhat elderly toast with more concentration than she felt this performance strictly warranted. After a moment or two he set down his mug.

"You seem in decent spirits, Doctor. Are we to take it that your patient is improved?"

Greta looked up from her plate. "A bit, yes. Whatever's... influencing... him, whatever's responsible for the eyes and so on, is still definitely helping him to heal despite his having been kicked out of the order. At first he was still going on about iniquity and wickedness and talking in scripture, but that seemed to pass off."

She made a face. Her unsettling little interview with the monk hadn't done much for her peace of mind. "He's having trouble remembering what happened to him, other than the bits we already know about, the blue light and the noise and being excommunicated. I was wondering, actually, if you would mind trying to thrall him, Sir Francis? It might get more actual information out, and I think he might be easier in his mind if he could remember things. Even if they're terrible."

Varney blinked at her—two tiny reflections of her caught in his eyes—and looked surprised. "I?"

She held his gaze, which was not the easiest thing she had ever done. "If you wouldn't mind. I mean, I quite understand your antipathy, he *was* part of the group responsible for your attack, but..."

"I, er," he said. "I suppose I could make an attempt,

although why you'd want me to do it when Lord Ruthven is quite capable, I'm sure I don't know."

He looked away. There was a very faint color high on his cheekbones, and he'd let the *Lord* slip—she knew he was trying not to use it because it embarrassed Ruthven, but doing so required him to make a deliberate effort. That was a discomfited vampyre-with-a-*y* if ever she had seen one, and Greta *hadn't* seen one before. He looked...different. Less remote. "I just think you'd get better results, that's all," she said. "It'll have to wait till he wakes naturally. I'm not going to haul him out of restful sleep for interrogation, but I'd appreciate it very much if you would have a go."

"Certainly," said Varney, and hastily finished his blood.

In point of fact Varney had made up his mind, yet again, to leave the house and take his awkward and utterly inappropriate *feelings* far away, but Ruthven had drawn him aside a little earlier and asked him point-blank to stay. *I think we may very well need you,* he had said. *Sooner rather than later.*

It was nonsense, of course; nobody *needed* Varney any more than they needed a bout of influenza, or some other unpleasant and debilitating condition, but he had to admit it felt pleasant hearing the lie. It was a kind lie, and Ruthven was a kindly host.

Varney watched Greta industriously consuming toast, and had to look away when she licked marmalade off her fingers in an unself-conscious sort of way. *I'm not going to haul him out of restful sleep for interrogation,* she had said. The white gauze bandage on her throat was very bright in the kitchen's warm illumination.

Without meaning to, he said out loud, "Why do you do this?"

Greta looked up. "Do what?" she asked, with her mouth full.

Varney was more than a little mortified, but made himself continue. "Why do you... help people like that creature upstairs? He would have *killed* you if he could."

She put down the piece of toast. "It's my job," she said.

"Why do you *do* it, though?"

"Because somebody needs to." Greta shrugged. "There really are not that many supernatural physicians in the area—in fact, there aren't many of us, period—and the need is never going to go away."

"But he's an enemy," Varney said, trying again. "I can perhaps understand the generalized motivation to provide care for a disenfranchised patient base, but *he* isn't a patient, he's an *enemy captive*."

"Firstly," said Greta, holding up a finger, "that's not quite accurate; he's been officially expelled from their nasty little murder club. And secondly, *it doesn't matter* what he is. He needs help, and I am trained to provide that help, and have in fact taken an oath to *give* that help whenever and however it is required. It's not always a superlative pleasure, but it is my job."

"And you still took the job, knowing what it would entail," he said.

"Yes." Greta pushed her plate away, looking steadily at him. "It was my father's job first, and I've always known what I wanted to do. It was simply a question of getting there."

Varney felt his hands curl into fists. "But we're *monsters*," he said, and had to close his eyes. It sounded so puerile out loud.

She failed to reply for long enough that he cautiously opened one eye to see whether she'd actually left the room, but she was still sitting across the kitchen table from him, looking almost evanescently tired. Varney felt a sudden sharp flush of profound dislike for himself.

"You are not human," she said at last, "but you are *people*. All of you. The ghouls, the mummies, the sanguivores, the weres, the banshees, the wights, the bogeys, everyone who comes to me for help, everyone who trusts me to provide it. You are all *people*, and you all deserve medical care, no matter what you do or have done, and you deserve to be able to seek and receive that care without putting yourselves in jeopardy. What I do is necessary, and while it isn't in the slightest bit *easy*, it is also the thing I want to do more than anything else in the world."

Varney looked very hard at the table, as if it could offer any sensible answers. He was conscious of the fact that nothing whatsoever in *his* life was necessary, including him.

"I don't know what to do about this," Greta said in a different tone of voice, and he looked up. "Any of this. The—attacks. The mad monks. Whatever is happening is *not something I can fix*, and—I am not very good at dealing with situations like that, I'm afraid."

"You seem to be dealing remarkably well," said Varney.

"I'm completely out of my depth. The only thing I *can* do is my job, so, yes, I am going to take care of our new acquaintance. And hope like hell that he can give us some answers, which is why I need you: I want you to do the thralling."

"I will," said Varney, too fast, too sharp. "I will. Absolutely. Anything I can do to help."

Greta smiled suddenly, and he had to blink. It was a little like watching a small and self-contained sunrise. "Thank you," she said. "I'm . . . very glad you're here."

Just for a moment, Varney thought that *he* was, too. For a moment.

Greta straightened up, back to business. "Someone's got to go shopping," she said. "Taking advantage of offered hospitality is one thing, but we've eaten Ruthven out of house and home."

Varney sat back from the table, both glad that the conversation had changed subject and wishing desperately that it had not. "And that wretch Cranswell finished off the coffee this morning," he said.

"Damn. I suppose I'd better go, if Ruthven lets me borrow the Volvo." She tucked her hair behind her ears again, looking as if she didn't relish the prospect in the least.

"I could go," Varney said, surprising himself.

She looked up at him, and he felt his face go warm, but made himself hold her gaze. "That is, if Ruthven would lend *me* his automobile. It would be . . . pleasant, to be of use."

"You sure?" Greta was smiling again, less intense but still present.

"If you would be so good as to write out a list of provisions, I will gladly go and fetch them," he said. "You have more important matters to attend to, Doctor."

"Well...thank you very much, in that case," she said, apparently convinced. "I appreciate the thought. Hand me that notepad? Let's see," she said, writing down "coffee" in a much nicer version of her normal handwriting scrawl, for clarity's sake, and not at all because it looked better. "What else are we out of?"

When he had gone, Greta began to tidy up the kitchen, conscious of doing so as an attempt to distract herself from the ongoing uncertainty of the situation. *You seem to be dealing remarkably well,* Sir Francis had said, and the hilarious inaccuracy of the statement was just about balanced out by how much she wanted it to be true.

It was a considerable relief, therefore, when Fastitocalon poked his head round the kitchen doorway and said, "*There* you are. Good. Can you come and look at one of the ghouls? Ruthven sent me to find you."

"Yes, of course," she said, a hair too quickly. "I'll get my bag."

As soon as she opened the cellar door, the baby's thin wailing was audible. She hurried down the steps, and then had to stop for a moment, blinking, to fully take in the sight of Edmund Ruthven cradling a very small ghoul in his arms. His expression was not one Greta could ever recall having seen on those patrician features before: a kind of besotted astonishment. Tiny green hands clutched at his shirt.

The rest of the ghouls were hiding in the shadows, other than Kree-akh and the ghoullet's mother, who was looking more worried than ever.

Ruthven looked up as she approached. "Greta," he said, and had to clear his throat and try again to get his voice sounding normal. "Could you have a look at this little chap? He's not tremendously well."

His armful wasn't screaming energetically, just wailing, a thin and miserable thread of sound. She looked from Ruthven to Kree-akh, who sighed and said something to the mother, prompting a flood of ghoulish that Greta couldn't even begin to follow. When it subsided, Kree-akh nodded. "Akha says you may examine him."

Apparently Ruthven had already been preapproved for ghoullet-holding duty, Greta thought, hooking her stethoscope around her neck and reaching into her bag for the thermometer. It made sense, of course. He was well-known as one of the *protectors* of the city, old and powerful supernaturals to whom one might appeal in dire need. Still, it made her smile a little. She'd never seen the vampire look quite like *that* before. It was also convenient to have someone else hold the baby while she did her examination.

Greta went through digital thermometer probes quite quickly; they simply didn't stand up to her patients' peculiarities of dentition. The one she had with her was relatively new and didn't take long to give her a reading. "Mm," she said, resetting it. "How long has he been feverish?"

More ghoulish from the baby's mother, this time a little slower; she could make out a few words. Kree-akh translated nonetheless: He'd had a cold for several days but it had seemed to be going away, before the blue monks had come, before the tribe had had to flee its home, and now he wouldn't stop crying and wouldn't eat his nice rat.

Greta nodded. She already knew what the trouble was likely to be, but just then the ghoullet let go of his grip on Ruthven's shirt to pull at one pointy green ear, removing all remaining doubt. She had a look in the ear nonetheless, and nodded again, turning off the otoscope. Absolutely classic acute otitis media, even if the eardrum looked a little different from the ones she had first encountered in med school.

"He's got an ear infection," she said, straightening up, "and given the general conditions, I want to start him on antibiotics right away. Has he ever been given them before?"

Again Kree-akh translated. "He's never been given *any* human medicine."

"Well, we'll start with amoxicillin and keep a close eye on him to see how it goes," she said. "I've got some with me. Poor little guy," she added, gently touching the baby's warm cheek. "I know, it's no fun at all, but you'll feel better soon. I promise."

She was a little surprised when the ghoullet blinked at her and let go of Ruthven again in order to reach out a small hand in her direction, still sniffling but apparently done with active crying for the moment. There were grubby handprints on the pearl-grey cloth of Ruthven's shirt, which the vampire either did not mind or had not yet noticed.

"He's curious," Ruthven said, amused. Greta looked at him, and he nodded. Not entirely sure of herself, she reached out and lifted the ghoullet into her arms, surprised at how *heavy* he was, dense-boned for his size. She cradled him against her shoulder, swaying gently in an instinctive rhythm, and was a little amazed that he didn't start crying again at once—she must be doing something right, if only by blind chance.

Looking up from her armful, she was aware of both Kree-akh and the child's mother—*Akha,* she thought, *her name is Akha*—watching her, and felt her face go hot. *He's curious,* Ruthven had opined, and Greta shot him a look before returning her attention to the ghoullet. "He's *lovely,*" she said.

One small starfish hand patted at the pale fall of her hair, and then the baby pressed his face against her neck and hung on tight.

A little while later, in the kitchen, Greta put on a kettle and watched Ruthven dab at the small greyish greasy handprints on his shirt. Most of the grime appeared to have come off on him; her own sweatshirt was in better shape.

"I think they may be indelible," she said. "Although you made a most touching scene, standing there with an infant in your arms."

Ruthven looked up, making a face at her. "You should have seen yourself. You came over all pink and breathless for a moment, cuddling him. He *is* going to be all right, isn't he?"

"Oh yes," she said. "Barring any nasty reaction to the antibiotics, he'll be fine. Kids get ear infections all the time, no matter what species they happen to be. Kree-akh will make sure his mother understands how often he's to be given his medicine and painkillers."

"That's a very fetching garment he has on," Ruthven said. "Kree-akh, I mean. The, ah. The rats' tails really make a statement, don't they."

Greta had to laugh. "Yes, they say *what a lot of rats went into making up this cloak*. I didn't know you were interested in ghoul fashion, Ruthven. You're full of surprises."

"I am," he said. "More things in Heaven and Earth, et cetera. I'm still a little shocked that you got Sir Francis to do the shopping for us. *There's* a surprise, if you like."

"I didn't *get* him to do anything," Greta said. "He volunteered. Nobly, I might add. I think he rather wanted an excuse to get out of the house, to be honest, even if it meant driving your Volvo."

"There's nothing wrong with my Volvo," he said. "Except the synchro on third is a bit temperamental."

"And it's hell to park. That reminds me," said Greta, snapping her fingers, thinking of the neatly arranged surgical instrument tray he'd prepared for her. "Did you *really* drive ambulances in the Blitz?"

"I really did." The kettle boiled, and he got up to make the tea. "And I can speak four languages fluently and a fifth and sixth extremely badly, darn socks, and dance the tango, not to mention all the excitingly dangerous neck biting—and the bat thing. Do not ask me about the bat thing. I cannot, however, fly a helicopter, play the piano, or compose lyric poetry, and don't ask me to keep houseplants alive. Ah, here's Sir Francis back from Sainsbury's, in fact."

Keys rattled in the lock, and Greta abandoned her attempt to picture Ruthven darning socks and went to help carry in the groceries.

CHAPTER 12

As it turned out, nobody had offered Sir Francis violence, religiously motivated or otherwise, and he'd
apparently managed the Volvo's intransigent gearbox without difficulty—Greta was quietly impressed—but the level
of tension in the city had been very evident indeed from the
attitudes of his fellow shoppers. Eleven murders and no end in
sight, and the police could apparently do nothing.

"It's getting worse," he said, handing Greta a box of tea bags.
"In the checkout line people were talking about getting out of
London entirely, at least for now, going to stay with friends or
relatives outside the city. Or sending their children away, if they
could not go themselves, the way people did during the war."

Greta blinked at him. The thought of Ruthven driving
ambulances in wartime was still near the surface of her mind.
She wondered briefly what Varney had been doing in the
1940s. "It's that bad?" she said.

She didn't spend a very great deal of time in what might be

termed *the real world*, her days given over to a job that did not involve ordinary humans or their opinions or activities, and it was a little strange to realize that in fact the situation *was* almost as bad for the regular inhabitants of London, who did not know the things she knew.

"There isn't...widespread panic," Varney said, apparently in an attempt to reassure. "But people are certainly frightened. The smell is unmistakable."

"The smell," she repeated.

"Humans in fear give off a very particular scent," Ruthven said over his shoulder, stacking tins in a cupboard. "It's quite distinctive. Not exactly unpleasant, but sharp."

Greta didn't much like the thought of that, but let it go. "Nothing else has happened yet, though?"

"Not that I could ascertain," said Varney. "There were no new murders in the papers I saw, and I only overheard mentions of the eleven victims, no further than that."

"I wish I could believe there won't *be* any more," she said, and couldn't help a shiver, frustrated all over again at the fact that she had *no idea what to do.*

They'd only just finished putting things away when Cranswell called down from the landing, for once not sounding particularly flippant. "Guys? You, uh, might wanna come up here. He's awake and talking."

The burned man was muttering and trying to sit up when Greta got there. She rearranged the pillows with brisk efficiency, propping him up. "Hey, easy, easy now. Relax. What is it? Have you remembered anything?"

She was aware of the others silently entering the room behind her, but her attention was focused on her patient. He seemed less vague and confused than he had the last time she had spoken with him, but not what she'd call totally lucid. At least he wasn't talking in scripture, which she thought was probably a good sign.

"Trying," he said. "I have...flashes. Bits. It's not *enough*..."

"You *want* to tell us about it?" Cranswell asked, sounding legitimately surprised.

His unpleasant eyes closed, reopened, and he nodded slightly. "No...reason not to, now. Already...already damned. Cursed of God."

Fastitocalon moved slightly, as if about to speak, but apparently decided against it. "Well, setting that aside for now," Greta said, "I think we can help you remember the parts that are missing. Will you let one of us...hypnotize you?" That was as close as any other description for what she hoped Varney could do.

He reached for her hand, and again she could feel that sick heat thrumming in him, feel it in her skin the way she felt the glow of his blue eyes, and she remembered Fastitocalon saying, *He's not human. Not entirely human, anymore.*

"Please," he said, and *that* sounded very genuinely human. She could also still recall with vivid clarity that he'd tried to kill her—and glancing over her shoulder at Varney she was a little surprised by the expression on the vampyre's face. There was anger there, yes, certainly, but there was also great weariness, and a sort of softening of the hard lines around his mouth that one might possibly call sympathy. It was not an expression she had ever pictured on those features.

"Sir Francis," she said, glad her voice sounded normal; she gently freed her hand, stepping away from the bedside. "If you would?"

Varney even moved as if that weariness were almost too profound to bear; it hurt her looking at him. She had seen people whose remaining days were measured in single digits move like that, deliberate and slow and with a terrible, painful care.

He sat down beside the bed, and the monk's blue eyes tracked down to meet his, and widened; the glow intensified for a moment. Greta read fear in the scarred face. Fear and fascination.

"Look at me," Varney said, and his voice was softer and more beautiful than any of them had ever heard it—a voice all of them instinctively wanted to obey. "Look closely at me, and relax. I will help you remember."

Watching, Greta shivered. Varney's pupils began to expand and contract, expand and contract, the reflective irises appearing to grow and shrink in a slow, gentle rhythm. Even from the side, not caught by anywhere near the full force of his gaze, she could feel the room begin to drift away from her into a vague shimmery space like a roomful of mirrors, reflections repeating themselves away into infinity. This wasn't at all like Ruthven's thrall had ever been. It was *much* stronger, much more powerful, and as she floated in the center of a world of gently shining images of herself, nothing seemed to matter in the least. Nothing…at…all.

Fastitocalon's hand touched her shoulder, and she jumped, finding herself abruptly back in the room. Gravity seemed to have been turned back on. He had to steady her for a moment as her balance tottered.

Varney was still talking in that low, incredibly sweet voice, repeating himself. "You are quite safe," he said. "No harm will come to you. Watch my eyes, and know that you are safe."

If she kept her own eyes shut and just listened, or made a conscious effort to look the other way, Greta found she could pay attention without actually coming under his thrall herself. The faint, ragged voice of the monk, when it came, was a sharp contrast from Varney's beautifully modulated tones. "Safe," he said, and sighed, sounding very young.

"Where are you?" Varney asked.

"Embankment... house."

"Who are you?"

"Excommunicate. Anathema."

"What is your name?"

Slowly he turned his head from side to side on the pillows. Either he had no name, or he could not remember it, or he was not allowed to do so. Varney took a long breath before returning to his questions.

"Where have you come from?"

"Under... city. Underneath. Tunnels underneath, chambers."

"Tell us about the place under the city," said Varney, with no emphasis whatsoever. "What is down there?"

"Light of God."

"What is the light of God? Tell us about it. Tell us everything you know about it."

She could feel it when Varney stepped up the power somewhat, like turning up a rheostat. The faint, vague murmurs in response to his questions strengthened into something more like ordinary speech. "In the room marked *Plant*. It is... inside a metal cabinet with a dial on the door. It is made of glass and it hums, all the time, never changing, even when it speaks in the voice of God." Abruptly he started to hum, a nasty whining sound, and beside her Ruthven sucked in his breath sharply. She was glad when the quiet catalog of information resumed.

"Inside the glass there is a spark, too bright to see clearly. It never stops moving. And it glows. It glows blue, and takes away our sight, our sins, our foulness. It burns away all that is... is *worldly*."

"Who are 'we'?" Varney asked.

"Brothers. Members of... holy Order, the Sword of Holiness, Gladius Sancti. Only those who have been purified by the light... may bear the blade."

There was the faintest catch in Varney's voice. "Tell us about the blades."

"The crossblade. Anointed with chrism. There are ten... nine, now."

"Where did they come from?"

"Don't... know." He turned his head on the pillows, eyes drifting shut for a moment. "Found. They were... found.

Brother Johann says...the finding of the crossblade and the secret of the chrism are a sign, that there is wickedness in the world to be excised."

"Was the Order formed before this discovery?" Varney asked.

"It was...above ground," said the monk, sounding slightly puzzled at the memory. "In sunlight. In...Chelsea? With... people, more people, before the Light came."

"Chelsea," Varney repeated.

"*Seminary*," he said, as if just catching the edge of the realization. "At seminary. Hall. *Allen* Hall. I...studied. Johann was there."

He looked confused. "Johann was there, and then...I wasn't a seminarian, I don't...I don't know how, but I was *ordained*. A brother."

"You don't remember joining the Order?"

"No," he said, the confusion on his face deepening. "I have always been in the Order, there is nothing else, I *was not* before the Order, but...I was at seminary, I *remember* that."

"It's all right," Varney said, gently, the beautiful voice very kind. "Never mind that now. Tell me about the Order. About the Sword of Holiness."

"We were...in sunlight," he said, again. "We met in the churches, but then Johann—*Brother* Johann—found the crossblade, and the sacred chrism, and after that there was no sunlight, no sunlight at all, no sky, but we did not *need* the sun for there was the light of God, the light that never dims or wavers or goes out, the endless light that burns *underground*.

The true light, truer than day, that speaks to Brother Johann of the holy teachings."

"What are the holy teachings?" There was a little urgency in Varney's voice now, but only a little.

"That...we know we are of God, and...the whole world lieth in wickedness," he said, and Greta recognized the change in tone that came with his memorized responses. " 'Break thou the arm of the wicked and the evil man: Seek out his wickedness...till thou find none. Give them according to their deeds...and according to the wickedness of their endeavours: Give them after the work of their hands; render to them their desert.' It is...our task...our burden...and our privilege. 'There is no darkness, nor shadow of death...where the workers of iniquity may hide themselves.' "

The last words of his recitation seemed to hang in the air of the room like curling smoke. Varney was silent; Greta ventured to open her eyes, and found that he looked more unbearably weary than she had ever seen him.

She didn't even realize she was reaching out before her hand touched his shoulder. Varney jerked in shock at the contact, as if she were a live conductor. He twisted around to stare up at her, and the bright numbness of his thrall flooded through her for just a moment before he regained control of himself and returned his attention and gaze to the man in the bed.

Greta blinked hard, trying to get the edges of things back in focus—but she had not taken her hand away from Varney's shoulder. All at once she had had enough of the blank blue stare, the rote-memorized phrases that didn't sound as if the nameless man believed them even as he formed the words. Most of all, she had had enough of wondering what *else* was in there, with the owner of those eyes. What might be looking back at her. What had taken over these people—for they had *been* people, arguably slightly mad and bent on reenacting a kind of thirteenth-century human supremacist organization as some kind of cult, but *people* for all that—and turned them into *this*. Into monsters.

She was so tired of *not understanding*.

For Ruthven the worst aspect of this...possession...had seemed to be the manipulation of these people's faith, the deliberate perversion of a deeply held belief. Greta couldn't forget how cold his eyes had been, how clear and how cold, lit with a controlled anger that was somehow worse than open fury. Now, standing by Varney and feeling him trembling faintly beneath her hand, Greta's own anger began to make itself known.

It wasn't ice-cold like Ruthven's; this felt more as if a small ball of metal in her chest were steadily being heated up by some invisible blowtorch, at first giving off just a sullen red glare and then a brighter and brighter glow, scarlet to red-orange to burning gold. Anger not so much at the fact that the thing had assumed the role of God for these people as that it had taken away their *names*, taken away who they were, rendered them mindless puppets of its design, rendered the world *nonsensical*. It had taken away their conscious identities, their will. That, to Greta, was worst of all: an insult to the very center of humanity. That this thing should *dare* seemed all at once unbearable. The heat behind her breastbone flared, gold to white.

She leaned forward, staring down at the ruined face on the pillows. "What is your name?" she asked, with deliberate clarity. "Who are you?"

The blue glow cut off, flickered, as he squeezed his eyes shut. "No..."

"It's very deep," Varney whispered. "He's fighting quite hard, Greta, I don't think—"

"Who are you?" she repeated, keeping her voice even with an effort, feeling as if the white-hot ball inside her should be giving off its *own* light, *her* skin glowing, her pupils hard dots of their own brilliance. "Where did you come from? Before you were in Chelsea at the seminary. Before this began."

He shook his head, beginning to squirm under the covers, and gave the terrible mewing cry she had heard for the first time in the church. "Your *name*," Greta pressed, her fingers digging into Varney's shoulder, heedless of his stifled hiss of pain, the way he held perfectly still despite it. "*What is your name?*"

"Greta—" Varney said, something in his voice she couldn't identify, but she leaned closer in, ignoring him. The anger roared with a blue-white flame now: *How dare it, how dare it steal his name, his conscious identity, the very center of his mind? How dare it make all this happen, set the balance of the world swinging out of true?*

He writhed helplessly on the bed, the blue light flaring irregularly now, jagged pulses of it blazing from beneath his half-closed eyelids. The room smelled like ozone, like thunderstorms. Even through her fury Greta could sense, almost *see* the struggle inside his mind, the effort of something battered and wounded and at the end of its strength still trying to pull itself free. The image was terrible and vivid: a point of white light, dim and wavering, in the grips of a poisonous blue brilliance. The blue spoke to her of ionized-air glow, the deadly shade of light given off at the moment of a prompt-critical burst; of the unearthly lambence of Cerenkov radiation, a cyan halo thrown by radioactive material underwater; of the killing endless blue of a desert sky at midday, vicious and inimical. It was so clear in her head that she wondered briefly if the contact with Varney were somehow lending her a little of what *he* might be seeing, with those odd reflective eyes.

But the struggles were still intensifying. Now the monk was no longer writhing but *convulsing*, huge clonic spasms, and his heart—already under terrible strain from his injuries—couldn't stand much more of this. Greta let go of Varney, turning to reach for her bag and the syringes and vials locked inside, but as she did the man in the bed gave a horrible choked gasp. His whole body stiffened, his back rising free of the bed in a rigid tetanic arch. Around her the others jerked back in shock.

Greta, trained to observe, was the only one who accurately witnessed what happened in the next few seconds. Afterward she would describe seeing three tendrils of something like bright blue-glowing smoke uncoil from his eyes and open mouth, joined by two thinner wisps of light rising from his nostrils.

The blue light flowed together into a cloud above his face, swirling angrily as if undecided. She had a very clear sensation that, whatever it was, it was *watching her*—it saw her very well, and marked her interference in the course of its affairs.

For a moment longer the glowing cloud hovered over his face; then something like a silent thunderclap shocked through the air of the room, and the light—and whatever it was that had made it—was gone.

Its host collapsed back against the bed, gasping, a trickle of bright blood tracing down his chin from a bitten lip—but the eyes he opened a few moments later, while ruined and weeping, were no longer blue.

His name was Stephen Halethorpe.

They'd gotten that much out of him before Greta sent everyone away. Whatever had been inhabiting him had been keeping his physical condition stable, and after its departure she was having to do some rapid work to restore that stability. The others had retreated to the kitchen, where Fastitocalon was trying to explain what the hell had just happened.

"Fascinating," said Ruthven, who had followed the explanation rather more closely than Varney or Cranswell. He was eyeing Fastitocalon thoughtfully. "When we have time—not now, but when we have time—I want you to go over all this in quite a lot more detail."

"If you like," Fastitocalon said. He had an absolutely clanging headache. Being in the same room as the recent events had been a bit like experiencing a metaphysical sonic boom.

"The parallels between the science of magic, more properly termed *mirabilics*, and physics are not complete but offer a useful viewpoint from which to begin examining the subject."

Varney seemed to have lost some of his melancholy distance. He was leaning into the conversation, frowning intently, even if he did keep rubbing at his shoulder as if it hurt him. Fastitocalon thought he was probably finding the sensation of being an active and valued participant in a group to be a novel, and not unpleasant, one. "This mirabilics business," Varney said. "Is it strictly relevant?"

"To a certain extent, I'm afraid," said Fastitocalon. "It doesn't require that you understand the whole of the theory behind it, just the concept of the laws that govern the behavior of pneuma."

"Pneuma being..."

Fastitocalon sighed. "You can use the Gnostic definition if you like, *spirit*, but it technically refers to the equivalent of matter on the higher planes. Each individual has a unique pneumic signature that can be identified and tracked. It's how I found our Mr. Halethorpe in the first place. Ordinary humans' pneumic signatures are easily differentiated from supernaturals' because of the behavior and interaction of certain particles and the resulting mirabilic field arrangements, which are perceptible to several nonhuman species and, under some circumstances, to individual humans with a certain type of genetic peculiarity."

"What Fass means, I think, is that we all have a...a specific identifiable code," Ruthven said. "Which can be called a spirit or a soul, if you want, and which varies based on the organization of these particles and so on. But an outside influence can actually alter that alignment, changing the code itself, which means that the way we ourselves interact with reality is changed. Am I close?"

Fastitocalon nodded. "More or less. It's like instant genetic engineering, in a way. Change someone's pneumic signature on the higher planes to indicate he's got a tail and bang, there he is with a tail on the prime material plane, for *as long as you keep the influence on*. That's important. Without it, the normal signature will reassert itself. This thing, whatever it is, made some pretty significant changes to Mr. Halethorpe's weight on reality, which have now been undone."

"That is the explanation for his apparent ability to see despite the injury to his eyes?" Varney asked.

"Yes, and now that it's gone he's probably stone blind. It's also been keeping him from succumbing to shock and infection despite the amount of abuse his body's undergone. I don't honestly know how long he's got without it."

"But he *is* mortal again," Varney said, looking distant. "He is human, and may receive absolution?"

"I should think so. Theology isn't really my division."

Ruthven tapped his nails on the table thoughtfully. "And you think this isn't related to Heaven or Hell, or at least not in any official capacity? As in, they aren't responsible for it and moreover aren't aware of it?"

"I don't know," Fastitocalon said. "I honestly don't. It doesn't *feel* infernal or divine, those are generally easy to recognize, but there have been instances of internal schism more than once over the course of existence and I suppose it's just possible that some ancient splinter of one or the other is responsible for this mess."

"Schism?" Varney asked, once more focused on the present. "There are doctrinal disagreements between demons?"

"Oh yes, that didn't stop with the Fall. It's happened more than once, but the last big shakeup Below was, oh, late sixteenth century." Fastitocalon closed his eyes for a moment, pushing away vivid memories. "That one had to do with a rogue faction directly influencing human interactions and events, partly camouflaged to implicate Heaven. Samael's response was…abundantly clear regarding his opinion of such activity. I can't see anyone from my side trying that again, not after what he did to Asmodeus. No, this is… something small enough so neither of them know about it, or know enough about it to *care*; otherwise it would have been caught and squashed before now. If we can just…quietly stop it without getting either side actively involved, it would save a great deal of political and bureaucratic bother."

Ruthven just nodded, apparently dismissing postvital political climate and the question of what might have happened to the unfortunate Asmodeus. "How precisely are we *going* to stop it? These Gladius Sancti people are not only armed with physical weapons that are capable of causing us major damage; they also now have whatever powers this supernatural influence has given them. I would not want to go up against more than one or two of them at a time, and there might be up to ten lurking under the city. Not to mention the...the thing itself, its physical location; that's likely to be guarded, and we don't know anything about it."

"Yet," Varney said. "We don't know *yet*. When he wakes again, he will tell us everything."

"We don't know if he'll be capable of that," Fastitocalon said. "This...forcible rearrangement business is extremely hard on the individual, and he's ill and hurt to begin with. It may have damaged his mind beyond repair."

"Assuming he wakes up at all," said another voice, and they all looked up. Greta was standing in the doorway, grey with fatigue.

"He's stable," she went on. "For now. I've done all I can, given the circumstances, but I can't...tell you when, or in fact *if*, he will regain consciousness. There's...a lot of damage. A lot."

Fastitocalon wondered if he had ever seen her looking quite so bleak, and thought briefly of the morning Wilfert Helsing had died, white sky and winter-barren trees, crows calling from the rooftops. His illness had been—perhaps mercifully—swift; Fastitocalon had not been there at the end, but he had *felt* him go, felt the change in reality as a familiar signature winked out.

That morning, when he had arrived to find Greta dry-eyed and blank, he had not hesitated a single moment before reaching out to touch her mind: the same instinctive gesture as an outstretched hand, open arms, *let me help, you are not alone, I'm here, I'm with you.*

"We'll pursue alternative avenues," he said, his chest tight with a pain that had nothing to do with pathology. "He *did* already give us quite a lot, remember. The seminary—Allen Hall—I know where that is, and it sounded to me as if this little sect started out rather more innocently than it ended up."

"There might be actual records of it," Ruthven said, and Cranswell looked from him to the others at the table.

"Or if not records, there have to have been other people *aware* of the group," he suggested. "We could maybe try figuring out if anybody knows what happened to them, where they went to ground, that kind of stuff."

Varney nodded. "And perhaps it might be possible to find out where Brother Johann located these peculiar knives, and if there are likely to be any more of them."

Greta was still looking almost evanescently worn, but Fastitocalon could see renewed determination under the tiredness. He knew very well that having a particular *task* to accomplish, a set of actions to undertake rather than trying to face the formless enormity of a situation, had always helped her cope.

"I know where the seminary is, too," she said. "Dad had a friend there years ago, when I was just a kid; we used to visit sometimes. I have to work out how to get there on the bus, though. Cranswell is right, I'm not going into any tunnels right now unless I have to."

"I'll drive you," Ruthven said. "I want to find things out just as badly as you do, but are you sure Halethorpe will be all right without you?"

"He's stable," she said again, but now there was guilt in her face as well as determination. Fastitocalon sighed. He could hear it as clearly as if Greta were shouting, the bright-burning thought at the surface of her mind: *I can't leave him alone.*

"He won't *be* left alone," Fastitocalon told her. "I'll keep a close eye on him, Greta. And if anything does go wrong I'm probably the one of us who can stop it going any *further* wrong, at least in the short term."

She brightened visibly. "I hadn't thought of that, but yes. Of course you are. You're *magic.* Or *mirabilic,* whatever."

There was a warm fondness in the words, and in fact Greta stopped leaning in the doorway and crossed the kitchen to kiss Fastitocalon firmly on the cheek.

"It's hideous," said Ruthven, staring across the street at the 1970s-era façade of the seminary building. "I mean, the brick bit on the left is bad, but the concrete egg carton attached to it is beyond contempt. I thought Catholics were supposed to go in for the *good* kind of architecture."

It was, in fact, pretty dire. Greta couldn't remember a lot about her occasional visits here with her father, decades back, only that the chapel had smelled of lilies and brass polish and incense the way Catholic churches always did, and the priests in their black suits had unnerved her with the *silent* way they moved. The front of the building facing Beaufort Street was mostly a low, unprepossessing yellow-brown brick structure, but the chapel attached to it with its concrete gridwork façade could only be described as grim.

"Are you going to be okay going in there?" she asked.

"My aesthetic sensibilities may need a stiff restorative drink afterward," he said. "Don't worry about the God thing. As long as I don't touch holy water or the Host I ought to be all right."

"No communion for *you*," she said, feeling slightly unhinged. "Or me, for that matter. I'm a heretic. Let's get this over with."

Inside it wasn't much more appealing than the external architecture had suggested, but Greta was rather acutely aware that even in a very nice (borrowed) coat over her jeans and sweater she was underdressed. Beside her Ruthven, in his quietly but extremely expensive dark clothing, fit in much less noticeably. She was a little glad when he stepped in front of her and smiled kindly at the man behind the desk. "Hello," he said. "I'm terribly sorry to bother you, but my friend and I were hoping you could help us."

The Roman Catholic Diocese of Westminster, it turned out, was less inclined to be helpful than Greta might have wished. Yes, they had had a Stephen Halethorpe studying formation with them, in his second year as a seminarian. He had left a little over two months ago. No, they did not have any information on his whereabouts. No, he had not said where he was going. No, they did not have a Johann on their books, regardless of surname. And no, they certainly were *not* aware of any student-run clubs or organizations interested in thirteenth-century armed monastic orders. As they had informed Scotland Yard more than once, they were not a home to cults of any sort, and who exactly had Ruthven said he was, anyway, and why was he so interested in their business?

At that point Greta was very aware of Ruthven taking a

deep steadying breath, and put in, "We're just worried about Stephen, that's all. I'm an old friend of his from ages ago, and he had stopped answering his letters. I wanted to find out whatever I could."

There were two men behind the desk, one of whom eyed the pair of them with cold pale blue eyes and emanated officious disapproval, and the other of whom—rather younger, with facial bone structure that reminded Greta of certain rodents she had met—looked a bit less inimical, but frightened of his superior. She was not entirely surprised when, on their way out, he caught up with them.

"I'm sorry about that," he said. "It's just—the police have been around several times asking the same sorts of questions. It's—this rosary business, at the murder scenes, they don't seem to understand that it has nothing to do with the Church, they just go *on* and *on* about religious cult activity and it's all very upsetting."

Greta made sympathetic noises, waiting for him to get to the point. "About Halethorpe," he said, eventually. "We *don't* know where he went, but he— Just before he left, he seemed to be less than sure of his vocation. Sometimes that happens. People *do*, er, *wash out*, I believe is the colloquial term. It— there was—when he did leave, his roommate was terribly upset, and in fact *he* left, too. That wasn't a very good time for any of us."

"His roommate?" Ruthven asked.

"Eric Whitlow. A promising student but—well. Perhaps a little unstable."

"Did Whitlow disappear, too?"

"Oh no," said the man. "No, but he...seemed slightly unhinged. I gather he is still in London, however. I can get you the last address we have for him."

"Thank you," Greta said, exchanging a look with Ruthven.

The building in which Eric Whitlow currently lived was not a great improvement over the seminary, architecture-wise, but at least it wasn't *supposed* to look either nice or welcoming: one of a row of grotty subdivided houses in West Ham. There were five doorbell buttons with hand-printed names beside them, stacked in a row beside the door. *Edging into garret territory*, Greta thought, and pushed the one marked WITLOW with no *H*.

After rather a long time the door opened to reveal a girl in pajama bottoms and a T-shirt advertising a band Greta had never heard of, who looked her and Ruthven up and down and demanded, "Yeah?"

"We're here to see Mr. Whitlow. Eric Whitlow. Is he in?" Greta asked.

"Him? He's *weird*," said the girl, eyes narrowing in suspicion. "He's not answering his door. Who are you, anyway?"

"I—" she began, but Ruthven cut her off smoothly, and Greta could *see* the change come over the girl's face as he applied a hint of thrall.

"We're friends of a friend," he said. "We just want a word with Eric, if that's all right."

She was already nodding, eyes wide and firmly fixed on

Ruthven's face. It was clear that Greta had ceased to exist entirely in her world, and that she had just joined the ranks of People Briefly If Hopelessly In Love With Edmund Ruthven. "Come in," she said. "I'm in the middle of studying, but I was just about to make a cup of tea, if you'd like anything?"

"That's very kind," he said, as she stepped aside to let them in, "thanks awfully, but we can't stay. If you could just show us to Eric's room, that would be wonderful."

"Of course," said the girl, and Greta could practically see the little hearts in her eyes. She sighed, following Ruthven up the stairs after his latest conquest. It was undeniably *useful*, of course, but sometimes Greta wished he wouldn't do that in front of her. It wasn't a comfortable thing to watch.

The girl led them to a door at the end of the hall and knocked. "Hey, Eric," she called. "You've got company, and I want that mug back, and it better not have green fur in it this time, okay?"

There was a muffled response that Greta interpreted as *fuck off*, and the girl sighed. "He really *is* weird," she said. "I'm sorry, it— Maybe you could come back later; he's usually up later in the afternoon or evening. *Eric*, come on, open the door, there are *people*."

This time the *fuck off* came from much closer range, and in fact they could hear the repeated click as several locks were unfastened. The door opened—a few inches, anyway. It was on a chain. Greta felt a flicker of profound sympathy for Eric Whitlow's housemates.

A pair of suspicious eyeballs regarded them from within a

quite extraordinary profusion of hair. It was difficult to tell where the hair on the head ended and the beard began; a kind of tangled shock of sandy growth seemed to have taken over most of his face. Greta was reminded, absurdly, of the *It's* man from the beginning of *Monty Python* episodes.

"Who are you?" Whitlow demanded.

This time Greta simply let Ruthven speak first. "We're friends of Stephen Halethorpe," he said, smoothly. "May we come in?"

Whitlow was a harder mark than his housemate, but after a moment the suspicious look relaxed and he opened the door properly. The view thus afforded was more than enough to verify the girl's classification of *weird*. It was, in fact, *bizarre*, but Greta said nothing other than "Thank you" and led the way into the room, leaving Ruthven to say good-bye to his new friend.

She stood in the narrow open space in the center of the floor, looking around. Every square inch of the walls, and some of the ceiling, was covered in devotional imagery. Plaster saints stood in a row on the windowsill and crowded the top of the desk and wardrobe, sharing the space with candles. There was a strong and distressing smell indicating that, if not the coveted mug, *something* in here was growing green fur; it was joined by a different if equally unappetizing smell given off by Whitlow himself, who seemed to have given up bathing as well as shaving quite some time ago.

He was short, thin—much too thin, Greta realized, clinically noting just how hollow his eyes were, how clearly the edges of his sternum were visible in the half-open V of his shirt—and even with the edges of Ruthven's influence acting as a mild tranquilizer, his fingers would not stop moving. They fiddled with the ends of his sleeves, with each other, with the mess of his hair, never staying still for more than a few moments. The nails were bitten right down to the quick, cuticles raw and torn.

Ruthven closed the door behind them, and with it a kind of relief visibly washed over Whitlow; he didn't stop fidgeting, but the anxious hunch eased a little, and he looked less *hunted*. "Who are you?" he said again.

"My name is Ruthven, and this is Greta. She's a doctor."

"Don't need doctors," Whitlow said, tugging at his hair. "Don't need anyone."

"We're not here to do anything to you," Greta said in her calmest and most reassuring voice, the one she used for frightened children of varying species. "We're friends of Stephen Halethorpe, like Ruthven said. We were hoping you could tell us a little about him."

"*Halethorpe*," he muttered, shaking his head. Dandruff flew. "Don't talk about him. Halethorpe's dead. Don't talk about him. Any of them. All dead. Better that way."

"He isn't dead," Greta said, leaving off the *yet*. "He's very ill, but he's alive, and I'm taking care of him. He was part of a religious group calling itself the Gladius Sancti, and we wanted to know if you had any information about them, since you and he were rooming together at the seminary."

Whitlow *stopped* fidgeting, staring at her with a hollow,

burning intensity. "Wait," he demanded. "You're saying he got *out*?"

"That's right," she said. "He got out. He's—"

She could see very clearly, just as clearly as with the girl a little earlier, the effect of Ruthven's attention, because at this point Ruthven cut it off, looking around himself for somewhere remotely unhazardous to sit, and Eric Whitlow's eyes widened very suddenly. His whole body seemed to *hunch*, as if preparing for some kind of terrible flight, and she could see the little hairs on his forearms all stand up at once in an intense flush of terror. He was sitting on the edge of what she had to assume was his bed, piled high with books and papers and crumpled-up clothing, and now he leaned back away from them.

Humans *did* smell of fear, Greta thought. There was a sudden sour tang in the air that even she could pick up. Ruthven was wrinkling his nose. "Hey," she said, gently, but with an edge on it. "Hey. Eric."

"Who *are* you?" he asked, shrinking away from them, and Greta's heart hurt when he reached behind him and grabbed a pillow as if it could offer some kind of shielding, scrabbling his way backward onto the bed, into the corner. "Who—*what* are you?"

Ruthven moved a little, but Greta made a sharp little gesture with one hand and he subsided. "Eric," she said. "We're not here to hurt you. Look at me. Look at my face, okay? Look at my eyes; you won't come to any harm. Look at me and tell me what you see."

He wouldn't, for another awful terrified moment, and then

hesitantly—she could see the effort, the courage that went behind it—he looked up at her.

"Tell me what you see," said Greta again, still low and kind, holding his gaze steadily.

"You're..." He trailed off, blinking. "You're a person."

"That's right," she said. "I'm a person. *Just* a person. Bog-standard ordinary person, but— Eric, I *believe you.* Whatever you saw. I believe you. I don't know the explanations for all of what's been happening, but *I believe you,* and I *want to understand.*"

For a moment longer he stared up at her, and then in a sudden terrible collapse covered his face with his hands, dissolving into violent, uncontrollable tears.

Greta said a couple of bad words under her breath and sat down beside him on the edge of the bed, putting a hand on his back. Beneath her fingers the knobbles of his spine were much too clear, much too sharp, shaking with the force of his sobs. "It's going to be all right," she told him, hoping it was true, and when he turned to her with a face twisted into a damp and miserable mask of fear she put her arms around him and pulled him close, and stroked the greasy tangled hair.

He cried in the hard and choking, almost retching spasms of someone very near the end of their endurance. It didn't take very long, though, before he subsided into hitching, juddering gasps and pulled away from her, mumbling something that sounded like *I'm terribly sorry* through the hair.

Greta's shoulder had been moistened by rather more unpleasant fluids in its time, but she was still very aware of its dampness as she stroked Whitlow's back gently. "It's all right," she said. "Eric—what you saw, whatever you saw—it was real. You're not—"

"Going crazy," he said, and parted the unlovely mess of his hair with both hands, wiping at his face. "*Gone* crazy. He— the *eyes*—and that *voice*—I didn't know what to *do*—what was your name, I'm sorry, I'm terrible at names—"

"Greta," said Greta, who couldn't help a little smile. "Tell me what you saw. I can perhaps—*we* can perhaps explain some of it, not a lot, but some. But I need to know what happened. You and Stephen were roommates at the seminary?"

Ruthven silently offered her a handkerchief, and she took the pristine square of lawn and pressed it into Whitlow's hand. He blew his nose, copiously, and she avoided looking at Ruthven as she went on rubbing his back. "Keep it," she said.

"Thank you," Whitlow said damply, and swiped the hair out of his eyes again. "It's—it was months ago, I've kind of lost track of time, but Stephen was...he started out so *ordinary*. You know? Nothing strange about him. Didn't smoke, didn't drink, came to the seminary right out of undergrad with a degree in classics or something. His idea of fun on a Saturday evening was discussing the minutiae of a passage's translation with a couple of his colleagues."

"And you wanted something else?" Ruthven said, and Greta could feel Whitlow tense under her hand as he shot a look at the vampire.

"It doesn't matter," she said, giving Ruthven a *let me handle this, okay?* look. "All we need to know about is the order."

"The order," Whitlow repeated, and gave a nasty clogged little laugh. "It was...fun, at first. Like a club. A little secret society that the faculty didn't know about. John came up with it. John Arbeiter. Said he'd found the idea in some ancient manuscript or other."

"The Holy Sword?" she said.

"Sword of Holiness, but yeah. It was...more interesting than the course of study, you know? A little time to...enjoy ourselves."

"The ceremonial aspect," Ruthven said.

Whitlow looked up. "Yeah, exactly. The...pageantry. Only on our terms. It felt...oh, fuck, I don't know. Rebellious and holy at the same time."

"Where did you meet?" Ruthven pulled his chair closer, across the unspeakable carpet.

"A bunch of places. We'd use the seminary chapel sometimes but mostly it was parish churches, around the city."

"Anglican churches?"

"John said God wouldn't mind. That He could hear us just as well from a C of E altar as from a proper Catholic one."

"How progressive," said Ruthven.

"Yeah, well." Whitlow coughed raggedly. "We were all a little dazzled, I think. John was good at it. At the preaching thing. Some people have it, you know, the, the ability to grab people's attention and hold it, and make them...believe things, at least for a little while."

"I can imagine," said Greta. "Go on. You and Halethorpe were part of John's congregation?" *Not Johann,* she thought. *John.*

"Yeah. It sounds stupid but it was all…fun and games, really, until he showed up with those fucking spike things."

"The crossblades?" Ruthven's eyes narrowed.

"He had…found them. Somewhere. Didn't tell us where. Just that God had led him to their hiding place, which— I mean, *really?* And some recipe for a magic potion that you were supposed to put on them. I was fine with all the…rhetoric, all the great smite-the-infidel shit, but then there were *knives.* I wasn't there for knives."

"But Stephen was?" Greta asked, her hand still on his back.

"Oh yes. Yes, Stephen was."

She exchanged a look with Ruthven, over Whitlow's bowed head, and felt the weight of uncertainty spinning down to a single, solid point.

"What happened after that?" she said.

"John wanted us all to take an oath," he said. "I could recognize bits of it. He was cherry-picking from Scripture. But the night he wanted us to sign this paper—"

He gave another racking, hoarse little sound halfway between a cough and a sob. "It wasn't John. Or, not just John. I could…I could have sworn his eyes were *brown* before, but that night in the church they were *blue.* And he—he sounded like more than one voice was speaking, when he talked. Like the demons. *Our name is Legion.*"

"What did you do?" she asked, gently.

"I said I needed to meditate on it. He didn't like that, but he let me go. I went back to our room and prayed. For hours. I was still praying when Stephen came back."

She and Ruthven exchanged a glance, but neither spoke. After a moment Whitlow sagged a little farther, burying his face once more in his hands. "He came back late at night. Early in the morning, actually. He was... different."

"Different how?" Greta asked, with a fair idea of the answer.

"His eyes were strange. Bluer. They had been grey before. I could have sworn they gave off *light*, how—I don't *know* what I saw, just—he said some things, some stuff out of Revelation, it wasn't *like* him at all. I asked what had happened and he said he'd *seen the light*, like one of those American preachers on TV, *do you see the light*, and he said he wanted me to see it, too, and his voice—like John's earlier, it wasn't just his voice, there was something else in there talking, something that wasn't Stephen—"

Whitlow broke off again, pressing his hands against his face. "And I saw him across the room, clear as day, and I saw—I saw the carpet underneath his feet, and there was *light* there, *he wasn't touching the ground*, he wasn't *standing on the fucking ground at all*—"

She could feel him shaking helplessly under her hand. "What did you do then?"

"I ran," he said, still hiding his face. "I ran, what the fuck do you *think*?"

It was late into the afternoon, getting on toward evening, when Halethorpe regained consciousness again. This time it was Fastitocalon dozing in the chair by the bed. The slight shift in Halethorpe's signature as he woke caught his attention.

"Hello," Fastitocalon said, sitting up properly. "How are you feeling?"

Halethorpe blinked several times, hard, the exaggerated blinking of someone trying to clear his vision, but the ruined eyes remained unfocused. His face was turned almost, but not quite, in Fastitocalon's direction.

"Who's there? I can't...I can't see, who's there?"

The voice was...different, now, subtly; it had lost a quality Fastitocalon realized had been something like an echo, a reverb effect. Now he just sounded tired and desperately ill, and very, very human. But recognizably *himself*, and not that other.

Fastitocalon was struck, again, by how tenacious the human race could be—against what odds it had managed to hang on over the centuries. "I'm Fastitocalon," he said. "I don't believe we've been introduced; I'm a friend of Ruthven and Dr. Helsing."

The blind face turned farther toward him, looking not at Fastitocalon's own face but somewhere just beyond his right ear. Without the blue glow Halethorpe's eyes looked even nastier. Visible ulceration had begun to spread.

"Not...with the mirror eyes?"

"No, that's Varney. Another friend. The chatty young man with the American accent is August Cranswell. I'm the antique in the beautifully cut suit."

"You're...grey," Halethorpe said, half a question.

"That's right. It's a constitutional thing, I'm afraid."

Halethorpe seemed to consider that, closing his eyes for a

moment. Fever spots burned in his cheeks, the shiny blotches of burn scars standing out starkly against the red. "I can't see," he said again. "Why can't I see?"

Fastitocalon sighed. "Well. It's rather a long story, and we were hoping *you* could tell *us* most of it, actually. Do you remember anything at all?"

"The...blue light underground. Light of God. *Voice* of God."

"You know it isn't really God," he said. "You know that, don't you?"

"It speaks...in your head. Speaks words. Voice of God... only not still or, or small. It *burns* you."

"It puts out a great deal of UV radiation," said Fastitocalon. "I gather you were...made to do vigil before it?"

"There was...there was a ritual." He seemed to be making an effort to speak, eyes still squeezed shut, but slightly more lucid than before. "Fasting and...prayer and...being allowed to enter the light. Be burned clean."

Fastitocalon watched as his hands on the bedclothes curled into fists. "Gave us...new sight. *Different* sight. I...I learned how to move again. To recognize where walls were, seeing *through* them..." He swallowed hard, and fresh tears spilled down his face. "Only...only the purified could carry the blade."

"Those blades, where did they come from? Who made them?"

Halethorpe shook his head slightly. "I don't know. Johann— Brother Johann—he found them. God *guided him* to find them."

247

Fastitocalon sighed. "You lived underground, then?"

"Yes. In the tunnels. Once we were burned...we stayed underground, except to do God's work."

"And God's work was to execute monsters."

"Evil," he said. "Yes. And...and the wicked. The workers of iniquity."

"The light determined who was wicked and who wasn't, I gather?"

"It spoke to Brother Johann. Those who failed to carry out his orders are...punished." The hollow between his collarbones pulsed with the rapid beating of his heart.

"Where is it? The thing itself?"

"Under the Underground," Halethorpe said. "Deep under. Some kind of...old tunnels beneath St. Paul's tube station."

Fastitocalon blinked. It had been *that* close to them, all along? The half a mile or so of space that separated Ruthven's house from St. Paul's Cathedral felt suddenly very, very narrow indeed.

"Thank you," he said, after a moment, gently. "Enough for now. You need to rest; you're safe here, nothing can harm you."

"Not safe. I'm damned. Cursed of God, anathema—"

"No, you aren't. Believe me, I would know. You *were* a creature other than human for a while there, but the thing that was inside you has gone; you are no more damned than any other man, and less so than some, I would say. Being excommunicated from the Gladius Sancti is a serious mark in your favor."

"How do *you* know?" Halethorpe sounded faintly peevish.

"I'm a demon. Well, mostly a demon. I felt it leave you."

Halethorpe's eyes widened, trying helplessly to focus. "You—"

"Relax. I'm not going to do anything demonic. Just take my word for it, your soul is intact: I'm looking right at it. What *is* in trouble with the Lord your God is the thing that caused all this mess in the first place. I'm almost certain that claiming to be the Voice of God when you are not, in fact, the Voice of God is something upon which Heaven frowns. The job's taken, you know."

"What is it?" Halethorpe whispered. "What is it inside the light? *What spoke to me?*"

"I'm not quite sure, but it doesn't feel entirely demonic, either. It's gone from you, Mr. Halethorpe. Spiritually I expect you could use a bit of a wash and brush-up, but you are not headed straight for the bottomless pit." He sighed. "You really had better rest now, or Greta will be cross with me. Do you want anything?"

"No. Wait. Water?"

Fastitocalon poured a glass from the carafe on the nightstand, helped him sit up to drink, aware of the sick heat of his skin even through layers of clothing, trying not to hurt him more than absolutely necessary.

"You don't...sound like a demon," Halethorpe said when Fastitocalon had let him go. "Are you *sure*?"

"Quite sure. Don't worry—it's not catching."

Halethorpe looked as if he were about to say something else, but just closed his eyes. He seemed both young and very fragile: barely out of childhood, heavily weighed down by the knowledge and the cruelty of what had been done to him.

Fastitocalon was suddenly aware of just *how* pale he was beneath the scarring, everywhere other than the burning fever spots high on each cheek; how rapidly and shallowly his breath came, and even as he noticed the blue tinge deepening in his lips, Halethorpe gave a little sigh and slumped sideways against the pillows.

Fastitocalon moved without thinking, reaching out his right hand to flatten the palm against Halethorpe's chest, fingers spread. He could *feel* the shaken, out-of-tune beating of the heart beneath his hand not simply with touch but several other senses as well. He knew how desperately strained that heart had been, how *tired* it was, how much it would rather be still.

No, he thought, *not now, not like this; for one thing Varney is right and you* can *and* should *receive absolution, and for another Greta left this duty to me, and I mean to do it.*

He closed his eyes and felt strength running out of him like water, *pushed* it, sending out reaching fingers of influence through bone and muscle, breath and blood, steadying and strengthening the flagging heart. After a few moments the beating eased back into a proper rhythm. The blue faded from Halethorpe's lips, his fingertips. Still that stuporous fever heat baked into Fastitocalon's hand through the thin fabric of his shirt.

Without taking his hand away, Fastitocalon fished his phone from his pocket and dialed one-handed. He had to wait for the stretch of three full rings before Greta's voice came on the line, sounding somewhat breathless. "Fass?"

"You'd better get back here," he said. "In something of a hurry. He's on fire; I've convinced his heart not to give up for now, but I can't hold it for very long."

"*Fuck*," she said. "On our way. Hang on, Fass, please hang on, for everybody's sake—and *thank you*."

CHAPTER 13

By the time Ruthven and Greta returned, Fastitocalon
had begun to lose sensation in his fingertips. He was
extremely glad when she arrived to take over, with her vials
and syringes, and told her what he could—which wasn't anything she didn't already know; there was just so *much* damage,
and at this point it was probably just a question of time. Even
if they got him to a hospital with all the supportive measures
imaginable, it was only going to be a question of *how long*.

He said as much to the others, coming downstairs. "We
know roughly where the thing is, at least. I don't think he
could give us much more information than that. He's—
wandering. But we know it's in a system of tunnels underneath St. Paul's tube station—"

"Christ. The *deep-level shelters*," Ruthven cut in, looking
disgusted with himself. "Of course. The old bomb shelters
attached to the Underground. I should have *thought* of that."

"Wait," said Cranswell, "what bomb shelters?"

"In the war people used the Underground stations to hide from air raids, which made perfect sense, but there simply wasn't enough room down there for everyone. So during the Blitz they started to build separate shelter complexes. There were supposed to be ten of them, mostly on the Northern line, but not all ten got built." He sighed. "I've even *been* in a couple of them, back in '44 when the bombing really got nasty—not the one at St. Paul's, but I imagine they're all much of a muchness. These days I think they're used for storage if they're accessible at all, but as a ready-built lair one could do a great deal worse."

"Why would a bomb shelter have one of these rectifier things?" Cranswell asked.

"Most of the electrical equipment down there ran on DC. Lift motors, fans, that kind of thing. What I don't get is why it would still be *working* after all these years."

"You said they're used for storage," said Varney. "Surely people would need to have the lights on in order to access whatever is being stored."

"I suppose so." Ruthven straightened his shoulders. "Well. We'd better go and do something about it, hadn't we?"

"Wait a minute. Let's consider the practical aspects of the situation." Fastitocalon coughed, wincing. "The ultraviolet light aspect in particular. Even without the mad monks and their envenomed Gothic-novel armament, you, Ruthven, are not going to be able to go anywhere near the thing. Sir Francis is less vulnerable to sunlight than you, but even so it poses a considerable problem."

Ruthven stared at him. "You know perfectly well I don't burst into flames in sunlight. That bit didn't come along until Murnau in 1922."

"You don't like direct sunlight and you can't be out in it for very long at all without getting a blinding headache and going shocking pink over all exposed surfaces," he said. "I've *seen* you with sun poisoning, back in the seventies, and that's *with* the atmosphere absorbing most of the ultraviolet in sunlight. This thing is putting out much, much more UV than that. Look at what it did to ordinary humans. Remember the burns? It would do you absolutely no good at all."

"I'll wear sunblock," Ruthven said. "If you think I'm going to let you and Varney go down there on your own, you're sadly mistaken, Fass. This is *my* bloody city."

"Fastitocalon has a point. I would not have you harmed for anything, L... Ruthven," said Varney. "If it is in my power, it is my duty to put an end to this wretched business myself. It was I who brought the trouble to your door."

"It's *everybody's* trouble, Varney, not just yours. I've been here over two hundred years now, and I'm not going to sit back and hide while everybody else protects me."

Fastitocalon leaned back in his chair, rubbing at his eyes. His fingers were still bothering him, and he was uncomfortably aware of having poured rather more energy into Halethorpe than he had necessarily meant to. "Could we possibly have the hero argument later?" he said. "Or preferably *never*. 'Never' works for me. We'll have to do this in an organized fashion, given the danger the rectifier poses; we need to deal with that first. I think that once the object that's transmitting the influence is physically destroyed, its power over them will cut off, but getting to it in the first place is going to be challenging."

"I'm coming, too," said Cranswell. All of them turned to look at him.

"No you're not," said Ruthven. "Don't be ridiculous. You're staying the hell out of this."

"I mean it," Cranswell said, the levity gone from his voice. "I'm pretty sure you guys can thrall me to the point where I don't know what the fuck's going on and keep me here while you take the opportunity to go play self-sacrifice tennis under the city, but, Ruthven, I'm telling you right now that if you do that, any trust I have in you is gone. Any trust my family has in you. That's what, two, three generations of friendship you're gonna throw away? How much of that do you have to spare?"

Ruthven clawed his hands through his hair, completely disarranging it for the first time Fastitocalon could remember seeing. He looked bleak and old, much older than usual. Under the tangle of black hair he had no color in his face at all except the silver of his eyes. "Ugh," he said. "Damn everything in the universe to hell. All right. You can be part of this, but you do *not* get to go up against those lunatics alone in unprotected hand-to-hand combat."

"Hopefully no one will have to," Fastitocalon said. "The first thing to do is to find the rectifier. Find it and break it, or turn it off, or whatever we can do to kill the light and the power it's putting out. I don't care how determined you might be, Ruthven. You aren't going to be able to do much of *any-thing* after you get in direct line of sight to that source."

"What about silk?"

All three of them turned to Cranswell once again. "What do you mean, what about silk?" Ruthven asked.

"It's an insulator." He shrugged. "Don't you guys ever read any proper occult mythology? I've seen it more than once. The Sidhe can touch iron if it's wrapped in silk, although they don't like it much, and in a bunch of the stories it's the same deal with weres and silver. I'm not gonna say that a silk veil is necessarily capable of *stopping* UV from doing bad shit to you, but it might cut down the effects for long enough for you to get in smashing range."

There was a brief silence.

"What a useful person you are, to be sure," said Fastito-calon with genuine appreciation, looking from Cranswell to the others. "He's right. The silk thing. We often use it if we have to touch anything significantly holy, and I'm fairly certain Above does the same thing with infernal artifacts. I ought to have thought of it myself."

"Next question," said Varney. "Where do we get hold of silk veils? I fear the current state of ladies' fashion does not allow for Dr. Helsing's wardrobe to offer much, even if she were willing to sacrifice a ball gown or two."

"I've got silk sheets somewhere," Ruthven said, waving a hand. "The dining room net curtains are silk, too. Yards of the stuff, no problem there." He gave an off-kilter little hiccup of laughter, covering his mouth hurriedly.

Varney raised an eyebrow. "What?"

"Nothing," he said, "just the mental image of wandering around tunnels wearing a bedsheet like a grimly traditional ghost is rather an astonishing one. I'd feel the need to rattle chains and gibber."

"Let's focus," said Cranswell. "Okay, so, you guys get draped in as much silk as we can find, we go down there—figuring out some way to get in without being noticed—and we go find the thing and break it. Vampires don't get mercury poisoning, do they?"

"I've no idea," Ruthven said. "Meanwhile the other occupants of the tunnels are somehow distracted, yes?"

"Yes," said Fastitocalon. "I think I may be capable of providing sufficient distraction. Briefly, anyway." He rubbed at his tingling hand, hoping he was right about that. "I'm almost sure that once the vessel's broken, they are likely to collapse and pose no further threat."

The way he said it got a curious look from Cranswell, but no questions.

Silence fell for a moment. "When are we going to do this?" Ruthven asked. "I'm inclined to suggest that any expeditions be undertaken after dark."

"Well," said Varney, "we know that they are active at night. But given their previous behavior, it's likely that several if not the majority of the—I keep wanting to call them monks, although I seriously doubt they have taken holy orders that would be recognized by any proper church—will be busy doing terrible things on the surface, leaving their headquarters relatively unguarded. And I agree. Access will be much easier after dark."

"There's still the question of sneaking into this place. This bomb shelter." Cranswell tapped his fingers on the table. "Two super-pale guys with weird eyes—one grey Edward Murrow–looking person in a vintage suit, and one regular human—are going to be pretty noticeable trying to climb down manholes or whatever, even at night. Can you do that don't-notice-me thing for all of us?" he asked, turning to Fastitocalon. "Like at the museum?"

"Not for very long, I'm afraid. And I need to try to keep as much strength in reserve as possible so I can use it for distraction-creating purposes." He had rarely been quite so *annoyed* at his own limitations.

"We'll wait for nightfall before we make a move," said Ruthven.

Fastitocalon looked from him to Varney, reflecting that Cranswell wasn't wrong: *two super-pale guys with weird eyes.* Of all the people he could have selected to accompany him in a highly dangerous activity involving a powerful source of ultraviolet radiation, a couple of vampires ranked near the very bottom of the list.

"Yes," he said. "In the meantime, I suggest you and Sir Francis have supper; you'll need all the strength you can get."

In the end there was very little discussion over who would stay behind to keep an eye on Halethorpe. Greta had already come to the obvious conclusion, and it did not make things easier to see the profoundly relieved expressions of the rest of them when she told them she would be staying. There were any number of very good reasons for this, and none of them made up for the crawling miserable awareness that *she* would be safe and comfortable up here while the others faced whatever they would find beneath the city.

"It has to be me," she said, biting off the words, "because I'm the only person qualified and capable of taking care of our guest, and because I have *responsibilities* to the rest of my patients and to London's supernatural community in general. I am not *replaceable*."

If she got herself killed chasing mad monks, her patients would have to find somebody else to provide specialist care, and for some of them that might not be possible at all. It was not lost on her that this would please whatever was running this whole wretched business *enormously*.

Greta had rarely resented the responsibilities of her job quite so much as she did just at this moment. She hated this like fire, both the fact that she had to be the one who stayed and the fact that she *knew* it.

"Quite right," said Ruthven, doing the annoying thing where he tipped up her chin with his finger. "The city needs you a great deal more than it needs any of the rest of us."

"It needs you, too," she said. "You know that. You've always known that, Ruthven."

"I don't intend to deprive it of the benefit of my presence and attention," he told her. "But if, in theory, it came down to losing you or losing me, I think both of us know which one represents the more significant hardship to the greater number of people."

She held his gaze for a long moment—which was damned difficult, he was looking at his most inhuman, silver-white eyes enormous—and then turned her head away from his hand. "Try not to get lost," she said. "In any sense."

"That at least I can promise," Ruthven said, letting his hand drop. He took a step away from her, and the place where his fingers had touched her skin felt absurdly, awfully cold, the instant of time stretching slightly out and then snapping back to normalcy. The clock struck half past eleven.

Cranswell had watched this little exchange in silence, but as soon as the clock's chimes ended he spoke up, arms folded, truculent. "Like I said, *I'm* coming with you. You guys are gonna need all the help you can get."

"They can see in the dark and they're considerably stronger than ordinary humans," Ruthven pointed out. "Like *I* said, you're at a distinct disadvantage."

"Which is why I'm gonna be carrying these," Cranswell said, turning to the knife block on the kitchen counter and removing a couple of Wüsthofs, which he brandished at the group. Ruthven went slightly paler.

"Put those back," he said. "I have had to overlook a number of personal inconveniences just lately, but I am *not* having you ruin the edge on my good knives by using them to chop up violent lunatics. If you insist on coming with us, go and get one of the damn swords over the dining room mantelpiece, and try not to hurt yourself with it."

Cranswell grinned. "Thought you'd never ask," he said, and hurried out, coming back with a very fine nineteenth-century cavalry saber. He gave it an experimental swish. Ruthven backed hastily out of range, looking as if he was seriously reconsidering the wisdom of this move. Greta wondered, briefly, where the hell the saber had come from, and who had last been using it, and if that previous owner would have approved.

The others were unarmed, but wearing silk gloves; Varney and Ruthven both carried a length of what had up until recently been Ruthven's best silk gauze curtains to use as veils against the ultraviolet light. Varney gave his a faintly suspicious look and tucked it into his pocket, or as much of it as would fit. "I hope you're right about this," he said.

"Me, too. Only one way to find out," Cranswell said. "Let's get going."

In the hallway Greta wrapped herself impulsively around Fastitocalon in a hug. "Bloody well *be careful*," she told him. "All of you. I— Just be *safe*. I need you."

"We'll do our best," he said, gently, and with that she had to be content.

From Fastitocalon she moved to Ruthven, who blinked at her but returned the hug, and to Cranswell, who didn't blink but grinned, and then to Varney—and stopped short. "Sir Francis," she said, and looked up at him. He was absolutely not the sort of person one embraced.

After a moment, though, he made her a courtly bow and took her hand in his—cold, hard, but very careful—and brushed the lightest of kisses over it. A shiver ran through her, racing down her arms and legs, all the tiny hairs on her skin standing up at once, and just for a second, as he straightened up, Greta saw herself reflected in his eyes. A wave of dizzying numbness washed through her, just as it had when she'd touched him in the middle of thralling Halethorpe, and she heard his voice again inside her head with that astonishing musical sweetness, very faint but unmistakable: *Thank you.*

Then he broke eye contact. Sound and light and time seemed to come back in a rush, and she stepped back, feeling herself blushing, powerless to stop it and barely able to fight down the rising threat of angry, frightened tears.

"Good luck," she said, keeping her voice from cracking with grim determination.

Varney simply nodded, and turned away with the others, and she noticed that his hair was mostly black now, just a little silver glittering here and there in streaks. She remembered seeing that hair spread tangled over the sofa cushions the night she had arrived—was it really less than a week ago?—all silver-grey with darker streaks; remembered him smiling unexpectedly up at her, changing his face for a moment into something memorable in a different way.

Ruthven opened the door on the darkness, and she watched them go. Out of the bright and into the black. The darkness seemed almost opaque, closing like ink around the four of them, as if they had never existed at all. For a moment she stood there, the night air biting at her face, before turning back inside. She thought helplessly of travelers setting sail across cold unknown oceans, passing beyond her reach, beyond her help, where she could not follow.

Greta leaned her back against the closed and locked door, and slowly slid down to sit on the floor, breathing deeply to try to clear her head. In a minute she'd go back upstairs and sit with Halethorpe. In a minute.

When her phone rang it seemed appallingly loud in the echo chamber of the hallway, and she fumbled it out of her pocket, suddenly sure it was one of the others calling to tell her they'd changed their minds, she should come with them anyway.

It was not. Greta sighed and lifted the phone to her ear. "Hello, Dez," she said. "I'm pretty sure I won't be in again tomorrow. I'm sorry to keep asking you to help—"

Nadezhda cut her off, her voice uncharacteristically sharp. "Greta, Anna's been hurt. I'm with her right now, at Barts."

Greta froze, the by-now-familiar hot-cold shock of adrenaline flooding through her yet again, dropping a weight into her stomach. "Hurt how?" she demanded.

"Some maniac with a knife. She was on her way home from the clinic. She's going to be all right, but she'll need to spend tonight here, possibly tomorrow night as well." The witch's voice was still sharper than usual, acerbic with worry. "I can take the clinic tomorrow but the day after that I have to be in Edinburgh, so if you're still out, either we'll need to shut down or call in somebody else to help— Greta, are you still there?"

"Yes," said Greta, tonelessly, staring at the far wall of the foyer without actually seeing it. Her fingertips on the phone were cold and numb. "I'm here. Forget the clinic coverage. Tell me about Anna."

"Like I said, she had locked up and was walking to the bus stop. She says she'd felt kind of uneasy all day, and it got worse as soon as she got outside—like she was being watched, or even followed, but she couldn't see anyone."

Greta could picture it very clearly: a dark shape invisible at night, the only hint of its presence two small points of blue light, watching Anna set the alarm and lock the front door and set off on her way—and following. Slipping soundless from shadow to shadow, avoiding the pools of light from streetlamps, slowly gaining on her, the short ugly blade of the poisoned dagger hidden in its sleeve.

"And someone came out of nowhere, she says, came up behind her and just *attacked* her. He didn't even try to steal her handbag. Just went after her with a knife. She has some pretty nasty lacerations."

Greta could imagine that, too. "Did he say anything?"

"Actually yes," Nadezhda said, after a moment. "She says he was *reciting* something, maybe saying some kind of prayer, but she couldn't make out what it was. It makes no sense. I can't see *why* anyone would want to stab Anna Volkov."

Greta knew the *exact* reason, and it was none other than Greta Helsing, MD, FRCP. If Anna had not been standing in for her, helping out at the clinic, she would almost certainly not have been targeted by the Gladius Sancti.

She closed her eyes, covered them with her hand, sick and

dizzy as she had been when this selfsame checkered floor tilted under her feet and tipped her into unconsciousness.

Everyone I know is in danger, because of me, and all I can do is sit here and wait until something happens. I cannot leave Halethorpe. I cannot go to be with my hurt friend in the hospital, hurt on my account, because there is no one else to take my place—and who knows what I might bring with me if I did go. I'm the target. *They want to kill monsters and I'm getting in their* way *because I'm the one who* repairs *them...*

"Greta?" Nadezhda was saying. "Greta, are you all right?"

"*I'm* just fine," she said, not entirely steadily, pushing away the spiral of useless reflection. "I'm glad they called you, to be with her."

"They tried you first, but the only number they had for you was the clinic landline, or something—whatever, they couldn't get hold of you—but Anna was able to tell them to call me instead. I'm going to spend the night here."

"She's not in danger, right?"

"No. Lost a lot of blood, and the wounds are nasty but they've cleaned them out and done as neat a job of stitching as I've seen in years. There's a lot of inflammation—they think there might have been something noxious *on* the knife—but that started to go down almost as soon as they began to irrigate and is continuing to resolve. She's about as comfortable as you can be under the circumstances."

"Did they find the knife?"

"No. Whoever attacked her must have thought she was dead, or dying, and run off again. I wondered if it could be the Ripper, but the Ripper murders have all been—well, *completed,* and there was no sign of that goddamn rosary anywhere. It's a damn good thing she's part rusalka," Nadezhda said. "I think that may have made a difference."

So did Greta, in the other direction. Ordinary humans did not have advanced healing powers, but then again they were also not directly vulnerable to the magical properties of the stuff smeared on the Gladius Sancti blades. She didn't know what the white-magic cocktail would have done to a full-blood rusalka, and she didn't want to know.

"Tell her I'm so *fucking* sorry this happened," she said. "And that I'll be there as soon as I can—which is not going to be tonight. If there was any way at all that I could get there tonight I'd already be halfway there by now."

"Are you *sure* you're all right?" said Nadezhda, sounding faintly taken aback. "What's going on?"

"*I'm* fine," she said again, squashing a totally unfunny little laugh. "And—I'll tell you once it's over. I'm sorry I can't do better than that right now, Dez, but it's—this is complicated."

"Okay," said Nadezhda, simply, and Greta had rarely been more grateful to her for *understanding.* Dez was half-in, half-out of the ordinary world in a different way than she herself was, but the overlap was significant, and both of them knew that there were times like now when *not asking questions* was the kindest action one could take. "*Do* you want me to open for you tomorrow?"

"No," said Greta. "I'm not having you put in danger as well. The clinic can close for a few days and the world will go on turning, I'm fairly convinced." She hated the idea of closing, but she also—and more immediately—hated the idea of any more of her friends coming to harm. It was bad enough that the others were off facing God knew what horrors under the city, and Anna was in the hospital seriously wounded because of her.

"All right. But give me a call if you change your mind, okay?"

"I will," she said. "Thank you. For a lot of things, Dez."

"You're welcome," said Nadezhda. "Look, *be careful*, whatever it is you're doing. Take care of yourself. I mean it."

"I will," she said again, not sure if *she* meant it. "Good-bye. Call me if there's—if anything changes with Anna."

"I promise."

Greta hung up. Her ear felt suddenly cold where she'd had the phone pressed to it, and her throat was tight and aching with the threat of stupid, helpless tears.

Being stuck here, now, alone and useless, was probably the worst thing Greta had ever gone through other than her father's death. Even then she had had the support of Ruthven and Fastitocalon and Nadezhda and the rest of them, and it had not been *her fault*; it had been terrible but it had been a thing that happened *to her*, and not a thing she had directly participated in causing.

(She wanted her father more than ever. If he were here he could be the one to stay with Halethorpe, safely out of the action, while she actually tried to do something useful.)

Greta leaned her head back against the door and took a

long, unsteady breath. He was not here; no one was here but her, and in fact she *did* have something useful to do. Even if it was so far from the action.

She thought of Ruthven saying *the city needs you*, of Varney asking *why do you do this*. Of trying to explain it to him. What it meant to be needed, and to deliberately accept the responsibility of trying to meet that need.

I can do something useful, she thought. *I can do my job.*

Greta got up, laboriously, using the doorknob to pull herself to her feet, and started up the stairs toward her solitary patient.

It was not a long walk from Ruthven's house to St. Paul's any way you decided to take it, barely a mile's distance. At this time of night there were not many people on the streets paying attention to their fellow pedestrians. Despite what he'd told Cranswell, Fastitocalon *was* expending energy he did not really have to spare in a very slight don't-notice-me field around the group, and as he did so he could feel both Ruthven and Varney also either instinctively or deliberately making themselves *unremarkable*. The way they did it was slightly different, and if Fastitocalon hadn't had other things on his mind he would have been interested to note more carefully the individual flavors of influence the vampire and the vampyre were exerting.

The vast bulk of the cathedral was having its own effect, bending the background mirabilic field lines around itself like a weight on a rubber sheet. As they drew nearer, Fastitocalon began to pick up the characteristic cyan traces of the monks' signatures beneath the city streets, and at the turn from Creed Lane onto Ludgate Hill, facing the cathedral's huge west front, he stopped to try to mark how many of them there were. He drew in his breath sharply.

"What is it?" Varney asked. Fastitocalon shook his head—*give me a moment*—and closed his eyes. At least two current traces, lots of older, fading ones, and something much more intense, much more powerful than any of the individuals. That one hadn't moved. That one had stayed right where it was.

"It's down there, all right," Fastitocalon said, starting to walk again. "Maybe a hundred feet down. Could be deeper; it's hard to tell with the cathedral distorting the fields. It's... it must have grown stronger just recently. I've passed by here I don't know how many times and felt nothing but the church. If it can drown *that* out, it's definitely gathering strength."

"Does it know we're here?" Cranswell asked.

"Not yet," he said. "I'm doing my best to make sure it won't until we're a great deal closer." Already the strain was audible in his voice. "There's just two of them down there at the moment; it could be worse."

"We'll have to take the lift-shaft stairs down," Ruthven said. "If it's anything like the shelters at Belsize Park and Clapham there will be a separate direct surface access shaft as well as the entrance from the tube station. Fass, can you tell—"

He had his eyes closed again, feeling for the shape of the spaces under the earth, reaching out with his mind as much as he dared without alerting anything to their presence.

"Ventilation ducts," he said, eyes still shut, and turned a little to point. "In the traffic island between Newgate Street and King Edward's Road. That way. Opens on a deep shaft. I can't see clearly but that's got to be it."

Cranswell was trembling slightly with excitement. "How are people not gonna notice us prying open the gratings and climbing inside?"

"You're going to do it very quickly," said Fastitocalon, "and since both Ruthven and Sir Francis can make themselves unnoticeable, you'll stay very close together."

"What about you?" Cranswell asked.

"I'm going to be giving the Gladius Sancti chappies a bit of a surprise," he said, feeling the edges of his strength, trying to determine if he could actually *do* what he planned to attempt. Maybe. Probably. It wasn't as if there was much choice. "At least I hope I am. We'll find out in a hurry, either way."

In fact it took surprisingly little time to get into the shaft. They timed it carefully, watching the traffic, and Cranswell stuck close to Ruthven as advised. The shaft rose up like a brick pillar—or a chimney—aboveground; there was an access door in the brick wall, fastened with a padlock that Ruthven twisted open as if it had been made of chewing gum. Inside, metal steps led down into the dark.

Into the *complete* dark. It was like walking into a cave. "I can't *see*," Cranswell hissed once they were all inside; he clutched the hilt of the saber at his hip and flattened himself to the invisible wall of the shaft.

"Yes, but we can," Ruthven said, and sighed irritably. Cranswell stared as two pinpoints of red appeared in the darkness, brightening rapidly, and blinked themselves at him. "There. Is that better?"

He had instinctively jerked backward, and his head bonked into the metal wall with a faint musical note. "Jesus Christ, Ruthven, how about you *warn* me when you're gonna do something ridiculously creepy, okay?"

The points of light rolled upward in exasperation and then vanished as their owner turned to face the other way, but the dim red glow they cast was still enough for Cranswell to make out the swells of rivets in the curved wall of the shaft, and the steps leading downward in a spiral around the narrow circular hoistway of the old lift. The cables were so rusty they looked as if a good tug would snap them in two.

Ruthven led the way down the staircase and Varney followed, and, after a moment, so did Cranswell, hand tight around the hilt of the saber. It was actually easier going than he had feared. With the red glow to see by, his night vision was just about up to the task.

"Assuming it was designed the same way as the other deep-level shelters," Ruthven said in an undertone, "this ought to lead down to one end of the shelter tunnel complex, which is probably directly underneath the tube station. The rectifier is probably located not very far away from the bottom of the shaft, because it and the transformer and rheostats run the lift and the fan machinery. I don't know which direction it will be, but we'll find out."

"Let's hope we don't find out that it's guarded by a brace of armed lunatics," Varney said sourly.

Cranswell was conscious of a certain gathering conviction, as they descended the staircase, that perhaps his insistence on coming along with the others might not have been his wisest-ever move. The hilt of Ruthven's sword was slick with sweat and felt entirely alien to his hand, weighing heavily on its belt, and he wished fervently that he hadn't eaten quite so much at dinner.

"Stop," Ruthven said softly. All three of them halted, listening intently for any sound from below.

"What is it?" Cranswell whispered.

"You. You reek of fear. I did tell you you shouldn't have come, didn't I?" A sigh, and then Ruthven came back up the steps past Varney to look him in the face. It wasn't any nicer looking at the red-glowing eyes close-up, Cranswell thought. In fact it was really kind of horrible, and he took another instinctive step backward. "Too late to go back now," Ruthven said. "Hold still, August."

"What—" he said, and then shut up, because Ruthven had taken his face between cold hands and the red eyes were... pulsing somehow, their light waxing and waning, and Cranswell was first dizzy and then warm all through, the weight of fear in his chest and stomach beginning to let go.

"You are going to be quite all right," Ruthven said firmly, somewhere a long way away. "I promised your father I'd look after you, and this whole mess is probably not exactly the best example of that, but never mind. You are going to be fine, and this will soon be over."

"Fine," he agreed, floating in the pale red light. "Over."

Ruthven said something else he didn't catch, something complicated that seemed to soar over his head, and then the pulsing slowed and stopped entirely. Cranswell let out his breath in a long sigh, feeling... really quite good about everything, as a matter of fact.

"Right," said Ruthven, with a searching look, and then just nodded and let him go. They crept farther down the stairs, slower now, as silently as possible.

The first intimation Greta had of the Gladius Sancti's presence was when the flaming bottle came through the bedroom window.

Fastitocalon had been right. It *was* only a matter of time. Even without an EKG she knew perfectly well that Halethorpe's heart was failing; would fail whether or not she got his fever down, and so far nothing she had done had had the slightest effect on *that*. She could hear the telltale crackles in his chest that meant fluid was beginning to collect in his lungs; several of the burns were unmistakably infected; the extent of the corneal ulceration had markedly spread. There was just too much damage. All she could do was try to keep him comfortable and wait for the end, and try not to think about what might be happening under the city.

Greta had been trying to read a book earlier, and found her mind skating over the words without taking any of them in, and given up in favor of mentally running through the surgery she was planning for Renenutet. She'd gotten to quite a complicated stage when the splintering crash of the window-pane and bright orange billow of flame made her scream.

In the bed Halethorpe's blind eyes opened. Greta seemed to be frozen in place, a dizzying flood of adrenaline pouring through her, for a matter of seconds; then he said something—cried out something, in Latin—and suddenly she could move again, her heart pounding, cold with thrumming shock. Everything went glass-clear and slow, as it had been once before in this man's company.

"*Go,*" he rasped. Dancing ruffles of flame were beginning to climb the curtains. "Go, it's them, it's the end of everything, they'll, they'll kill you, get away, get far away—"

"Not without you!" She reached for his IV lines; it seemed as if he could see again, at least a little, because he caught her hand in his without a moment of hesitation and pushed her away. Both of them were coughing now, black smoke beginning to gather under the ceiling. The glassy clarity was beginning to splinter into bright shards of panic.

"*Go,*" Halethorpe said again, more strongly, more strongly than she would have thought he could speak—and somehow he sat up, curled a hand around the tubes, and yanked them free. Blood spattered. "They...will have the house surrounded," he said, with visible effort behind each word. "Go... underground. Cellars. There are...things down there...who will shelter you."

Greta was crying, half with shock and fear and half with the acrid smoke. He turned his horrible piebald face to her.

"Go," he said one more time as the flames leaped up, and gave her a little shove toward the doorway.

Greta went.

He was right. The house was surrounded; as she ran down the stairs, another flaming bottle, this one thrown from the back garden, smashed through a window. *Ruthven's house,* she thought, nearly tripping on the stair carpet, breath sobbing in her throat. *All his things. Oh God. All of everything.*

Then there were voices and footsteps *inside* the house and Greta stopped thinking completely and scrabbled for the doorway to the cellar, half-fell inside, and slammed it shut.

A constellation of red pinpoints blinked at her, and then the light clicked on. Some of Kree-akh's people had been sleeping; they scrambled to their feet. She stumbled down the stairs, her knees threatening to give out, and a ghoul caught and steadied her as she reached the bottom. "The house...the house is on fire," she gasped. "There are things out there trying to get in. There's a man upstairs who's probably dying, or dead..."

They all spoke at once—or hissed—and then Kree-akh rattled off a rapid stream of ghoulish she couldn't catch at all, coming over to join Greta at the foot of the stairs. He took her by the shoulders, cold, hard hands digging into her flesh. "Are you hurt?" he demanded.

"No," she said, still dazed, glad of the support. "No, but Halethorpe—and the *house,* Ruthven's house, all his *things,* all his *books*—"

"Where are the others? Are you alone?"

"They're gone," she said. "They're—they've gone to break the thing, the rectifier, the electrical thing that makes the blue light, they know where it is now—"

"Blue light," another ghoul hissed—younger than Kree-akh, almost certainly his son judging by the bone structure—"blue *fire*," and Greta blinked at him.

"It's a spark," she said, "or kind of a spark, in a glass bulb. It's in some kind of old air-raid shelter under St. Paul's tube station. That's not important now. The *house*—"

The ghouls spoke rapidly to one another. "I think you are wrong," Kree-akh said after a moment. "I think it is *very* important. Mewleep, take her and Akha and the young one, get them safely away, and tell Dr. Helsing what you have seen. *We*—the rest of us—will hold Lord Ruthven's house."

Greta wanted to ask questions, a lot of them, but she could not seem to organize the words into coherent sentences; her mind felt like a cauldron full of poisoned soup, chunks of thought swirling and bobbing chaotically in an unpleasant murk. She was still trying to figure out what she wanted to ask first when Mewleep, now accompanied by the ghoullet and his mother, took her wrist in a clawed hand and led her around the bulk of Ruthven's furnace to the low, dark mouth of a tunnel. He fished out a piece of what looked like rotting wood from a pouch hanging on his belt. It glowed a thoroughly unearthly green, giving off enough light to show her the tunnel's walls. Blocks of stone and bricks had been set in neat piles around the opening. It had clearly been carefully bricked up, and only recently reopened.

The last thing she saw, looking over her shoulder, was the pitifully small band of ghouls starting up the cellar steps to whatever awaited them beyond.

Greta had to walk bent over, shuffling along under the low tunnel roof. It was completely black except for the green ghost-light and the dim red pinpoints of the ghouls' eyes. She followed Mewleep in silence, still dazed by the shock of the fire and the way Halethorpe had seemed to be able to see again, sit up on his own, as if the strength of the dying had come back to him all at once; the *force* of his words, as if a whole lifetime of effort were behind each one.

He's dead, she thought. *He's almost certainly dead.*

And, after a moment, *It's better this way.*

His injuries and infections had been so massive, so comprehensive, that she knew even with the best of care he would not have had much time, and the questions that would have been raised at the hospital were questions that inevitably led to discoveries better left undiscovered. And she thought perhaps it *was* better for him, that he should go out this way, facing the people he had once fought alongside, rather than sinking slowly little by little.

He should have had the consolation of the last rites, should have had that reassurance, before he went, but maybe that didn't matter; maybe he would not need to be *given* absolution after all, maybe he had bought and paid for it himself in the end. Greta would have cried for him, if she had been able to form tears. They seemed to have gone dry.

The tunnel opened out into a larger passageway, the roof

only just high enough for Greta to walk upright. As the imme-diate urgency of escape faded, sour, spent adrenaline throbbed in her head, and she couldn't help thinking of Ruthven's lovely house burning to the ground with Halethorpe inside it, and wondered where the others were. And what they would think if—no, *when*, damn it—*when* they made their way back up to the surface to find the house a smoking ruin containing a human skeleton. Ruthven had left her in charge, entrusted it to her, and hadn't she done just a *bang-up* job of protecting his possessions?

Anna was badly hurt because of me, she thought again. *She could have been killed, and Ruthven's house is dying.*

The haze of misery blotted out constructive thought. It was only when Mewleep paused to let the other ghoul, Akha, catch up, the pallid glow of foxfire catching the planes and angles of his face, that she remembered Kree-akh standing in Ruthven's cellar talking to him. *Tell Dr. Helsing what you have seen.*

That thought helped. Greta's vague and unhelpful mental processes seemed finally to cohere into something approach-ing constructive reasoning. "Mewleep," she said. "What did you mean, *blue fire?*"

CHAPTER 14

Mewleep's English was significantly less fluent than his father's, but nonetheless Greta could piece it together without much difficulty, standing in the darkness and listening to the story he told.

The ghouls knew almost every corner of the undercity, from the sewers to the subway to the old Pneumatic Dispatch conduits to the miles and miles of 150-year-old utility tunnels that crisscrossed the metropolis. They were very, very good at practicing the art of *not being seen* by the humans who regularly visited these underground spaces. They had to be. And they had very sharp ears and eyes.

He had been hunting for fresh rat for Akha's baby—ghouls didn't *like* fresh meat, exactly, preferring it to have gone a little runny first, but at least a live healthy rat was less likely to contain poison than a dead one—in the Northern tube line near Belsize Park station, and had heard men's voices coming not from the station platform itself but *under* it. Voices filtering up through the ground.

Mewleep had known there were some deeper tunnels dug beneath the Underground here and there, but they were mostly shut up very firmly, *bricked* up sometimes, and there was too much man-smelling *stuff* in there—and not enough rats—for the deep tunnels to be considered as potential haunts. This one had people in it, however, and he was curious. He had made his way down through a tangle of ventilation ducts until he could see into the old shut-up, rusty-walled tunnel below.

He had never seen the lights on in one of these places before. Ghouls could see in the dark very well indeed, but the humans went blind almost immediately without these bright stinging lights. There were two humans in there, talking to each other, but what Mewleep saw beyond them was *much* more interesting.

"Blue fire," he told Greta. "Blue fire in a...flask? A bottle. *Lectristy.*"

Beside him Akha hunched her shoulders and held the baby closer. She was shivering. *"Lectristy,"* she repeated in a hiss, emphasis on the first syllable, as if it were the name of some terrible enemy or a deadly disease.

"Fire in a bottle," Greta said, intensely focused. "In a bottle about so high, with legs sticking off the bottom of it?"

Mewleep nodded. *"We see it before,"* he said. "Blue fire underground, *lectristy*, we see it before, all my father's tribe, it kills two of us when they touch a thing in a tunnel that they should not touch, blue fire leaps at them and they *dance* and they are burned and they are dead."

"Fear it," Akha rasped. "*Ware* it."

"But here the fire is *caught in a bottle*," Mewleep said. "In a bottle, and it does not leap at the humans, and they do *not* ware it, like there is nothing to fear. It is sorcery."

"It's electromagnetism," said Greta, feeling dizzy, thinking of Fastitocalon explaining parallels. "That...thing you saw. It's not the only one under the city. There is at least one other, and *that one* is sorcery, all right, it's...what's behind everything, all the murders, all the raids on your people. That's where Ruthven and the others have gone. To break it. To end it."

Akha was shaking her head, holding the baby tighter; he began to cry softly. "No," she said, and then went into a rapid-fire crackle and hack of ghoulish. Mewleep listened.

"She says, they break the bottle and let out the fire, and *everyone* will dance and burn," he translated. Greta sighed.

"I can see why you'd think that," she said, "but it's—it can't live outside its bottle. It won't escape and kill anyone, it'll just *go out*, like a blown candle, and stop...being dangerous, except the whole mercury contamination angle, which I am not going to think about right now. They *have* to shut it down, or break it, either way."

"Shut it down?" Mewleep said.

"Yes. It has to *stop*."

"Kill power," he said, as if to make sure.

"Yes. That. Shut it down, turn it off, kill the power, throw the goddamn *switch*, whatever phrasing you like," she said, and heard her voice rising, and hated it.

"*I know how.*"

In the dim light of the rotting wood he held, Greta could not make out his expression as clearly as she would like. "You do?" she said.

"The humans in the tunnel are talking," he said. "I do not listen at first but then one says *kill*, and then I am listening hard. They are talking about power. They are talking about a box and a switch that *kills*, and where this box is found, outside the tunnels."

Greta stared at him. If Ruthven had been right and the shelters were all laid out close to the same way— Why hadn't they *thought* of that, God, they didn't *have* to go walking right into the thing's lair armed only with a cavalry saber and a couple of silk veils, it—

"Do you remember—" she began, and didn't have to finish. He nodded.

"I listen," he said. "I listen very well, Dr. Helsing. I am hearing everything they say, and I *remember*."

"We have to get to the St. Paul's tube station," she said. "That's where it is. Underneath. If it's the same kind of shelter the switch will probably be in the same place. Can you take me there, Mewleep? Can you take me there *right now*?"

Fastitocalon stood very still in the shadows of a shop doorway on Newgate Street, not seeing the familiar pavement beneath his feet at all. In his rather more complicated vision the surface of the street was merely a translucent intimation, a line drawn on a layered diagram. He could see the lift shaft with its staircase coiling down into the dark, and the peculiar vertically stacked platforms of St. Paul's station proper, and below that—

Below that was a tangled pulsing knot of brilliant blue, staining and filling up the bores of the abandoned shelter complex. The comings and goings of the blue monks were recorded in their looping and returning traces, like the tracks of animals, and Fastitocalon could *see* where they had crept from tunnel system to tunnel system on their deadly errands, moving under the city with a kind of blind, insectile determination. The blue trails converged on the throbbing heart of the glow, where whatever it was that had done this to them— to the mad monks, to the murder victims, to Varney and Greta and God knew who else—lay waiting.

He did not think it was aware of them, just yet. He was putting out quite a lot of energy into holding a shield around Varney and Cranswell and Ruthven as they crept down the turns of the staircase, and there was nothing in the pulsing light that indicated it knew he was there. Fastitocalon knew better than to hope, but he had been dwelling here on the skin of the world for a long, *long* time, and some human habits were hard to break.

He could see, too, the blue points of the two monks still present in the shelter tunnels. When the others had reached almost the bottom of the staircase and stopped to wait for his signal, Fastitocalon took a deep, painful breath—*everything* hurt now; he was running on empty and he still had so much to *do*—and focused on the two blue points.

A moment later there was a muffled bang like a car backfiring, as the air where Fastitocalon had been collapsed suddenly in on itself.

He found himself surrounded by a dank, chilly blackness, the dense lightless atmosphere of places under the earth. Not that he needed light to see any more than the Gladius Sancti did. To him the tunnel in which he stood was a transparent outline on a kind of moving blueprint.

He was quite aware that the two monks, who had frozen at the sudden disturbance of his arrival, were now approaching him with their crossblades drawn and ready, and he let them get quite close before he *changed*.

Through all the centuries he had spent on earth, Fastitocalon had looked very much the same from age to age, grey-pale, fiftyish, respectable, *unremarkable*. Human. Now he very deliberately took that seeming off and the blackness of the tunnel was suddenly lit with moving, flickering orange light.

The wings felt strange, after so long without them. In fact the whole form felt strange—not unpleasant, simply unfamiliar. Fastitocalon, now not even remotely mistakable for a middle-aged human accountant, floated a few inches off the floor and spread his wings as far as they would go, filling the tunnel bore from side to side.

The wings of demons, contrary to supposition, can look like

pretty much anything the owner wants them to. *Leathery and batlike* had of course been in vogue on and off forever, and some people went in for complicated hymenopteran versions with lots of little iridescent veins, but Fastitocalon's were the same white as they had been since the flames of Lake Avernus bleached their color away all those ages ago, the morning of the Fall. The feathers were a little tatty, perhaps. In need of a good preen. Mostly the flickering orange light that limned each one of them hid the wear.

The two monks had frozen as soon as the light show had started up, and were staring at him. Their eyes were blank, a boiled-egg white behind the blue glow, like Halethorpe's had been, and Fastitocalon could remember very clearly saying, *Your soul's intact. I'm looking right at it.*

He was looking right at theirs now, and there *was* something there inside, tangled and overgrown with mad buzzing blue.

"*Angel*," one of them whispered. The blades were drooping forgotten in their hands.

This might actually work, thought Fastitocalon, doing his best to smile. And then reached hard, *hard* into both their minds, sank his grip into the lashing blue tendrils wrapped around each, and *pulled.*

He could feel the others nearby, and as he pulled, he shouted at the top of his mental voice, *NOW!*

It was loud enough to make all three of them jump, though none of them had heard a sound. Ruthven looked from Cranswell to

Varney, apparently making some final decision of his own, and nodded, and together they plunged down the last curve of the spiral staircase and into the light.

Into the light. The *blue light*. Finally into the play of the cold-burning glow under the city, the light that killed germs, burned skin, spoke words into the minds and hearts of men and changed them into something no longer entirely human.

Cranswell had time to realize that it hadn't been *expecting* them, that Fastitocalon's shielding had worked; that they had come as a surprise to it, and that it did not like surprises. Then the others hunched away, shielding their eyes from its brilliance, and the light fell full on Cranswell's face, and thought went away entirely.

He stood transfixed while the light poured through him, through his heart, through his head. Instead of the warm redness of Ruthven's reassurance his mind was flooded with a wave of bright, cold blue. Sensation dwindled; he lost everything except the hum and the blueness and the dancing spark at the heart of the glow.

It was huge, bigger than he had imagined, the heavy glass bulb with its angled legs almost three feet tall from the base to the top of the dome, clamped within its metal cabinet. The hum it made filled all the world, filled up the spaces in the bones of his head, resonated in the roots of his teeth, sent ripples through the clear jelly of his eyes.

He took a step farther, and then another step, into the glow. He could understand the blue monks now, understand their...passion. Their *adoration*.

Then hands like iron closed around his shoulders, and he was wrenched around to stare into a pair of eyes that even through the silk veiling looked like polished metal balls. Varney's teeth were bared, very sharp and very long and very white, and something deep in Cranswell's brain responded with a pulse of deep and primitive fear that seemed somehow to drive away a little of the blue fog. "*Hold,*" Varney said, or rather snarled. The sweetness was entirely gone from his voice, leaving only command. "Cranswell, you *hold*, do you understand me?"

"So beautiful," he heard himself say. His mind felt full of shattered ice and quicksand, all sharp edges and dull helpless sliding at once, *poisoned* with blue, drunk with it.

"August Cranswell, you know damn well that thing's a jumped-up lightbulb, nothing more than a bit of engineering with ideas above its station," Varney said, and *there* was the sweetness, the mellifluous beauty back again, and instead of warm pink clouds Cranswell found himself abruptly in a place with mirrored walls. It was like cool glass against burning skin, better than Ruthven's thrall, better than the bright shock of adrenaline.

In the mirrors he could see more clearly, see the rectifier for what it was, and hear the voice in which it spoke without—quite—falling all the way under its spell. "You have to do it," Varney said, echoing in the halls of his mind. Behind them Ruthven had staggered all the way back to the doorway, hiding his face. Even over the thing's hum Cranswell could hear him gasping. "I can't get close enough on my own," the vampyre said, "and he can hardly stand. It has to be *you*, Cranswell. *Can you do it?*"

He blinked, his eyes stinging—the stink of ozone in here was so strong it took the breath away—and felt for the hilt of the saber.

I have to, he thought. *There isn't any choice. I must, so I can.* "Yes," he said out loud, and Varney squeezed his shoulders hard enough to bruise.

He could see blisters rising on Varney's face through the silk, felt his own skin burning. Thought of the man they had left behind in Ruthven's house, who had spent hours, perhaps, in vigil, kneeling within inches of this thing. Thought of the uncertain wavering voice, reciting bits of scripture cut and pasted like ransom note letters into a set of new and hideous commandments.

For wickedness is in their dwellings, he thought, *and among them.*

He turned from Varney, back toward the moving core of the light in its glass castle, the hilt of Ruthven's dining room saber blood-warm in his hand.

They were *schoolboys.* In Fastitocalon's mind the edges of both monks' memories were vivid, clear, even through the writhing poison-blue of the foreign influence. One of them was barely nineteen, the other in his early twenties. Both had wanted very much to be priests. To serve God. To do *right.*

He held on grimly, pulling against the blue glow, feeling

the adhesions between human and inhuman beginning to tear. Fastitocalon had watched Stephen Halethorpe do this on his own, wounded and sick and at the end of his strength, and now that he himself was having to try to separate two relatively healthy individuals from the clinging, questing tendrils of whatever was behind all this misery, he was astonished that Halethorpe had managed it at all. That he had somehow even found the determination to *try*.

That Halethorpe was dead Fastitocalon had known for some little time now. He had felt that particular point of light wink out of his mental awareness of the city. The others were okay—or not *okay;* he didn't at all like how bad Ruthven's signature felt—but *there*. Cranswell, Varney. Greta.

He could feel her in his mind as he had always felt her, since that cold, bleak morning when he had first offered that support, saying *you are not alone*, saying *I'm here, I'm with you*. She was a small bright weight on reality that for some reason always made Fastitocalon think of rain-washed air, the clarity of light after a storm. He couldn't spare much attention for wondering how *she* was handling the night's eventualities, not with the entity in the rectifier fighting him for control of two men's souls. He would have to trust Greta to take care of herself. At least she was out of it, safe back at the house.

He was so tired, and the thing was hanging on so tightly, and he could feel the monks' pneumic signatures beginning to crack and craze from the incredible strain on them, and it did not occur to Fastitocalon to wonder what the *rest* of the

Gladius Sancti might be up to this fine evening until it was too late. He did not even sense the approach of four other blue-eyed monks, shielded as they were by the blue-lit power of the thing he had come down here to destroy, the thing that had summoned back its servants to deal with this unscheduled intrusion; he did not even hear them coming. There was only a split second between the sudden unspeakable *realization* that they were *right behind him* and the blank, thudding shock of the crossblade in his back; and after that there was, quite simply, nothing left to think.

Cranswell was barely five feet from the rectifier when he heard Ruthven say, "Oh God," half-choked and strengthless.

"*Edmund*," Varney said, sounding horrified, and in the same moment that Cranswell turned to look back, suddenly and completely the clear cool mirrors in his mind all went away at once.

Because Varney's attention was no longer focused on Cranswell at all. It was directed instead at the three monks standing in the tunnel just beyond the doorway, holding their poisoned knives. The one in the middle had something staining his blade all the way to the hilt and beyond, black in the cyan light, glistening on the man's knuckles. Still wet. As Cranswell watched, a drop ran down the edge of the blade, paused for a moment, swelling at the tip, and fell silently to the floor.

Ruthven took a step toward the door, hands curling into

fists, and Cranswell had time to see the silver eyes blaze scarlet before a voice like a thunderclap spoke in his head.

Look at me, it said, buzzing in his teeth, his bones. *Look at me, look into my light.*

He could not stop himself from turning. He felt his tendons creak like dry leather straps. He was suddenly and completely aware that if he fought against that pull hard enough, he would break his own bones.

Look at me, said the thing inside the glow, and Cranswell's eyelids would not obey his frantic efforts to close them. *Look at me.*

He had no choice. He looked. He *saw.*

All the world went blank and terrible blue.

The pain was huge; the pain filled all the world, on every plane; every sense, every way of seeing was flooded solid with raw, agonized sensation.

Fastitocalon lay on the gritty tunnel floor, one wing broken and twisted under him, and felt his own blood moving warm and liquid in his lungs: heard the bubbling of air escaping the wound in his back, breath he could no longer draw.

The pain was not the worst of this. He could bear pain. Had borne it. The worst was the sure and certain knowledge that he had failed—failed everyone: Ruthven and Varney and Cranswell, who were certainly the returning monks' next targets; failed Greta, who had been counting on him to *help* the others; failed the two young men whose pneumic signatures he had been attempting to free before the crossblade buried itself in his back. Failed himself, even, not that that mattered in the slightest.

He coughed, bringing up dark and bitter blood, and thought: *Asmodeus was right, after all: I was a mistake.*

The thought brought with it less pain than he expected. In fact, Fastitocalon realized, the pain was receding, drawing away from him like a slow tide, and in the darkness around him one by one he could see stars. One by one, and then ten, twenty, a hundred, a *thousand* stars, blinking into existence, scattering the dark tunnel with points of diamond light.

He could not feel his hands, his feet. As he watched the stars come out, the numbness crept over him, taking away pain and sorrow and grief. He rolled over to look up at the brilliant constellations above him, the wound in his back no longer hurting at all.

It's so beautiful. Like Hell, a spring night in Hell, with all the crystal spheres chiming as they turn, and the flames of the lake like a floor of moving opal. He tried to reach up with one hand, to see if he could touch them, but he couldn't seem to move.

Oh, Sam, he thought, thinking suddenly, vividly of Samael standing on the water stairs at the lake's edge with a wreath of pale flowers in his hair, all gold and white and blue, lit by the rippling glow of the water itself and by his own warm light. The image took his breath away. *Oh, Samael, how I miss it. How I miss it all.*

Around him the wings were slowly fading out of existence—but the feathers remained, dropping one by one to the tunnel floor in soundless drifts of white. *Samael,* his mind echoed. *Samael,* distant now, the word and the name going away from him, out of one world, into another.

Oh, Sam, I want to go home.

Fastitocalon watched the stars and thought, dimly, of a white sky and crows calling. Thought of Greta, far away now, of the *determination* of her, that cold morning; and, still thinking, began to drift away.

In the end Mewleep carried her as they ran: carried her on his back, like a child, because ghouls were *designed* to run through low tunnels in pitch blackness, stooped over, carrying heavy weights. They would have lost time Greta was certain they did not have to lose if the party was limited to a pace she could manage on her own two feet.

It was not the most pleasant experience of Greta's life, bumping and jouncing along on Mewleep's back in complete and utter darkness, having to trust to ghoul sight and ghoul instinct. Akha and her baby—who did not yet have a name, apparently; they did not name children until a certain age because so many ghoullets died in infancy—ran behind them. The only sound in all the world was the slap-slap of feet on the tunnel floor and their quick, sharp breathing. She had not realized just *how* fit they were; Mewleep had been running hard for maybe ten straight minutes, carrying a heavy weight, and while his respiration was rapid it was in no way distressed.

Greta had no idea where they were, or what the tunnels

actually *were* that they ran through. Without light one hollow black space was much the same as another. Several times they had turned left or right down winding ways, and once they had had to slow right down and negotiate a passageway so low Greta's back scraped along the ceiling. She had squeezed her eyes shut and hung on very tight and waited for it to be over, and when they emerged into a much larger tunnel bore and Mewleep could straighten up she had been very strongly aware of her own heart racing much too fast, sour adrenaline and fatigue poisons sloshing in her brain.

She had no way of knowing how much time had passed, either, when he finally slowed to a trot and then to a walk, and then let go of her legs; she half-slid off his back and had to steady herself against the unseen tunnel wall. A moment later he took out the sliver of glowing wood again, and in its feeble light she could make out the fact that they were in a cast-concrete corridor rather than a brick-arched tunnel. Wires and conduits draped in multicolored swags along the walls, and there was—

—there was a shoulder-high metal box against one wall, its color indistinguishable in the faint glow of foxfire, but Greta knew it would be the blank grey-green of electrical equipment housing all over the world.

The corridor shook as a train passed by in a tunnel very close, very close indeed. Dust sifted down from the ceiling as the last of the cars went rattling past, the sound fading off into the distance. *We must be just below the Underground*, Greta thought, and looked back at the metal box standing against the wall, at the fat electrical cables that fed into it on both sides.

"In there," Mewleep said. Behind him Akha was watching her intently, more intently than Greta would really have liked. "The men in the deep tunnel are saying, in the box in access corridor north of the shelter is the cutoff switch."

It was locked, of course, heavy padlocks preventing any unauthorized entry. "To the whole station, or just to the shelter?" she asked.

"Shelter," he said, and then turned and said something to Akha in ghoulish, his tone completely different. Greta heard both reassurance and what sounded like the ghoulish version of *Please?*

Akha looked from him to Greta to the box and back, and then down at the baby in her arms. "You say *lectristy* will not burn us," she said, returning her gaze to Greta. "Not come out of bottle Mewleep is seeing, and . . . escape."

"It won't," said Greta. "I promise that it won't. Breaking the glass won't set it free. Breaking the glass will put it out. I don't want you near this box when I throw the switch in case anything *does* happen, but can one of you please *open the lock for me.*"

Akha sighed, the deepest sigh Greta had ever heard a ghoul fetch, and handed the baby to Mewleep, who at once began the unconscious practiced sway of someone used to the task. She knelt in front of the box and took the lock in her left hand, and belatedly Greta noticed that her claws were much longer than most ghouls' were, longer and very sharp, their tips black like porcupine quills. One of them was not completely straight, with some zigzag notches filed into its sides, and it was this claw that Akha inserted carefully into the first padlock's key slot and twisted very slightly.

Greta had been expecting them to simply yank the lock off the door and toss it aside, the way a vampire would, but as she watched Akha work she realized how important—how *vital*—it must be to the ghouls' safety and livelihood to be able to open and close locks without leaving a trace. She thought of Gandalf, *keep it secret; keep it safe*, and almost laughed, jagged with exhaustion.

As she watched there was a faint but decisive click from inside the lock, and the shackle sprang free. Akha dropped it and began to work on the second lock, which lasted even less time. When she had them both open she stood and retreated from the electrical box, and took the half-asleep baby back from Mewleep, cradling him against her shoulder.

Greta was lost for words. "Thank you," she said, after a moment. "I— Thank you."

"*Do* it," said Akha. "Doctor. Make it *stop*."

Greta nodded, and swung the doors open, and despair sank into her stomach at the complexity of the equipment revealed—how the hell could she hope to know *which* of these switches to throw—and then Mewleep said, "Second from right, top row."

"Thank you," she said again. "Can you give me the light, and then go back down the tunnel a safe distance, please, all of you?"

He gave her the piece of rotting wood, which felt as if it should be either hot or cold to the touch, giving off that eerie green light, but which felt like any other splinter: quite ordinary and unremarkable. Their hands touched briefly, and then Greta was alone.

She held the wood up to the electrical switchgear, trying to read the curling, ancient Dymo tape labels, unable to make out more than a string of useless numbers and letters on each one. *It doesn't matter,* she thought. *Mewleep* heard *the men say it. Second from the right, top row.* She would have to trust his recollection.

The switches were huge, old. She closed her fingers around the Bakelite handle of the one she needed.

Oh God, she thought. *If this doesn't work—*

But her hand was already moving, and the switch came free of the ON detent in a crack and fizzle of sparks, and slammed into OFF with a sound that seemed to Greta much, much too loud: loud enough that people on the *surface* might have heard it, loud enough to crack the concrete tunnel around her and send the earth cascading in.

Cranswell hung in a blue void, unable to move, unable to scream, as the thing inside the light unpeeled his thoughts and memories slice by translucent slice. It was *in his head.*

It saw everything, all of the small and shameful perfidies of childhood, everything he had ever hated, every time he had failed, each flare of lust and envy, each deliberate insult, dissected out in a clean and clear unseaming and set out for his own view, one by one.

This is what you are, August Cranswell. This is all that you are.

No! he thought. *I'm not like that! I've never—*

Never what? said the voice, amused. *Never lied? Never cheated, stolen, envied, hurt?* One by one it showed him flickers of his own memory, example after example after example.

I've never killed!

Oh? said the voice. *What about Mrs. Jennings's dog, when you were nineteen and driving your mate's car and fiddling with the stereo system instead of looking where you were going?*

That was an accident! He could see it in his mind's eye, very clearly, presented for his approval like a wine bottle in a restaurant: his younger self on his knees in the gutter beside what had recently been a dog, the stupid car's stupid stereo still belting out the song he had been trying to skip over, dog blood soaking into the knees of his jeans, mouthing, *I take it back, oh God, I take it back, I'm sorry, I'm sorry, please, I take it back—*

I didn't MEAN to! he howled, inside the light. Tears ran down his cheeks.

Could just as easily have been Mrs. Jennings's little son, August, couldn't it? Couldn't it? You weren't looking *where you were* going, *and a man who will run over a dog will run over a child.*

I didn't mean to, Cranswell said again, dully now, strengthless, and he could *feel* the thing drawing itself up for its next attack, feel it relishing the sick misery from that day years ago and searching his head for more—and abruptly, suddenly, with no warning whatsoever, the light cut off.

Total blackness filled the room, a darkness so complete it felt *solid*, as if the air had gelled into some impenetrable substance. In that dark Cranswell could hear the faint roaring of some huge fan slowing as the blades spun down toward stillness, could hear his own breathing, panting like a man who has run up several flights of stairs. His mind was his own again, a book closed from prying eyes; he was alone in his head once more, and he had time to think, *We will never find our way out of here, we are lost under London, lost in the dark, and they have* poison knives *and we have just one sword I don't know how to use* before the spark in its glass bulb flickered back into existence.

The light grew, and with it the voice, like a volume knob being turned up. Cranswell could feel it beginning to pull at him once more, the tears still drying tacky on his face, but it was *weak* now. He could see its edges.

He took another step toward it, and another, Ruthven's sword still in his hand, and even as the voice in his head scaled up and up and up he wrapped both hands around the hilt and drew the sword back over his shoulder.

Mrs. Jennings's dog was off its lead, he told the voice. *It should never have been in the fucking street, that was an ACCIDENT, and YOU are NOT THE VOICE OF GOD—*

Cranswell brought the sword around in a baseball swing

that had his full weight behind it, and the voice screamed, *No, you do not DARE, YOU DO NOT DARE, YOU MUST NOT,* but nothing in the world or out of it could have stopped the saber now as it sang through the air to make contact, at last, with the pregnant curve of the rectifier's bulb.

Not so very far away, Greta Helsing snatched her hand away from the power switch, now slammed back from OFF to ON, and clutched at her head with both hands, eyes squeezed shut. "Fass," she said, voice wavering on the edge of tears, "Fass, I—I undid it, I put it back, I turned it on again, where *are you*—"

There was a hole in her mind where Fastitocalon *should have been.* His presence, quietly protective, *safe,* was the one thing she had always been able to count on, after her father was gone. *I'm here, I'm with you,* he had said, and through the numbing, bitter shock of grief she had *felt* that, felt herself drawn into a mental embrace, held and steadied, reassured: *You do not have to bear this all on your own; you do not have to* be *alone. I've got you.*

In the years since then she had always *known* he was there, and now she had thrown the switch and in the moment when it slammed into the OFF detent he had simply vanished. A line cut, a lamp blown out: just empty nothingness in the back of her mind where he ought to be.

"I'm sorry, I didn't mean to, Fass. Come *back*, fucking come *back*, please, this isn't funny, *I need to know if you're okay*, I know you can read minds, just please..."

The mental socket where he should have been felt cold,

empty, raw. She was barely even aware of Mewleep and Akha kneeling down beside her, of their chilly, strong hands on her shoulders, still preoccupied with trying to find any trace of him in her head. It wasn't until the baby woke up in his sling against Akha's chest, woke up and protested in a wail that he was hungry, that Greta came entirely back to the present. She felt scoured-open, ancient, more lonely than she knew what to do with. Empty.

"Are you hurt?" Mewleep said, still holding her shoulder.

"No," she said. "No, I'm not hurt. But I have to get in there, Mewleep. Into the shelter. Do that for me and then—I don't know what's happened, what I did, what any of us did, but you—and Akha and the baby—you should get well clear of here."

"Not leaving you," he said.

"You have to. The baby's hungry and the others in there will keep me safe. You did what Kree-akh asked," she said. "Thank you. Thank you so much, both of you."

"Not thank us yet." Mewleep watched as she reclosed the locks on the electrical cabinet and then stood up, giving Greta a hand to her feet. "Not until all are safe. I take you to the shelter—"

"And then go," Greta said, hollow-eyed in the last of the foxfire's light. "Get far away from here. There may be humans, coming down to see what's going on. I want you all safely gone by the time they get here."

Mewleep nodded after a moment, and turned. "This way," he said. "Not far."

*   *   *

Cranswell would remember for the rest of his life how the cracks raced outward from the point of impact through the glass envelope of the rectifier, crazing spidery pathways around its swollen bulb. The whole of it hung together for a long and terrible moment before *imploding* in a musical crash of glass. The awful voice in his head *screamed* like nothing Cranswell had ever heard, or ever wanted to, as, for the second time, the light cut off completely like a blown-out lamp.

This time there was no rekindling of the spark, but the voice remained, no longer contained behind the glass. The scream grew louder and louder, filling the sudden darkness with anger and fear and hate and all of the thousand miseries human beings are capable of visiting upon themselves, upon each other. Grew until he thought it would break the bones of his skull the way opera singers broke wineglasses, the way he himself had just shattered the envelope in which it dwelled. Grew until it blotted out all other sensation—and then just as suddenly, in a devastating flare of brilliant actinic light, cut off.

I am having a stroke, Cranswell thought, pressing his hands over his eyes against the force of that light. *In a moment I will lose consciousness entirely and then I will die, and I never even got to see my stupid museum exhibit go up.*

It occurred to him that this was not a very noble dying thought to consider, and then a moment later that he was, in fact, still around to consider it, and that the blaze of light seemed to be fading. Sure enough, when he took his hands away from his face, he could make out the edges of the room they stood in, the shapes of Ruthven and Varney, through the glaring afterimage of that first sun-bright burst of light.

He could also, very clearly, make out the fact that they had been joined by another figure. It was just as clearly not a human. The wings were a dead giveaway, huge and snowy-white and folded neatly, arching over the newcomer's shoulders. The wings, and the blank, pupilless red eyes. Without those it could probably have passed for a very beautiful golden-haired young man, wearing an irritated expression and a white chiton clasped at the waist with a snake-shaped girdle made of gold.

It was holding out a hand over which the source of the brilliant light hung in midair, slowly turning. With an impatient little gesture the figure shooed the point of light up to hover near the ceiling and looked around the little room with undisguised dislike.

"What a complete hole," it said. "Are any of you hurt?"

Cranswell watched as Ruthven and Varney looked at one another, and then down at the crumpled robes lying at their feet. Apparently the monks had reacted rather badly to the destruction of their idol.

Neither vampire nor vampyre looked even close to okay, but Ruthven was visibly worse off, swaying a little, all his visible skin burned an angry red. Cranswell remembered Fastitocalon saying, *I don't care how determined you might be, Ruthven. You aren't going to be able to do much of* anything *after you get in direct line of sight to that UV source.* As he watched, Varney stepped over an unmoving monk foot and got an arm around Ruthven's shoulders to steady him. "I believe you have the advantage of us," he said, the beautiful voice seeming more incongruous than usual in these surroundings.

"I generally do," said the figure, and sighed. "Sorry. My name is Samael, and I promise I will do my best to explain, but there's something rather important I've got to sort out first."

CHAPTER 15

Greta had no idea how long they had been down here, or what might be happening in the world above, and right now she did not care in the slightest; she followed Mewleep with her teeth clenched and her hands curled into fists, still searching with grim determination for the missing touch in her mind. The rattle and clatter of trains in the tunnel above them grew louder as they went along.

She was sore all over, every muscle aching as if it had been her and not Mewleep who had made that run in the dark, but pushed the pain away. *Doesn't matter. Nothing matters, not now, except Fass. And the others. But Fass most of all. He's all I have of family without Dad. I can't have lost him, too.*

The ghoul stopped in front of a ventilation grate let into one wall and looked at her. "Are you sure?" he asked.

"*Yes,*" she said. "This is the way in?"

Mewleep nodded. "The shaft splits. Take the left fork." He

sniffed. "I am not smelling blue-men-with-blades. Not living ones."

She did not know whether that was reassuring or not, and was about to ask what he *did* smell, and then just sighed. "Thank you," she said. "Go, both of you, get the baby safe away from here. Thank you, so much, for your help."

Akha was bouncing her son gently on one bone-sharp hip, and pushed past Mewleep to look Greta in the face. It was difficult to hold that gaze; she was sure Akha wanted nothing more than to be shut of this entire miserable evening's business, but the ghoul simply stood looking at her for a long moment—and then reached out to touch her cheek with a chilly claw tip.

"Come back safe," she said, the sibilant hissing between needle teeth. "You are... needed."

Greta was appalled to feel tears threatening, and blinked hard. "I will," she said, and looked down at the little creature in Akha's arms, patting at his mother's chest with a small green hand and grizzling faintly. "Go now," she said. "Don't forget he needs his medicine right after you feed him. I will see what's happened, and *deal* with it. I hope Kree-akh and the others are not hurt, and no matter what I find in there I *will* come back to help as soon as I can. I promise."

Akha nodded and looked up at Mewleep, who lifted the ventilation grate aside for Greta and then ducked his head in the brief bow she had seen some of the ghouls give Kree-akh from time to time. Then he turned, with his arm around

Akha, and the sound of their footfalls retreated, leaving Greta alone again with the last of the guttering foxfire's light.

Air touched her face in the darkness, moving sluggishly, and somewhere nearby she could hear the faint rattling vibration of a fan. *Electricity's working,* she thought. *I hope that's a good thing.*

Greta took a deep breath and crawled into the shaft. The glowing wood was all but useless. She dropped it and crept forward on both knees and one hand, reaching the other out in front of her to feel for obstacles. It took her much longer than she had expected to reach the place where the shaft forked off to the left, and she was beginning to feel the first swells of panic—*I'm lost, I'm lost in the darkness and no one will come to find me*—when she realized she could, in fact, see her hand in front of her face.

The shaft was very faintly lit with red, like a darkroom's safelight. Greta crept forward, the light brightening all around her, until she could look down through another set of air intake louvers into a proper tunnel, dimly lit with red emergency lamps.

At first she couldn't make out what it was she was looking at, and then she shivered as she recognized the scarring and lesions of Gladius Sancti monks tumbled in a heap of burlap robes. Nothing was moving. That was good, right? They weren't...active.

Greta leaned as far over as she could to try to see down the tunnel, and then went very still. She *knew* the wingtip shoes that were just visible lying a little farther along the floor, in a dark and sticky puddle. Knew them, and their owner.

Shaking her head in stupid, mute negation, she thrashed around in the shaft until she could get her back against the curving wall and kick out at the grate with both feet. The noise was terrible, a clang and screech that couldn't help drawing the attention of anything left down there, but she was a little way beyond caring about that now. It took two more kicks before the ancient metal finally gave way, spilling her out into the deep-level shelter tunnel to land in a heap not far from Fastitocalon.

He lay on his back surrounded by a drift of inexplicable dingy-white feathers, the pool of blood around him too dark and sticky to be human. There was so *much* of it, Greta thought, helplessly, trying not to do calculations about blood volume in her head, trying not to think of how much someone could lose and go on breathing. She felt it soaking, thick and already cold, into the knees of her jeans as she bent over him and reached for the pulse beneath the angle of his jaw.

Part of her had still been expecting to find one.

He was... cool to her touch, utterly still. The tightness that had crept around Greta's chest in the time since she had lost his mental touch sharpened suddenly, abruptly, as if a screw had been turned, a fist had been clenched just under her breastbone. Her eyes burned, dry, as she looked down into his face.

In the tunnel's red emergency lights, he was all black-and-white, no color left in him at all. The sharp contrast took away fine detail. The lines that bracketed his mouth and ruled his forehead were still there; nothing could erase those completely. But the exhausted, pinched, above all *worn* look was gone; the expression of someone at the very end of their strength, tired almost beyond rest but gamely hanging on because there was simply *no other choice*, was no longer there. His eyes were closed, the deeply grooved parallel lines between the eyebrows smoothed out. His mouth was stained with blood, but the lips curved ever so slightly in a smile.

There was an awful and beautiful peace in that face, a quiet contentment she'd never seen there before. Never known he was capable of. It was the calm smile of an alabaster effigy, silent and still. The thought stirred up more fragments of phrase from half-forgotten texts: *peace that passeth understanding.*

She had never really understood what that meant, and she still did not. All she could understand right now was that he was dead. That Fastitocalon was dead. All of everything was over, because he was dead, and gone beyond her skill, and he was—had been—all she had left.

She couldn't breathe; her throat closed painfully. Now, finally, the tears came, sending the world into a wavering blur. Greta knelt beside him, her hands fisted in the lapels of his jacket, as terrible raw sobs ratcheted out of her chest. She didn't care if there were more of the blue monks coming to stick a knife in her as well; didn't care if the tunnel caved in around them. She buried her face against his still chest and cried for everything lost, everything ruined, everything thrown away, wasted, unwanted.

Shantih shantih shantih.

*   *   *

Cranswell heard it before they even turned the corner into the main tunnel, following the brilliant hovering light: somebody crying, and crying very hard indeed.

Samael led the way. He had turned the wings and gold-girdled chiton into an exquisitely cut suit of white silk, which was a little easier to deal with, but Cranswell was still aware of being so ludicrously far out of his depth that he couldn't even see the shore.

Ruthven was still leaning on Varney, his face and hands puffed and blistered, his hair hanging over his forehead in dusty tangles. Cranswell was vaguely surprised to see how long the front actually was when he hadn't got it combed straight back. The disarray made him look somehow younger, his odd eyes huge. Varney was in slightly better case, but only slightly. Cranswell himself had the world's worst headache and a nasty sunburn, and his hands still tingled and buzzed with the reverberation of the saber's impact.

The dim red glow thrown by the emergency lights was drowned out entirely by the white glare from the hovering ball of light over Samael's shoulder. It was as bright and mer-ciless as a floodlight at a crime scene: Cranswell could very clearly see two more dead Gladius Sancti sprawled in a heap, and a little farther onward Greta Helsing kneeling, bent over something that looked like a crumpled pile of old clothes. The sounds she was making were terrible, involuntary, violent.

The clothes looked...very familiar. That thought drove

the singular question of *what the hell she was doing down here, she was supposed to be staying safely out of this* from Cranswell's immediate consciousness.

He said something under his breath and took a step forward, aware of Ruthven and Varney doing much the same, but Samael held up one perfect hand and they halted at once. He walked closer to the woman crouched on the floor, the globe of light staying where it was, and Cranswell realized that Samael *himself* was actually giving off visible light. The white silk suit seemed to glow.

"It doesn't, you know," he said, more gently than Cranswell would have thought possible. His voice was not loud, but somehow it cut through Greta's choking sobs as if he'd shouted.

She twisted around, revealing a face drawn into an ugly mask, red and wet with tears and snot, and looked up at Samael. "W-what doesn't?" she managed, breath coming in hitches. "Who the fuck are *you*?"

"Peace," he said. "It passeth not understanding. Anyone who believes that hasn't tried hard enough." The faint but visible nimbus of light around him faded slightly. "My name is Samael, and for the purposes of the current situation it's probably best if you think of me as the Devil."

He took a step around Fastitocalon's limp body and knelt down on his other side, the beautiful white silk trousers taking no stain from the pool of blood. Cranswell only caught the edges of the gaze he had turned on Greta, but even so he blinked and had to shake his head to try to clear it. Instead of bright red cabochons, Samael's eyes were now the eyes of an ordinary man—except that the irises were a shade of brilliant, iridescent, shimmering butterfly-wing blue.

"He's *dead*, don't you get it?" Greta said thickly. "Leave him alone."

Samael paid her no attention, turning that blazing blue gaze down to Fastitocalon's face. He bent closer and cupped one hand to the slack grey cheek. "Oh, Fass," he said, again so terribly gently. "Fass, why didn't you tell me you were this ill, why didn't you come *home* and let us renovate you properly, you stubborn old reprobate, why did you let things get this bad? It's enough to make me go all fucking *despondent*."

He leaned down to kiss Fastitocalon's forehead very lightly, leaving a brief point of light where his lips had touched. Then, with the air of someone rolling up his sleeves in preparation for a difficult and time-consuming task, Samael sat back on his heels, shut his eyes, and brought his hands together palm to palm. When he spread them slowly apart, a web of gossamer threads of light stretched between them.

Greta drew back, wincing at the brightness, instinctively scrambling out of the way. The web of light drifted down over Fastitocalon's body, first outlining and then appearing to sink into him, vanishing beneath clothes and skin. Samael placed his crossed hands on Fastitocalon's chest, closing his eyes.

There was a sense of collectively held breath, of something gathering its strength for an unknowable effort, and then there was a kind of silent thunderclap as every golden curl on the Devil's head stood out straight in a brilliant aureole with bluish sparks dancing at the tips. Blue fire rippled over Fastitocalon's still form. Through all the confusion Greta felt a flicker of coldness touch her spine at that blue light, but it wasn't the bright actinic blue of the thing in the glass bulb. This was a softer, somehow kinder shade, a blue that brought to mind the shimmer of peacock feathers or the shifting glow caught in the depths of a moonstone.

Then it was over. The light cut off abruptly, as if it had never been there, and something like the smell of burned tin filled the tunnel. Samael sat back, panting, as if he'd just run a couple of wind sprints instead of putting on a light show; when he opened his eyes they were that blank bright red again. He took his hands away and shook them briskly, with a little wince.

And Fastitocalon opened *his* eyes.

"Ow," he said. "That...really stings."

"Serves you right." Samael's hair was rearranging itself, coiling back into its proper curls. He shook his head to settle them, looking tired. The globe of light, which had been huddling near the ceiling for the past few minutes, returned to hover over his shoulder. "Why you let matters get to this state is entirely beyond me. You were practically worn to nubbins *before* you used up what was left trying to free those two idiots in Benedictine drag."

Greta was still frozen, staring, as Fastitocalon propped

himself up on his elbows and stared at the white-suited figure beside him. The terrible hollow place in her mind, like a bleeding socket, was filled again. He was *back*.

"*Sam?*" he said.

"Well done, that demon. Full marks for observation."

"What...happened? Why are you here?"

"Because, you utter ass, you summoned me," Samael said, with what sounded like fond exasperation. "I don't think you actually meant to, but you did, and then you died, which was a little hard to ignore."

"You can't have been...paying attention to *me*. Of all the demons."

"It's the falling-sparrow thing. I know where all of you are, every last one of you. Makes for an unavoidably noisy head at times."

"Mmh." Fastitocalon poked at his chest, experimentally, and then seemed to become aware that they had an audience; he looked up at the three who were standing, and then over at Greta, who hadn't moved. Her breathing was still coming in those juddering gasps, although the tears had stopped.

"*Greta*," he said. "What the hell are you doing down here? How did you get in?"

She didn't think she had ever been this angry. Her voice was thick and clogged, when she managed to make it work. "You...I thought you were *dead*, Fass, goddamn it I thought you were *dead*, you fucking bled out and you *died* and I couldn't *do anything to help you and I was all alone*—"

"I'm terribly sorry," he told her, and sat up, wincing a little, looking sheepish. "I didn't *intend* to, you know. Die, I mean. I think this suit has had it."

"*Fass*," she said, and scooted closer through the mess of feathers, close enough to take him by his shoulders and shake him violently. Samael got up, white silk knees showing no evidence of bloodstains or any other filth, and glanced over to the three observers.

"If you would care to join me," he said, "I think I can explain at least the outlines of what's been going on."

They followed the gleaming white suit—and the floating point of light accompanying it—through an archway to another tunnel, this one still half-full of bunk bed frames from the days when this had been a shelter for ordinary people, not cultists. Cranswell sat down on a creaking, rusty bed frame and watched the Devil take out an enameled cigarette case, remove a cigarette that was an improbable shade of teal-green, and light it with a fingertip. He drew in the smoke, eyes closing, and sighed it out with the air of someone coming to grips with an unpleasant necessity.

"Right," he said, opening his eyes again; they were back to being brilliant blue. "What you've just seen is the sort of thing we try very hard not to have happen, for obvious reasons. I'm terribly sorry you had to deal with this on your own, although I am frankly impressed by your resourcefulness, and I am also sorry that so many people have died. It may come as some small consolation that you have undoubtedly *saved* a much larger number of lives by stopping it when you did—as far as I can tell, it was planning to burn the city down, which is not only atrocious but unoriginal. We would, of course, at that point have realized what was going on and taken steps to address the situation, but my London surface op has been away from his post and I'm afraid this sort of thing doesn't ping on our radar until a fairly significant death toll has accumulated. London owes all of you rather a large debt of gratitude—which, of course, it must never be permitted to know about."

He sounded genuinely rueful. "I can at least reassure you that the entity responsible for this whole mess is now controlled and will not be allowed to make a nuisance of itself again on this or any other plane. Obviously you'd worked out that it was using that glass thing to project its influence over its followers, because you went to what must have been considerable personal peril to smash said glass thing, thus releasing said followers. I'm afraid none of them seem to have survived the experience."

Cranswell watched him tap ash; it vanished in faint sparkles before it hit the floor. "I'm here for two reasons: to see to Fastitocalon, and to tidy up this nasty little mess. The entity is…what we call a *remnant*, something left over from the beginnings of the universe that does not fit anywhere within it. Mostly the remnants are inert, do nothing, cause nothing to happen, but this one must have been a leftover from the creation of something intelligent and aware, because it developed its own awareness over an eon or so. Enough to be capable of identifying its own hunger, and acting upon that."

Ruthven looked up at this latest intelligence. His eyes were puffed almost shut, like a man in the middle of a nasty allergic reaction. "Then it's as old as creation itself?" he asked.

"Yes. And this isn't even close to the first time it's been active in this world, either; it had developed a particular and specific taste for fear—and hate, and anger. It's been very busy over the past couple of millennia."

Samael glanced at the hovering ball of light above his right shoulder. "Haven't you?" he added, and lassoed it with a smoke ring; the light pulsed briefly, resentfully, and Cranswell realized what exactly it was they'd been looking at all this time. "You needn't worry," Samael went on, still looking up at the light. "I've got it firmly under control. I happened to have been inadvertently summoned here by Fastitocalon, not that he intended to bother me, and when I showed up I thought it expedient first to simply catch the thing and stop it scuttling off to infect any *other* minds, and *then* see to Fass."

"I'm still a bit unclear on how all this works," said Ruthven, a little unsteadily, but only a little. "Fastitocalon told us about the...balance, between the sides, and that both sides are actively engaged in maintaining this balance. Neither of you knew about this business until now?"

Samael exhaled smoke again. "I'm afraid not. It's been very good at hiding its tracks and at the moment things are a little fraught in terms of infernocelestial politics; this couldn't have come at a less opportune time. The angels aren't at their best, either."

"Angels," said Ruthven.

"Mm. It's somewhat sensitive," Samael said, and lit another cigarette, this one pale pink. Cranswell thought he recognized them as Sobranie Cocktails, and wondered half-hysterically if Sobranie of London was aware of this particular celebrity patron. "I think this time I *am* going to have to request a meeting with Gabriel in person, which is going to be immensely tiresome. He won't like it one little bit, but then Gabriel never likes anything I do. I really am sorry you had to sort out this wretched business on your own, it's unconscionable, but you *did* do a remarkably good job and prevented a lot more deaths, and it cannot ever happen *again*."

Beside Cranswell, Ruthven sighed. "One other thing, though. I thought 'Samael' was the name of the Angel of Death, not the Devil himself."

"Well, technically I *am* an angel," Samael said, "or an ex-archangel, anyway, and the lovely thing about human scripture is its varied and extremely versatile potential for interpretation. You lot are so endlessly creative. As it happens I'm in charge of a group of archdemons who run various aspects of Hell, which I'm afraid I really ought to be getting back to, if you don't mind; Fass needs looking after properly and I've got to shout at Asmodeus about his Monitoring and Evaluation protocols."

Cranswell looked up at the golden hair, the peacock-blue eyes. He thought he could make out Samael's wings, even though they weren't being completely visible: a sort of faint shimmer in the air, a change in refraction, like looking at the edges of ice under moving water. He was aware of something not unlike thrall lapping at his perceptions, numbing him from feeling the kind of awe that might ordinarily strike an observer dumb and breathless—or maybe his capacity for wonder had just been saturated by the night's events.

"I have a question," he said, raising a finger.

"Yes?" said Samael.

"I quit a couple years ago, but...can I bum a cigarette?"

Fastitocalon's suit was, in fact, a lost cause. "Even if I could get the blood out," he said, looking dolefully at the ruined jacket in his hands, "which I can't, there's no way the hole could be repaired. I really am cross about that. It's fifty-six years old and completely irreplaceable."

He was sitting on the floor of the tunnel, stripped to the waist, while Greta examined his back. Once she'd cleaned away the blood, there was only a minor reddish bruise marking where the knife had gone in: no sign of scarring, no intimation that the skin had ever been broken at all. She ran her fingers over it: almost no swelling. And the ever-present rustle in his breathing seemed to have stopped. When she put her ear to his back to listen, he sounded clearer than she had ever heard him.

"I mean," he went on, wiggling a disconsolate finger through the hole torn in the back of the jacket, "they could have been more considerate." His shirt was also beyond repair, but apparently he minded less about that.

"What, would you have rather they let you take your jacket off before they stabbed you?" Greta asked, sitting back on her heels. She was still furious, but the clinical fascination with what had just *happened* was currently eclipsing the need to shout at him. "'One moment please, Mr. Violent Lunatic, I don't want to get blood on my nice suit'?"

"Well, yes," he said, as if this were an obvious and rational statement. "I can be repaired, but good tailoring is very difficult to find."

"*Repaired*," she said. "Why didn't you *tell* me you could... what, come back to life? That...person...said you summoned him."

"Mm," said Fastitocalon, wincing. "I really am sorry. I thought you *knew*. I didn't realize you'd be so worried."

"You thought I knew? How the hell would I have known?"

"I assumed Wilfert had told you," he said. "And I don't remember summoning anybody, but the sparrow thing is apparently actually *true*. Sam must have sensed I was in trouble and decided to come and lend a hand."

"The sparrow thing," Greta repeated, and just stopped herself in time from tucking her hair behind her ears; her hands were still sticky with Fastitocalon's blood. Her father had known about this? And hadn't bothered to *tell* her?

"Mm," he said again. "He knows where all his demons are, all the time. I think he feels ever so slightly guilty about the whole business with Asmodeus, when I was first exiled; every now and then he tries to get me to come back to Hell permanently."

"And you don't want to go?" Greta asked.

"It's not a question of *wanting*," he said, bleakly. There was a little color in his face, but to Greta he still looked unwell. "I'm not the same *thing* as I used to be. It's not home anymore; I don't fit there, much as I miss it. I don't fit here, either, but I've been here so long it's difficult to imagine being anywhere else."

Greta looked at him—grey, shirtless, disheveled, covered in blood, his perfectly combed hair a tangled mess—and her tears brimmed over. He stifled a curse and reached for her, and Greta let him steady her with a thin hand on her shoulder. She closed her eyes for a long moment, fighting for calm, for control.

When she could trust her voice, she said, "We have to get you out of here. And the others. Ruthven and Varney looked terrible. I need to see to them, and we all have to get the hell out of this goddamn tunnel before anybody *else* shows up. I— Oh *fuck*."

"What?" said Fastitocalon, letting her go. "What is it?"

"Ruthven's *house*," she said. "They set it on fire. The monks. I just hope Kree-akh and the others got out safe, but, Fass, he left *me* in charge of it and it burned to the fucking ground. He's going to be *devastated*."

"You don't know that," he said, but he had gone noticeably paler. "It might be destroyed; it might just be damaged, there's no way to know until we get up there and see. Don't go borrowing trouble. But I agree that we ought to vacate the current premises; if you'll help me up I think I can probably manage independent ambulation."

Greta nodded and pushed herself to her feet, offering him her hands. She had to take quite a lot of his weight, but once he was upright he seemed relatively stable. Still, she was very glad to see Fastitocalon's improbable boss leading the others around the corner. She had no idea what he'd *done* with that whole light-show business, but it had worked, and if Fass happened to experience a sudden relapse she wanted Samael nearby, freaky eyes and all.

She turned her attention to the rest of them, and winced. Ruthven looked dreadful, worse than she'd ever seen him. His face was bright scarlet, puffy, blistered all over, his big silver eyes red and glittering with tears. She thought of the rectifier, of how *much* UV it must have been putting out, and how much damage it would do to someone with his level of severe sensitivity: That was a clear case of sun poisoning if she had ever seen one. He was leaning on Varney, who also looked bad, but significantly less so.

Before she could say anything, Samael had crossed the chamber to them and was looking critically at Fastitocalon, the point of light still bobbing along a few feet above his shoulder. At close range the gold and white gorgeousness was really kind of overwhelming, especially since he seemed to be glowing faintly. Greta narrowed her eyes, unwilling to let go of Fass despite being loomed at. She had a horrible feeling that he might simply vanish.

Samael took Fastitocalon's chin in his hand, tilted his face slightly, peering into his eyes. Whatever he saw seemed to satisfy him and he gave a little nod. "You'll do," he said. "I'm taking you home; I want Faust to look at you properly, and you're going to spend at least a week at the Spa doing absolutely nothing."

"I'm all right," Fastitocalon protested.

"You *will* be. Come along and don't argue. I am not even slightly in the mood."

"But—" he said, and then his shoulders slumped. "If you insist."

"You're taking him to get proper medical attention?" she asked Samael, looking up at the brilliant blue eyes with some difficulty. They narrowed for a moment, and she had the strong and unpleasant conviction that he could read every single thought in her head. It felt a little bit like being thralled without the pleasant pink fog or the cool mirrors; this was not in the least gentle, a glaring searchlight inside her skull.

Then it cut off, and the Devil smiled a little. "I am," he said. "Dr. Faust is my personal physician, as well as being medical director of the Erebus Health System. Is that good enough for you, Greta Helena Magdalena Helsing?"

"Greta," said Fastitocalon in a warning tone.

She held Samael's gaze for a moment longer, and then nodded. "Yes, of course. I would love to have the opportunity to speak with Dr. Faust at some point, if that would be at all possible."

"I expect that can be arranged," said Samael. "And now we really must be going. Fass?"

Fastitocalon gave her a look Greta couldn't read clearly—there was apology in there, and affection, and not a little worry—and then just sighed and closed his eyes. Samael put an arm around him, pulled him close, and made a small sharp gesture with his other hand. There was a brilliant flash and then a small thunderclap as the air collapsed in on itself, and Samael, Fastitocalon, and the captive ball of light were gone.

"Didn't he have nice *manners*," said Ruthven into the subsequent silence, sounding slightly hysterical, and fainted dead away.

CHAPTER 16

Ruthven came around fairly quickly, in time to catch Greta telling the others about the house fire, whereupon he promptly fainted again. Kneeling beside him, she felt the pulse in his throat and looked up at the others grimly. "We need to get him out of here. Sooner rather than later."

"What's wrong with him?" Cranswell asked.

"Other than the burns—shock, dehydration, UV poisoning. He shouldn't have come down here in the first place. Fass was right."

"He and Varney were fighting off the monks together," Cranswell said. "Without both of them here I'm pretty sure we'd all be dead right about now, or at least permanently insane. Can you fix him?"

"He needs blood," she said. "And not to be here. There's— I think there's some of that poisonous stuff in the *air*. It's almost certainly contaminated most of the surfaces; it's not doing him any good at all. How did you get down here?"

"We took the stairs," said Varney, and looked at her, blinking. "How did *you* get in? For that matter, *why* are you here in the first place? I thought it had been agreed that you were to stay on the surface."

"The ghouls brought me," she said, sitting back on her heels. "I had this idea based on something Mewleep had said that it might be possible to turn off the goddamn rectifier the easy way, by flipping a switch, but it doesn't matter now. You killed it."

The quality of the sudden silence struck Greta as strange. "What?"

"You turned off the power somewhere? Down here? Just now?" Cranswell demanded.

"I turned it off and then right back on again, because, well, that was when Fass kind of vanished from my head," she said, looking up at them. He was still there, in her mind: very faint now and far, but *present*. "And the obvious mental linkage was that I'd fucked up somehow by flipping that switch, logic or no logic, so I turned it back on. Why?"

He and Varney were staring at one another. "When—" Varney began. "Just at the end, for that one moment—"

"—it dropped out," Cranswell finished for him, and then returned his gaze to Greta. "We didn't know why, but the power just kind of flickered out briefly, and we could actually kind of think again without that voice yelling in our heads, and more importantly we could *move*, and before it could grab us again I got close enough to hit it with my sword."

"Which I doubt he would have been able to do," Varney

said, "without the momentary flicker in its attention. It was... *strong*. Stronger than we anticipated. I think we all owe you rather a large debt of gratitude."

"It *worked*?" said Greta, blinking.

"It sure as hell did," Cranswell told her. "That probably saved everybody's collective ass, right there. 'Thank you' sounds puerile, doesn't it? Samael said a whole bunch more people would have died if we hadn't stopped the thing, so, that's kind of on you, I think. Well done."

"Thank Mewleep, not me," Greta said. "He was the one who knew about the switch panel and also not only where it was but which one of the goddamn switches I needed to pull. Look, never mind that for the moment. We really do have to get Edmund out of here."

She tucked her hair back, feeling about four thousand years old, and tried to consider logistics. "We'll have to carry him up the stairs—shit, there won't be any *light*; this is going to be impossible—"

"Allow me," said Varney, kneeling down beside her. He gently nudged her aside, and she proceeded to watch in astonishment as he hoisted Ruthven's limp form over his shoulder as if the vampire weighed nothing at all.

Greta and Cranswell exchanged looks. "Lead on," she said to Varney, pushing herself to her feet, and took a last look around the tunnel: the heaps of feathers, the black bloodstain on the floor, the bodies of the two Gladius Sancti monks Fastitocalon had been trying to free. "It's over, isn't it? It's over."

"It is," said Varney, and as she turned to follow him out of the shelter, Greta thought, slightly to her own surprise, that she believed him.

The journey up the spiral staircase in the dark was not something Greta wanted to recall with any clarity afterward. It was not completely dark, but the light thrown by Varney's eyes was barely enough for them to make out the stairs, and Cranswell and Greta had to move slowly, feeling their way. It took what felt like hours, every muscle in her body aching as she forced herself up one more step, and one more, and one more.

Cranswell's watch was broken; she had no idea how long they had been down there, underneath the city. It might be midday in the world above. It might be the *next* night. She was so tired she could not think in straight lines, and it did not help that the staircase was a twisting spiral, dizzying and endless. Nor did she have any idea what kind of state the world might be in when they emerged, though she could not seem to muster the strength to care so terribly much.

Greta was so lost in her own swirling, treacle-thick thoughts that she didn't notice the darkness of the shaft slowly changing color. She almost walked into Varney when he stopped and held up a hand.

In front of them, light outlined some kind of door. She could hear things. Sirens. The sounds of a city: people, cars.

Varney very carefully pushed the rectangular door open a little, letting in dim greyish light that nonetheless hurt Greta's eyes with its brightness. He peered through the crack and pushed it open all the way, then stepped through.

She followed, and Cranswell after her. They were—she blinked, looking around—they were on a traffic island between Newgate Street and King Edward's Road. The tower of Christ Church Greyfriars stood across the street, its spire catching what Greta realized must be the light of dawn.

It was London. Still there. Still in one piece. Although as the three of them stared around themselves a fire engine went past with lights and sirens blaring, and the smell of smoke was heavy in the air. Greta could see two—no, three—columns of black smoke rising over the rooftops.

They didn't just hit Ruthven's house with their firebombs, she thought. *They must have had a busy night.*

She looked down at herself. She was covered in grime—luckily most of the blood just looked *black*, less alarming than it might otherwise have been. The others were just as filthy. Ruthven, still draped over Varney's shoulder, gave a little moan, and Greta felt the jagged edges of despair opening up, threatening to swallow her. He needed to be in *bed*, he needed medical attention, and his house was probably a smoking ruin, and they didn't have anywhere to *go*.

"What do we do now?" asked Cranswell. Whitish dust powdered his hair, turned his dark face ashy. "Not to point out the obvious or anything, but we're kind of in bad shape."

"We are going—" began Varney, straightening up with the air of one making a decision. "We are going to the Savoy."

Greta stared at him. Under the grime his expression was unreadable. "Where I will engage a suite of rooms suitable to accommodate the entire party," he went on. "I believe that would be an acceptable option?"

She and Cranswell looked at one another. "Uh," he said, "we're not exactly dressed for five-star hotels at the moment."

"One thing I have found to hold true across the centuries," said Varney, "is that people are willing to overlook all *kinds* of eccentricities if you present them with enough money. This way, I think." He nodded down the street and started to walk, still carrying Ruthven without apparent effort.

"Is he for real?" Cranswell asked, staring after him.

Greta shook her head slowly in wonder, finding that she was not, after all, too old and worn and battered to smile. "You know, I rather think he *is*."

Dawn had run a wash of pale rose and lemon-yellow light up the eastern sky by the time they reached the river, and despite the haze of smoke in the air—she could see another column of it rising somewhere over in Southwark—Greta thought it might possibly be the most beautiful sunrise she had ever seen. The water was a flat sheet of silver, mirror-calm. No breeze stirred the branches of the trees along the Embankment. The glass capsules of the Eye, still and unmoving, glittered like jewels on a giant's bangle.

She had been dreading the sight of Ruthven's house, or what was left of it. In her mind's eye it had been reduced to a blackened cellar hole with half-burned beams jutting out of it like broken teeth. Greta knew perfectly well that the fire was not her fault, but it felt that way nonetheless, and she could not stop worrying about Kree-akh and his people, and wondering where *they* were now.

There were still fire engines parked in the street ahead, firemen striding around and doing things with hoses, and a small crowd had not yet drifted away. Greta made herself stop and look over their heads at the remains of the house, and could not breathe at all for a moment in a sudden and shocking wave of relief. It was still *there*.

The roof was gone. She could see the sky through the front windows of the top floor, and the entire front of the house was blackened with smoke—but as she watched, a fireman leaned out of the second-floor windows and called something down to his colleagues on the street below. There *was* a second floor, then. Maybe not *everything* had been destroyed.

"Jesus Christ," said Cranswell. "Is—the monk. Halethorpe. Is he still in there?"

She hadn't even thought of that. "Probably. *Fuck.* If—if they find anything left of him, if he can be identified, Ruthven is going to have to deal with even more problems than his house burning down."

"Greta," said Varney, and hoisted Ruthven higher on his shoulder. "Sufficient unto the day is the worry thereof. We will deal with the difficulty of the house and whatever and whoever it may contain *after* we have had a chance to recover somewhat."

"I hope the ghouls are safe," she said, her voice sounding thin and small.

"So do I, but there is nothing we can reasonably expect ourselves to do for them just now."

"He's got a point," said Cranswell, and put an arm around her. "Let's not stand around, okay? We're kind of noticeable."

In fact they were far from the only filthy and dazed refugees wandering the streets after the night's chaos, and Greta was grateful for that as they stumbled along, Ruthven's house left behind them. She thought she had never been so tired in her entire *life*, dizzy with it, grateful of Cranswell's steadying arm.

Varney had been right. It was astonishing how quickly things started to happen once you threw large sums of money at them; as soon as his black credit card made an appearance he became "Sir Francis" to the suddenly deferential staff of the Savoy.

Ruthven had woken up a little upon being deposited in a chair so that Varney could charm check-in clerks, and he had in fact made it up to their suite under his own steam, but it was very obvious that he was feeling dreadful. Greta wished she had even her basic black bag with her—that was back in the house, or whatever remained of it—but what she had was the services of a five-star luxury hotel, and it would have to do.

She got him into bed, and by the time she had finished carefully cleaning his burns the first of her room service requests had arrived. "There, now," she said. "In a minute you can have a nice cocktail of extremely expensive red wine and several other useful ingredients, but before that you ought to have a couple of pints of blood. I'll go first."

Ruthven blinked painfully up at her, his eyes red and glassy. *Photokeratitis,* she thought. The light had burned not only the skin of his face but his corneas, possibly even the retinas themselves, like a mountaineer gone snowblind. "What?" he said. "No. You can't. *I* can't. I won't be able to *stop,* Greta; don't even think of it."

"Yes you will," she said. "For one thing, it's *you,* and for another, there's Sir Francis handy to detach you if you do lose control, and you need this rather badly at the moment, so shut up and bite me. Neck or wrist?"

He closed his eyes tight. "Greta—"

"Neck," she said, "or wrist?"

After a long moment, eyes still closed, Ruthven said reluctantly, "Neck."

She leaned over him, tilting her head to expose the great vein in her throat, and although she had been prepared for it, expected it, the sudden *force* with which he struck took Greta's breath away. He held her tight in his arms; she could not have pulled away if she had wanted to.

There was pain, at first, quite a lot of it—he wasn't in any condition to be gentle, and she was fully conscious and unthralled—before the anesthetic in his saliva turned the pain into a spreading sensation of warmth.

She had been bitten before, several times, but you did not ever quite get used to the feeling of your own blood not *flowing* out on its own but being *drawn.* It was a different kind of sensation than ordinary phlebotomy, and that was partly due to the sudden noticeable drop in blood volume; even half a pint was enough to make you feel decidedly peculiar.

Greta knew roughly how fast he was drinking, and how long she could let him go on doing it, and when that time approached she said, "Ruthven," and was not entirely surprised to receive no answer whatsoever. "Ruthven," she repeated, sharper. "That's *enough*, Ruthven. Stop."

Nothing. Damn; she *was* going to have to yell for Varney, and it was going to be embarrassing. "Ruthven. *Edmund*. It's me, it's Greta. *Stop*."

This time he shuddered, hard. She was about to start calling for help when she felt the change: the sudden pressure of his tongue against the wound in her neck, and a sharp prickle as the clotting agent he secreted went to work.

He unwound his arms from her and raised his head, gasping, and she made herself sit up *slowly* to avoid passing out, blinking through a wave of sparkles. The change was remarkable, even with only about a pint's worth in him; the angry redness of his skin was visibly fading, and as she watched several of the smaller blisters simply shrank back into the skin and disappeared.

"Greta," he said, sounding stricken. "I'm so sorry, I—"

"Hush. You were fine," she told him. "You needed it. You still do, as a matter of fact. Let me get Cranswell, and then you need to rest. We all need to rest. And *shower*."

Ruthven laughed a little, and looked surprised at himself, and then laughed some more; after a moment Greta found herself joining in. It felt surprisingly good, even if she was sore all over; it felt like incontrovertible evidence that she was, in fact, still alive.

She got up, carefully, hanging on to the bedpost until the dizziness passed, and went to tell Cranswell it was his turn; she was glad that only one task remained to her, and that it was one she could perform without *moving*. It took a little while for her battered mind to dredge up Nadezhda's number; her own phone had been lost somewhere in the tunnels between Ruthven's house and the deep-level shelter, but Greta got it right on the second try—and was grateful that it went straight to voice mail. This was not a story she felt capable of recounting at any length just now; nor was she up for answering questions, no matter how well-intentioned. She told Dez's answering machine about the fire, and asked her to take care of the ghouls, and left it at that. *Sufficient unto the day,* Varney had said, and that would have to do.

Someone was talking, not very far away. Greta rolled over in bed and buried her head beneath the pillows for a long moment, before it occurred to her to wonder where the hell she was.

Memory came back in shreds and snatches. She emerged from the pillows to find the slant-light of late afternoon falling in a long bar across the bed, and sat up, taking in her surroundings: a gold-and-white hotel room large enough to hold a small board meeting, with a view out over the river. Someone was *still* talking not very far away. In the next room.

Greta got out of the palatial bed and stifled a string of curses. She was stiff and sore all over; everything hurt. At least she was *clean*, and wearing a clean hotel bathrobe. She vaguely remembered showering, having to sit down in the shower because she'd been too light-headed to trust herself not to fall; she didn't remember actually getting into bed.

Hobbling like a mummy, she made her way over to the half-open door, listening.

" '… and while the investigation is not yet complete, we are confident that the individuals responsible for last night's multiple cases of arson are no longer a threat.' Good news there from Scotland Yard this afternoon, Sheri."

"That's right, Neil. While the Met is still not sharing many details of their investigation, sources indicate that the rash of arson fires and the Rosary Ripper murders are, in fact, related."

"But is this the end of the terror? Public opinion of Scotland Yard has been at an all-time low over the past six weeks. Above all, people are asking the question, *Is it safe to live in London?* We asked residents to share their thoughts on the string of gruesome tragedies, and we'll have that and more when we return. For BBC News, I'm Neil Davis."

"You're a prat," said the voice of August Cranswell. She pushed the door the rest of the way open and was rewarded by the sight of Cranswell in a matching white terry-cloth robe with SAVOY on the pocket, sitting at a table and consuming room-service bacon and eggs. "Not you," he clarified, looking over at Greta. "*Him*. Hairspray and nuclear-white teeth and stupid goddamn questions. How are you feeling?"

"Old," she said, and came over to join him. "Stiff all over. What about you?"

Cranswell poked vaguely at the square of gauze taped to his throat, stark white against his skin. "Not bad. Still kind of woozy, but it's getting better."

"Good," she said. "Drink lots of fluids, take some vitamins, don't try to do anything terribly energetic for a week or so. He took more from you than me, I think." The gauze wasn't really necessary—the little wounds made by Ruthven's teeth healed very fast into slightly itchy bumps—but at least it stopped him scratching at them. "What else did the news say?"

"Basically just that," Cranswell told her. "They don't know what the hell was going on, but they aren't going to say so, and it seems to be over."

"It *feels* like it's over," Greta said. "It feels…ordinary. I didn't know how much I missed *ordinary*. It's been the longest week of my entire life. What time is it, anyway?"

"Just gone half past three," he said. "They apparently serve breakfast whenever you want it, however, which is useful to know if you ever happen to become disgustingly rich."

"I'll remember that. Did anybody call?"

"Yeah, while we were all still asleep," he said. "There's a message. I didn't listen really close, 'cause it was for you, but your friend with the weird name has everything under control, apparently?"

"Oh, thank God," Greta said, and stole a piece of bacon on her way over to the desk. According to the display, Nadezhda had called a couple of hours ago. On the machine she sounded tired but in decent spirits.

"Greta, I'm assuming you're still asleep, after what you told me this morning. Everything's all right—I'm at the clinic. I've got Hal Richthorn here to lend a hand, and all but two of the ghouls have been treated and released—burns, smoke inhalation, one broke a leg when a bit of debris fell on her, but they're mostly in decent shape. I've postponed the trip to Scotland, so I'll be here to help as long as you need. And don't worry about Anna; they're letting her out of hospital today and I will make damn sure she doesn't try to come to work until she's properly recovered." Nadezhda paused. *"Give me a call when you get a chance, okay? I want to know if you're all right."*

Greta put the receiver down slowly, the wave of relief making her dizzy all over again. She didn't *deserve* friends like this, but she was very, very grateful for them.

"Everything okay?" Cranswell said, looking at her inquiringly. She nodded, straightening up, and realized how hungry she actually was. The last time she'd eaten anything was... good Lord, sometime early the previous evening? And then she'd donated blood. No wonder she felt loopy.

"Apparently so. I'll call her back when I've had something to eat," she said. "And coffee. Do you want more coffee?"

"Of course I want more coffee," Cranswell said. "I don't know when the others are going to be back, they went...shopping."

"Shopping," said Greta. "Ah. Yes. Ruthven *likes* shopping. How was he, when they left?"

"Seemed fine, maybe a bit tired. All that sunburn actually turned into a really faint tan, that—that was kind of amazing. He went from being seriously not okay to 'let's go max out Varney's credit card' in the space of a few *hours*."

"That's more or less what I would expect," Greta said, picking up the phone again. "That kind of vampire healing is *fast* when it's working properly. One day I'll write a paper on comparative tissue trauma recovery rates in the classic draculine and lunar sensitive subspecies of sanguivore. Hello, room service?"

Ruthven did, in fact, enjoy shopping. A great deal.

Even if it wasn't technically *his* money, just at the moment, that he was spending. He had begun to say something to Varney about paying him back as soon as he got the banks to issue him replacement cards and Varney had cut him off with an expansive gesture, *It's the very least I can do after all your kindness and hospitality, and in any case I have rather more than I could easily spend on my own.* It was a vampire thing, and also apparently a vampyre thing. Very long life and wise investments tended to go together.

First, of course, they had bought him a new phone, which he had used to set in motion the tiresome and exhausting work of dealing with insurance agents, and then gone round to the banks—and then Ruthven had begun to shop in earnest.

There were so many things he *needed*, after all. A computer, clothes, shoes—a car could wait, he would weep for the Jag later and the Volvo had probably earned its retirement anyway, but for the moment cabs would suffice for transportation—hair products, accessories, the list went on.

By the time they returned to the Savoy that evening, laden with bags, Ruthven felt not *good*, exactly, but something close to *himself* again. Varney was looking a trifle shell-shocked, which was not uncommon for people who found themselves accompanying Ruthven on shopping trips, especially since it was his credit card that had taken most of the damage. Ruthven made a mental note that the first thing he would do when he got the new MacBook out of its box would be to pay Varney back via online transfer, and he was briefly and vividly glad that such things were possible in the modern age.

He was quiet as they rode up in the elevator, thinking. One week. A lot could happen in a week. A lot *had* happened, to him and to all of them. He was tired, but not exhausted—and almost pleasurably aware of the difference. The thought of the house still hurt, but the hurt was cushioned, insulated, behind the knowledge of the work he had set in motion to repair, to rebuild, and to replace.

When they got to the room he only just managed to put his bags down safely before Greta—still wrapped in her hotel bathrobe, the clothes she had worn under the city having been beyond the hope of repair or rescue—hugged him so hard his ribs creaked.

He held her close, vividly remembering what it had been

like to hold her the night before, remembering her saying *Neck or wrist*, remembering her cool hands on his burned skin, and made another mental decision. She had never asked him for help, never even mentioned the idea of a loan, but he knew her practice was struggling to stay afloat, that she wanted very badly to renovate and expand the clinic, and as he stroked Greta's hair Ruthven thought of both her and her father before her, and what they meant to the city, and wondered why it had taken him so damned long to get around to doing this.

"What?" she demanded, when he let her go. "You're looking smug about something, Ruthven."

"I have decided to take a more active philanthropic role in the life of the city," he said—possibly smugly, she might have a point there—"or at least in one very specific aspect thereof. What do you need to fix up the clinic? New equipment, renovations, supplies?"

"A new X-ray setup," she said immediately. "And a proper 3-D printer to make bone replacements instead of having to sculpt them all by hand. And the roof leaks, and I'm still using a computer system from 2009, and honestly a dental operatory chair and air drill system would be perfect for the mummies, and I'd like to be able to give out more medication for free but the pharma companies just keep jacking up the price, and—oh, a solarium built on the back of the property, and—Ruthven, what are you doing?"

"Making notes," he said, holding up his new phone. "I don't think I got all of that; you might need to review the list and see what else you want to add to it before we start placing orders."

"*What?*" Greta demanded, staring at him.

He put the phone away, took her face between his hands, and kissed her firmly on the forehead. "I am going," he said with exaggerated clarity, "to buy you *whatever you need* to do your job to the best of your ability, my darling infant, for the benefit of all monsterkind. Stop goggling at me, and come sit down and let me show you the rest of our haul."

Some time later Greta closed Ruthven's new computer and set it gently aside, rubbing at her eyes. Outside the full moon had risen, spilling a flood of silver across the city, turning the river into polished glass. Varney had drawn a chair over to the tall windows and sat basking in it with his eyes shut, paying no attention to the light in the room.

She had been looking at medical equipment websites, and had had to stop, for a little while at least. It was overwhelming to keep realizing that she could actually buy the things she needed, *new, under warranty* even. She was conscious of feeling slightly light-headed with excitement as well as blood loss. The prospect of being able to actually *repair* all the things at the clinic that were stuck together with tape and superglue, of being able to replace her old equipment with gloriously efficient state-of-the-art versions that worked without needing to be thumped and called names, was...well, it was huge.

She had never asked Ruthven for help before, because it had simply never occurred to her. All her life she had made do with what there was. Hand-me-down clothes, secondhand cars, used medical equipment from two decades back. It was just how things were, and always had been, and the idea of actually being able to have the things she wanted instead of just dream about them opened up such an enormous array of opportunities. Greta would finally be able to offer her patients the kind of treatment she had been wanting to provide ever since she took over the practice.

She just wished Fastitocalon were here to see it all.

Somewhere a cork popped, and there was murmured conversation; she paid no attention until Ruthven said, "Greta?" and she looked up to see him holding out a glass of champagne—every inch the host, even temporarily homeless and dispossessed. He had regained that irritating vampire ability to seem both entirely at home and completely in charge of the situation, and she had never been happier to see it in her life.

She got up, taking the glass. "What's this for?"

"Celebrating," he said. "Mostly the fact that we're all still alive, to varying extents. *Let us condole the knight; for lambkins, we will live.* Come and be sociable."

Cranswell was sitting cross-legged on the floor in a drift of wrappings and boxes, playing with Ruthven's new phone. Both he and Greta were wearing the clothes Ruthven had bought to replace their ruined things, and all in all she had to admit there was a very Christmas-morning feel to the air. The dark jeans and sweater she had on were quite a lot nicer than anything she had previously owned, and fit perfectly.

Ruthven was pouring more wine; she picked up a second glass and drifted over to where Varney sat by the windows. He opened his eyes, blinking up at her. In the moonlight they were not just *metallic*, those eyes, but *iridescent*; she found herself thinking of black pearls, oil-slick rainbows, the sheen on a raven's wing.

She offered him the glass, and he took it—without breaking eye contact. Greta could feel the faint shimmery edges of his thrall, just for a moment, there and then gone again. "Thank you," he said, and sounded as if he meant more than *for this nice glass of fizzy wine*.

"You are most welcome," she said, and sat down on the arm of his chair, and Varney caught his breath. Beyond her, Ruthven had settled into the corner of one long white and gold sofa, draping himself aesthetically against the cushions, and raised his glass.

"If I may," he said, drawing their attention. "I'd like to propose a toast."

"To what?" Cranswell wanted to know. " 'No more crazy monks—cheers'?"

"To absent friends," Ruthven said, mildly. "Greta, you spoke to Nadezhda earlier?"

She nodded; she had called Dez back and spent half an hour on the phone going over case management. "Kree-akh and his people are going to be all right. A couple of them are still at the clinic, but everyone is going to pull through, and Anna's been released from hospital."

"Thank God," Varney said, and Greta looked down at him

and saw that he apparently meant it. The weariness in his face was still there, but subtly lessened. He looked more... present, in the world, she thought. Less of a disinterested observer.

She thought of him asking *why do you do this job.* Thought of him putting groceries away, hypnotizing Halethorpe with his eyes, bending over her hand to brush his lips lightly over her skin; thought of him lifting Ruthven over his shoulder without apparent effort. Of him saying *sufficient unto the day is the worry thereof.* Saying her name. No one had ever said her name quite like that, quite the way he did.

"And I understand that Fastitocalon is in the best of hands," Ruthven continued. "So: to absent friends, who are dearly missed but *safe*, and to present ones, whom I appreciate rather a lot just at the moment."

"That I *will* drink to," said Cranswell, and leaned up to clink his glass with Ruthven's. "Cheers."

"To friends," said Varney, apparently tasting the word like an unfamiliar delicacy, and looked up at Greta. She smiled, sore but illogically happy, and touched her glass to his, and drank; for a moment absolutely nothing else needed to be said.

It was Cranswell who broke the spell. He yawned, leaning back against the edge of the sofa, and swirled his champagne to watch the bubbles glitter and fizz. "What are you going to do now, Ruthven?" he asked. "I mean, where are you gonna live?"

"Once my flat has been decontaminated," Varney said, "which I expect to have to pay quite a lot to have done, you have a standing invitation to stay there as long as you see fit."

"Thanks," said Ruthven. "I very much appreciate the offer, as I appreciate your current generosity"—he gestured at the suite's elegant furnishings—"but I think I might take the opportunity to travel."

"What?" Greta looked up from her glass, distracted. "You're leaving? Where?"

"It is going to take many days for the insurance people to do their business, and many weeks for the various builders to come and go and do what they need to do in order to render the house even slightly habitable," he said. "And while I love this wretched city a great deal, for all its faults, I think I could stand to be somewhere other than London for a few weeks. I have now acquired the bare necessities to keep body and soul together, thanks to Sir Francis's generosity."

"Not at all," said Varney, eyeing a bag full of Bumble and bumble hair products with a doubtful expression.

"And the next thing I think I shall buy," Ruthven went on, "is a first-class plane ticket. Four, in fact, if you three would care to join me."

"*Where?*" Greta asked again. The idea of Ruthven making travel plans was something of a shock; as far as she knew he hadn't spent much time out of the country in nearly two hundred years, not since the awkward and much-publicized business with Miss Aubrey.

He was smiling a little, as if contemplating some private joke. It was an expression that she hadn't seen on that face for a while now: not quite serenity, but *contentment*. Satisfaction. He didn't look either anxious or angry—or bored.

In the past week she had seen him both absolutely enchanted and coldly furious, both confident and more helplessly miserable than Greta had known he could look, but in all the terror and exhaustion of the whole miserable adventure, not once had she seen boredom cross his face. It was remarkably beautiful in its absence.

"Well," he said, and met her eyes, still smiling. "I've heard that Greece is delightful, this time of year."

EPILOGUE

The afternoon sun turned the old Cretan harbor of Chania into crushed sapphire, glittering with tiny wavelets driven before a freshening wind.

It had in fact rained three of the five days they'd been here, but at least the rain hadn't been *London* rain, and had fallen vertically instead of horizontally, failing to rime everything with ice. Ruthven, philosophically, had remained indoors with the hotel's balcony windows open and the gauze curtains blowing, filling the rooms with the smell of sea salt and petrichor.

Crete in the off-season was refreshingly devoid of holidaymakers towing shrieking infants or getting noisily drunk. Stripped of the throngs, the island itself was revealed: an old and strong place, its bones showing, sleeping in the sun. Ruthven went around in a wide-brimmed floppy hat and enormous sunglasses, and was pleasantly aware of feeling for once very much younger than his surroundings.

Even Varney seemed to be cheered by the change of scenery. Their hotel looked out over the harbor, the bleached-white domes of the little seventeenth-century mosque visible to the right, facing out at the lighthouse at the end of its long breakwater. He and Ruthven sat on the balcony, under the shade of an umbrella, drinking a very creditable wine and watching a speck of white out on the water beyond the lighthouse.

"Are you sure they know what they're doing?" Varney asked for the second time. Ruthven swirled his glass, watching the light catch and ripple, and then looked up.

"Reasonably sure. Stop worrying," he said. "They look like they're having a nice time sailing the bounding main."

Greta and Cranswell weren't doing too badly, although the water beyond the lighthouse was noticeably choppier. He watched them steer the rented boat in circles for a while before looking over at his companion, whose face held such a hopeless expression of longing that Ruthven had to blink and glance away quickly.

Varney cleared his throat. "They seem to be getting on quite well together," he said.

It was intended to be wry, but only managed mournful. Ruthven looked back at him, measuring the expression, wondering if Varney really *hadn't* seen certain of the things that were right in front of his admittedly strange eyes. "Her affections do not that way lie, my friend."

"What do you mean?" Varney frowned.

"I mean," he said, sitting back and picking up his glass again, "that among other instances I happened to notice Dr.

Helsing in Athens visiting an extremely expensive boutique of the sort that purveys nightdresses. Of the frilly, diaphanous, and possibly even underwired persuasion, suitable for moonlit rendezvous."

"What on earth are you saying, Edmund?" The formidable brows were drawn together.

He couldn't help smiling. It sounded an awful lot better than *Lord Ruthven.* "There's a full moon tonight," he said. "You might consider the fact that her balcony adjoins this one."

"I'm sure I don't know what you're getting at," Varney said, still frowning mightily, but there was that faint flush of color high on his cheekbones again, and the glass in his hand was not entirely steady.

"Ah, well." Ruthven looked complacently at the tiny ripples in the dark surface of the wine. "I think I'll dine out tonight. Young Cranswell was going on about that retsina place he'd seen on Yelp."

"You're very kind to him," Varney said, obviously grateful for the change of subject. Out in the harbor the white speck was no longer a speck, but a boat; Ruthven could make out Greta's pale hair tugged by the wind, Cranswell's dark head bent close to hers as she drove.

"His father was a good friend of mine," he said. "I promised I'd look out for him, which, to be bracingly honest, I don't think I have been doing very well of late."

"Is it really over, do you think?"

Ruthven looked bleak for a moment, and then his smile came back, wry now, a little crooked. "No. It's never going to be *really* over; as long as we exist, there will be people determined to try to remedy that condition. But this part of it is done with. Kree-akh and his people are safe back in their old home. I got an e-mail from Greta's witch friend saying that everyone's been released from the clinic and recovering nicely. Anna Volkov should be back at work in a couple of weeks. Even that slightly deranged kid Whitlow will be okay. He's being cared for."

"'Peace, the spell's wound up'?" Varney said.

"Something like that. You heard the Devil; it's unlikely to happen again."

"I'm having difficulty believing any of that was real," Varney said. "The... the Devil bit."

"I know." Ruthven finished his wine, set down the glass. "But Greta said that Fass told her a little bit about Samael, about how the structure of Hell works. I gather there is a rather complicated bureaucracy keeping the place running, and sophisticated cities, and in fact a Lake Avernus Spa and Resort where demons go to take rest cures. Frankly, in a world where rebellious remnants of creation use 1940s electrical technology to broadcast their ill will upon the earth, I'm willing to believe quite a few improbable things before breakfast. And, really, I have to think that at least if I've been thoroughly put out and personally damaged and had my property destroyed I have at least not recently been *bored*."

"You are remarkably efficient at finding silver linings," Varney said.

"I find that if you dig deep enough you can almost always

find something worth the effort. And, well, it is nice, to know one is not alone. Nice to have friends."

Varney watched the sleek white shape of the boat on the dark water, watched the little figure of Greta ready with the rope as they drifted up to the dock, watched her leap ashore. "I shall have to work at getting used to the idea," he said.

"Do." Ruthven smiled at him across the table, and was pleased and only a little surprised when Varney smiled back. It changed his face, warmed the melancholy eyes, took a few years off his apparent age.

They watched Cranswell finish tying up and join Greta, both of them walking slowly back toward the hotel—and then saw her stop dead still in her tracks and stare.

Along the path at the water's edge a third figure was walking toward them: a man, tall and thin in a pale linen suit, a straw panama tipped rakishly on his head.

The figure looked up toward Ruthven and Varney and gave them a little wave, just before a ballistic Greta flung herself at him and knocked his hat off. They watched him hug her off her feet, spinning her around in a delighted circle, and then put her down, protesting, in order to shake Cranswell's hand. Even from a distance they could see the expression on his thin face. Beside Ruthven, Varney's own smile was brighter than ever, almost the expression of a living man.

They looked down from the balcony together at Greta and Cranswell, now wearing Fastitocalon's hat; and watched Fastitocalon take the outstretched hands they offered him, and let them lead him home.

The story continues in...

BAD COMPANY

A Dr. Greta Helsing Novel

Keep reading for a sneak peek!

ACKNOWLEDGMENTS

The evolution of this book has been a long story in itself, and involved the help, support, and encouragement of a great many people. In particular I would like to thank AnnaLinden Weller, best of readers and measure of my dreams; Stephen Barbara, best of agents; Kelly O'Connor, who first saw its potential, and Lindsey Hall, who brought it to fruition; Jane Mitchell, who was there almost from the very beginning, and whose character development and insight I am grateful for borrowing; Audrey, tireless beta-reader and advisor, who stuck with it for draft after draft; Melissa Bresnahan, best of cheerleaders, whose encouragement made me actually finish telling this story; Joyce Ritchie; Von Waldauer; Jesse; Julian; Roach; and everyone who ever left me a comment or took the time to tell me that they liked my stories. Thank you for coming with me this far, and I hope you stick around.

extras

orbit

meet the author

Photo credit: Emilia Blaser

VIVIAN SHAW was born in Kenya and spent her early childhood in England before relocating to the United States at the age of seven. She has a BA in art history and an MFA in creative writing, and has worked in academic publishing and development while researching everything from the history of spaceflight to supernatural physiology. In her spare time, she writes fanfiction under the name of Coldhope.

if you enjoyed
STRANGE PRACTICE,

look out for the sequel,

BAD COMPANY

A Dr. Greta Helsing Novel

by

Vivian Shaw

CHAPTER ONE

There was a monster in Greta Helsing's hotel bathroom sink.

She stared at it, hands on her hips, and it stared back at her. After a few moments it apparently decided she wasn't an immediate threat, gave a froggy *glup* sound, and settled down in the marble basin for what looked like an extended lurk.

"What on earth are *you* doing out of a well?" she inquired of it. "You ought to be guarding treasure, not preventing me from brushing my teeth."

It blinked at her—its eyes were large, also froglike, with a coppery iridescence to the irises—and then shifted a little to reveal that it was in fact guarding something: Greta's amethyst earrings, which had been sitting beside the sink and were now clutched tightly in a clammy grey-green hand.

She sighed. "I need those. If I get you something else pretty to hang on to, can I have them back?"

Another slow, coppery blink. She went back out to the bedroom and returned in a few minutes with the watch she had been meaning to have repaired for several months now and that had not benefited from rattling around in the bottom of her handbag for the duration. It was at least still fairly shiny, even if it didn't work, and when she held it out to the wellmonster it reached for the watch right away, grabbing at it with both little hands, her earrings forgotten. Before it could change its mind she reached into the sink and rescued them.

"Which still doesn't explain what you're doing in my *bathroom*," she told it, putting the earrings on. They were only a little damp, not slimy at all. "I don't think that was on the Le Meurice hotel prospectus. How did you even get in here?"

It wasn't very big, either: the size of a half-grown kitten, small enough to fit easily into the basin. The European wellmonster, *Puteus incolens incolens*, seldom got larger than a human toddler—and unlike the New World species, *P. incolens brasiliensis*, which was equipped with large pointy teeth, had few dangerous characteristics. This one looked to be in reasonably good shape, if entirely inexplicable: How *had* it found its way into a fourth-floor hotel bathroom without anyone noticing?

Glup, it said, and wrapped itself tighter around her broken

Bulova. Greta sighed again, and reached out to stroke it gently. "All right," she said, "you can keep that safe for me. *Depositum custodi.*"

The monster licked her hand.

"*I* don't know," she said that evening, looking into the same bathroom mirror as Edmund Ruthven pinned up her hair. "It was gone when I got back from the first session of the conference, taking my watch with it, I might add, and leaving no trace as to how the hell it got here in the first place. Ow."

"If you would hold *still*," said Ruthven, "this wouldn't hurt and would also take up far less time and energy. And I will buy you a new watch, as I have been threatening to do for months; I know perfectly well you were simply never going to get around to having that one repaired."

Greta made a face at him. She was wearing a black velvet dress she personally would not have picked out, but which, she had to admit, did quite remarkably nice things for both the bits of her it concealed and those it exposed. There was a certain Madame X air to the whole thing, especially when Ruthven finished with the pins and hair spray: Her neck and shoulders were very white against the rich blackness, and he had somehow managed to get almost all of her hair into an elegant loose knot with several wisps artfully escaping here and there.

The makeup was also much nicer than she would have been able to manage on her own. He had attacked her with an eyelash curler, ignoring her protestations, and she grudgingly had to agree that it made something of a difference.

"I look like a high-priced courtesan," she said, meeting his eyes in the mirror. Ruthven was just about as tall as she was, and Greta knew perfectly well nobody was going to look at *her* when he was present: He was much prettier than she was, delicate features, black hair and big shiny white-silver eyes with dramatic dark rings around the irises. He rolled them now and glowered back at her, almost offensively perfect in a bespoke tuxedo with tiny ruby studs winking from the starched shirtfront.

"You look," he said, "like a very expensively soigné young woman. Which, all right, I'll admit there is some thematic overlap. Stop making faces and put your jewelry on, we haven't got much time, and remind me where the damn wellmonsters come from in the first place."

"They get summoned," she said, turning to get a look at the back of her head in the hand mirror. "By people who happen to need guardians for various shiny objects. They do breed, but very rarely, and for the most part it's all done with chanting and runes and cobwebs and frogs' blood. Not difficult once you've got the ingredients."

"Cobwebs are easily come by," Ruthven agreed, "but frog phlebotomy strikes me as a lot of effort. So somebody summoned that creature?"

"Presumably. No way of knowing who or why." The silly dress came with an even sillier purse, a tiny slip of a thing, and Greta eyed it dubiously before stuffing her wallet and phone and compact inside. She felt ridiculously naked despite the snug velvet and the matching wrap Ruthven offered her; she was used to hauling around a handbag the dimensions of a good-sized mop bucket and just about as elegant, stuffed full of everything from journal articles to mummy-bone-replacement castings, and not having that comforting weight on her shoulder was unsettling.

At least they'll mostly be looking at him, she told herself again, fastening the ruby drops Francis Varney had given her into each earlobe. *That's pressure off me. And it's* Don Giovanni,

I've always wanted to see that, and *at the Palais Garnier.* Greta scowled at herself in the mirror. *So bloody well lighten up and have a nice time, Helsing. You deserve it for presenting this paper on no damn notice.*

Ruthven straightened his tie in the mirror and offered her his arm. "Madam, will you walk?" he said, and she had to smile.

"Yes," she said, "yes, sir, I will walk, I will talk, I will walk *and* talk with you."

Together they left the suite, and it was a good twenty minutes before something very hairy clambered in through the half-open window and went to hide under her bed.

The Grand Staircase of the Palais Garnier *should* have been an overwhelming, chaotic jumble of color and texture and shape. Every surface in the vast five-story atrium was either painted, gilded, inlaid, carved, or some combination thereof. Huge spiked candelabra jutted out from the four walls of the atrium and were thrust aloft by seminude bronze women posing on the newel posts of the staircase itself; the balustrades were dark red and green marble, the columns and pilasters of the atrium walls carved from two separate kinds of complicated, veiny, butter-colored stone, with layers of wrought-iron lacework forming balconies between them. High above, the ceiling was painted with dramatic scenes of allegories in saturated color. It *should* have been a cacophonous mess of design elements, and instead, somehow, it all *worked.* The over-the-top opulence offered the same kind of uninhibited, glittering cheer as a polished drag queen's performance.

It was at its best when thronged with people. In the golden light each surface glowed with rich warmth, the polished stone and dark bronze providing a thoroughly complementary setting for the herd of humanity passing through. Glittering jewels, bare shoulders, snowy shirtfronts brilliant against black: a moving kaleidoscope of color, accompanied by the clamor of a great many people talking all at once, being seen in the act of seeing.

From the vantage point of a fifth-floor balcony, the people on the staircase were doll-size, inconsequential. Easily blocked out by the tip of a thumb held at arm's length.

Corvin leaned on the stone parapet, following the progress of two heads through the throng: one dark, one fair. The dark head was glossy, sleekly combed, with a part in it that might have been drawn with a ruler. He closed one eye a little, squinting, and gave his outstretched thumb a vicious little twist, the gesture of a man squashing some small and importunate insect.

The object of this pantomime paused for a moment on the landing, glancing around, as if Corvin's attention had somehow registered on his senses. He was short, very pale, impeccably dressed, and even from here Corvin could see red fire wink from his ruby shirt studs, see the pale eyes flash as he looked around. They were very pale, those eyes, so light a grey they looked silver, with a dark ring around the iris. Corvin knew them very well.

The man's companion, a blonde in a black velvet number, had continued a few steps; now she turned to look back at him: *What's the matter?*

Corvin watched as the man shook his head, dismissing whatever had caught his attention, and offered the woman his arm once more. They passed on up the staircase out of sight, and Corvin was about to detach himself from the balcony parapet and go to find his own seat when the man and woman reappeared on a second-floor balcony across the atrium, this time holding drinks.

They seemed to be enjoying themselves.

Corvin's fingers tightened on the stone edge, and there was a faint sound as a crack arrowed through the marble underneath his grip. Not tonight. Not tonight, but he was *going* to get his chance to talk to Edmund Ruthven *very close-up indeed*—

"Ooh," said someone directly to his left. "Varda the omi palone."

Corvin jerked involuntarily in surprise, and swung around to glare at his lieutenant, who had silently appeared beside him, leaning on the parapet. He *hated* it when Grisaille did the silent-sneaking-up bit. He'd *said* so, multiple times.

"What the fuck are you doing here?" he demanded. "You're supposed to be back at headquarters."

"Isn't he pretty, though," Grisaille said, nodding to the distant figure of Ruthven. "I can see why you want to pull his head off. It's a nice head."

"*Grisaille*," said Corvin.

"Devout and humblest apologies, dear leader." Grisaille sketched him a little salute. "Bad news, I'm afraid: It's Lilith. She is throwing yet another massive tantrum for reason or reasons unknown, and I've been sent to fetch you home to sort it out." He shrugged, returning his attention to Ruthven and the unknown woman on his arm. "Who's the dolly-bird with Mistress Bona?"

Corvin pinched the bridge of his nose. "God damn it," he said. "I told Lilith to lay *off* the fucking junkies. And I don't know. Some human whore."

"Oh, not just *some* human whore. Look, he's all into her, all solicitous and caring. It's touching. In a *barbaric* sort of way." He paused, as if waiting for some particular response, and then sighed. "I don't suppose you saw what I did there."

Corvin ignored this. "You suppose she's important?"

"Could be, could be." Grisaille seesawed a hand in the air. "Shall I make inquiry?"

"Yeah. Do that, and keep an eye on them, damn it. I suppose I have to go and see what's wrong with Lilith this time. I'm getting pretty tired of this shit."

"As you wish," said Grisaille, with another little salute. "Don't worry. You're not missing much with this opera— spoiler warning, he ends up going to Hell at the end."

Corvin straightened up, absently setting aside the little piece of marble he'd broken off the parapet's edge. "So do we all, Grisaille," he said. "So do we all."

if you enjoyed
STRANGE PRACTICE,
look out for
PRUDENCE
The Custard Protocol: Book One
by
Gail Carriger

When Prudence Alessandra Maccon Akeldama ("Rue" to her friends) is bequeathed an unexpected dirigible, she does what any sensible female under similar circumstances would do—she christens it The Spotted Custard *and floats off to India.*

Soon, she stumbles upon a plot involving local dissidents, a kidnapped brigadier's wife, and some awfully familiar Scottish werewolves. Faced with a dire crisis (and an embarrassing lack of bloomers), Rue must rely on her good breeding—and her meta-natural abilities—to get to the bottom of it all . . .

CHAPTER ONE

The Sacred Snuff Box

Lady Prudence Alessandra Maccon Akeldama was enjoying her evening exceedingly. The evening, unfortunately, did not feel the same about Lady Prudence. She inspired, at even the best balls, a sensation of immanent dread. It was one of the reasons she was always at the top of all invitation lists. Dread had such an agreeable effect on society's upper crust.

"Private balls are so much more diverting than public ones," Rue, unaware of the dread, chirruped in delight to her dearest friend, the Honourable Miss Primrose Tunstell.

Rue was busy drifting around the room with Primrose trailing obligingly after her, the smell of expensive rose perfume following them both.

"You are too easily amused, Rue. Do try for a tone of disinterested refinement." Prim had spent her whole life trailing behind Rue and was unfussed by this role. She had started when they were both in nappies and had never bothered to alter a pattern of some twenty-odd years. Admittedly, these days they both smelled a good deal better.

Prim made elegant eyes at a young officer near the punch. She was wearing an exquisite dress of iridescent ivory taffeta with rust-coloured velvet flowers about the bodice to which the officer gave due appreciation.

Rue only grinned at Primrose's rebuke—a very unrefined grin.

They made a damnably appealing pair, as one smitten

admirer put it, in his cups or he would have known better than to put it to Rue herself. "Both of you smallish, roundish, and sweetly wholesome, like perfectly exquisite dinner rolls."

"Thank you for my part," was Rue's acerbic reply to the poor sot, "but if I must be a baked good, at least make me a hot cross bun."

Rue possessed precisely the kind of personality to make her own amusement out of intimacy, especially when a gathering proved limited in scope. This was another reason she was so often invited to private balls. The widely held theory was that Lady Akeldama would become the party were the party to be lifeless, invaded by undead, or otherwise sub-par.

This particular ball did not need her help. Their hosts had installed a marvellous floating chandelier that looked like hundreds of tiny well-lit dirigibles wafting about the room. The attendees were charmed, mostly by the expense. In addition, the punch flowed freely out of a multi-dispensing ambulatory fountain, a string quartet tinkled robustly in one corner, and the conversation frothed with wit. Rue floated through it all on a puffy cloud of ulterior motives.

Rue might have attended, even without motives. The Fenchurches were *always* worth a look-in—being very wealthy, very inbred, and very conscientious of both, thus the most appalling sorts of people. Rue was never one to prefer one entertainment when she could have several. If she might amuse herself and infiltrate in pursuit of snuff boxes at the same time, all the better.

"Where did he say it was kept?" Prim leaned in, her focus on their task now that the young officer had gone off to dance with some other lady.

"Oh, Prim, must you always forget the details halfway through the first waltz?" Rue rebuked her friend without rancour, more out of habit than aggravation.

"So says the lady who hasn't waltzed with Mr Rabiffano." Prim turned to face the floor and twinkled at her former dance partner. The impeccably dressed gentleman in question raised his glass of champagne at her from across the room. "Aside from which, Mr Rabiffano is so very proud and melancholy. It is an appealing combination with that pretty face and vast millinery expertise. He always smiles as though it pains him to do so. It's quite...intoxicating."

"Oh, really, Prim, I know he looks no more than twenty but he's a werewolf and twice your age."

"Like fine brandy, most of the best men are," was Prim's cheeky answer.

"He's also one of my uncles."

"*All* the most eligible men in London seem to be related to you in some way or other."

"We must get you out of London then, mustn't we? Now, can we get on? I suspect the snuff box is in the card room."

Prim's expression indicated that she failed to see how anything could be more important than the general availability of men in London, but she replied gamely, "And how are we, young ladies of respectable standing, to make our way into the *gentlemen's* card room?"

Rue grinned. "You watch and be prepared to cover my retreat."

However, before Rue could get off on to the snuff box, a mild voice said, "What are you about, little niece?" The recently discussed Mr Rabiffano had made his way through the crowd and come up behind them at a speed only achieved by supernatural creatures.

Rue would hate to choose among her Paw's pack but if pressed, Paw's Beta, Uncle Rabiffano, was her favourite. He was more older brother than uncle, his connection to his humanity still strong, and his sense of humour often tickled by Rue's stubbornness.

"Wait and see," replied Rue pertly.

Prim said, as if she couldn't help herself, "You aren't in attendance solely to watch Rue, are you, Mr Rabiffano? Could it be that you are here because of me as well?"

Sandalio de Rabiffano, second in command of the London Pack and proprietor of the most fashionable hat shop in *all* of England, smiled softly at Prim's blatant flirting. "It would be a privilege, of course, Miss Tunstell, but I believe that gentleman there...?" He nodded in the direction of an Egyptian fellow who lurked uncomfortably in a corner.

"Poor Gahiji. Two decades fraternising with the British, and he still can't manage." Prim tutted at the vampire's evident misery. "I don't know why Queen Mums sends him. Poor dear— he does so hate society."

Rue began tapping her foot. Prim wouldn't notice but Uncle Rabiffano would most certainly hear.

Rabiffano turned towards her, grateful for the interruption. "Very well, if you persist in meddling, go meddle."

"As if I needed pack sanction."

"Convinced of that, are you?" Rabiffano tilted his head eloquently.

Sometimes it was awfully challenging to be the daughter of an Alpha werewolf.

Deciding she'd better act before Uncle Rabiffano changed his mind on her father's behalf, Rue glided away, a purposeful waft of pale pink and black lace. She hadn't Prim's elegance, but she could make a good impression if she tried. Her hair was piled high atop her head and was crowned by a wreath of pink roses—Uncle Rabiffano's work from earlier that evening. He always made her feel pretty and...tall. Well, taller.

She paused at the refreshment table, collecting four glasses of bubbly and concocting a plan.

At the card room door, Rue reached for a measure of her dear mother's personality, sweeping it about herself like a satin capelet. Personalities, like supernatural shapes, came easily to Rue. It was a skill Dama had cultivated. "Were you anyone else's daughter," he once said, "I should encourage you to tread the boards, *Puggle dearest*. As it stands, we'll have to make shift in less public venues."

Thus when Rue nodded at the footman to open the card room door it was with the austere expression of a bossy matron three times her age.

"But, miss, you can't!" The man trembled in his knee britches.

"The door, my good man," insisted Rue, her voice a little deeper and more commanding.

The footman was not one to resist so firm an order, even if it came from an unattached young lady. He opened the door.

Rue was met by a cloud of cigar smoke and the raucous laughter of men without women. The door closed behind her. She looked about the interior, narrowing in on the many snuff boxes scattered around the room. The chamber, decorated without fuss in brown leather, sage, and gold, seemed to house a great many snuff boxes.

"Lady Prudence, what are you doing in here?"

Rue was not, as many of her age and station might have been, overset by the presence of a great number of men. She had been raised by a great number of men—some of them the type to confine themselves to card rooms at private balls, some of them the type to be in the thick of the dancing, plying eyelashes and gossip in measures to match the ladies. The men of the card room were, in Rue's experience, much easier to handle. She dropped her mother's personality—no help from that here—and reached for someone different. She went for Aunt Ivy mixed with Aunt Evelyn. Slightly silly, but perceptive, flirtatious, unthreatening. Her posture shifted, tail-bone relaxing back and down into the hips, giving her walk more sway, shoulders back, jutting the cleavage forward, eyelids slightly lowered. She gave the collective gentlemen before her an engaging good-humoured grin.

"Oh dear, I do beg your pardon. You mean this isn't the ladies' embroidery circle?"

"As you see, quite not."

"Oh, how foolish of me." Rue compared each visible snuff box against the sketch she'd been shown, and dismissed each in turn. She wiggled further into the room as though drawn by pure love of masculinity, eyelashes fluttering.

Then Lord Fenchurch, unsure of how to cope with a young lady lodged in sacred man-space, desperately removed a snuff box from his waistcoat pocket and took a pinch.

There was her target. She swanned over to the lord in question, champagne sloshing. She tripped slightly and giggled at her own clumsiness, careful not to spill a drop, ending with all four glasses in front of Lord Fenchurch.

"For our gracious host—I do apologise for disturbing your game."

Lord Fenchurch set the snuff box down and picked up one of the glasses of champagne with a smile. "How thoughtful, Lady Prudence."

Rue leaned in towards him conspiratorially. "Now, don't tell my father I was in here, will you? He might take it amiss. Never know who he'd blame."

Lord Fenchurch looked alarmed.

Rue lurched forward as if under the influence of too much

bubbly herself, and snaked the snuff box off the table and into a hidden pocket of her fluffy pink ball gown. All her ball gowns had hidden pockets no matter how fluffy—or how pink, for that matter.

As Rue made her way out of the room, she heard Lord Fenchurch say, worried, to his card partner, "Which father do you think she means?"

The other gentleman, an elderly sort who knew his way around London politics, answered with, "Bad either way, old man."

With which the door behind her closed and Rue was back in the cheer of the ballroom and its frolicking occupants—snuff box successfully poached. She dropped the silly persona as if shedding shape, although with considerably less pain and cost to her apparel. Across the room she met Prim's gaze and signalled autocratically.

Primrose bobbed a curtsey to Uncle Rabiffano and made her way over. "Rue dear, your wreath has slipped to a decidedly jaunty angle. Trouble must be afoot."

Rue stood patiently while her friend made the necessary adjustments. "I like trouble. What were you and Uncle Rabiffano getting chummy about?" Rue was casual with Prim on the subject; she really didn't want to encourage her friend. It wasn't that Rue didn't adore Uncle Rabiffano—she loved all her werewolf uncles, each in his own special way. But she'd never seen Uncle Rabiffano walk out with a lady. Prim, Rue felt, wasn't yet ready for that kind of rejection.

"We were discussing my venerated Queen Mums, if you can believe it."

Rue couldn't believe it. "Goodness, Uncle Rabiffano usually doesn't have much time for Aunt Ivy. Although he never turns down an invitation to visit her with a select offering of his latest hat designs. He thinks she's terribly frivolous. As if a man who spends that much time in front of the looking glass of an evening fussing with his hair should have anything to say on the subject of frivolity."

"Be fair, Rue my dear. Mr Rabiffano has very fine hair and my mother *is* frivolous. I take it you got the item?"

"Of course."

The two ladies drifted behind a cluster of potted palms near the conservatory door. Rue reached into her pocket and pulled out the lozenge-shaped snuff box. It was about the size to hold a pair of spectacles, lacquered in black with an inlay of mother-of-pearl flowers on the lid.

"A tad fuddy-duddy, wouldn't you think, for your Dama's taste?" Prim said. She would think in terms of fashion.

Rue ran her thumb over the inlay. "I'm not entirely convinced he wants the box."

"No?"

"I believe it's the contents that interest him."

"He can't possibly enjoy snuff."

"He'll tell us why he wants it when we get back."

Prim was sceptical. "That vampire never reveals anything if he can possibly help it."

"Ah, but I won't give the box to him until he does."

"You're lucky he loves you."

Rue smiled. "Yes, yes I am." She caught sight of Lord Fenchurch emerging from the card room. He did not look pleased with life, unexpected in a gentlemen whose ball was so well attended.

Lord Fenchurch was not a large man but he looked intimidating, like a ferocious tea-cup poodle. Small dogs, Rue knew from personal experience, could do a great deal of damage when not mollified. Pacification unfortunately was not her strong point. She had learnt many things from her irregular set of parental models, but calming troubled seas with diplomacy was not one of them.

"What do we do now, O wise compatriot?" asked Prim.

Rue considered her options. "Run."

Primrose looked her up and down doubtfully. Rue's pink dress was stylishly tight in the bodice and had a hem replete with such complexities of jet beadwork as to make it impossible to take a full stride without harm.

Rue disregarded her own fashionable restrictions and Prim's delicate gesture indicating that her own gown was even tighter, the bodice more elaborate and the skirt more fitted.

"No, no, not *that* kind of running. Do you think you could get Uncle Rabiffano to come over? I feel it unwise to leave the safety of the potted plants."

Prim narrowed her eyes. "That is a horrid idea. You'll ruin your dress. It's new. And it's a Worth."

"I thought you liked Mr Rabiffano? And *all* my dresses are Worth. Dama would hardly condone anything less." Rue deliberately misinterpreted her friend's objection, at the same time handing Prim the snuff box, her gloves, and her reticule. "Oh, and fetch my wrap, please? It's over on that chair."

Prim tisked in annoyance but drifted off with alacrity, making first for Rue's discarded shawl and then for the boyishly handsome werewolf. Moments later she returned with both in tow.

Without asking for permission—most of the time she would be flatly denied and it was better to acquire permission after the fact she had learned—Rue touched the side of her uncle's face with her bare hand.

Naked flesh to naked flesh had interesting consequences

with Rue and werewolves. She wouldn't say she relished the results, but she had grown accustomed to them.

It was painful, her bones breaking and re-forming into new shapes. Her wavy brown hair flowed and crept over her body, turning to fur. Smell dominated her senses rather than sight. But unlike most werewolves, Rue kept her wits about her the entire time, never going moon mad or lusting for human flesh.

Simply put, Rue stole the werewolf's abilities but not his failings, leaving her victim mortal until sunrise, distance, or a preternatural separated them. In this case, her victim was her unfortunate Uncle Rabiffano.

Everyone called it stealing, but Rue's wolf form was her own: smallish and brindled black, chestnut, and gold. No matter who she stole from, her eyes remained the same tawny yellow inherited from her father. Sadly, the consequences to one's wardrobe were always the same. Her dress ripped as she dropped to all fours, beads scattering. The rose coronet remained in place, looped over one ear, as did her bloomers, although her tail tore open the back seam.

Uncle Rabiffano was mildly disgruntled to find himself mortal. "Really, young lady, I thought you'd grown out of surprise shape theft. This is most inconvenient." He checked the fall of his cravat and smoothed down the front of his peacock-blue waistcoat, as though mortality might somehow rumple clothing.

Rue cocked her head at him, hating the disappointment in his voice. Uncle Rabiffano smelled of wet felt and Bond Street's best pomade. It was the same kind of hair wax that Dama used. She would have apologised but all she could do was bow her head in supplication and give a little whine. His boots smelled of blacking.

"You look ridiculous in bloomers." Prim came to Uncle Rabiffano's assistance.

The gentleman gave Rue a critical examination. "I am rather loath to admit it, niece, and if you tell any one of your parents I will deny it utterly, but if you are going to go around changing shape willy-nilly, you really must reject female underpinnings, and not only the stays. They simply aren't conducive to shape-shifting."

Prim gasped. "Really, Mr Rabiffano! We are at a ball, a private one notwithstanding. Please do not say such shocking things out loud."

Uncle Rabiffano bowed, colouring slightly. "Forgive me, Miss Tunstell, the stress of finding oneself suddenly human. Too much time with the pack recently, such brash men. I rather forgot myself and the company. I hope you understand."

Prim allowed him the gaffe with a small nod, but some measure of her romantic interest was now tainted. *That will teach her to think of Uncle Rabiffano as anything but a savage beast*, thought Rue with some relief. *I should have told her of his expertise in feminine underthings years ago.* Uncle Rabiffano's interest in female fashions, under or over, was purely academic, but Prim didn't need to know that.

He's probably right. I should give up underpinnings. Only that puts me horribly close to becoming a common strumpet.

Speaking of fashion. Rue shook her back paws out of the dancing slippers and nudged them at Prim with her nose. *Leather softened with mutton suet, resin, castor oil, and lanolin*, her nose told her.

Prim scooped them up, adding them to the bundle she'd formed out of Rue's wrap. "Any jewellery?"

Rue snorted at her. She'd stopped wearing jewellery several years back – it complicated matters. People accommodated wolves on the streets of London but they got strangely upset upon encountering a wolf dripping in diamonds. Dama found this deeply distressing on Rue's behalf. "But, Puggle, darling, you are wealthy, you simply must wear *something* that sparkles!" A compromise had been reached with the occasional tiara or wreath of silk flowers. Rue contemplated shaking the roses off her head, but Uncle Rabiffano might take offence and she'd already insulted him once this evening.

She barked at Prim.

Prim made a polite curtsey. "Good evening, Mr Rabiffano. A most enjoyable dance, but Rue and I simply must be off."

"I'm telling your parents about this," threatened Uncle Rabiffano without rancour.

Rue growled at him.

He waggled a finger at her. "Oh now, little one, don't think you can threaten me. We both know you aren't supposed to change without asking, and in public, *and* without a cloak. They are all going to be angry with you."

Rue sneezed.

Uncle Rabiffano stuck his nose in the air in pretend affront and drifted away. As she watched her beloved uncle twirl gaily about with a giggling young lady in a buttercup-yellow dress— he looked so carefree and cheerful – she did wonder, and not for the first time, why Uncle Rabiffano didn't *want* to be a werewolf. The idea was pure fancy, of course. Most of the rules of polite society existed to keep vampires and werewolves from changing anyone without an extended period of introduction, intimacy, training, and preparation. And her Paw would never metamorphose anyone against his will. And yet…

Prim climbed onto Rue's back. Prim's scent was mostly rose oil with a hint of soap-nuts and poppy seeds about the hair.

Given that Rue had the same mass in wolf form as she did

in human, Primrose riding her was an awkward undertaking. Prim had to drape the train of her ball gown over Rue's tail to keep it from trailing on the floor. She also had to hook up her feet to keep them from dangling, which she did by leaning forward so that she was sprawled atop Rue with her head on the silk roses.

She accomplished this with more grace than might be expected given that Prim *always* wore complete underpinnings. She had been doing it her whole life. Rue could be either a vampire or a werewolf, as long as there was a supernatural nearby to steal from, but when given the option, werewolf was more fun. They'd started very young and never given up on the rides.

Prim wrapped her hands about Rue's neck and whispered, "Ready."

Rue burst forth from the potted palms, conscious of what an absurd picture they made—Prim draped over her, ivory gown spiked up over Rue's tail, flying like a banner. Rue's hind legs were still clothed in her fuchsia silk bloomers, and the wreath draped jauntily over one pointed ear.

She charged through the throng, revelling in her supernatural strength. As people scattered before her she smelled each and every perfume, profiterole, and privy visit. *Yes, peons, flee before me!* she commanded mentally in an overly melodramatic dictatorial voice.

"Ruddy werewolves," she heard one elderly gentleman grumble. "Why is London so lousy with them these days?"

"All the best parties have one," she heard another respond.

"The Maccons have a lot to answer for," complained a matron of advanced years.

Perhaps under the opinion that Prim was being kidnapped, a footman sprang valiantly forward. Mrs. Fenchurch liked her footmen brawny and this one grabbed for Rue's tail, but when she stopped, turned, and growled at him, baring all her large and sharp teeth, he thought better of it and backed away. Rue put on a burst of speed and they were out the front door and onto the busy street below.

London whisked by as Rue ran. She moved by scent, arrowing towards the familiar taverns and dustbins, street wares and bakers' stalls of her home neighbourhood. The fishy underbelly of the ever-present Thames—in potency or retreat—formed a map for her nose. She enjoyed the nimbleness with which she could dodge in and around hansoms and hackneys, steam tricycles and quadricycles, and the occasional articulated coach.

Of course it didn't last—several streets away from the party, her tether to Uncle Rabiffano reached its limit and snapped.